CW01498937

THE
GLORIOUS
DEAD

THE GLORIOUS DEAD

JUSTIN MYERS

RENEGADE BOOKS

First published in Great Britain in 2025 by Renegade Books
An imprint of John Murray Press

1

A CIP catalogue record for this book
is available from the British Library.

Hardback ISBN 978-1-408-74918-0

Typeset in Caslon by M Rules
Printed and bound in Great Britain by
Clays Ltd, Elcograf S.p.A

John Murray policy is to use papers that are natural, renewable and
recyclable products and made from wood grown in sustainable forests.
The logging and manufacturing processes are expected to conform to
the environmental regulations of the country of origin.

Carmelite House
50 Victoria Embankment
London EC4Y 0DZ

The authorised representative
in the EEA is
Hachette Ireland
8 Castlecourt Centre
Dublin 15, D15 XTP3, Ireland
(email: info@hbgi.ie)

www.dialoguebooks.co.uk

John Murray Press, part of Hodder & Stoughton Limited
An Hachette UK company

For Nana and Grandma,
two glorious women.

'The truth is rarely pure and never simple.'

— OSCAR WILDE

Overture

Boredom and an empty house are a dangerous combination. Your mind starts rapping on doors it has no business noticing, doors you should never unlock. But that's how adventure starts. Pushing the boundaries, wading into water at twilight when you can't even see the horizon in the distance.

And that's how I discovered it. Bored, nosy. Scroll, sweep, click. Gasp. The truth about him. The truth about everyone. Pages and pages and pages of the reality behind that smile, that smart mouth, his benevolence. I wouldn't say I was shocked, particularly; we can all lash out, speak out of turn, take brief dips into vulgarity and dishonour before carefully falling back into line, and it doesn't mean anything. The ones we love forgive us. The ones with more to lose take an oath to conceal.

But to see these secrets shaped into words, years and years of them, from before I knew him right up to the present day, it was like they'd been carved in stone. There was no explaining them away.

If he were being this brave, this candid, this fierce, this ugly, it could mean only one thing. He'd lost control. He didn't care any more. He was willing to throw it all away. Everything he'd earned, everything he'd built, he was prepared to see it fall.

And it wasn't just himself he was ruining. The bastard was willing to take us all down. The whole sorry lot. Scorch the earth, death warrants signed, heads on spikes up and down Shaftesbury Avenue.

And, you know, the funny thing is, the more I read, the more I learned, the more the truth opened itself to me like a filthy, sordid lotus, the more I thought, maybe I should let him.

Let them burn. Every last one of them.

One

January

Jo

Laurie is dead. There's no doubt about it. Laurie has an aura, if you like, a presence. Usually, Jo can feel it before Laurie walks into the house, before even the slamming of the cab door and the urgent trot (or woozy shlep) up the garden path. The impatient scrabbling for keys. The door's squeaky hinge yawning in recognition. The flop of Laurie's bag and coat on the chair installed in the hallway for that very purpose – he doesn't like reaching for coat hooks, says it strains his deltoids. The sigh as he kicks off his shoes, if he remembers to take them off at all. When Laurie is on his way, the air changes, warns you he's coming. Warned you, rather. It wouldn't again. Jo just saw the evidence for himself, in the depths of the hospital, in the dark room windowless save for one looking out onto Laurie's body, lying under a sheet that had at one corner,

Jo noticed, a small stain. They said Jo could touch him if he wanted. He didn't.

Jo walks to the kitchen, gently placing his keys on the hook by the kettle. Jasper raises his head to greet him but does not, as he usually does, turn and search the air for his other master. Instead, the grizzled labradoodle burrows his head back into the bobbled fleece of his bed, blinking sadly. The rush of wind, the kaleidoscopic hurricane that usually brought Laurie to him, will now be still for ever.

It's late. What now? You tell people, don't you? Better to be told than find out. Jo's grief barely has a shape, but soon it won't belong only to him. Laurie isn't a star, but he's not nobody. Guaranteed a dimming of the lights in the West End at least, an obituary in the *Guardian* for sure. Would it be drafted already? At forty-five, Laurie is a touch too young to have a posthumous 'best bits' in the vault. Was. Forty-five. It's nothing. Half a life.

Who first? Jo can't call Laurie's mother, not at this hour. Viv, then. It's wrong to leave Laurie's best friend sleeping while her world is falling apart. The phone feels clammy in his hand as he scrolls for her number. He counts the rings. Seven. She sounds groggy. Not just tired. Drunk-ish. Maybe she was with Laurie earlier, the last person to see or speak to him. The last! Such finality.

'Viv, it's Jo.' It feels like the first time he's spoken to another human in years. Viv starts off bright in her reply, like he's woken her with a tray of eggs Benedict and the papers. Her tone shifts slightly when she realises there's no sunshine straining at her blackout curtains. Laurie would probably remind him, if he weren't lying in a chiller cabinet in the Royal Free, that nobody calls at four in the morning to say congratulations, so he should get to the point.

'There's been an accident.' She's crying already. He should've gone over. There are probably rules about how to do this. He's never broken the news that someone's dead before, least of all his own husband. He thinks it: my husband is dead. It sounds like his mind doesn't belong to him. Back to business. He parrots what the young police officers told him.

'Lost control of the car, Viv. Went through a wall. Well, into it. Er, Highgate somewhere. No, I don't know what he was doing there.'

Laurie had friends everywhere, but nobody he liked well enough to visit that late, approaching midnight. Midnight. If the crash happened before midnight, it was already another day. He died yesterday. He is yesterday.

Maybe Laurie was brainstorming. He was prone to grabbing his car keys and coasting along the streets at night, when he needed to think – although he'd done it less often since being pulled over as a suspected kerb crawler and ending up as a blind item on a gossip website. The police didn't believe his excuse, that he was groping for his dropped glasses on the car floor. They had both laughed uproariously because the idea of Laurie crawling kerbs for anything other than a craving for fried chicken was almost as ridiculous as the idea of him being dead. Yet one of those impossibilities is now true.

Viv wants to come over. He asks her not to. The neighbours opposite have a new baby; comings and goings might disturb them. Last week, through a tense smile that looked like a committee decision, they mentioned they'd heard Laurie slamming a cab door and singing the same two bars of a Vengaboys song as he searched for his house keys.

'You know how it is when you have kids,' the disappointingly hot dad of the couple told him while his wife explained the bizarre sleep technique they were trying out on their pink-faced progeny.

Laurie loved babies but was unrepentant: 'Five months of renovation those fuckers put us through before they moved in. Drove us insane. They can cope with me boarding the Vengabus every now and again.'

Viv hangs up. Jo puts the kettle on, knowing she'll ignore him and drive round anyway. Twenty minutes later, her fists are beating on his door. Jo opens it, finger to his lips like a primary school teacher, and Viv hurls herself into his arms. She is still in pyjamas. Zebra print. Silk. A present from Laurie. Her red curls squished under a baseball cap. She holds out her arm.

'Pinch it,' she says. 'Hard as you can, proper playground bully style.' Jo begrudgingly obliges. 'Ow. I was hoping it wouldn't hurt.'

She sinks to the floor in the hallway and sits, legs splayed. Jasper wanders over and begins licking her hand, an action that usually sends Viv running for the sanitiser, but this time she looks straight ahead and strokes Jasper's ears, saying his name quietly over and over, like a mantra, because what she really wants to say is Laurie's name. Jasper yawns and lets loose a cloud of halitosis. They've been trying him on new food to make his daily excretions less tricky to pick up with a poo bag.

'Fucking hell, Jojo.'

'I know, he stinks, sorry.'

'No, I mean fucking hell. This. It's real. Is it real? It is, right?'

'Yes.'

They sit in the back lounge, the 'messy room' off the kitchen that looks out over the garden. It's still dark outside. Jo makes tea, then pours Viv a gin, then pours that away because he remembers gin makes you miserable, and gets her a vodka instead. They look at each other a while. Laurie's lifetime love and his oldest and best friend, bound together in this weird, timeless purgatory waiting for the world to wake up. It's like there's no future to think of, just an endless now.

'The police were nice,' says Jo, just to make a sound. 'Kind.'

'Surprising.' Viv considers herself an anarchist, even when she's photographing Tory politicians for Sunday supplements.

'They were so young.' Jo is back for a moment in that mortuary, the room bare and soundproofed, lights respectfully dimmed. Laurie so distant. So dead. He didn't look like himself. Not just the slight swelling on his head, but Laurie was in perpetual motion: eyebrows always Groucho Marxing in his sleep, twitching and writhing and scratching himself at weddings and funerals. And now so still. That stain on the sheet.

Viv talks about Laurie in present tense, like he's stepped out of the room. A party they're going to next Tuesday. Jo can't feel anything. It's not numbness, it's a powering-down. His body preparing him for the wave. It's like the comedowns that blighted their twenties. Lifetimes ago.

'Viv. I need to tell Belinda.'

'Let's do it together. When it's light. Not on the phone. You can't tell someone their child is dead over the phone, when it's dark outside. Do you feel okay to drive?'

He does. A stray bird starts tweeting. Although ravaged by a chilly January, the garden still looks beautiful. Frost clinging to the blazing red shoots of the plant whose name he can't remember. Fire and ice. Light from the back door hitting the bronze leaves of another. The trees naked but dignified. From where he's sitting, by the window, Jo can see along the side of the house that juts into the garden, and the window of the smaller study, still in darkness. They won't be alone long. Laurie's office will burst into life in a few hours, without him. He's forgotten who's on the rota, whether it's Rosy or Byron coming in today.

The contrast between Laurie's two part-time assistants will be all the starker this morning. Viv's daughter, Rosy, is fresh, young, energetic. Byron, Laurie's friend since the years of no hangovers and sharp features, is weary, embittered, usually angry at the morning for not being the bright new dawn he was always praying for. Today, he'll have a right to that anger.

If it's a Rosy day, Jo usually hangs on to see her, but if it's Byron, Jo times it to perfection so their paths never cross. Byron always lets himself in through the garden door to the back of the house to Laurie's offices, clicking on the lamp in the window that Jo sees now, then dives into Laurie's various inboxes, tutting as he clears coffee cups and sweet wrappers from Laurie's writing room. Rosy, however, bombs straight into the kitchen, makes a fuss of Jasper, and spends the first hour of her working day at the kitchen table scrolling through emails, so long as her mother has managed to penetrate Rosy's soundproof dreams and drag her out of bed.

As if reading his mind, Viv says, 'It's not Rosy today. She went to a rave or something. Wasn't back when I left the house.'

Jo is suddenly aware of how little he knows about the protocol. Tracey, Laurie's agent of the last two decades, never sleeps. Jo tells her the news robotically, like he's calling from the electricity company for a meter reading. He'll get used to this, he thinks, sadly, as the words spill out. There'll be a long version and a short version. He will never mention the stain on the sheet. Tracey screams. Poor Laurie has made two women cry in the space of two hours. He'd be crushed.

They drive to Laurie's mother's house. It is crisp and somehow inappropriately bright. Belinda opens the door, fully dressed, perfume leaking out into the cold morning air. She smiles in surprise until she notices a darkness to their faces, realises this is not a social call. Viv and Jo enter and, as tenderly as they can, over hot, sweet tea, they ruin Belinda's life. Viv asks her to come back with them. Jo is relieved when Belinda refuses. She wants to stay steeped in memories of the only child of her three who truly understood her. Life without Laurie would be like never hearing her favourite song again.

Driving, Jo calls the café, and immediately regrets putting his young, vibrant staff on speaker. Life goes on, with gusto. Alif sounds jolly. Jo can hear Zosia in the background singing a song she's surely too young to have even heard of. Jo and Viv almost manage to smile with their eyes as they hear Zosia tackling the high notes.

Jo says the words, pausing for the inevitable gap between them hearing the news and understanding it. On the retelling, Jo will time it perfectly, he knows, same as he always knows when the panini is ready, five seconds before it starts to smoke. It's like being onstage again; Jo was never the best actor but he'd always known his lines. 'I'm afraid he didn't make it.'

As he's about to hang up, Zosia shouts out, 'Love you, Jo,' and Jo pulls over and puts his head on the steering wheel, because a simple expression of love in this moment when everything's been taken away seems so fucking weird and alien. Viv does not move or speak. Jo pushes the ignition and they're off again.

Back home, they hear Byron moving in the back of the house. It's always bothered Jo that he has a key, even though Rosy has one too. Byron's been around way longer, but Rosy is family. Jo was glad when Byron went part-time to 'concentrate on his fiction' and Rosy came on board for the stuff Byron refused to do, like social media and being pleasant over emails.

Leaving Viv catatonic in the kitchen, Jo slips through to the back of the house and breaks the news. Byron sinks slowly into his ergonomic chair, readjusting the seat on autopilot.

'I only spoke to him last night. Why didn't you call?'

'I know you like your eight hours.' Jo feels immediately guilty at this needless barb which also reveals that Laurie talked about Byron behind his back.

'I need to get his things in order.'

'What things?'

'His office.'

'I'll go through it myself.'

Jo feels sorry for him; it's good to pity someone else. 'Come through, help make calls. Viv's here. We haven't told Rosy yet, even.'

Byron slopes through to the kitchen – Jo hears Viv's vulpine scream as she sees a familiar face – and Jo goes into Laurie's writing room, stopping in front of the great oval desk in the middle of the room, like he's awaiting a telling-off from a headmaster. Posters on the wall, of both Laurie's own productions and ones he admired. A couple of his less prestigious awards on the shelf. Books everywhere. Desk cluttered with fragrances, hand sanitiser, pocket tissues, notebooks, some cigarettes – not the usual brand he pretended not to be smoking – and a lighter. Post-its, some scrawled, some with neat cursive, others in regimental block caps, decorate the edge of his large screen, which is smeared with fingerprints. On the rare occasions Jo came in while Laurie was working, it felt like gazing at the exposed innards of a magic trick, or a living art installation. Now, it's a museum.

Laurie's landline starts ringing. Jo's own phone vibrates in his pocket. In the kitchen, alerts start chiming on Byron's. It's started. In fewer than twelve hours, Laurie has gone from being a person to news.

Heading to the kitchen, every step feels laboured, wading through rapidly drying cement. His stomach churns with hunger, tiredness, and the future's sharp jab to the abdomen.

God, he thinks, as the doorbell rings. Oh God. What the fuck, Laurie? What the hell happens now?

Two
February

Vivienne

'*Hey, this is Laurie. Thanks for your call which, sadly, I've missed. Please don't leave a message after the tone, text me instead. Or email. Or try again later. Or call my office. But if you do leave a message, make sure you say the important stuff in the first five seconds because that's all I can bear. I'm sorry. Love you, possibly.*'

Viv hangs up, like she has the previous fifty times or so over the last couple of weeks. She'll speak one day, she knows she will. But not today. What would she say?

'Hey, Lulu, I'm on my way to your funeral.' His funeral. Sounds so weird.

Arriving in their car, behind the hearse, Viv tingles with irritation to see the street packed with mourners in bright colours and blow-dries. She hates this trend of dressing for funerals like it's a day at the races.

Laurie didn't leave instructions, but on the few occasions they talked about it, Laurie only said, 'If anyone tells you to be happy and smiling and celebrating my life or whatever, tell them to piss off. I don't want anyone in fucking fuchsia. I want black. Dour faces. Everyone paralysed by grief. Okay?'

Inside, people cram round the edges of the church, or squeeze onto pews. It would've thrilled Laurie to see a full house for his curtain call. All those relationships Laurie must've had day to day. His barber, the guy in the deli who made his lunch, favourite waiters and bar staff, the receptionist at his doctor, his one-time drug dealer even. Parts of Laurie that Viv can never touch. At least their grief will be fleeting. Maybe they'll reminisce happily one night, over a glass of wine, but they'll move on, think about something else. Viv is stuck with this for ever.

The carpet running up the aisle is bright red. It could almost be a premiere. If they'd set up a step-and-repeat board, doubtless plenty would've posed in front of it.

They take their seats. While Jo avoids looking at the wooden box containing Laurie, Viv can't take her eyes off it. Laurie's in there. Laurie in a box. It would almost be funny if it weren't so horrifying. She recognises that photo on top. Wedding day, she reckons. Laurie smiling, slightly clammy from dancing, strands of his dark blond hair reaching for his powder blue eyes, his face almost purple from the sunburn he'd picked up the previous day.

There is a rustling as the vicar's microphone is made live and she fusses with her robes. 'Welcome, everyone, to this celebration of the life of Laurie Blount.'

Celebration. Honestly. Someone barks out a large cry from a few rows behind. Rosy squeezes her hand. She's been gentler than usual. Rosy does her crying in the shower. Viv has heard her, seen her emerge with red eyes.

'It's the shampoo,' she said.

*

Viv's started smoking again, despite ditching cigarettes well over a decade ago. When she's been over at Laurie's – well, Jo's now – Jo doesn't make her go out into the garden; he lets her stand at the door. She likes to imagine the plumes of smoke comfort him as they billow and float past the window, remind him she's there. They've known each other a long time; Laurie was the love of both their lives. But there's an understanding between them that neither will ever say out loud: that they both wish the other had died instead of Laurie.

Jo didn't want to speak at the service. Neither did Viv. She regrets it now, listening to theatre's most shameless show-offs over-enunciate impersonal passages from books Laurie never read, or their own hackneyed eulogies. There was much more to Laurie's life than this circus.

'Not just a client, not just a shining star, but a friend, and a good man,' says Tracey, her voice much smaller and younger than it ever sounded when Laurie had her on loudspeaker, miming a gun to his mouth because she was ordering him to appear on a panel somewhere. Tracey fiddles with her wedding ring the entire time she's speaking. Viv has heard the wife has a bed in her studio.

Ned Lanford next. He'd made Laurie's dreams come true and been the root of a few of his nightmares probably.

Viv can't help herself. 'Poor Ned. Ageing like a banana. He's starting to look like Frans from Guess Who.'

Jo turns to her. 'Viv! I can't believe you said that.' But there's a glint. Laurie's spirit hangs round them in a fog. He'd have enjoyed today. Shame he can't be here to see it, that you never get the attention you crave until you die. Not that Laurie was ever starved of it, with rave reviews, fancy parties, glowing plaudits and gushing letters from fans desperate to know his 'process'.

Ned looks spruce and gaunt, as always. His usual waxed

twink straightening his tie for him before he approaches the lectern. Or is it a pulpit? Whatever. Ned's hair is almost completely white now; he has the telltale tan of someone who sneaks off to the Caribbean straight after New Year.

Laurie once told Viv that Ned hardly ate and spent the spare calories on vintage Châteauneuf-du-Pape.

'They have terrible genes,' Viv says, whispering Laurie's exact words to Rosy now. 'All the other Lanfords are oval and riddled with gout. They usually collapse around sixty.'

Rosy squeezes her hand, tighter this time. A hushing mechanism.

After reminding everyone he discovered Laurie's talent, Ned recites a few lines from one of Laurie's plays. The big one, that changed everything. *The Cruelty of Daylight*.

'Grief is the echo of the love you felt when they were alive. The harder you loved them, the longer and louder the echo. You can't run from grief. You must allow yourself to build your world around it.'

Byron is up last. Poor By-By, thinks Viv, we should've got him a box to stand on. Two decades she has known him and she always forgets how short he is until he's right next to her. Byron repeats stuff said earlier by other speakers, with less sincerity but more oomph. He talks, with a fondness that teases at Viv's tear ducts, about the three of them working late in the Sonata Bistro up by Chancery Lane in their younger days, and there's an overlong, and untrue, anecdote about Laurie rechristening him 'Lord'. Byron started that. Nothing sadder than a nickname you give yourself. Viv is suddenly furious nobody else can corroborate, and that Laurie died in such a stupid way. In a car. Not even a very nice one. He'd be livid.

Rosy starts the applause when Byron's done; it rings out and fills the room. Everyone is smiling and cheering, not for Byron, but Laurie, and because the service is more or less over, and they can get a drink.

'Silver Springs' by Fleetwood Mac starts up. Viv reckons Laurie would've picked 'Is That All There Is?' given the choice; she regrets not speaking up but she had to leave the room every time someone talked about 'the arrangements'. She stares in disbelief as Laurie's coffin trundles away, making his final exit with more subtlety than he ever showed alive. Laurie liked you to know he was leaving a room.

This is so fucking unfair, thinks Viv. There's so much still to say. Who will she laugh with now? Who can she be horrible with? Not *horrible* horrible, just horrible in that affectionate way. The declarations of love that leave bite marks. Nobody else does that. Rosy doesn't get it. Too earnest. Nor Jo. Too pragmatic. As for Byron, he can give, but he can't take. Only Laurie had the perfect balance. How could he leave her?

Jo

Jo has spent the last couple of weeks in an invisible goo he can't wash off. The weight of grief. Usually, he'd scuttle about, getting a million things done, running out the door, compiling a schedule for the week in his head. Now he's resigned to moving through this cold, messy, sticky treacle for as long as it takes. Grief keeps its own schedule, its timeline a zigzag. Zosia and Alif update him on things at the café but he can't take in anything other than what's happening right in front of him.

Like this room. Usually dressed for weddings, the management obviously had a mild panic and tried to eliminate every scrap of pink and ivory, covering tables in weighty dark plum fabrics to signify the seriousness of death. Strange really. Dying is a much easier commitment to make than marriage, and he should know; he married Laurie twice. Kind of. People are certainly dressed for a less sombre occasion. Jo has been to umpteen funerals over the years – grandparents, friends' grandparents, long-lost acquaintances, that shock death of a former schoolfriend that always happens in your early twenties – but he's never seen quite so much animal print and crushed velvet. And that's just the men. Fascinators too. Maybe he's not used to being around theatre people any more. He stopped red carpet peacocking years ago, got tired of standing awkwardly in theatre foyers, fingers sticky from canapés, watching people's eyes either dim or blaze up depending on how interesting or useful Laurie was to them. No more book launches, screenings or private parties. Laurie was disappointed, said he liked to have Jo on his arm, but he'd take Viv instead, or Byron or Rosy sometimes. Jo only went to first nights and awards if Laurie was nominated. He didn't miss them. He was invisible beyond velvet ropes anyway.

Jo's parents made the trip from Derbyshire and, judging from their stony faces, argued all the way down. Jo shakes a lot of hands. So many people come, one by one, dispensing aphorisms about grief, or love, or death. A few are instantly recognisable as song lyrics, or quotes off the back of a book jacket; Jo remembers one from an episode of *Doctor Who*. Grief is a tribute, love is beyond the physical, death is not the end, he's in a better place, they say, over and over, pitching slogans for fridge magnets or tea towels. So many words, Jo doesn't know what to do with them.

It was unsettling to hear the tributes during the service, talking about Laurie as if he weren't right there in the coffin next to them. They all performed well, even if Ned and Byron ran a little too long, but that's what it was: a performance. Did any of them really capture his magic? Ned's reading, from *The Cruelty of Daylight*, was beautiful, but quite pretentious, too, like a lot of Laurie's writing. Laurie was amazed that reviewers, patrons, producers, actors and just about everybody immediately declared it a seminal work. His first smash, despite it featuring zero laughs. It had the desired effect, though: a cotton salute of handkerchiefs filled the room and even Ned faltered a little reading the last line.

A year or so ago, Jo and Laurie attended a funeral for a formidable journalist who'd interviewed Laurie a few times and became a favoured bar-hopping pal. Jo gawped while Laurie filled him in on the people eulogising her, and at least one terrible thing each of them had done. If these reprobates were exalting this woman, who'd apparently been a giant-hearted legend, a rare talent, and a force of nature – all words used about Laurie dozens of times in the last hour – was she actually a good person at all? If you're judged by the company you keep, aren't you judged even more by those willing to stand up and lionise you once you're gone? Would people say that about Laurie, after listening to Ned Lanford, with a dating history so murky it needed its own survivors' helpline? What about Tracey – fabulous, an angel, but also responsible for many a smear campaign against her enemies? And Byron, with his habit of leaving fake one-star reviews of rivals' books on Amazon? Your mourners help set your legacy.

'Laurie changed my life,' says one man, who Jo recognises as an early alumnus of Laurie's scholarship for actors and writers from underprivileged backgrounds. Named the Valenti, after Jo, in recognition of the very first underprivileged actor he'd bailed out. 'Without him, or the Valenti, I wouldn't be where I am today.'

'That's so kind, thank you,' autopilots Jo. Then he remembers his manners, and actors' fragile egos. 'Great to hear you're doing well.'

The actor beams again. 'Laurie was one of the good ones, you know. Well, I'm sure you already do.'

'I do,' says Jo, as the man retreats into the main throng. He isn't wearing socks. It's February.

'Rosy, can we go?'

Rosy breaks off from chatting to a vaguely familiar young man, one of the zillion strangers from the church who will be for ever emblazoned onto his brain now.

'Yup, sure. Some people are coming back to the house, close friends only. That okay, Uncle Jo?'

He supposes it'll have to be.

Two hours later, anyone who couldn't get close enough at the first reception now corners him in his kitchen, drinks splashing onto the floor, which Jasper will no doubt lick up later and get sick from. Grief is a tribute, love endures, mourning is a process. Nonsense. Grief is smiling beatifically while a congregation crane their necks to see if you look sad enough. Grief means standing in your own kitchen unable to tell grinning well-wishers to get the fuck out. Why can't they finish their martinis, hit pause on their eulogies, gather up their funeral garb and go home?

Holden, Jo's oldest friend, has telepathically received the memo.

'Think we're going to shoot off.' He signals at his lovely wife Sian and their children, who all try not to sigh too heavily with relief.

'Sure.' Jo smiles gratefully at his best friend. And ex-lover, of course. Laurie could never understand staying friends with

anyone who'd seen you come, or had come on you, sitting round
the table like nothing ever happened. When Laurie left lovers
behind, the cord was irrevocably severed. There's no question of
a reconciliation; Holden actively disconnected from the label of
bisexuality about fifteen years ago, around the time he started
using his surname as his first name, although there have been
aberrations.

'Remember, Laurie wouldn't want you to wallow.'

'I know. I won't.'

Jo watches them go, preparing his best stoic smile in case they
turn round and wave. They don't.

Laurie's brother Ray has made one concession to formality
and foregone his denim obsession to wear what is likely his
only suit, purchased some time before dial-up internet was
invented. His sister Evangeline has finished talking to a good-
looking actor who did the Broadway run of *Cruelty* and now
approaches Jo, clutching a wine glass smeared with fingerprints.
Her teenage children sit uncomfortably waiting to get back to
their version of the world where everyone is young, and dies
only in video games.

Jo smiles at Evangeline and watches her son, on the cusp of
fourteen and slurping full-sugar Coca Cola out of a gigantic
tumbler. 'Bless him.'

'We think he might be like Laurie, y'know,' says Evangeline,
tongue struggling to make the words with layers of red wine
coating it like emulsion.

'A writer? Brilliant!'

She laughs. 'No! Gay!' She starts to do the wrist action but
stops herself. 'I'm not sure how to tease it out, or if I even should.
Laurie said to throw a football in his general direction and if
he ran away screaming, he was probably gay. If he kicked it,
straight. Picked it up, bisexual. He was the living end.'

Jo imagines Laurie's clipped tones delivering this expert opinion and smiles. 'Yes, he was,' he murmurs, and is glad to lift his drink to his mouth as a distraction.

Jo spies his mum at the kitchen sink, looking round anxiously. Theatre people can be a bit much if you're more of a 'ready meal in front of a gameshow' type. He feels a rush of sympathy and affection.

'Don't even think about washing up.'

'I can load the dishwasher?'

'Someone's coming to do that. Do you have to leave tonight?'

Jo's mother winces. She wants to stay. 'Your dad needs his own bed. Don't you, Bob?'

Jo's father sidles up and tips cold tea down the plughole, not rinsing out the sink after. Jo remembers living at home and swearing into the bathroom mirror because his dad spat toothpaste into the washbasin but never swilled it away. Old habits. 'You'll want some time to yourself, Jo.'

'I have the rest of my life to myself.' How grown-up and serious, to be a widower. He's never asked what his parents really thought of Laurie. They aren't talkers, not like Laurie's mother. It's more what they don't say. Looks. Sighs. How they close a door. A spoon clattering round a cereal bowl, scooping up milk dregs. He decides to ask.

Jo's mother is not shocked by the question. 'Um, Laurie was clever, and ... smooth. Smooth, Bob, wouldn't you say?'

Bob twitches ever so slightly. 'Yep.'

Jo remembers their wedding video. For the 'upgrade' – not the civil partnership a few years earlier. As Jo and Laurie kissed, the videographer panned across the luxurious room to take in the collective joy, but for some reason paused on Jo's parents, and zoomed on Bob's face. Lips pulled in tighter than an appendix scar. Looking on as Laurie's tongue swirled round the mouth of his only son, the same mouth that had said 'Dada!', had eaten fish fingers off the 'choo choo train' fork, and may well, in Bob's mind, have sucked a thousand dicks a day before meeting Laurie. He doesn't need to know what his father thinks of Laurie; his face told him, ten years ago, on that video.

Jo leaves them and hears running water and the clink of glasses as his mother begins to wash up.

As the house clears, Jo heads to the garden to check the smokers are using ashtrays. The door to Laurie's rooms is open.

'Ned.'

Ned Lanford jumps. Rosy has shown Jo videos of cats leaping almost as high when someone points a cucumber at them.

'Jo. Sorry. I was feeling nostalgic.' He traces his finger across the top of the computer screen. No dust. Diana the cleaner was in at six this morning.

'I understand.' But he doesn't. Not really. Ned and Laurie's friendship – or whatever you'd call it – played out on their favourite tables in any number of Soho's restaurants, not here. There isn't a barman in a ten-mile radius they weren't on first name terms with. 'Anything I can help with?' Jo has an urge to frisk him. What would possibly interest him in Laurie's messy little office? Ned could buy everything in there a billion times over.

'Jo, if you need anything, let me know. I'll drop by whenever I can.'

'Honestly, there's no—'

Ned grips Jo's hand tightly. Everyone is determined to man-handle him today. 'You know Laurie meant a terrific amount to me, don't you?' Jo nods. 'He'd want me to keep a close eye, look after you. I won't let my old friend down.' He raises Jo's hand to his mouth and kisses it, before walking back through

the kitchen and clicking his fingers, calling his young com-
panion to his side as Jo might to Jasper to let him know his
food was ready.

Jo tries to conjure up what Laurie's response might have been,
and as Viv watches Ned float by, she locks eyes with Jo and he
can tell she's thinking the same. For the first time since Laurie
died, Jo can't bring anything to mind. Life will be like that from
now on, he realises. Gaps in the air where Laurie would have
spoken, but won't, not any more.

Daddy Issue

Laurie

When Tracey floated the idea of doing an autobiography, or whatever this ends up being, I was disgusted. Imagine releasing some awful cash-in, gurning on the cover, holding one of my Oliviers or a Tony. It's not like I've climbed Everest, or cured cancer, or survived ten years on a desert island, I told her. I don't need to reel off my achievements, like I'm applying for VIP access at the pearly gates. I got lucky: I had the talent, and the chat; I exploited both, and people liked the result. If anyone wants to know more, see one of my plays, watch one of the ghastly movie adaptations, or pop on the soundtrack to my two (very successful, thank you) musicals. I'm absolutely fucking everywhere if you look hard enough. She sold it to me eventually; she's good at that. I've never been able to say no to a charming lesbian in good lipstick.

'Think of it as a personal memoir, Laurie, not your CV.

Vignettes. A collection of essays on your life, thoughts, feelings. It doesn't need context, you're the context. Anything.'

Anything. What a strategy. I could use my plays as inspiration, she said. Name a chapter after each one. A gimmick isn't a plan, I told her, but here we are, I'm giving it a go. A stab at a memoir. Why not, eh? Forget the hard-luck stories or 'plucky young upstart' bullshit that paints my life in a much duller hue than it's felt to live it. My life isn't worthy or wholesome, or even beset by scandal. It just is. Probably best left alone, but I like a challenge. Let's get the childhood out of the way.

My mother has a nice saying that I put in one of my early plays so it gets quoted back to me in interviews, or reader questions, or even as epigraphs in books by newer, less jaded writers. 'Everything begins with a broken heart.' It doesn't make sense but it's pretty and poetic – which expertly sums up dear Belinda.

My mother's own heart broke each time she gave birth, but my arrival – her third and final go in the stirrups – smashed it into the smallest smithereens. Imagine being a heartbreaker, sticky and amniotic, before you've barely squawked your first complaint to the world. I'd like to say I started as I meant to go on, but for a long time the only heart getting broken was mine. My father died when I was sixteen – not a heartbreaking moment, by the way. If this sounds cruel, you're underestimating the crude selfishness of a teenager's commitment to their own horn. He died at the start of summer, and I was on the cusp of a sexual awakening, knowing my schoolfriend's older brother would, as he did every summer, sprawl shirtless in their back garden, trying to catch a tan, the magic amulet he used to get the attention of every teenage girl in a five-mile radius. Watching him bronze those delightfully perky tits all day long the previous year had finally inspired the pink penny to drop inside me, two days before the weather turned chilly and they disappeared back under his Firetrap T-shirt, so I was primed for this summer.

Alas, my father's death meant I'd spend most of it indoors, respectfully grieving. You can't mourn on the patio, in Bermuda shorts, apparently. Doesn't look right. Worst of all, my father chose to perish while mowing the lawn – usually my job, but I'd stamped my foot and fled to London to buy CDs and baggy jeans. It was left to a (different, non-sexy) neighbour to witness my father's collapse and phone Mum at the travel agent's. I couldn't even peer across to where my by now coppery neighbourhood Adonis lay without conjuring up a sketch of my father clutching his chest, no doubt cursing my name as he fell to the earth that would become his permanent home seventeen long days later.

So instead of perving, I picked up a pen. That's how it started. The only notepaper in the house was the tear-off pad my mother wrote shopping lists on, and it didn't seem appropriate to nip out and buy stationery. I dug out an old telephone directory – carbon dating myself to the neolithic period there – and wrote over the print in the bluest pen I could find. I invented a man who was sad about his daddy. My first play. So I have him to thank, really.

I knew I wouldn't miss my father. He was not an unkind man, but distant and preoccupied. He embraced dullness and order. I was the only child to inherit my mother's taste for excitement and adventure and sequins, the enlivening third and final act in a disappointing production. My siblings were, like my father, dour and unimaginative. A scarf, to them, was for keeping warm and nothing more, but to me it could be anything! A hat, a kite, a sail on my enchanted boat. My mother grabbed my passion for the extraordinary with both hands, like she'd been starved of colour from birthing two greyed-out dullards before me.

I'd tried to win Dad round, asked to do things I thought he might like. I remember begging him to take me and my tiny bike into London so I could ride round Hyde Park and feel part of something special. He refused. I had to settle for the local park, which in the eighties was all discarded foil and needles, scraps of pornographic material in the bushes, verges unkempt, or scarred by nature paths, paving unloved and fissured, accentuating every bump of the stabilisers right up my then-bony bum. My tears at his funeral were a mixture of relief that the house had one less person in it to disappoint and genuine sorrow at being prevented from objectifying the neighbour.

He'd have hated the gay thing. Interesting, really, because it was his fault. More or less. I was fascinated by men from an early age, before I felt even a sexual tingle. My father worked with a man called William Fossett, not particularly attractive, but my first alert to a man's physical possibilities. He was so different from my pa. He was huge, and brutal, hair sprang from the neck of his shirts like electrified wire, but there was a gentleness; he kissed my mother hello on both cheeks – outrageously continental then – and used a coaster without being asked. His dreary business attire looked like it was preventing something wild and exciting from escaping. My father was lithe – despite eating like a horse; I suppose on reflection the arteries were doing the heavy lifting – and his own suits seemed to be encasing something unpleasant. I never craved the approval of adults or liked joining in; I had a cousin who would roll his belly and do puny muscle man poses, but I was never willing to play the tart for coin. But when William Fossett used to come round to watch sport on our TV, I'd use long words to impress him, and clamber onto his lap on our vile brown sofa and ask for a story – aged eleven. I was quite undignified about it. He didn't have a wife ('not yet' was his official stance) so Dad took this young bachelor under his wing.

My feelings and my body were beginning to confuse me. It had been a long road: my sister Evangeline caught me dancing to 'Rocket to Your Heart' in her bedroom when I was about eight and said that's when she knew. Literally the only time she's ever been right about anything; I expect she treasures the memory. I was blissfully unaware for years to come, however, until something about my inner workings caused me to draw further away from my father and William Fossett.

I became more shy in William's presence, wouldn't kick the ball back if he lobbed it my way, shrank from his ruffling my hair, awkwardly refused offers of piggybacks on the lawn that would one day kill my father. He stopped coming round when I was about fourteen, for reasons never disclosed. I fretted I'd driven him away, by picturing his face as I humped my pillow every evening. I've fantasised about looking him up a million times, but life has been disenchanting enough; I hate to think of William Fossett ageing, barely remembering the gawky brat who showed him his poems.

My dad eschewed Vivaldi or a slow one from the Beatles for his funeral. He picked 'Your Silent Face'. New Order. Quite edgy for him. A glimpse into the supernova one explosion too late. Far too long, though. It cut off after the first verse, so before the swearing.

When I think about my father dying now, I see it through a modern-day lens. You know, why didn't anyone help me and my mother process his death in that ugly house in Greenford? Did we have PTSD? We endured it. I wonder sometimes if I grieved at all. He was thirty-five when I was born. He always seemed so old but people did back then. You looked fifty as soon as you hit thirty. People of his era had been too close to the ones who'd lived through horrifying wars, seen too much. Inherited trauma. Maybe I still carry it.

He never saw my success, and however you get on with your parents, that's all you want, isn't it? To show the people who made you that you were worth the bother, that they created something beautiful or useful? Or both.

Starmaker

Laurie

I was nineteen when I started working in the Sonata, a scuzzy little bistro up the Gray's Inn Road, watching barristers conduct extramarital assignations over linguine and cheap, treacly red wine. Nineteen! Scribbling away during any downtime, and sometimes during the uptime, if Vivi or Byron covered for me, which they did. On paper, we had nothing in common other than our shift patterns, but the horrible and the damaged always find each other somehow, like serial killers do. Vivi was a beautiful, formerly spoiled disappointment to her uptight upper-middle-class Surrey-dwelling parents – she'd go on to disappoint them even more when she got pregnant by the gorgeous (married) chef Asaad and gave birth to what her horrible racist bitch of a father would call 'a brown baby' (Rosy). We shared a passion for reciting movie dialogue at each other – *Withnail and I* and *Breakfast at Tiffany's* were favourites – and clicked straight away.

As for Byron ... oh Byron, ironically named by a time-travelling parent with a sense of humour perhaps. Byron was allegedly our manager, a mere two years our senior and host to an impressive amount of inferiority complexes. He lived – still lives, in fact – in that filthy bit of Earl's Court that's resistant to gentrification, and had ambitions to be a writer, a painter, a restaurateur, a sculptor, you name it. All ambitions he was doing nothing about other than talk about them. He expected success to find him, rather than seek it himself, a risky strategy that didn't pay off. Vivi and I came round to him, though, despite his fondness – which he maintains to this day – for calling us by our surnames as if we were corporals to his sergeant major. He controlled the rota and, luckily, he favoured us over other waiters, who were more talented and beautiful than us but had richer parents, which Byron resented, though he wasn't exactly impoverished – he was paying some ancient aunt a peppercorn rent for his west London hovel. In all the years I've known him, he's never picked up the dinner tab; as my Irish granny used to say, he'd peel an orange in his pocket, that one. When the bistro closed at night, Byron would always say, with the true desperation of someone who never has anywhere to be, that he had plans but couldn't be bothered, so would join me and Vivi as we half-heartedly mopped, downing the aforementioned woeful red wine and plotting the downfalls of enemies we had yet to meet. I remember thinking as I swirled that fetid swab over those faded tiles: I simply have to make it. This couldn't be all there was.

One day the owner, a moustached man who wore cheap tweed and was always scratching himself, told us the bistro was being sold, to someone who wanted to go upmarket and would probably fire us. That someone was Ned Lanford. Everybody's heard of Ned Lanford, not always for the same reasons. Vivi, Byron and I made a pact to stick together and somehow avoid

the sack. Vivi because she'd just had a baby – I cried with happiness and have been madly in love with Rosy since she was
born – and Byron because he'd certainly never make it as anything else. And me? Because I knew that Ned Lanford's family
just happened to own three theatres. I already had one play
under my belt, *Daddy Issue*, staged for buttons in a tiny space
up the Caledonian Road thanks to Vivi mildly embezzling her
parents and us relying on favours from every actor and techie
we'd ever shagged (a fair number). Now I was working on my
second, better one – yes, that one – and had literally no idea
what to do next. Fate had dealt me an ace for the first time.

 Ned was your typical posh boy, teeth like blank scrabble tiles,
familial rejection burning a hole in his heart, which lived at the
bottom of his pocket. He was too pretty for politics, too ugly
for showbiz, too queer for Daddy's love and too pedestrian for
his mother to be excited by having a gay son. So he acted out by
pumping his money into the arts and his rage into boyfriends
who barely lasted longer than mayflies. He had fingers in un-
countable theatrical pies but still enough digits free to terrorise
the waistbands of young drama students up and down the country. We bonded over both being thwarted actors. Oh, I always
deny it, but I wanted to be a performer. To act. To sing. Take
the stage. A few small problems there: I couldn't act for shit,
nor sing for toffee, and compared to other bright young things
flunking auditions, I had a face like a slate layer's nail-bag. I
had no chance. So I got other people to say the words. I could
show off on the page. Writing's all I can do now. I love making
beautiful people say ugly things. Controlling the emotions,
making characters speak and move and live and die and fuck
and buy coffee and cheat and cry and run down hills and climb
mountains I'll never see. I wrote my way out of my old life and
into the arms of a community that may not always love me but

it understands me and respects what they kindly refer to as my brilliance. And it used to get me laid.

I digress.

As a trio, we charmed Ned. It was quite calculated. We were in that stage of life where you assume your youth is extremely desirable to others – he was over thirty, which seemed like a million years old to us. We laughed at his jokes and gently ribbed him about his playboy lifestyle, pretending to be interested in any gossip from the parties and launches he was always attending in an attempt to get into *Tatler* or at least the society pages of the *Standard*. (He managed it a few times, deploying anglepoise contortions to leer in the background of various paparazzi frenzies outside nightclubs; the photos used to make us howl.) He popped in most days, seeking our counsel on the imminent refurbishment, and even confided in us about a possible new Soho opening, which made our collective self-interested heartbeat quicken. One evening, Vivi was off at postnatal aqua aerobics or something, and it was just me and Byron, wiping down tables.

'You're gonna have to take one for the team, Blount, if we want the Soho jobs,' said Byron lasciviously. 'You know he's gay, right?'

Of course I knew. Sometimes you can't tell with majorly posh men; they all got buggered senseless at public school after all. Ned was the real deal. Everything gave him away: the way he sat on chairs, how he spoke, his coffee order. Nobody but the gay or lactose intolerant were asking for soya milk back then. So I resigned myself to it, asking if I could drop by and see him for 'professional advice'. He invited me for a drink at his club, and I took my dog-eared printout of *Daddy Issue*, and the latest draft of *The Cruelty of Daylight* with me, expecting them to be quickly tossed aside so he could begin sexual overtures. I wasn't unused to sleeping with men I had no interest in – I liked my teeth rattled at least twice a week, it didn't always matter who by – but I didn't want to do this. He was waiting on a banquette, his shirt unbuttoned one rung lower than usual. I was bleaching my hair then, I liked to stand out, but I felt cheap and conspicuous as I made my way to the table, trying not to gawk too much at my surroundings: the tasteless art cobbled together by members too tight to pay their bill, the odd minor celebrity, and attractive but frigid waiters who knew I absolutely didn't belong this side of the partition. A quaking subject approaching the king.

Ned read them in front of me, in silence, while I sipped deathly pale rosé like a teenager sneaking booze at a wedding. We didn't eat.

'These are extraordinary. I can't imagine the work that went into . . . ' – he flipped back to the front of the manuscript – *'The Cruelty of Daylight.'*

I hadn't yet learned the sweet balance between confidence and self-deprecation back then. I became slightly manic.

'This? This is just a 3 p.m. idea. This is cobbling something together while waiting for my toast to pop. My best ideas come after midnight, 2 a.m., later, when I'm climbing into bed and the rest of the world's unconscious. I mean, I don't even know if you're ready for 2 a.m. me. Honestly. I don't know if my body can take it either. So 3 p.m. will have to do.'

'Well, 3 p.m. is just fine.' He laughed. 'I prefer to be direct, Laurie, so here's what I'm going to do. I want to make the plays happen. I can introduce you to some very influential people.' He suggested another run of *Daddy Issue* with a bigger budget while I finessed *Cruelty*. And he did exactly as he promised. Not a single move made, didn't even thumb the hem of my bootcut jeans. I was astounded. I was primed to hold my nose and go face down and star-shaped in the name of art, but the debt was never called in. Not in that way, anyway. Looking back, he must've decided my talent was more valuable than my arse. I owe him, I know that; he saw something no amount of mirrors could help me see in myself, but it was a mutual benefit. I gave him cachet, depth, accentuated his cool and, crucially, attached professionalism and respectability to how he usually operated. Much easier to wow an impressionable young actor by saying he helped put plays on stage than persuade them home to see his impressive library, with not one spine cracked. I wonder sometimes whether I'd have been better off fucking him that night, and erasing him from my future. We live and learn.

Vivi and Byron were delighted for me when I told them the next day. Well, Vivi was. Perhaps Byron was hoping I'd be brutalised and discarded like a Kleenex. I wondered if he'd considered trying it himself – he was ostensibly straight but most men I met in the hospitality industry were happy to look up at the ceiling and pretend someone else was tearing at their zip fly. Maybe he'd have had more luck. While I was whisked off into the heady world of theatre and began the baby steps towards making my name, thanks to the cold hard cash, time and energy of Ned and his array of backers, movers and shakers, the bistro closed and Vivi and Byron didn't get the Soho transfer.

Luckily, they never held it against me, keeping their powder dry in case I really did turn out to be the next big thing and, well, we know the rest. No need to dwell. But the realest, biggest thing was still yet to come. Jo.

Three
April

Jo

Rosy's bought Jo a book of affirmations. He's been trying it out, reading one to himself from the slim, square paperback every day. It's what Laurie would call woo-woo bollocks, but Jo finds it oddly gratifying, in a very neutral, unemotional way. The positive energy dissipates by the time he arrives at work, on the days he bothers going in. Even understaffed, the operation has become slicker in his absence. Has he been holding Zosia and Alif back all these years? Jo is a gooseberry. Alif is now in the habit of telling Jo to take a break and banishing him to a corner of the café with a panini.

'Of course, we should really be calling it a panino when it's just one,' says Alif. 'I keep telling you.'

Three months on, and he still hasn't let Byron go; he's literally paid to sit on a laptop at the house, reading celebrity news.

Laurie wouldn't have minded. Viv comes round most days. She isn't working, and she hates being in her house alone, so Jo is happy to have her there, to retread old anecdotes. Neither of them experience enough of the outside world to bring anything new to the table. Watching Viv and Byron interact is like spying on an old married couple. They pre-empt the other's next thought or emotion. Viv finishes a story about Laurie hiding in a mop cupboard during the lunchtime rush to read his own dialogue aloud and Byron already has a tissue prepared for her to whip out of his hand once the memory makes her cry. She insists on cooking for Jo almost every night, and if Byron is there, she prepares an alternative, minus the ingredients that he can't stomach. They don't laugh at each other's jokes, though, aware, perhaps, the jokes aren't as funny now Laurie isn't here to build on them.

One day, Viv suggests clearing out Laurie's wardrobe. She's just finished a book by a woman who believes the key to happiness is folding socks into threes and throwing away most of your possessions.

Viv and Jo stare at it, doors closed, like snakes wait within. Viv is saying ridiculous things.

'Honestly, I can help with anything Laurie used to do. What about the garden?'

'We have a young couple come and do that.' Sarah and Bruce, they wear yellow dungarees and have smiled nonstop since birth. 'Do you really think Laurie helped with the rockery? He didn't even know it was there.'

She laughs. Having never lived with Laurie, she recalls his general domestic inertia as a fond anecdote, rather than a daily irritant.

Finally, Jo wrenches the wardrobe doors open. Laurie's moss-green cashmere overcoat is hanging there. Jo puts it to his face and sniffs it. He breathes deeply, awaiting a tidal rush of memories, a scent forging a trail back to happier times. But nothing. A vague trace of cologne. But no essence of his husband. Just the weight of the fabric on his skin. He peels it away. He's grateful to breathe regular air again, air that isn't trying too hard to be someone else.

'We should start small. Sock drawer?'

Viv peers in. 'So many! Oh, I bought him these.' She holds up some bright pink suit socks with a green trim.

'His favourites,' lies Jo.

'Honestly, I want to help.'

Maybe Viv is looking for someone to tell her it's okay to sit and do nothing. Laurie would've expertly turned this back round. Jo begins taking out socks; most are not in pairs. 'The only thing I need help with is staff for the café. I need a new barista.'

'Maybe I can do that!' Viv is animated and enthusiastic, like someone just finishing their second airport pint. 'Why would a man need so many socks? It's ridiculous. None of my boyfriends ever owned more than five sets of black socks. Bobbly or threadbare usually. All these colours. Even his socks were full of life.' She snorts, balls up a pair of socks and flings them back in the drawer. 'I can't. Not today. It's too soon. Isn't it? Don't you think?'

On his free afternoons, after an hour or so reading, or tidying, or babbling at an impassive Jasper, Jo usually becomes paralysed by loneliness. He's tried, a couple of times, to watch pornography, see if he can get things moving. He's scrolled through interminable obscene thumbnails, searching for something semi-suitable, jeans off and folded on the bed next to him. He doesn't like tattoos, or saliva as lubricant. Everything feels sordid and inappropriate. Too soon.

Usually, he takes himself to a small, but clean and nicely furnished bar round the corner from the house. Gentrification's tendrils reaching out again. He's glad to see chicken shops and tatty convenience stores holding firm among the vegan bakeries and yoga studios, even though Laurie buying a house there only accelerated that problem. On arriving at the bar, he has learned just the right amount of force to liberate the door from its resting place without wrenching it open and causing its locked twin to vibrate noisily. He approaches the central aisle leading to the bar as if it's a catwalk, staring straight ahead, although nobody ever looks up. It's the kind of bar that pops up in a long-vacant shop and has never taken cash. Its tables and chairs don't match, no doubt rescued from the houses of the dead pensioners the neighbourhood's social renovators gobbled up for buttons. Jo always orders a cocktail, different every time to avoid the curse of becoming a creature of habit, which Laurie always said was like leaving a voicemail for death. Laurie also claimed people-watching was a dullard's idea of a hobby, but it's one of the few pleasures Jo shares with both parents, although Mr and Mrs Valenti tend to stare at their fellow humans with envy and disgust, rather than Jo's reflective fascination.

Jo misses the time before phones, before in-person conversation with strangers became weird and unpleasant. Sometimes, while the bartender makes flat small talk as he works up to asking for money, Jo longs to hear someone else's voice. It doesn't matter whose. A change from the indifferent politesse of shop assistants in the supermarkets he wanders around with an empty basket, or people barking 'excuse me' and sweeping by as he stands squinting vacantly at a building that somehow reminds him of Laurie.

Transaction over, he takes himself to as central a table as he can, easing out one of the four assorted chairs to avoid scraping on the stone tiles. Between sips he will look around him, pretending to admire the unambitious artwork on the walls, taking in his fellow drinkers. Usually he raises his glass to whoever's at the next table and asks them an innocent question, nodding at their cocktail and purring, 'That looks delicious. What is it?'

He only does this with couples; he leaves solo drinkers alone. Even though he'd be delighted if someone pitied him enough to strike up a conversation, he doesn't want to give the impression of a pest. The couples, usually young, always desperate not to reply, will trill back the name of the cocktail – French martinis are still in vogue, Jo notes. Never ready to break the connection, even though he spent two decades mixing cocktails for Laurie and his friends and whoever else ended up back at the house after a press night, Jo plays dumb. 'Ooh, what's in that?'

The couples smile, their reply friendly but clipped. They might ask about his cocktail in return, or they might not. After a minute or two, they chuck out a breezy 'well . . . ', and tell him to 'have a lovely evening' – what Laurie would call a 'fuck you on a silk cushion'. Jo knows when they've turned away they'll give each other the 'oh no' eyes, drink faster than they had before Jo interrupted them, then leave.

One afternoon, he's just finished interrogating the drinkers of an old-fashioned and an amaretto sour when he feels a tap on his shoulder.

'Drowning your sorrows?'

Tracey, Laurie's agent. He's so pleased to see her he's almost embarrassed by it.

'Trying to. Turns out they're strong swimmers.'

A consoling smile. 'Can I join? By which I mean, let's sit outside, so I can smoke.'

She's been visiting one of her authors, she says, as she scoops up Jo's drink and moves it to a table in unbearable direct sunlight.

'Talented beyond measure on the page, but can't do small talk. The slurping of my noodles was deafening.' She peers back into the bar. 'Were you trying to pick those two up?' She smiles at his gasp. 'No judgement. Me and the wife sometimes put the pugs in kennels for the night so we can have an overnight guest.'

'Tracey! No, I was just chatting.'

'Rosy says you're hanging round the house all day. I'm in the café sometimes, never see you. You're not even going to the gym.' She clasps her hands over his. 'Rosy told me that, I mean. I can't tell. I don't look at men's bodies, you're all floating heads to me.'

Jo finds himself caught in the curse of being desperate for company and conversation but not this exact combination. 'I know I have to do something, not sure what.'

'If I can offer some life advice? Someone else dying is the end of their life, not yours. Dig out some, uh, long-dormant ambition and try to make it happen.'

'I've already been to Disneyland.' At Holden's insistence, their one holiday together.

'I don't believe in bucket lists, far too morbid, but ...'

'It's always "go to New York" or "jump out of a plane", isn't it?' says Jo. Did Laurie have a bucket list? His goals were creative and professional; he never expressed a desire to see the sun set over Angkor Wat.

But there is something he wants to do. Something he's barely thought about in years. It will sound silly. Tracey pushes. She's good at it. It's how she earns her living.

'I always wanted to go to university. Like, properly. Study something.' His further education consisted only of acting. His father warned him he'd never use it. They came to one of his plays when it toured, tight-lipped and mortified in the stalls of the Lantern Theatre in Sheffield, flinching at the swearing.

'Brilliant! Be a mature cheddar, slouching in corridors and

fraternising with people who still drink cider for pleasure! Study what?'

'English, maybe? Or . . .' He doesn't want to say it. It's too tacky. Disrespectful. Weird. Slipping on a dead man's jacket. Tracey taps the table impatiently. 'I used to write. Maybe I could again.'

Tracey's right eyebrow lifts a millimetre and she immediately grabs her phone and begins tapping. After a minute or five of oppressive silence as Tracey's impressive manicure skitters across her phone screen, she sits back and lights a pink Sobranie. 'Sorted.'

'What?'

'You should get an email in the next couple of days from an amazing bird called Laura Parr, leads a fantastic creative writing course at North London Uni. I'll get you on it. I've, uh, done it before for old friends, no trouble. Great launchpad for a writing career.'

A rush of excitement Jo hasn't felt in a long time. 'I don't want a career. Don't I need to sit exams or something?'

Tracey shrugged. 'You're forty . . . uh, what are you now? Older or younger than Laurie?'

There it is. That punch to the gut. 'A year older.' But next year he'll be two years older, then three years older, then . . . Laurie is frozen at forty-five.

Tracey is oblivious to Jo's sudden nosedive into the dark place. 'Right, well, just pop in for a chat, write a couple of short bits, and you're in. What do you reckon?'

'Tracey, is Laura one of the overnight guests you farmed out the pugs for?'

Tracey rears her head in laughter. 'Not for the want of trying. Look, take my advice, do the course and take control of your bloody life, darling.'

Jo can't help but feel he's cheating, using nepotism to parachute into a course he might flunk.

Tracey rolls her eyes. 'Laurie would want you to. He'd be so proud. He'd have done this for you. So let me instead.'

She's hoisted him back from a brink he didn't even know he was teetering on. She's right, Jo's life isn't over. By grieving for Laurie, he's not honouring him, he's making his death worthless. He won't squander this precious gift by moping. Laurie would give anything for another crack at life, and Jo can't waste the opportunity.

'Thank you, Tracey. Honestly. Thank you.'

Night Zero

Laurie

Life-changing moments. They're funny. At the time, are you even aware how pivotal that moment is? Mostly, no. You can't be. So you don't drink it all in, you're on power-save. If only you knew how often in the future you'd long to relive those precious hours or days. You'd take in every detail, push your brain to its limits. I knew, though. I did. That entire night, the night I met my beautiful boy, it plays in my head like a movie anytime I want.

To coin a cliché I've never been afraid to use, the day started like any other. I woke up next to somebody. The last man I'd fuck before Jo. If I'd known, I might have given my promiscuity a better send-off than a drunken fumble with someone who couldn't remember my name. When I opened my eyes, he was looking at me with a strange curiosity, like he was peering into a sock drawer searching for a specific pair, and he said, with emetic overfamiliarity, 'Morning, sleepyhead.'

Three minutes later, I was in my pants, in my kitchen – a tiny flat in Kennington; I miss that bijou dive. I watched him write his name and number on the little yellow pad pinned to my corkboard. He finally said my name for the first time, seeing it on a gas bill – unpaid – tacked right next to it.

'Laurie Blount.'

'It rhymes with "shunt", not "mount".'

'Oh, sorry. Cool name.'

'It was given to me,' I said, spikily. I'm not a morning person. 'I'm glad you like it.'

'I do,' he said, sizing me up like I was a kebab at 3 a.m. 'And I like you.'

Silence. He winked, coughed and left. I looked at his note. Marcus. I knew I wouldn't be calling. I didn't like the way he wrote his sevens.

But still: all of it, the whole day, in cinematic clarity. Lunch with Vivi somewhere generic. Rosy was about two, and she sat and grizzled in a high chair while I filled her mother in on my night. Back then, my life was a soap opera to Vivi. Like a little old lady who sits in front of reality TV, gorging on chocolates, agog at a life she'll never lead, Vivi would sit open-mouthed as I regaled her with tales of who did what to whom, and for how long, and how hard.

We were firm friends by then, but we still had the ability to surprise and shock each other. Vivi was drifting, working front-of-house at an awful restaurant near the river. She hadn't found her passion. I wasn't in a position then to make it happen, I was still nobody. Made up for it later, of course. Things were hard for her, bringing up Rosy on her own, trying to date again. Unrequited tragic crushes on men whose wives didn't understand them, or fumblings with commis chefs in rusting cars overlooking places of natural beauty. She deserved better. Once we'd talked each other's heads off to our natural tolerance level, she was gone, all scarves, handbags, pushchair and disorganisation, off to deposit Rosy with a sitter so we could go out that night.

We were seeing a play. Some dreadful *Trainspotting* rip-off; there were still a lot of those in the early noughties. Utterly dry of humour and charm. I think that's why *Daddy Issue* was doing so well. It was cheeky. This was around the time someone called me the next Joe Orton for the first time, which was quite terrifying in a way. Better than 'enfant terrible', though; I know what that means: cunt.

Byron had suggested dinner before the theatre, which should tell you how amateurish he was. Going for dinner before a show isn't just the height of bridge-and-tunnel behaviour, it's asking for trouble if the show doesn't hold your attention. Your full belly will have you nodding off before the end of act one. The time to dine is after the show, so you can dissect the performances and shred the story line by line. I like my audiences' stomachs rumbling. So I ignored that request and met Vivi and Byron in the theatre bar. The place smelled like piss on a hot pavement. Byron was still waiting tables then. Writing too, of course, but he hadn't even had his first rejection at this point. I remember, still, the charged mist of excitement all around me. Ned Lanford was going to be there. By now he'd helped me make a success of *Daddy Issue* and was in the process of emptying his deep purse all over *Cruelty*, which was next to open, and I had a new idea to run by him that would eventually lead to us setting up a production company but ... I'm getting into the technical details now and nobody wants that. Onward.

I saw Ned as we walked in. He did the 'drinky' motion which,

I already knew, meant 'don't bother me now, I'll see you at the party after'. I was quite impressed by his commitment to the arts: he hardly ever missed a preview, liked to catch everything he could. I would one day realise this was one of his pick-up methods: haunt a disastrous first night then lend a sympathetic shoulder to whichever young actor's life had just been dashed to pieces.

So the main event! No, not the play. It was as I feared: under-written, and over-performed. A story desperately in search of a neutral heart and a red pen. There was one saving grace. Jo. It's incredible to me that there was a time when I didn't know his name, a name I've said over and over every single day since that night. Then, on that stage, doing it once more with feeling, he was just a slim, dark-haired boy who delivered his lines perfectly adequately. He was playing a tortured soul, addicted to an un-named drug, and spent a lot of the show cowering and frowning. He looked utterly miserable, which I didn't ascribe to acting talent, more his general situation. I watched him so closely; I can see every frame now, all these years later. His hair, laden with product to make it seem unwashed, resisted any attempt to control it and fell over his eyes, like a proper romcom cliché. His stern brow, pointing down to his bright Aegean eyes. He was skinny, but in that very defined, athletic way that was popular then. I'd heard a lot about the thunderbolt moment, when you see someone across a crowded room and it's like your brain, your heart, your gut and your dick instantly form a hit squad whose only mission is to possess that person, but if I'm honest, I didn't feel that way. Not at first. Still, I was determined to speak to him at the party, especially after I noticed Ned Lanford sitting up very straight in his seat every time the rueful young scamp appeared on stage.

Once the flutes of second-rate fizz had been handed out – we

were still in the grip of cava in those days, Prosecco yet to slip
on its strangling gloves – I ditched Byron and Vivi and searched
for the object of my affection. He was in a corner, talking to a
rat-faced boy I now know to be Dan Holden. I've never been
particularly shy, but my stomach fluttered as I barged into whatever was going on and congratulated Jo on his performance. He
was even better close up, a pout jutting proudly, acting as joist
to his annoyingly perfect nose. Men who look like this have
no choice but to become actors; it seems a shame to see them
breaking hearts from behind a bar, or delivering parcels. Beauty
belongs where it can be seen and appreciated. I can hear our conversation clear as a bell in my head. Well, our parts anyway. I'm
sure Holden interrupted because he can never resist jamming
an oar into even the narrowest gap, but I've blanked him out.

'You look like Alain Delon in *Plein Soleil*. Even though you
still have your shirt on.'

Tiniest hint of a smile at the corner of his mouth. 'I haven't
seen it.' Not Scottish, as he'd been in the play. A northern
accent, one I couldn't place. I didn't want to place it, didn't want
to wreck the illusion, but I wanted to hear it for ever. Corny?
Look, if you'd been there, you'd get it.

'You know it's a compliment, right?' Looking back, I sounded
patronising. I was twenty-three. Everyone is patronising at
twenty-three, a defence mechanism against not knowing
enough and being terrified of anyone else finding out.

'Course I do. Alain Delon. Nobody's going to turn you away
for saying that.'

You could talk like that when you were young and hot.
Nobody cared how corny your lines or how cruel your jokes
were; to be noticed was a compliment. But once your skin
starts to sag and your belt strains, you have to rein yourself in.
It's not cute to be flirtatious, it's creepy. They run from you.

Even if you're Alain Delon. I suppose there's also the other point that I've never met a man who looked as knockout as Jo did that day, so any flirting I've done since has been for ever tarnished.

Ned Lanford hovered, stuck talking to someone too influential to be dismissed. Now was my chance. 'I'm a writer.'

Tiny smile again. 'Cool.'

He didn't ask what I wrote, which was annoying, but I pressed on. 'Hmm, I've a new play coming. We're moments from casting.'

He looked at Holden a second too long. 'Cool. Good luck with it.' I remember that sense that I was losing him, it was too much to bear. I still get it sometimes, in the aftermath of a row. Ned Lanford grew closer, saliva gumming up in the corner of his mouth. I always think of him as being ancient, but he's barely ten years older than me. God. Savage youth.

'I'd like you to audition.' Which he knew.

He laid his hand on my arm. The first time he ever touched me. I imagine I still feel it sometimes; that gentle tap had a half-life of a billion years. 'Look, Mr ... '

Mister! Like I was an old man! We were peers! He had already noticed an imbalance between us.

'That's kind of you, but I'm giving up. That was my last night onstage.'

'What? Who's doing the rest of the run?'

He laughed then. A peal of silver bells on a summer's day, with a trace of grit. 'Rest of the run? It's not happening. We both know it's a load of shit.'

Again, it enveloped me, the fear that after this evening he'd slip out the door into the night and would live, for ever, without me. 'But you're so good.'

'I'm not.' He shrugged. 'It's fine. I don't wanna act anyway.'

'What do you want to do?' I could practically feel Ned Lanford's hot breath on the back of my neck. 'Write, maybe?' Most actors I'd met did.

I remember Holden piping up. 'He wants his own little tea shop, don't you, Jo?' Now I knew his name. 'Wants to serve coffee and fairy cakes to the proles. That's a good name for it actually, Fairy Cakes.'

'Shut up, Dan.'

I handed Holden my empty glass. 'Would you do the honours, squire? My mouth's drier than a Pompeii bathhouse.' And off he fucked. 'Is that really what you want to do?'

He looked embarrassed to be caught out. 'Yeah, kind of. One day. Not a tea room. Ignore that prick. A cool coffee place. Good food. Grab a little breakfast. You know?'

I loved his vulnerability, and hated Holden for exposing it so cruelly. 'Nothing wrong with that.'

'I wasn't asking your permission.' That northern brusqueness. We weren't quite sparring, but not flirting either. I was tingling. His gaze tracked to a spot over my shoulder. 'Your friend's coming.'

I only remember the next half hour as terrible. Trying to keep my cool while Ned unleashed his full charm offensive upon Jo which, back then, I believed to be irresistible. I watched Jo's face as Ned spoke. A wry smile. Blinking slowly. Letting those blue eyes drift occasionally to me. Were we conspirators or rivals? I couldn't tell. I knew he was about to excuse himself any minute and the thought devastated me. When Jo sidled off to the bathroom, Ned snaked his hand round my waist and brought me in close.

'I've had my eye on young Mr Valenti a long while.' Valenti. Now I knew his surname, I could swot up on him after this was done.

'Have you?'

'Yes. Terrific talent. He's got big dreams.'

'So he was telling me. He should audition for me.'

'For us,' he corrected, pressing his fingertips into my hip bone. 'Great idea. Was that all?'

I asked what he meant but he couldn't bring himself to admit he was warning me off. His eyes said enough. Dark and sad, used to getting what they wanted. I could push Ned a little, have fun with it, though I was discovering there were limits. 'Don't worry, Ned, I won't steal him away.'

He was reassured. Maybe I meant it. Hard to gauge in the cold light of day, decades later. Ned needed only say the word and *The Cruelty of Daylight* would remain in the dark.

Ned was called away by a loud man with a martini glass in each hand. To my surprise, delight, joy, Jo came back.

'Your friend gone?'

Again with the 'friend'; it sounded like an accusation. I wanted to show I was different, not some wealthy arsehole who could buy people. 'We're in business together. He has the money, I have the ... uh ...'

'The talent?' That sardonic smile yet again. I blushed.

'The words, I was going to say. He wants you to audition too.'

'I don't give a fuck what he wants.' The bluntness shocked us both and we laughed like teenagers on a weed-spliff high. He held out his hand for me to shake. 'I'm Jo.'

'Laurie. Laurie Blount.' No flicker of recognition. 'Can I have your number?' I'd never, ever asked for a number in my life, I didn't have to. The numbers came to me. Always. 'Or I can take you for a drink.'

His face set hard in an instant. 'I don't fuck for parts. Which is probably why I don't get any parts. Anyway, I told you, I'm done with it.'

'You don't have to fuck anyone. Can I not persuade you?'

'The drink or the audition? Or the fuck?'

'Any. Both. All.' I was jack-knifing this lorry out of the danger zone, I could feel it.

He read out his number to me. I typed in his name. J. O. E. 'No E. Just J and O. Valenti.'

'That's a lovely name.' I cringed, remembering that morning's conquest scrawling his own digits in my kitchen, a lifetime ago.

'Grandad was from Barcelona. It's just a name.'

'Do you want mine?'

'I'll have it when you call me, won't I?' He looked about the room for his friend. Holden was now standing at the bar swaying dangerously, a telegraph pole in a hurricane. I've seen many a good young man lost to a free bar, and plenty of bad ones too. 'I meant it about the audition. I'm not interested.'

The boldness of youth swelled in me. 'What about me?'

That smile. 'I have to go backstage, get my stuff.'

'I can wait for you.' I had no shame. The thunderbolt had been engaged.

'I'm not going home with you, Mr Blount. Laurie. Sober up, and if you still feel like calling, call. Bye.'

I felt the turning of the earth beneath my feet and looked up to see Ned staring across the room. Both of us knew that everything was different. This isn't hindsight talking, I felt it.

I'd been fuelled by bravado, but Jo stripped away that facade. He turned me back into that sixteen-year-old alien pining for his hot neighbour. Until I met Jo, I went home with the men I thought I deserved. I was attractive but still aimed low; I liked to win first prize in any pageant I was in. But that night, that burning summer when every car blasted 'Crazy in Love' on gridlocked streets, in that clammy and tired little theatre with greasy walls and arse-numbing seats, I reached for the moon.

I knew I'd never sell myself short again. Jo held a mirror up to me, he always has, for better or worse; he taught me I could be who I wanted, that my charm was my power. In a way, that was his first mistake.

Four

May

Vivienne

Feeling heavy and tired, but glad to be doing something, Viv takes the Tube to the counselling centre, in Waterloo. She makes a slight commotion yanking at the door until a disembodied voice trills from a hidden speaker, asking her to wait for the buzz and then pull, gently. Viv is red-faced and clammy by the time she's greeted by the friendly receptionist. The place looks underfunded. The linoleum is scuffed and the walls need a good couple of coats of paint. There's a bulb out in one of the wall lights. She would've gone private but Laurie was a huge fan of the NHS. Back when they worked in the bistro, they'd reassured him a lump on his left bollock was merely a cyst and not imminent death, so it would've felt disloyal. Details details details – perfect distractions from whatever is going to happen in that room.

A few people wait, shifting uncomfortably in the chairs, which creak in sympathy. Everyone is old, except for one very young-looking person, early twenties maybe, in a huge scarf, and a man in his thirties who glances up at Viv impassively. They stare at each other for a second or two too long, before he returns to his phone. The counsellor, a woman in knee-high boots and in desperate need of leave-in conditioner, trots out to reception, introduces herself as Mandy, and invites them to follow her. They troop into a peach-walled room with mood lighting and nine chairs, a box of tissues lurking ominously beside each one.

I will be expected to cry here, thinks Viv.

'You not joining us?' the counsellor says to someone hovering at the door. It's the man she exchanged glances with earlier. He mumbles a reply and walks away. 'Right you are.'

Viv wonders if she'd be better off bailing too. Some of the group are reaching to the floor for a tissue already, and nobody has said a word. Viv is worried. She can't try to feel something here, in this impersonal room that smells faintly of herbal tea. She feels Laurie everywhere else, cinematic snapshots of days gone by for almost every second of the journey there. Outside Brixton Tube, Laurie standing in dog poo the first time he wore his olive suede boots – 'This is God telling me to take cabs.' The rhythmic rocking of the train carriage and watching Jo and Laurie burrow their hands down into the seat between them and touch knuckles, in case a violent homophobe was watching. Stepping out at Waterloo and seeing ghostly versions of Laurie and herself everywhere, from glamorous nights on the balcony at the National, laughing at actors' jokes, to their younger days barrelling into twenty-four-hour shops to get cheap wine or giant bags of dusty salty popcorn. But here, there's nothing to hold on to.

As she does every time she walks into a roomful of strangers,

Viv imagines the others are better at this than her. One man, hair white and fluffy and combed over like angel hair pasta on a poached egg, is at the water cooler filling a large Evian bottle, and some smaller cups, which he dishes out to everyone, including Viv, before taking his seat and cradling his bottle like it's the head of his dead spouse, assuming that's why he's here.

There are introductions. Names, pronouns, some announce ages and jobs, or what they did before they retired. Viv instantly forgets most of their names. They recount their stories in fragile agony. Holding hands as they slipped away, bedside vigils, final declarations of love, nurses quietly switching off nightlights with kindly smiles.

This is how Viv would've imagined Laurie's death, if forced to. Jo there too, old, grey, withered, weak bones groaning as fingers interlocked, a half-century of friendship, maybe more, behind them. It wasn't supposed to end like this, so dramatically, horrifically. While Laurie was crunched against the steering wheel of his car, staring blankly through the shattered windscreen, Viv was at home, oblivious, reading the Sunday supplements from the weekend before, tipping Picpoul down her neck. As devastated as these people are, they foresaw this ending. Viv had no idea Laurie was about to leave her; they were supposed to live for ever.

One man keeps talking about how things haven't worked out with chapter two. An author! 'Can't they ever talk about anything else?' Laurie would scoff. But then another person mentions chapter two and another, and Viv worries she's come to a writing workshop by mistake.

When it's her time to speak, Viv takes in her audience as if noticing them for the first time. 'My doctor said I should come. It was a locum. Dr Richardson wasn't in. He didn't even read my notes properly, asked about antidepressants. I mean, I've been on anxiety meds since before Lady Gaga rose to fame.' An old Laurie joke. One person titters politely. Tough crowd. 'I told him, I tried to explain. I'm not in denial. I know he's dead. It's been four months. I'm still getting up, going to work, all that.' The lie comes easily. 'I'm just sad about it. Counselling won't change that, will it?' She can't help herself now, the bottom lip starts going, the tang of shame hits her eyes and the tears fall. Fuck, she promised herself she wouldn't even speak, let alone cry. 'I think I should stop now.'

Mandy smiles sweetly and says it's fine, that they can pick things up next week, because she thinks she'll be back, and doesn't know, as Viv does, that she'll never return. 'Actually, can I ask,' Viv says. 'What does chapter two mean?'

'It's what happens after you've lost someone,' says Mandy. 'Your other half dying isn't the end of your story, you see, just that first chapter.'

Viv doesn't see it that way. Surely everything coming now will be the inferior sequel that taints the original?

The young person, still swaddled in their scarf, goes next, introducing themselves again as Kris with a K. They lost their mother, the only one who understood them. Kris doesn't get on with their siblings and was fired from their job in a café for taking too much time off. Kris speaks quietly and carefully as if painstakingly mining for each word in their deepest soul.

'Mum was everything to me,' says Kris. 'She never came back from work. A heart attack. On her own. In a way, I'm glad I wasn't there. I wouldn't have known what to do, might've made things worse. But I hate that she was by herself.'

Now there's somebody who knows the inside of my head, thinks Viv, as Mandy wraps things up with wise words about not allowing guilt to creep into your thoughts, advice which will be ignored by everyone present.

Viv thinks of what Laurie might do if he were sitting here. He'd go round suggesting activities, or offering them a free ticket. For young Kris, he'd say, 'Do I have the thing for you!' Because she does.

As they leave, Viv stops Kris, holds out her hand to shake. 'I'm sorry about your mum. I know of a job, a nice place. Good people.'

Kris looks at Viv's hand like she's holding out a dog turd. 'Are you a pervert? Or a cult or something?'

Viv laughs and it's a surprise to hear it out loud. 'No. My, uh, my friend owns a café. He needs someone to do a few shifts. I can give you his number. He's lovely, honestly, just lost his husband, so he's kind of in the same boat. Or in the same storm at least.'

'What's his name?' They smile finally, showing a wide gap between their front teeth. 'I'm Kris . . . '

'With a K, yes, I remember. He's Jo, without the E. I'm Viv. Well, Vivi. Depends who you ask. Call the number, say I sent you.'

Kris takes the details and ambles off, calling out thank yous as they go. Viv hugs her coat closer even though it's not cold. She's done a good thing, it wasn't a complete waste of time, but she won't come back. She can't sit here trying to explain Laurie to strangers. You had to live Laurie to love him.

In gentle springtime drizzle, Viv walks across the river and up Charing Cross Road, thinking she might pop into Foyle's, get a hardback, retune her radio to the present day. Then she sees it, a poster for *Daddy Issue*, Laurie's first play – bawdy and sweary and clever, revived at a small theatre off Long Acre. She remembers seeing it in an even smaller place, a zillion months pregnant with Rosy, Laurie sweating pure fear and adrenaline, certain everyone would hate it. An hour later, Viv's in the small auditorium, rapidly filling with the matinée crowd who'll see anything to get out of the rain.

Laurie always spoke fondly of daytime theatregoers. 'Sweetie wrapper rustlers, chardonnay slurpers, demonic talkers, but I love 'em all! They keep the lights on.'

The theatre darkens and the stage lights dazzle. A lone actor in a white vest, sitting on a stool with a cheeky grin, takes a deep breath and begins to deliver the opening monologue, a salacious tale about the young man's adventures the night before. Viv sits and listens in the darkness to the words Laurie sat and wrote twenty years earlier. She realises halfway through her cheeks are hurting from smiling. Not only because the monologue is funny and the actor is delivering the lines with a wry grin, but because she knows Laurie will always be there. In the words, no matter where she goes. The shock of it makes her cry.

The Gleaming

Laurie

Harking back to the good old days, whatever your definition may be, makes an insane amount of money. Jukebox musicals, nostalgia acts at festivals, revivals of plays that should've stayed long dead – mine included. The past, given we know the outcome, carries less anxiety than the future, which is still ours to ruin if we try hard enough. There's something tacky about time travelling to your personal paradise, free of responsibilities, before you knew the agony of mounting bills, back pain, and lying to your GP about how many units you drink a week. Yet I go back to those early days with Jo time and time again, wishing I could bottle that splendour.

He made me wait for our third meeting – 'This isn't a date' – before letting me kiss him. And even though I'd engineered the date, sorry, *meeting*, to be round the corner from my flat, at the Little Apple, he politely turned down my offer of coffee back at mine – reader, I had no coffee – and hopped onto a 159, solo, before I could protest.

But once we came together – literally, those were the days – what a time we had. His awful play inevitably shut down in thousands' worth of debt, and Jo started working in a sandwich shop on Berwick Street. He had Sundays and Mondays off and didn't like buttering crusty cobs with a hangover so asked that I leave him alone through the week. I met him from work on Fridays, taking him for dinner somewhere shabby-fancy, before dutifully putting him on a Tube back to the Acton hovel he shared with Holden and three girls I never actually met. Oh, that youthful infatuation! We parted and reunited with the intense emotion of wartime sweethearts. Although Jo was always a much cooler customer. On Saturdays, I'd be waiting, tapping my foot. We'd eat limp, leftover sandwiches or sometimes he'd make something specially for us and hide it until closing, then we'd sink a few pints on Old Compton Street and head to a club.

I was still in Kennington, renting a formerly luxurious dive with scratched laminate flooring and a door entry system smashed by frustrated youths desperate to steal my laptop. It had a fire escape, which bizarrely went up to the flat roof – how you'd avoid a fiery demise up there I don't know. Jetpack? Jo and I would float in from the club and lie on my sofa, or on the rug. We'd talk nonsense and stroke each other and think about fucking, but instead of fucking we'd climb the rickety stairs to the roof and sit drinking whichever beer was trendy – and on special offer – at the time, halving pills and feeding them to each other, listening to old disco tunes, watching the sky lighten over the huge gas towers. In that full flush of euphoria that came both from being high and falling in love, I'd never felt so alive, and so aware that one day I wouldn't be. I've always struggled to let joy just be joy for its own sake. Being happy always reminds me that one day the sun will rise without me. Nothing lasts for ever. Except me and Jo, I would say to myself, and that would make it better. I'd turn my face to the light once more, then open my eyes to look right at Jo, the imprint of the sun still blazing in front of me, framing him like a halo.

We'd be in turns light and deep, trivial and utterly serious. We made promises. Agreeing never to go to bed on an argument, for example, or avoiding jealousy at all costs. Commandments we were fated to break.

'Secrets kill a relationship,' we used to say. 'Let's never have them.' Idiots.

Sometimes, if she could get a sitter for Rosy, Vivi would join us, and we'd laugh too loudly until we'd hear the telltale whoosh of a sash window from a neighbouring block being opened in anger and someone popping their head out, ordering us to shut the fuck up. Byron tagged along occasionally, but could never let loose. He'd be busy turning the music down, or clearing glasses and cups while we were still chewing our faces. Byron has never walked into a party he hasn't wanted to shut down. His ideal night out is in a restaurant, exacting revenge on the hospitality industry by constantly sending meals back to the kitchen over some petty complaint.

Once the sun was up and the noise of traffic and real life surrounded us, we'd troop back down the fire escape and fuck for what felt like hours. Jo's body tasted even better than it looked. It seems impossible to me now, shifting uncomfortably in my chair because I refuse to acknowledge my love handles and go up another size in my trousers, that we were ever so young and sexy. After a few hours' sleep, we'd do it all again, if slightly more low-key out of respect for it being the Lord's day: a couple of hours' dancing in Vauxhall, devouring every inch of each other all night, then out for lunch, nursing bloody Marys to stave off the tremors. I remember that blissful ache all over my body, patches of soreness, tenderness and heat from where Jo's mouth or hands had lingered too long. I loved to look at him, opposite me, clothed and respectable and quiet, reading a paper, and recall where my tongue had been. It's an underestimated perk of being with someone, I think, knowing exactly what they look and feel like under their shirt, how they react when you push their buttons. The parts nobody else sees, territory you've conquered. Every time I fucked Jo I was driving a flag into him, staking my claim.

Sexual chemistry was new to me. Nobody ever stayed around long enough for me to commit their bodies to memory. Jo's is mapped in my mind for ever. The small, but very dark, freckle by his right nipple; that beautiful contour when he raises his arm above his head, from his elbow down his torso to his hip; the sheer cliff-face jawline I loved to brush my finger along, hoping to cut myself on it to have a scar to remember him by. I talk about him as if he were just a body to me but it was merely the casing on a very satisfying package. My perfect boy.

We quarrelled, of course. We seldom agreed on the optimum time to leave the club – I liked to rip the arse out of it, Jo preferred to exit before boredom set in. My foolish reaction when another hopeful gay would dance too close to Jo in the hope of catching his eye. I'd move in tighter, become more tactile.

Jo would scowl. 'Touch me because you want to, not to show ownership.' He always was good at bringing me to heel.

We had a similar sense of humour then, but sometimes I'd take it too far. Jo's a master of respecting, and setting, boundaries. Back then, he defended the underdog. Byron, who'd just lost thousands on a falafel stand venture in Hammersmith, was temping in the City and trying to get an agent. He was prolific, biking at least one novel outline and a couple of essays over to me a week. When he learned to email them, I was soon swamped. I rarely opened them. One day I found Jo reading through a printout of Byron's opinion pieces – actual paper, can you imagine? Jo's always been staunchly analogue, typing out emails with a puzzled squint and his tongue lolling between his teeth.

'What do you think?' he said. 'Can he write?'

I took the pages and tossed them onto my kitchen table, overflowing with empty cans and beer bottles and whatever else we'd made our way through that weekend. We drank a lot. Barely ate for two days, though, which is probably how we kept our disco bodies. 'He can write fine enough, but I'm not sure he has anything to say.'

It was true then, and it's true now – his editor deserves the George Cross. Byron is big on volume, short on depth; he's a huge fan of mind-numbing detail, but has always forgotten you need the devil to make the words shine. Interminable descriptions of a character's curtains or stultifying scenes where nothing happens – page after page of someone striking a match to light a cigarette. Honestly, he makes me shout.

Jo tutted as he concentrated on the words. 'It's sad, this one. The part about struggling to break into writing.'

'He writes what he knows.'

'Isn't that good writing advice? Why shouldn't he write what he knows?'

'He doesn't know anything.'

'Laurie, Byron's your friend. Be supportive.'

Byron's trouble? He dashed this stuff off and expected miracles to happen. Half-hearted essays and typo-strewn manuscripts – he wanted to be seen, but not put the work in. He was obsessed by what others thought of him. I know for a fact he sometimes sits on trains with headphones in but no music playing, to check what people are saying about him, only to find nobody is talking about him at all. Why the fuck would they? I didn't want Jo to be mad at me, though, so I resolved to offer Byron constructive feedback and spent untold hours coaching him on turning his sow's ear into a silk purse. I'd do anything for my Jojo. Still would, despite everything.

Five

October

Jo

Jo's classmates are friendlier than he was expecting. He was nervous on his first day. You can have as many middle-aged students in sensible jumpers and supermarket trainers roaming the corridors as you like, but universities are designed for young, strong bones and fresh, curious minds. Laurie always complained that queer men were like high-pitched sounds in a hearing test – once you hit a certain age, you disappeared. Not all his classmates are young anyway. There's a woman with grey hair who continually rakes through a sequinned pencil case, and another guy, who lurks as far into corners as he can, not as old as Jo or pencil case woman, but older than the others, the faintest peppering of grey in dark curly hair, ink-black eyes staring out at nothing, usually. Neither of them socialise with the group.

Jo made a valiant effort at first. He assumed he'd be an

outcast, a dinosaur, but they seem to respect his opinion, listening to him intently in seminars. Maybe they're still young enough to confuse advanced age with authority and knowledge. He's invited along for drinks a couple of times, but outside class, the generation gap is a canyon. They're a welcoming, spirited and diverse bunch of people, sparkling and exciting in that way you can only be when you are actually young and not just playing at it. Laurie enjoyed being around younger people, preferred 'their energy', he said, which was both a very youthful and a very outdated thing to say, depending on who was listening. Jo's fellow students like drinking in shitholes. They're both proud of and horrified by their parents. Their problems, which vacillate between traumatic and piffling, are the worst experiences of their life so far, because they don't yet know worse will come. So sure are they that things can only get better, they use up joy like it's cheap bubblegum. When they discover Jo had a husband who died a mere eight months ago, it's a concept as alien to them as having limbs made of Styrofoam. Widowhood is a status that belongs to their grandparents, maybe, aside from one guy whose mother died when he was a child. It marks Jo as more emotionally sophisticated; they're in awe of it, and maybe a little turned off too. Jo feels barriers rising.

Rosy did her best to prepare him for her generation's quirks. She talked him through a few trending topics, patiently answering his questions about anything hugely unrecognisable from his own youth. It could've been mortifying, and patronising, but it wasn't, and Jo enjoyed being her mentee. He and Laurie had spent the last two decades offering some semblance of moral and social guidance, and now she was repaying the debt; he'd never felt closer to her, or prouder. She even jokingly taught him a few slang words, which he promised never to use. He doubted he would need most of them anyway.

That night Viv had 'just popped in', as she did every day at exactly the same time, and ended up cooking a three-course dinner. She watched Rosy and Jo chuckling as she slurped loudly on her jasmine pearl tea. 'Slang is a barbed wire fence, isn't it, basically?' she said. 'Keeps us cringey old people out. Me and Jo don't need your words, Rosy. We have our own.'

They don't, not really. She and Laurie spoke their own twisted Polari, but though he's known her almost half his life, Jo and Viv have few unique shared references.

When Jo told Byron he was going to university, he almost recoiled. Jo wasn't surprised – every time a new writer appears on the literary scene, Byron considers it a personal slight.

'Writing?' he said, closing all his browser windows at lightning speed. 'But that was … I mean, since when were you interested in writing?'

'Just exploring something for myself. I've got time now.'

Byron bristled. 'You always had time. You didn't need to work, not really.' Every now and then there are hints of how Jo featured in Laurie's private conversations with his friends. It's illuminating, but he prefers the details hazy.

Now it's been a few weeks and Jo has settled in at university, he keeps interactions with classmates to corridors and lecture halls. Premature self-imposed exile feels preferable to an inevitable eventual shunning. At least he doesn't have to listen to their scarily frank dissections of how good everyone else is in bed, as they quickly form branches of their own fuck tree.

Instead, Jo spends free periods pacing the neighbourhood around campus, trying to look like he's on his way somewhere, not an aimless loner. He finds a very small park, set back a couple of streets from the bustle of the Holloway Road. Unremarkable, really, except in the middle stands a war memorial, similar in shape to the Cenotaph in Whitehall, but much smaller and no coffin on top, Jo is pleased to see. There's a café too – well, a wooden shack bordering the park at one corner. Its main entrance and a few tables are round the front, but there's a serving hatch and two picnic tables at the back for anyone too lazy to travel the extra steps through the gate out of the park. Jo imagines the place lush and pungent in summer's fullest bloom, but now, in autumn's grip, it's a feast of sludgy brown. There's nobody there except for a man watching his French bulldog sniff tree trunks and, on one of the benches, reading, the man from his course, the guy from his classes who prefers corners, or at least a seat where he can observe without being overlooked.

'Like a cat,' Jo says to himself.

They've never spoken, or even nodded, but Jo has caught the man looking over sometimes. An old customer, maybe. Jo sees them everywhere. He decides against saying hello, and buys a small salad from the café's hatch to eat at the picnic bench, opening his Joan Didion, and sneaking a look up at the man every now and again. The man's jumper is old, it has holes in the cuffs. Obviously a beloved garment, or he's poor. His skin is light brown, but naturally; it's not a suntan. Turkish descent maybe? Jo doesn't like to speculate – he's always hated explaining where his name comes from while potential bigots work out how polite they have to be. The man has two faint lines across his forehead and a few round his eyes but otherwise his skin is smooth. His hair is cut short round the sides, but curly and shiny on top. Jo cannot see his eyes, they're hiding behind thick lashes and staring down at his book.

If Laurie were here, he'd nudge Jo, tell him the guy must be 'one of ours'. You just know. Posture. Demeanour. A near imperceptible grace, a watchfulness.

Jo goes back to *Play It As It Lays*, trying to absorb Californian sunshine off the pages to blank out the gloom. After a couple of minutes, he hears the gritty crunch of footsteps.

'You're on my course, aren't you?'

Jo looks up as if he didn't notice him. His first acting job in a very long time. The man is extremely handsome; it's unsettling. 'Oh. Hello. Yes. I am. Hi!'

'How are you finding it?' He smiles warmly.

Jo doesn't know much about being a student but he gets the feeling you're not supposed to act like you're enjoying it too much. 'Good! Well, you know.' He pulls a face. 'You?'

'Not easy being the old fart in the room.' He sees Jo's face drop an nth of a degree. 'Me! Not you! Of course.'

Ice definitely broken, 'the man' introduces himself as Theo. He's thirty-three. They shake hands and Jo smells tobacco. This is Theo's third attempt at higher education.

'Timing wasn't great before. Family stuff. This time I'm gonna crack it. Gonna soak it all up. Let myself be amazed.' There is something about Theo's casual openness that makes Jo want to sit somewhere else, but Jo misses chewing the fat with a good-looking man, and Theo is beautiful, so he stays put. 'And if it don't work, I'm gonna listen to the universe, you know?'

Jo doesn't know – the universe has never spoken to him directly – but loneliness seems to pour from the man so he invites Theo to sit. With the hushed brevity of small talk at a party, Jo gives him an edited synopsis of the last few months, leaving out any details of who Laurie was, not that he expects Theo to have heard of him.

'That must've been rough. I've been through similar.'

Jo is torn between preserving a near-stranger's privacy and finding a kindred spirit whose grief is unconnected to his own. 'Have you?'

Theo takes a breath and Jo holds his, expecting everything to come flooding out, but Theo shakes his head. 'Ancient history. But you keep going. Helps to do something positive, something for yourself. Right, better go.'

Jo feels selfish now, that he's unburdened and this man will walk away with his own troubles unhalved. 'I'm a good listener if you ever want to . . .'

Theo smiles, with friendly dismissal, and rises, gathers his things. Jo's eyes track down Theo's body, the way his jumper hangs off him, a little too big, the belt tied tight round his slightly baggy jeans. He feels a lump in his throat. It's strange to evaluate a man's body, feels like he's being unfaithful. Something he's finding it difficult to get his head round since Laurie died – they're still married, but no longer on the same plane.

'You okay?'

Jo realises he's staring into space. 'Sorry, yeah. Nice to meet you.'

'Yeah. Good to put a name to the back of the head.' Theo looks around as he heaves his tatty bag onto his back. 'How did you find this place?'

Jo detects a hint of objection to the intrusion. He's probably being paranoid. 'Just wandering about. I can't stand the canteen.'

Theo seems to immediately understand. 'I like everyone. They're good kids, but . . . I don't know. They're loud in a way I can't relate to. Like they speak in a different pitch.'

It's true. Anyone passing the university canteen at lunchtime might assume it was on fire and everyone was trying to escape. Shrieking, whooping, yelling – Jo doesn't remember ever being that way, although older people never do.

'What about you?' asks Jo. 'How'd you find it? You a local?' Is this how people talk? Jo is aware for perhaps the first time of the limitations of his own personality. A lifetime of standing next to someone never lost for words has dulled his social skills.

He's never had to try. Not for a long time anyway. Where's that wit of his younger days?

Theo seems surprised to be asked, as if there is nowhere else he could possibly be. 'I like to get to know an area, especially if I'm gonna spend a lot of time there. If I'm honest, it's a safety thing. Escape routes. Looking for fire exits when you walk in a place.' Theo catches Jo's surprise. 'You never done that then?'

'Not for a long time. I know what you mean, though.' As a younger gay man, in unfamiliar towns or pubs with reputations, he'd cast a quick eye about to check there was another way out. With Laurie, security was always someone else's problem. 'What are you escaping?'

Theo shrugs. 'I won't know until it catches me.' Deep. Also slightly ridiculous. Theo checks his watch. 'I've got to head. See you in the poetic form seminar tomorrow, though, yeah?' He pauses, like he's willing himself to say the next part. 'You want to grab some lunch after? Here, I mean.' No man has asked Jo to 'grab' lunch in over twenty years. This is like role play. Maybe he dithers too long. 'You don't have to.'

'No, I'd like that. I mean, yes, I'd like that.' Jo realises that by the time the lunch comes around he might actually be telling the truth. Rosy warned him most people spend their second year at university avoiding the friends they make in the first – would Theo be Jo's first clingy student friend? He's too cool to be clingy, surely? Enigmatic, almost, in lectures and seminars. Fresh air clearly did something to him. Should Jo have said no?

Theo walks away, fists clenched, propelling himself forward with his arse and hips rather than striding and using his whole body as an engine. It's kind of slouchy, adolescent. Jo notices the trousers are too baggy to see the shape of his backside and is ashamed of himself for looking.

Inviolate Hearts

Laurie

Around eight months in, we met the parents. A huge moment for Jo, who said his sexuality was something he'd always left outside on the (ironic) welcome mat when visiting home. I never thought I'd do parental introductions. I couldn't imagine falling in love with someone, meeting superannuated versions of them, peeking into their childhood bedrooms. We got the train to Derbyshire and stayed in a hotel to avoid having Ma and Pa Valenti agonise over whether they should allow us to bareback in their guest room.

They were nice enough, on the surface. Polite. The dad had been good-looking in his day, I could tell. The mother still something of a beauty. I saw the components that had gone into the making of my handsome boy. Every feature they'd donated worked much better on him. Small-minded, though. I told Jo he'd almost certainly been conceived through a hole cut in a sheet, which made him choke with laughter all the way home.

On the few occasions I've been left alone with them, we chat politely, I can make Jo's mum giggle at will, but it feels like they're dying to say, 'We know you fuck our son.' Most mums and dads know their kids have sex, obviously, but blank it out somehow, fading to black before their imaginations confront body parts colliding, and the grunting and mess. The Valentis, though, dwelled. I could be quite sadistic about it. I once gave Jo stubble rash from gnawing at his throat too long and I could see big Bobby V staring at the smear of bright red, framed beautifully by Jo's white, open-necked shirt that clung to his hard body like paint.

'You've caught the sun,' he said. 'Just there.'

Jo clutched his neck as if pearls were dangling there and the look between us told Bob everything he didn't want to know.

My mother adored Jo the minute she laid eyes on him. I watched her take in every detail, like I had that first night in the theatre. She found out Jo was short for Josep, and has delighted in calling him by his full name ever since. Jo caught on very fast that airs and graces were not legal tender in Belinda's house. His face was a picture when whichever pug was around at the time sat on his knee and left a dirty mark – the worst kind – on his pale trousers.

'No, really. Um, it's fine.' He was even cute when trying not to retch.

My mum screamed with laughter. 'A little souvenir of your visit, Josep.'

The tight little petals of his inhibition began to open up, his taut smile relaxed. 'I'll never wash them again,' he said, as Belinda whooped with laughter.

She took me aside in the kitchen later. 'He's ever so handsome. Bit quiet, though, isn't he?'

Not when it matters, I thought. 'Mum. Your dog just shat

on his leg and he's still here. I'd call that a victory.' She still mentions it now.

Jo hardly talked about his early years in London. Not quite evasive, and not exactly enigmatic, more the kind of person who'd never think to dissect his own life. Most people are the same, think themselves so unremarkable that their experiences aren't worth picking over. Not that it stops them writing memoirs if the money is right. Living with Jo is one long game of pass the parcel; over the years, layers have been unwrapped, a few details revealed. If I were to guess, I'd venture Jo did some things he wasn't proud of. But haven't we all?

Aside from nights with Vivi and Byron, and sometimes Holden, worst luck, Jo and I socialised alone that first year or so. We went public for the first night of *The Cruelty of Daylight*. Rented white tuxes, had facials at a spa on Marylebone High Street. It was the first time Ned Lanford saw us together. He'd heard rumours, I'm sure; he knew stuff about you before you knew it yourself. One thing I'll say about him, he was gracious in defeat. Either that or his face was frozen from Botox. Ned couldn't make enough of a fuss, telling us how handsome we looked in what he called our 'brave' choice to wear white in a winter month. He had a new twink circling him that night, at a safe distance in case he was photographed. Ned said he didn't like to think of his bank manager or the man who serviced his cars knowing he was a poofter. Seemed plausible at the time, most things did. Life is a series of long, painstaking calculations that serve up the final answer only when it's far too late to be of any use, I have discovered.

We watched the crowd mingle a while before curtain-up. I was trying not to talk because I was so nervous about reviews. Jo leaned in and asked if Ned and I had ever got together.

'Don't be ridiculous. I'd rather lick the floor in a Berlin piss club.' Jo's jealous streak excited me. He gave so much physically and we could talk and laugh for hours, but there were still many doors left to unlock; it was a thrill to peep behind one for free. 'Would you mind if I had?'

Jo smiled and shook his head. 'No, of course not. I just wondered.'

He knew as well as I did that success like mine didn't just happen – as modest as it was then, still yet to explode. There was always something more; something had to be given away, or taken. It was a reasonable assumption that I'd fucked Ned, or at least let him watch me fuck someone else.

'Ned's not a talented person, Jo. I don't mean that in a horrible way. He appreciates talent in others, gets something out of it, but he doesn't always want to fuck them. In fact, the less talented you are, the more likely he'll screw you, going off previous boyfriends. He's a collector, likes owning things. He prefers my brains to my body. He could have anyone he wanted, except me. And you.'

Cruelty changed everything. You'll already know that, if you're reading this. It's probably *why* you're reading this. Once, we were in a bar and a young guy approached and said he loved my plays. Jo didn't appreciate the interruption and stood glowering until the fan had scuttled away.

It was a rush then, but now, there's a few seconds after someone tells me they love my work when it feels like a trap. What am I supposed to say? Do I agree that, yes, I'm wonderful? Or do I bow my head and say, 'Oh, really, are you sure?' like a starlet saying a polite 'no thank you' to the flat, velvet box of diamonds she's dreamed about since she was four?

When it came, success came fast. I won't list it, look it up. I loathe bragging. That first movie script I did – an insane amount of money for something redrafted by so many other people that I think around four of my lines made the final version. I went through the motions, chased the dollars, but preferred Hollywood at arm's length. The movie business likes the stink of its own shit too much. Those coked-up bozos still act like they're making dreams come true in one-mule backwaters, with a single screen picture house on Main Street allofeeding plucky, hay-chewing hicks the myth they can be whoever they want to be. Theatre is more real. More me. Anyway, the movie begat a novel adaptation; got paid silly money for that, those were the days. Then the National put on *Break Out the Bombazine*, which ran and ran and ran thanks to Ned's expert schmoozing and the internet – which was generally less insane then – giving it a thumbs up.

I did what anyone would do with instant success: I made dreams come true. I bought my mum a house. Got Vivi some help for Rosy so she could study photography, introduced her to literally everyone with an ounce of influence, and we drank (cheap) champagne every night for about a year.

Poor Byron took my success the hardest, like I was thriving to spite him, but he still accepted my offer of a writing coach and, years down the line, a part-time job answering my emails and making adequate coffee. I bought a flat. No more fire escape or long nights squinting at sunrises over the gas towers. There was one more thing I wanted to do. I got a bit of help from Ned's network of contacts – spread across London like threads of clover smothering a manicured lawn – though we agreed to keep his part in it between us.

Jo and I had been together two years. We'd already done the anniversary: two candles squidged into a Battenberg and a magnum of (not as cheap) champagne. Not long after, I met Jo from work and bundled him into the tatty Ford Focus I'd bought for bombing around in. (Eventually I more or less stopped driving and took up my rightful role as one of life's passengers; the nation's pedestrians breathed a collective sigh of relief.)

'How was your day?' I didn't want him to hear the traces of nerves in my voice.

'Oh, not bad. New girl started. Just graduated from Arts Ed, obviously. She's nice, but far too theatre. Every time she came back from the big fridges into the main shop we could practically hear her counting herself in – "a one, two, three, four, here's the Milano salami", you know?' Noticing I didn't laugh, Jo finally became aware of his surroundings. 'What are we doing in Camberwell?'

'You'll see.'

We pulled up outside a little café on Denmark Hill, opposite the sexual health centre. It was more or less empty and hadn't been open for a month or so, but the shutters were rolled up and a lamp on the counter gave a glimmer of hope among the gloom.

'It's shut.'

'For now.'

My heart was racing as I fumbled for the keys. I didn't dare look back at Jo as I strolled to the door. I heard him follow me in, uncertainty ringing out with every footstep on the laminate.

'Laurie.'

Without looking in his eyes, I closed the door behind him and stood at the counter watching him take it in. Dirty marks on the wall where pictures had hung. The scratched floor, from a billion chairs scraping in and out. The dilapidated and ancient coffee machine that would probably look incredible with a polish. I reached under the counter and brought out the two miniature bottles of cava one of Ned Lanford's associates had left for me.

'Is this what I think it is?'

I can write romantic scenes but I'm no good at being in them. I had words tumbling around my head but I didn't want to sound phoney, or like one of Byron's stories – people talking like characters, not living and breathing souls with their own feelings and motives and doubts. But I had to give it my best shot. 'Jo. I love you.'

'I know. You haven't bought me a coffee shop, have you?' He sounded almost robotic. I realised he was frightened.

'Not exactly. It's a lease. If you don't want it, I can get out of it.' Well, Ned could. Maybe. 'But it's for you, yeah. Time to be your own boss, do whatever you want.'

He made objections. Set-up costs. His lack of business acumen. Fear. But there was something else. 'I always thought I'd do it myself.'

I told him he was doing it himself, I'd have no involvement beyond being an investor. What the hell did I know or care about serving coffee? All I wanted was to get him started.

'It's a big commitment. A business, I mean.'

'Not just that, though.' I reached into my pocket for another set of keys.

'What are they for?'

I honestly cringe whenever I think of this, but I wanted to reply 'my heart'. Jo would've probably walked out. Even though I didn't say it, my body tenses in revulsion every time I remember wanting to say it. Instead, I said, 'My flat. Our flat. I want you to move in. Friday to Monday isn't enough, Jo.'

That same sliver of a smile from night zero. 'A new job and a new place, in one day? Is there anything left in my life I actually control?'

I cringe about this too, but I actually did say it. 'Yeah. Me. And I love it.'

'Laurie . . .'

'Don't be pissed off, Jojo. I got excited. Is this bad? It's not about control. Honest. I love you. I want to make your dreams come true. Like you did mine.'

'Barf!'

'Nobody says that any more.'

Convincing him took longer than I expected, but was quicker than I deserved. We sat on the counter and drained the mini cavas. I ruffled his hair, he kissed me on the forehead, called me silly, and impulsive. I wanted to please him so badly, I'd have given him anything. He was frightened I'd given him too much. I went to the chip shop and by the time I got back he'd made up his mind. He said yes to the café, and yes to moving in. That night, it felt like we could take over the world.

Six

October

Jo

Theo and Jo have now had lunch in the park together four times, to discuss whichever class they've just left. Theo struggles with a Dylan Thomas seminar.

'Love and death. Two things I've never been good at dealing with.'

'He's not the cheeriest.'

Critiquing poetry, books, or anything really, feels like Jo's interfering in somebody else's business. Obviously Laurie always asked what he thought of a book or a play, but other than 'I loved it' or 'It has real potential', Jo never found the words. His opinion never mattered anyway; he didn't pay for his tickets, got free copies of the books, and had no sway. Among the rest of his class, and Theo, as they weighed up Thomas's 'A Refusal to Mourn the Death, by Fire, of a Child in London', Jo half expected Theo to pull a face and ask what the fuck he was talking about. Instead, he nodded, said 'good point', or 'I like the way you see things'.

They watch a squirrel fling itself into a pile of leaves. Theo sighs. 'I thought it would move me more. The poem. Mourning.'

It's as if the sturdy wooden bench beneath them rests on the thinnest of ice. Jo's used to being gentle around others' grief. He and Rosy can talk openly about Laurie all evening, laughing until their sides hurt; it's like therapy to her. But when Viv comes round to cook dinner, as she still insists on doing most nights, she and Byron act around him like you might treat someone dying of a terminal illness. It reminds Jo of when Liza, their first dog together, was ill and Laurie kept spelling out 'cancer' phonetically lest she hear. What are they afraid of?

During previous lunch breaks, Jo has been trying, ever so gently, to go beneath the surface with Theo. So far, every time he's close to a breakthrough, Theo hits a wall. His dark eyes, which have seen clearly much more than his thirty-three years on Earth should've allowed, crinkle in pain, his voice becomes tight, and he expertly steers the conversation elsewhere. One time he managed to convert Jo's question about cremation into an anecdote about winning a hot sauce tasting challenge at a barbecue restaurant. Undaunted, and perhaps inspired by Dylan Thomas, Jo decides to try again.

'We all mourn differently, don't we?' No movement from Theo. 'I don't feel sad reading about grief, or looking at gravestones.'

Theo looks up. 'Oh?'

He could never say this to Viv, or Byron, but being with a near-stranger, in a place he barely knows, he can dare. 'The living upset me sometimes. Carrying on, regardless, oblivious, while my Laurie ... well, you know.' Not only that, but reminders of Laurie round the house. Laurie's favourite mug, a glued-together Creme Egg one. A couple of Post-its on the hall mirror in his handwriting with emergency numbers on and the alarm code (0-0-0 ENTER). The things that aren't there too. Sounds. Like the swearing as he thumps and yanks open the door to the downstairs loo, which has been stiff and awkward for over a decade. No more *thunk-thunk-slap* of his shoes and coat hitting the tiles in the hall. A new kind of silence, bleaker because it's scarred by the noise it used to know.

'I know.' Theo stands and shakes crumbs from his chicken flatbread. 'Stupid stuff brings it all back.' His voice is slightly higher. Jo waits. It's coming. Theo is trying to find the words, mouth pulled tight like a scratch. 'I lost my brother. It was a while ago now.' Theo's face is panicky, like he regrets being so open. 'And, er, well, the Queen dying was a big one. Like, I'm not into the royals or nothing, but ... that sense of something ending. The spectacle, you know? All that emotion. I couldn't really understand it.'

Jo remembers Laurie rushing home from wherever he'd been that afternoon, both sitting glued to rolling news, spotting that Buckingham Palace had lowered the flag before the presenter had even announced it. It felt like anything could happen next.

'I suppose that's what they wanted, to get us in the feels,' says Theo. 'Mourning keeps us from revolting.'

Jo can't help but think this is a very sixth-form opinion, underdeveloped, parroted from someone else. He looks over at the café, its hatch spilling over with pumpkins. Soon it will be time for sparklers, then mince pies. Jo has never been so aware of the earth's ceaseless spin as he has these last ten months or so. He checks his watch. When she found out Jo had the afternoon off, Viv said she'd be round earlier today. If he isn't there, she'll call him and he doesn't want her to, not when he's with Theo.

'Like, one of my earliest memories is Princess Diana dying,' continues Theo, awkwardly. 'I must've been six? My mum was crying like it was her best friend who was gone. I remember thinking she was like an angel. All the jewels sparkling and her big smile. Huge personality. A superstar. Gone. I never thought I'd know that feeling again.' Jo notices how stilted he is, now he's getting dangerously close to baring his soul. This could be about to get very interesting, but he stops like he's revealed too much, despite saying nothing at all. 'Er, I've got to go.'

They talk over each other as they gather their things. Theo is anxious to get away, Jo wants to let him. He's embarrassed by Theo's clumsy attempt to open up, and his part in provoking it. 'See you Friday then.'

Theo is already walking off. 'Yeah. I'll see how I feel. I'm working Thursday night.' He turns back. There are words piling up in his mouth. Jo wills him not to say something that will make them both feel awkward. 'Thanks for, uh, being ... I find it hard to make friends. Don't you?'

It's irksome and a comfort to be so easily read. Jo can't remember the last time he made a friend. A proper one, anyway, that he didn't employ. Holden aside, does he even have his own friends? Everyone else was attached to Laurie first. 'It's hard, yes. In London. At our, um, my age.'

Theo holds out his hand. 'I'm glad I've made a friend. Well, I mean, you're a friend to me. No, I mean ...' He was more eloquent raking over the poetry of long-dead men than his own feelings. 'I hope you feel we're friends.'

Jo's unused to this. He doesn't look at interactions under microscopes. At a loss, he takes Theo's hand and shakes it. 'Of course.'

Theo clasps his other hand over Jo's. His palms have a roughness that is not unpleasant. After the limp handshakes at the funeral and from so many commiserating strangers since, Jo realises how much he's missed the confident grip of a man's hand over his, unembarrassed by skin contact, unafraid of the emotion it betrays. 'I don't really . . . I don't wanna sound weird. A lot of people don't get me. I'm not great at being a person, being in society. I don't feel like I see the world like everyone else. So I appreciate the chats. Hope that's not weird.'

Having this conversation with anyone else, or a few months earlier, Jo would be mortified for them, desperate for the light dusting of cynicism that keeps everyone safe from their own emotions. Laurie was always so good at defusing such bombs. But somehow Theo's childlike earnestness is touching, and Jo always felt sorry for the loners in the playground, so he covers Theo's hand with his spare and lies that it definitely isn't weird.

'Anyway, better move.' Clearly embarrassed, Theo springs back and scoots away.

Through a tiny gap in the bushes, Jo watches him amble down the road, until Theo is a speck, his red coat blurring into the rest of London, everyone getting on with their lives.

Charming Young Men

Laurie

I think they tell you that the day you get married is the happiest day of your life to make sure you turn up. Not that I wasn't happy, and not that Jo wasn't a vision in the white Gucci suit I bullied him into wearing, but it was a hugely chaotic day. My mother, in a hat larger than an oil tanker, kept reminding me men change once they get a ring on the finger. Vivi was having some kind of relationship crisis with whoever she was shtupping at the time.

'Nearly two years,' she said, spilling the last of the table wine down her front, 'and I've never seen inside his flat. Not once.'

Talking her down off the figurative ledge, I remember thinking, I bet I won't remember that man's name this time next year, and sure enough, when we were packing to move to the big house, I spotted his face in the wedding group shot and drew an absolute blank. That's showbusiness, darling. Vivi has endured countless beaux over the years, from bright-eyed striplings seeking a Mrs Robinson to oleaginous old farts who imagined her an earthbound Barbarella. None stuck. She's always said she could never find someone who looked after her as well as me but, really, any boyfriend (understandably) floundered in our poorly ventilated closeness. That, and Vivi hates being told what to do, and likes her quiet time.

Later, as the wedding band honked out a slightly incongruous cover of 'Since U Been Gone', Vivi clung to me in a death grip and made me promise things wouldn't change.

'I still need to see my Lulu. And I hope you still make time for Rosy. I adore Jo, you know that, he's so hot and lovely. But I don't wanna lose you.'

I suppose she had a point – when you marry, you're divorcing your old life. I did my best to reassure her.

Ned Lanford brought a handsome young actor, who sadly ended up dead a few years later – drugs, I think – and told me no hard feelings. As if he ever had a chance with Jo! I hadn't exactly stolen the great love of his life, and Ned had not spent the last few years mourning. But at funerals, christenings, weddings and first nights, you must be gracious, generous and gay, so I changed the subject and told him, for some bizarre reason, how much he meant to me and how I couldn't have done any of this without him. I didn't specify what 'this' was. He was buoyant anyway, and not just because of his young actor friend, who remarked to me on more than one occasion how handsome Jo looked in his suit, as if I were standing before him dressed in takeaway cartons and bin slime.

Ned had just met a royal. One of the Kents, I think. There'd been a photo in the *Standard*.

'Did you see it?' he had the gall to ask on the happiest day of my life.

'Oh, I barely recognised you side-on.' I paused, knowing he'd be waiting for the punchline. A little game we liked to play. 'You're so impressive from the front that it didn't seem possible that ordinary profile could be you. Lighting issue, I assume.'

He squeezed my arm. 'Of course, you look great from every angle, dear Laurie, but we especially love to watch you leave a room.' The shit. He sailed off into the throng.

We left disposable cameras on the tables and upon processing I found one of Ned slumped in a corner, his crotch dark and soaking. Saving that for a rainy day.

Byron, eyes greener than ever, spent all evening congratulating me, even though I wasn't 'actually married, just civil partnered'. As everyone was realising they should've gone to bed two hours ago, Byron grabbed the mic and announced his book deal. A self-help book of sorts. The irony. I was happy for him, but had to wrench the microphone away when he started quoting snippets.

'Save some for publication, By-By. Don't spoil it for us!'

Byron studied me through those expressionless eyes, and clambered off the stage, falling into my arms. 'A bruised banana is showing you its vulnerability, but still tastes as sweet.'

Despite such razor-sharp insight, the book went on to sell fewer than 200 copies, but, still in blissful ignorance, we got drunk on the idea of the fame and fortune coming Byron's way.

It took a good year to convince Jo to weld himself to me. Civil partnerships were new and Jo was sore about them, said they felt fake. I promised I'd make it real, would call him Mrs Blount at every opportunity and turn the television up every time he tried to speak to me, as my father had done with my mother.

Holden was thrilled we got married, partnered, whatever. Probably because he needed £15,000 to finish off his loft extension and wanted Jo in a good mood before he asked him (us) for it. He'd married Sian the year before; she was way too good for that vapid failure. Holden was desperate to be part of some terrible, clichéd coupled-up quadrangle, instigating 'movie nights' and 'date nights', ten-pin bowling and pub quizzes. It still seems a disgrace to me that they fucked, regularly, that Holden's hairy, sausagey fingers have wanked off my Jo. He's so stupid, beaming that great big mooncalf smile; I know for a fact I paid for those igloo-white teeth of his.

Now I had Jo, I couldn't believe it. Mum was right, though: things shifted once we were official. Jo began overseeing the renovation of the new place in Streatham, tearing between it and the café in Camberwell. I was busy, breezed in and out, nodded through the estimates and gave vague compliments on sketches and swatches. Now Jo had less time for me, I reduced my effort in response. He'd try to involve me in bannisters and coving and I'd make a terrible joke that they sounded like position of the fortnight from my sister's teen magazines and instead of laughing he'd scold me, 'I'm being serious, Laurie.'

Jo started ducking out of the canapé trail – the silly parties, premieres and launches we'd always loved doing with Vivi and Byron when we were skinter and slimmer. I can talk to anybody, but Jo claimed he had nothing to say, that the hangers-on were only interested in me anyway, and blamed me for the rudeness of others. I always tried to include him, thrust him forward, but once he'd answered the three standard questions you'd ask someone who owned a café, there wasn't much else.

He never raised his voice or got angry, but it was a firm disconnection from that side of my life. 'I'd rather focus on the house right now.'

When it was finished, he led me round. I could see why he'd had no time for silver salvers and small talk. It was extraordinary, breathtaking. I don't think I realised how well he knew me until I saw the contents of my own head translated into the walls and floors and furnishings. The renovation had felt nothing to do with me beyond the financial outlay, but he'd been listening all this time. All I wanted, I suppose, was a house nothing like the charmless semi I'd grown up in, sharing the front bedroom with my brother and his football magazines and crunchy tissues in his bedside drawer.

'Shit, I should be taking photos of your reaction,' he said, around halfway through the reveal.

'Shall we pretend you have? Start over?' I hugged his wiry body tightly, his ribs eventually finding mine through the thin layer of dough I was accumulating now I'd sailed past thirty.

'It's okay. I'll remember your face for ever.'

There was no unifying theme or style. It was like a person, full of contradictions and clashes that somehow work as a whole. The minimal front lounge, for entertaining, cool enough to intimidate anyone who didn't take me seriously, but welcoming enough to make friends feel at home. The huge kitchen, which I would never cook in, really, but loved to sit in while Jo twirled around it clanking pans and burning his fingers on the oven door. A more relaxed lounge overlooking the garden with huge sofas and a giant TV that was modern for the time. Then my rooms at the back.

One of the hardest things about writing is translating the thoughts that sound so wonderful in your head as faithfully as you can when committing them to the page. It's a gamble, and never a pure conversion. Somehow, Jo had acted as master interpreter, and my dreams were right there, within those walls. First, a small anteroom where one day I'd have an assistant, maybe, and then my writing room at the back. A huge orange slouchy sofa for me to do my thinking on – I recognised it from a series of *Big Brother* a couple of summers before, although sadly it was damaged by a dropped cigarette years later and ended up in a skip – and a beautiful retro desk for me to write at, and an antique bureau in one corner for me to keep my notes.

'Jojo, this is wonderful. You've outdone yourself. You've worked so hard.'

He looked very serious. Stroked my face. 'I wanted to do something for you for a change.'

'You do everything for me!'

We opened wine, turned the music up, twirled and tripped and whooped as we danced to Rihanna on the deep-pile rug. I'd missed dancing the night away with him. Hiding with Vivi in corners bitching about shitty leading men and Ned's gymslip boyfriends was fun, but now this was over, Jo could rejoin the madness.

Jo sighed with the tension of a thought long held but so far unexpressed. He'd support me whenever he could, he said, but his days of chasing down flutes of fizz in function rooms with bad acoustics were over; he was happier off the circuit.

'It's not fun for me, Laurie. I know you like it, I get it. Look, a deal. I'll let you off bowling nights with Holden and Sian? You hate them.'

'Jojo, I do not hate Holden and Sian! Well, not Sian.'

'I meant the bowling!'

So I carried on without him, and he, Holden and Sian made a threesome. Yes, I'd hated those nights, but now I was annoyed he hadn't fought harder to force me to attend. Mind you, I used to like it when he'd stay up and I could tell him what I'd been up to, almost as much fun as having him there. I've always loved an audience.

In the end, I enjoyed a home life and a work life that felt distinct. It was comforting, steadying. At home with Jo, I could be myself and didn't have to perform. Sometimes the worlds collided, obviously. Other gay couples who used to party with us were also chasing the choke of heteronormativity and invited us away for weekends in tasteful rented houses. Hiking once or twice, even. We still see some of them now, occasionally. So strange that the waifs from my youth, who I'd once gyrated and shared cubicle cocaine with, have transformed into thick-set, outdoors-loving bores in coordinated cagoules. I remember their bony hips and willing boners grazing mine as plain as day and now all I see are dull fogeys suspended in cloudy aspic.

Maybe you're too comfortable when you get married. Complacent. Commitment seems so adult that you cast aside your reckless youth to embrace stability. There's a marked difference between ageing and maturing, a balance I'm not sure I've ever aced. Time to grow up, yes, but not grow old. Not ever.

Seven
October

Vivienne

'You need to give Jo some space, Mum,' says Rosy one morning.

'He's got loads of space, in that big house.' When did it start, that reversal between them, when Rosy felt emboldened to talk to her like an equal, but not always in a good way? 'He likes my cooking, always has.'

'But bugging him to see what time he's getting home ... He has a life.'

Unlike Laurie, she wants to say, but she can't deal with the ensuing eye roll from Rosy. 'I don't want it to go cold!'

'Dropping round when he's out at uni?'

'What? I like to have lunch with my daughter. What's wrong with that?' It's a lie. Viv enjoys being in the house, around Laurie's things. It's stupid, but she likes to touch whatever he touched, sit where he sat, breathe in deeply in the hope of catching traces of him in the air. The whole house is a safety deposit box packed with her memories. She even drank out of his mug for a while but became frightened of breaking it.

'All I'm saying is . . .' Rosy chews the inside of her cheek, like she's deciding just how honest she should be. 'Work must be picking up. I'm sure there's loads of stuff you could be getting on with.'

Getting on with. Viv remembers patronising her own parents like this, as if they were the stupidest, most emotionally stunted people on the planet. Okay, so she had maybe fudged the truth a little, and claimed not much work was coming in when really she's said no to shoots she could've done in her sleep. Yes, she had a much lazier summer than usual, mornings at the lido in Brockwell Park, or yoga at the church hall, and afternoons at the cinema watching comedies, sitting at the back so nobody could see her crying. And, fine, maybe September slipped away from her too. But her life has been turned upside down, and not just once; it's in constant turbulence. 'You know one day, Rosy, you'll sit and look at photos of me and cry, wishing you could take back every time you spoke to me like I was some moron on social media.' Not that photographs are ever enough; they're too posed. Viv has found herself trawling Google Street View trying to find Laurie tramping the streets of Soho or popping to his local shop, but nothing yet.

Rosy swallows hard. Maybe Viv's mortality has occurred to her for the first time. 'Okay. Sorry.'

'Jo has actually invited me over today. I can show you the text if you like.'

They're giving emptying the wardrobe another go.

'Ruthless, this time,' she says, not meaning it, as Jo hands her a mug of coffee.

'Definitely.' He doesn't mean it either, she hopes. 'By the way, Viv, take whatever you want.'

They sit cross-legged on the bedroom floor for about thirty seconds before Jo admits defeat and grabs cushions. 'Forgotten how hard it is to sit like this. Not done it since school assembly, I think.'

Viv unfolds sweaters and trousers, checking for damage. She won't find anything – as soon as Laurie spilled so much as a drop of wine on himself, the offending item would be dispatched to a charity shop.

'I can't go round looking like I can't find my mouth,' he would say.

How evocative Laurie's clothes are, lying in a pile before her. Viv never remembers noticing his outfits, but now, free of context, everything rushes back. It's like a biography, laid out before her; she can conjure up every scene in fifty-foot CinemaScope. The bright green crew neck from the day he poured wine into a mean critic's manbag, the houndstooth trousers he wore tumbling from Rosy's childhood pogo stick, drunk, at her eighteenth. She looks up. Jo's eyes teem with similar memories.

'I read that Laurie was writing an autobiography when he died. Doesn't sound very him.'

Jo looks confused. 'Where'd you see that?'

'Online somewhere.' Jo does not need to know that she googles Laurie's name at least three times a week to make sure the embers of his good memory aren't fading too fast.

'Doesn't sound very him, no.' Jo holds up a blue cardigan that must've been an impulse buy; Viv never saw Laurie in it once. 'He always knew when to stop talking about himself, didn't he?'

She takes shoes out one by one and begins to pair them, and comes across a gold pair of Nikes. Another impulse buy? She suddenly wonders if Laurie was hiding a shopping addiction from her, and how many other things she doesn't know. 'Trainers! I never saw him in these?'

Jo smiles. 'I bought them. He was never casual. Thought he might ... I don't know. He was always talking about feeling old before his time. I think that blue cardy is mine by the way. Forgot I had it.'

Viv is relieved her knowledge of Laurie's taste has gone unchallenged. She holds the trainers up to the light. They haven't even been laced. 'Rosy has quite big feet, maybe they'll fit her. He loved his brogues, clip-clopping about like a show pony, didn't he?'

The room is charged with their shared memory. 'Liked you to know he was there.'

'It all tells a story, doesn't it? This stuff. Doesn't mean anything to anyone else, though.'

'No.' Jo's voice is strained. They're running out of things to say to each other that aren't fused with the lingering shockwaves of Laurie being dead.

'Y'know, I'd give anything for even an arsey text. Shouting at me for waking him up, or for being late, even though—'

'He was late every single time he came to meet you.'

'Yes!' She spies something on a shelf in the wardrobe – a plain, wooden cube. It has a lid; she can see hinges. 'What's that?'

Jo blushes immediately. 'Laurie.'

Viv's body tries to do too many things at once – choke, gasp, cry, shout. Laurie? In the room with them all this time? Right there? In the wardrobe? Hidden away? Plonked on a shelf amid the scarves? Shouldn't he be somewhere more dignified, more prominent? On display? This is his house! It's all Viv can do not to scream.

Jo reads her mind. 'I didn't know where to put him.'

The flagrant disrespect. Talking about Laurie like he's an awkward piece of furniture he hasn't the space for. Why didn't he call her? She could've helped him pick the perfect spot! It's so thoughtless, so uncaring. The man you've lain beside for over twenty years dies and you shove his sacred remains in the bottom of the wardrobe with outdated fashions you prefer to forget? Laurie's socks were treated with more reverence. She wants to grab the box, stand up and sweep everything off the mantelpiece and place Laurie upon it as if laying the crown on a monarch's head. Have him looking out over the bedroom, watching the husband he adored suffer a thousand sleepless nights.

Jo is oblivious. 'I thought me and you could scatter them . . . eventually.'

She reminds herself she's not in charge, it's nothing to do with her, nobody asked. Rosy would tell her to know her place. Still.

'Okay. That would be nice,' she says through clenched teeth, swallowing the rage she was ready to unleash. She folds the last jumper back up and pushes it to one side, knowing, as Jo does, yet again, the clear-out will not happen today. 'I feel like I'm the last person alive that speaks this really obscure language.'

'I'm still here, Viv.' Jo reaches for her hand and squeezes.

She feels instant guilt for the outburst that never came. 'Sometimes before I go to sleep, I . . . well . . . it's not praying, but I ask him to come and see me in a dream.' Jo knits his brow. 'Usually after wine, yes.'

'Does he? Come see you?'

'Sometimes. But it's not very, um, spiritual. We're always in a theatre, and he's always shushing someone for talking during the performance. There was a full-scale ruck in one dream. Do you dream about him?'

'Erm.' Jo looks awkwardly down at his own pile of Laurie's clothes. 'Weirdly, I don't. I wish I did.'

He certainly would if he had to stare at that box every day. Viv paints over her resentful undercoat and smiles. 'You will. It's probably all too raw.'

'Yeah.'

She stares at the wooden box again, as if waiting for it to move or make a sound. But nothing, only the rustle of the plastic bags destined for the charity shop – clear ones, Viv thought black bin liners were too barbaric. She resolves to stuff those houndstooth trousers in her bag, and maybe even sneak a scoop of the contents of that wooden box, in case this is the last time she gets this close.

Eight

November

Jo

Rosy doesn't sit in the office at all now, says it's too quiet without Laurie's furious *tap-a-tap-a-tapping* at his keyboard – plus it's freezing out and the radiator in the office has developed an unlikeable personality. She prefers sitting at the big kitchen table, Jasper curled at her feet, headphones on, nodding her head to music as she goes about her daily tasks, while Jo, or Diana the cleaner, bustle around her. It takes a while for Jo to realise that although Rosy's grief for Laurie is more pragmatic, knowing that the best tribute is to mitigate your sadness by living life to the full, she is lying about the silence, doesn't mind the cold; she just wants the company.

Jo is fine with it. Before Laurie died, he felt like he couldn't get near Rosy. As a child, she always ran to Laurie first. They always had their own thing going on, Jo a mere observer, waving hello as he left for the café with no idea what the two of them got up to all day. Once, years ago, he came home to find Rosy passed out on the back lounge sofa and Laurie, totally plastered, trying to bring her round by waving a can of air freshener under her nose.

'Her first boozy lunch,' he said. 'Ned Lanford cancelled. I didn't wanna waste the table.'

'She's in her school uniform, Laurie!'

'I know! Camp! Lunch with 1999 Britney Spears!'

Jo felt like he was looking at them through glass. As an only child, Jo found mixing with other kids tricky. He was a reader when gaming was starting to take off. He wore the wrong kind of clothes, his mum shopped at the market, and his dad wouldn't let him watch *Fresh Prince of Bel Air* because, Jo suspected, it had a Black cast. He always craved the company of adults, running off to London to find them aged seventeen, so dealing with children has never been his strong point. Laurie spent his boyhood fighting, and winning, countless battles against his siblings; there wasn't any child he couldn't win over.

If Laurie could see them now, sitting at the table, chatting happily, he'd presume some kind of conspiracy. Jo remembers Rosy showing him a video she made. She must've been about fifteen; she had a natural talent for it. Jo rewarded her with a homemade doughnut. Fun happening in a room he wasn't in was a bat-signal to Laurie, who emerged from his office to see what was going on.

'All this mutual appreciation, very touching,' he said. 'Two premiership footballers high-fiving at a spit-roast.'

He laughed, but there was a certain timbre to it that served as a warning. It was the strangest thing about Laurie sometimes. You always wanted him to notice you, but attract his attention on the wrong day and you might live to regret it. There were no more doughnuts for a while.

Now, Rosy sifts through various social media platforms, sighing at the gross comments men leave under her posts, when it occurs to Jo that, other than be in the same room, they haven't done anything together since Laurie's death.

'Why don't we go for lunch?'

Rosy looks up. 'You hungry? I can order something in.'

'No. I mean go out. Somewhere nice. Just us.'

A flicker of confusion on Rosy's face. They've been alone together countless times, but they don't really do that. Haven't for years. Not since Jo might have taken her for an ice cream or stopped off at a McDonald's after picking her up from school. She rights herself quickly. 'Okay!'

'Mind you, what if your mum pops by? She'll wonder where we are.'

'Uncle Jojo, let her wonder. She needs to get a life of her own. You need a day off.'

Jo isn't comfortable this side of the fence, betraying Viv, but he doesn't want to kill Rosy's enthusiasm. 'Cool. Where'd you wanna go?'

'Where would you usually go?'

A shadow over her face as she decodes the 'you'. She deliberates, shuffling a deck of potential venues in her mind.

'We used to go to Uncle Lu's club.'

'We can do that. If you want. I'm a member.'

Rosy looks surprised. 'Do you ever go?'

Jo feels a tingle of embarrassment remembering his last solo visit. Even if you hand over the money every month, wear the right clothes and have the preferred accent, places like that have ways of letting you know you don't belong. Waiters linger at other tables, avoid eye contact, or explain the menu like you have a reading age of an embryo. He waited thirty-five minutes for his order to be taken before getting up and leaving.

'Laurie got a cheap deal for the two of us. I didn't use it. Not much.'

'We can go somewhere else.'

'No,' says Jo, sharper than he intended. More softly: 'It'll be nice. Let's go.'

The club has had a refurb since Jo was last here. Beyond the authentic Georgian lobby and its gleaming bannisters and spotless tiles, the kernel's decor has tinges of bordello – he's never seen so many cushions in one room. The lunchtime crowd is sharing secrets on bulging sofas, or conducting business deals over lunch, gobbling up tiny plates of safe, anodyne reproductions of global favourites and large glasses of pale pink wine. Rosy and Jo are shown to the least appealing table in the corner, in a back room, nearest the toilets. Over a very average soup starter, Jo asks Rosy about the mean comments. Jo hasn't opened an app in years. Zosia forcibly removed his access to the café's social media accounts because of his unsophisticated photography. He uses his phone only to set alarms, text and read news stories while waiting for the kettle to boil.

'I might stop posting pics, you know,' says Rosy. 'It's brutal out there.' Jo raises an eyebrow. 'Men sliding into my inbox giving it "nice thighs" or whatever. You can see one centimetre of my leg in the pic. Desperate.'

'Not much better than your Uncle Laurie's pickup lines, to be honest.'

A smile spreads glacially over Rosy's face and Jo sees she's gone to another place, one where she's telling Laurie this story and he's got a brace of gold-star comebacks ready for her to deploy next time a creep messages her. She snaps back into the present day.

'See, I know I'm pretty.'

Jo laughs at this charming immodesty but stops when he sees Rosy is about to be very serious.

'But a man telling me I'm hot is meaningless. They want something. So instead of saying thanks, I start replying, "I know". And you know what happens?'

Jo shakes his head.

'He takes the compliment back. Tells you you're not all that. Too big for your boots. Only he can say you're hot, you can't know it yourself, he decides. Men want you to pretend you think you look like Shrek and only he can turn you into Princess Fiona. Fuck that. I'd happily die without ever hearing a man call me beautiful again.'

Wow. Every now and again Rosy reminds him why Laurie loved her so fiercely. 'Rosy, why do you care what men think?'

Rosy's laugh rings hollow. 'Uncle Jojo, we have to care, these fuckers rule the world.'

The waiter clearing their bowls recognises Rosy, says he hasn't seen her in a while. While they do those polite volleys between regulars and waiters – the how are yous, what have you been up tos – Jo looks round the room, drinking in the young people on laptops absentmindedly scooping salad into their mouths or daintily pouring tea from heavy silver pots. There are a couple of people Jo's age, but they're from serious money, dressed in clothes they didn't pick out themselves that morning. Jo is annoyed that he's so intimidated by what is basically a chain pub behind a velvet rope. He imagines Laurie here, at a better table in a more luxurious room, nodding hellos and leaning back in his chair safe in the knowledge that places like this would always feel like home. Probably why he spent so much time here.

Rosy is watching him. 'You're squirming in that chair. You're allowed to hate it, you know.'

'It's lovely. Did you come here a lot?'

'Can I say something?' Jo laughs. It's rare for Rosy to ask permission. 'Me and you. It's not gonna be the same. We don't have to do whatever me and Laurie used to do.'

Ah, that familiar feeling of being picked last for football at school. 'Oh. I just . . . '

'You don't have to try to replace him. Big shoes. Laurie was like this huge, I don't know . . . presence. But not that word. You know what I mean.'

From anyone else this would feel like an evisceration, but this is just Rosy being Rosy. Honest. She always told you how you looked without being asked.

'I thought you might be missing an ageing guncle.'

'I know. I am missing him, yeah, but look, me and you, it's a different energy, and that's not a problem. Don't call yourself a "guncle", that's rank.'

'Understood.'

They sit up as the waiter deposits their lunch plates, bows and sods off.

'But do you understand? Really? I like you for you, not as a stand-in. We're a team of our own. I'll miss Uncle Lu for ever, but that part of my life, with him, it's gone. I've, like, had to shut the door on it. Now I have to start something new.'

Jo feels a wave of relief, like he doesn't have to try as hard. He allows himself romantic visions of meeting Rosy and her friends for drinks, of her bringing home a serious girlfriend or boyfriend for his blessing, of walking her down the aisle even. He asks Rosy about her love life. It feels like intrusion, uncharted territory.

Rosy shrugs. 'Nobody worth chatting about. What about you? You got a new man?'

She says it so innocently, as if the whole concept of Jo having a 'new man' isn't a potential firebomb. He doesn't know what to say. A few lunches in a scruffy park with an enigmatic classmate, not exactly *Giovanni's Room*. There's no indication it's anything other than an extra, slightly more intimate studying session. But he doesn't want to lie. She can take it, she gets it.

'How would you feel if I did have a new man, as you put it?'

Her finger lightly drums on the table. Her eyes fill with knowing. 'Oh. I'd be happy. Seriously. Have you, then?'

He has known Rosy far too long, and respects her candour too much, to be evasive. But it doesn't stop him. 'I have a new friend, you could say.'

'A friend. That's all it is?'

'Yes.'

'For now, you mean? But it could be something more?'

'I'm not some drippy teenager.'

'Neither am I.'

Suddenly he wants to tell her everything. 'Sorry, I don't know how to answer questions I haven't even asked myself.'

She is unfazed by his reaction; she's wheedled much bigger secrets out of people she knows a lot less well than him, he can tell. 'Where did you meet?'

This has escalated. Isn't it too early for an origin story? Don't you need a fixed destination first? Jo is suddenly aware of work-shopping, live, half-formed feelings he doesn't quite understand, and blushes. 'It's not ... it's not anything, really. Friends. We study together.'

'Ooh, does he carry your bag for you? Have you carved his initials on your locker?' She is suddenly serious. 'Is he ... um ... I'm sorry I can't think of a way to ask this that doesn't sound like I'm calling you a paedo, but, is he young?'

Jo smiles. 'It depends whether or not you think I'm old.'

'I don't even know your age. Uncle Lu told me never to ask, because you were so ancient.'

They both burst into laughter. The tension evaporates.

'He's not fresh out of A-levels if that's what you're worried about.' He pauses for her to make a crude joke, but she gazes back innocently. 'He's a mature student, like me. Thirty-three. And I'm forty-seven. Like I say, we're just friends.'

Rosy nods thoughtfully. 'That's still quite . . . that's a big gap, isn't it?'

This has been whirring in the background, during their little talks. Hearing Theo read his date of birth over the phone to his bank was levelling. But Jo knows men and women his own age who can barely get dressed in the morning and still rely on parents – or best friends – for payouts. He's been trying to put himself in the position of a casual observer watching the pair of them do circuits round their little park, wondering if the age difference looks ridiculous. It's a blow to hear Rosy confirming it out loud.

'It's like me dating someone who's thirty-seven or so, right?' She wrinkles her nose. 'No offence. Couldn't be me. It's jarring. Imagine if I brought some middle-aged person round and said, "Hey, this is my new lover." How would you feel?'

Jo doesn't know which is worse, that Rosy's seen through his own self-doubt so sharply, or that she thinks thirty-seven is middle-aged. But she's right, isn't she? He'd be horrified, they all would. Even though it's so common, especially in the world where Laurie made his fortune, there's still something icky about it. It's perfectly legal, yet creepy. How many years have he, Laurie and Viv spent rolling their eyes at Ned Lanford's array of young sidekicks? What's so different? He's relieved to find the answer he's looking for.

'A twenty-three-year-old and a thirty-seven-year-old will have very different life experiences. At twenty-three, you've a lot of growing up to do. There'll be stuff you haven't done, or seen, or felt, that a thirty-seven-year-old would've.'

'And?'

'That puts him, or them, sorry, at an unfair advantage. I think. There's a power imbalance.'

'Because I'm a woman?'

This is difficult. Laurie would be better at this. 'Uh. Maybe.'

'So why's it different for you?'

Jo thinks of Theo's eyes, the way they look haunted sometimes. How he bats away careful enquiries about his grief, how whenever their conversations take a dive into the deep and gloomy, Theo does all he can to break back to the surface where the water is frothy and exhilarating, back to sunnier childhood memories and cultural influences. Back to safety. They may be different ages, but Jo senses they're on similar wavelengths. If anything, because of what he's been through, or what Jo assumes he's been through, Theo is way ahead when it comes to emotional maturity. He's definitely more jaded.

'We're friends. That's all. But once you hit a certain age, your experiences kind of plateau. Your learning curve levels out. It's why time starts to fly once you hit, I don't know, thirty. You feel like the same person day in, day out, because your bones have stopped growing, a lot of those huge life events are behind you. Age starts to matter less.'

Rosy dabs at the corners of her mouth with her napkin, and looks exactly like her mother while she does it.

'But if you were, say, thirty-five, and he was twenty-one, that would be ... I don't know ... grim?'

'Rosy, are you asking these questions because you genuinely don't know the answers, or because you think I need reminding?' Jo feels his skin has a light film of filth all over it. 'Being old isn't "grim". But, yeah, it would be different. There's power imbalances in all relationships, and not just age.'

There's money, confidence, health, mobility, skill, emotional maturity.'

'What was the imbalance between you and Laurie?'

One day her frankness will get her into trouble, but she deserves an answer. 'You'll know this, but when you're gay ... or any LGBTQ person, I suppose, some people figure out who they are earlier, and it can put them slightly ahead, even if they're the same age.'

'So he was more confident because he came out first?'

Confidence isn't the right word. 'He was better at pushing himself forward. More ambitious.'

'So he was more successful? That was the imbalance?'

Out of the mouths of babes, thinks Jo. He's being waterboarded. 'Not exactly.'

'But you worked well.' Her voice cracks. 'What about the new man? Where's the imbalance?'

Jo isn't ready to think about that. Too soon to tell. He doesn't know enough about him. Maybe that's the imbalance, that he'll never know what he's thinking. Laurie was an open book, Theo is locked away in a vault.

'His essays are better than mine.'

'Shit answer, but you're keeping things close to your chest. Got it. But for you, personally, right now, is it giving "midlife crisis fling" or, umm, "true love defying the generational divide"?'

'Generations? Christ, Rosy! It's not love. We are friends.'

'Sounds like you've thought about it, though,' she says, reading him with ease. 'You had your sugar daddy defence lined up.' She laughs, so he does too. 'Do I get to meet him?'

'Told you. We're just friends. But, sure, one day.' What would that look like, introducing Theo, a member of his new world, to everyone who lived in his old one?

Rosy stands up. 'Cool. I'm gonna go take a ... go to the loo, then can we get out of here? Let's go somewhere with a bit more life.'

'Brilliant.' Jo watches her walk away, and try as he might to shake the thought, he can't help but feel there was a ghost with them at lunch.

Mondegreen

Laurie

I judge a man by the force of his piss. Always have. Better a monsoon gush thundering into the bowl than the timid tinkling of a watering can over limp petals. Much more appealing, more manly. I was cringing at the next urinal to Ned Lanford – the sound of lapsang souchong trickling from a miniature bone china teapot, if you're interested – when the idea of a scholarship came up. Charitable deeds are how rich and successful people offset their guilt for either no longer being poor or having never been. You can attend as many galas and make as many ludicrous bids for signed memorabilia at dreadful charity auctions as you like, but they won't grant you immortality. I fancied pencilling in a lasting legacy for my sixties, maybe, arrange a plaque on a wall somewhere, plant a tree, but Ned wasn't having that.

'You've had a great deal of success in a short amount of time, you need to give something back,' he said, mid-spray in the downstairs loo at Black's.

I didn't love this suggestion I was an out-of-touch brat. I'd worked hard for my spoils, and I didn't hoard; Vivi always dropped a grand on the odd telethon on my behalf. I'd love to know the percentage of Lanford millions going into hungry mouths – other than silencing them. Ned said I needed something visible, useful, and not a vanity project. A scholarship would acknowledge my own hard work, he said, and cause a stir, present me as a visionary and a maverick, staving off the influx of entitled or connected writers and actors. Irony detection had never been the multimillionaire heir Ned Lanford's strong point. The idea was simple enough to be brilliant: a grant, coaching and networking for one actor and one writer a year, and a guaranteed role in our production company somewhere for a year after.

'I'm a writer. Can't it just be writers?' I saw more than enough actors in rehearsals; I didn't want to mentor them too. I fantasised about a terrified, mousy little scribbler from Basingstoke coming to my office once a fortnight to show me their dog-eared notebooks.

Ned laughed so hard I thought his cheek implants might explode. 'Laurie, darling. Most writers look like pigs in wigs. Think of the publicity campaign. Actors are more visible, more likely to take off, become a rising star. Get a pretty swan in to fund all your ugly ducklings.'

Pigs in wigs. Ned had all the grace and charm of a train toilet, but paranoia hit me. My hands instinctively went to my face. I was a little bloated. Had a bit more wine that afternoon than usual.

'My office can take care of everything,' said Ned. 'You'll barely need to do a thing, except be the face, hand over some dough.'

'The face? A pig in a wig like me? Actually, can they be like me? Gay, I mean? Or lesbian, of course. Or bi, or transgender.'

'Absolutely. I'd encourage that. Now, names. A brand. The Laurie Blount Award? Foundation, even?'

My chest puffed up. Not a vanity project, Ned had said; I was feeling too much pride, and didn't want to fall. Plus, I didn't want the scheme to become rhyming slang. Who inspired me the most, to be better? Who did I desire and respect more than anyone else?

'No. The Valenti. After my Jo. He's the real star working behind the scenes.'

I relished that tiny spark of envy in Ned's eyes. We decided to keep the branding under wraps, and surprise Jo. Ned said he didn't need me for the first interviews, but I went anyway. The first guy, for the acting part, was that unbearable bastard you see everywhere – an ugly, friendless child who got hot and tall overnight and realised they didn't need a personality after all. I'd once seen him shouting at a waiter at a party at the BFI after some screening. I said no.

Then there was a statuesque young lady with a breathy voice who claimed she was shy but walked into that room with the energy of Bette Davis striding up to a chicken to wring its neck. I understood where she was coming from; actresses often have to pretend they're a nerdy goofy klutz at heart so nobody gets threatened. Fuck that. I want an actress who looks like she can steal my husband. My gay husband. I want an actress who cuts brake cables to get parts, even though her talent can be seen from space, and knows exactly what she fucking wants. I went to school. I know nerdy goofy klutzes don't succeed. They just don't. Anyway, I liked her.

The final interviewee for the acting award was Elliott Bannerman, the young slip of a boy Ned brought to our civil partnership. Lovely and charming, but once he'd left, I asked Ned what the hell was going on.

'I thought we were wiping out nepotism, not rebranding it.'

Ned told me not to be silly, Elliott was on the ascent and would make a great success story for our first year. 'He grew up in a massive tower block.'

'I don't think Porchester Place counts, Ned.' But I caved. 'What about the writing award?'

Ned waved me away. 'I've lined up a delightful young lesbian from Skelmersdale, don't worry. You're too close to the art. Let me handle this.'

Even at that stage in my career, I was still powerless next to the money men. The feeling I was being hoodwinked by Ned, and occasionally struggling to remember details after a lunch-time rosé, led me to start taping conversations around this time. I'd always got inspiration from real-life encounters, but hurriedly scribbling notes became more difficult depending on how much malbec was sloshing inside me. Having an indisputable record was a comfort and curse. I've been back often to listen to this anticlimax. I still feel that disappointment; I'd wanted something to get my teeth into. Next year, I told myself.

At the launch, upstairs at Kettner's, my speech didn't have enough jokes, and the ones it did have didn't find their audience. We got a West End Wendy who was off *Les Mis* with strep throat to whoosh away the curtain and reveal the logo. Jo couldn't take his eyes off it, transfixed by the huge, sparkly swirls and points, his name glimmering under the lights.

Ned glided over like a Roomba on polished parquet. 'Fame at last, dear Jo!'

Jo threw his head back and laughed like I'd never seen before, which made me realise, instantly, I was in trouble.

He ignored me and chatted to the driver all the way home,

becoming monosyllabic as I poured him a large gin in the back lounge, and appeared on the verge of an aneurysm as he slunk upstairs. I can't go to bed on an argument, let alone one that hasn't actually happened. I was waiting as he came out of the bathroom.

'I thought it was an elaborate joke at first. Like full-on hidden camera shit.'

'Jojo, I don't see the problem.' Which was, apparently, an even bigger problem.

'You've named an award for developing talented actors and writers after me, a failed actor, and a writer with a hundred page-ones in the top drawer of my brain but fuck all else.'

'I've never seen you as a failed actor.' He gave up willingly, despite his talent, not through lacking it. 'You barely tried.'

I attempted to explain. I named it after him because I was proud of him. I wanted everyone to see that I knew how lucky I was, that someone as wonderful as him was willing to put up with me. Also, I was selflessly handing over my only shot at immortality.

His eyes blazed, his legs wide apart in streetfighter stance as he loomed over me in his shorts. Silk. Bought by me. 'If you want to be remembered, call it the Laurie. You're just reminding people of who I never was.'

Ned, delighting at my being in the doghouse, refused to change the name. 'It's snappy, exotic, and the branding cost twenty-five grand.'

Jo could never be mad at me too long. He eventually saw it as a compliment. I still smarted from misreading the situation so badly. The first time you put a foot wrong is so unsettling and upsetting – there's a reason babies never touch that hot flame twice. I wanted to make it right. I delved into my bank of brilliant ideas and past wins and came up with one that made things even worse.

The day of Byron's birthday party. We were getting ready. I tried to keep it casual, watched him spritz fragrance on his throat, and told him about a lease I'd taken on a new café, how I'd already got shopfitters in, that it would be ready on our anniversary. Looking back now, I can see it was petrol on a fire that had almost burned itself out.

'Remember last time?' I said, carefully taking the very heavy bottle of cologne from his hand lest he fracture my skull with it. 'You took a bit of convincing, but once you were in, you were in.'

He reminded me he'd been annoyed. 'It was romantic, yes. Lovely. But you can't just expand my business for me!'

'Isn't the whole point of starting a business to grow an empire? Otherwise it's just a hobby.'

He turned away and rested his hands on his washbasin, pushing on them full force like he was about to do push-ups. Even in this moment, I couldn't help appreciating the taut line of his body.

'I'm perfectly happy with the café I've got! Do I have to be a ... a ... mogul?'

This was the first time I remember feeling Jo switching to a cipher I couldn't decode. Hadn't he been yowling only weeks earlier that I thought him a failure? The antidote to failure is success! Also, it was two units, not exactly a multinational.

'You could be so much more.'

He looked at me again, eyes raw and tired, defeated. We were married, for God's sake; how could there still be so much to learn about each other? 'Aren't I enough?'

He refused to come to Byron's party. Not the worst move in the world – Byron had been sick by ten and, as I left, was reading out sex scenes from *Hollywood Wives* and damning to hell anyone who hadn't turned up. Vivi wasn't a sympathetic ear, chastising me for patronising Jo and keen to remind me I was a donkey to Jo's racehorse.

'Watch yourself. Jo's not short of admirers. The best rides have the longest queues. You don't want to end up at the back.'

I sulked in the taxi all the way home, as a radio phone-in blared with idiots moaning about the unfinished Olympic stadium. Something in me triggered my self-destruct protocol. I felt like a wretched character in a book with no redemption in sight, who decides to go fully nuclear. A few drinks and Vivi crowing in my ear had somehow convinced me I was utterly in the right and Jo was a miserable shrew. If I'd known that the next morning he'd wake up and apologise for being so sour, ask me to drive him to the café (in Notting Hill, thanks Ned) so he could gaze in awe at his new outpost, things would've been different.

But I didn't know.

I got home to find not Jo, but Holden, in my writing room, in his boxers, helping himself to a large glass of my favourite Polish vodka. He and Sian had been only too happy to come over and act as a double set of shoulders for Jo to cry on – I hadn't even noticed they weren't at Byron's party, such is their magnolia wall energy. Too hammered to drive home, and too miserly to call a taxi, they'd stayed over, and our respective spouses were now safely tucked up in bed.

It was not Holden's first vodka of the evening, or possibly even the previous five minutes, so he was showing off more than usual. He slinked round me, like a mink stole brought back to life and now powered by throat-choking diesel. Every syllable was a toxic waste cloud of menace, branding me 'flashy' and claiming I should be on my knees thanking him for 'talking Jo out of packing his bags'.

What utter bollocks. I was feeling quite spirited myself, so asked the question every man wants to ask the ex of the love of his life. 'You hate me, don't you, Holden?'

He laughed and flashed the teeth Jo had paid to get fixed for his wedding. 'Why would I? You try to buy Jo. That's never been what he's about.'

It was definitely what Holden was about, though. His wedding venue was Sian's parents' garden – and when I say garden, I mean meadow. Plus, we had just 'lent' Holden the money for a new car. I said something regrettable.

'How much would it cost to buy you, Holden? I reckon I've enough change in my pocket to cover it.'

He walked over to me, a contemptuous smirk on his thread-thin lips. He put his hand in my pocket. He rummaged for change. He found something else.

I wish things had been different. Still. Even now. God. It comes back to me in waves, sometimes, all these years later. Being on the wrong side of that door. Those ratty boxers on the floor. His face pressed against my keyboard, the intermittent warning bleeps seeming to sound in time with the breathing, fast and shallow and urgent and resentful, the air rushing in through my teeth as I fucked that smug bastard on my desk until we collapsed on the floor in a heap of flesh and treachery.

Even then, as the shame descended, I knew he'd never tell. He needed Jo almost as much as I did. I regret ever being part of it. Looking back, it was the beginning of the spiral. The magic was escaping. Once you've done something so terrible, felt that agony of betraying someone who means the world to you for the sake of one ridiculous hate-fuck, you know no sin that comes after it will ever feel as bad.

Nine

November

Jo

Jo stands very stiffly and straight and tries not to blink as the cameras flash. Tracey talked him into this, said if he didn't represent Laurie, someone else would: Ned Lanford maybe or, even worse, Byron. Rosy wrote his speech; he didn't dare do it himself, not with everybody watching. She's smiling encouragingly, like a proud parent, as he reads her brilliant words. He hasn't lost his touch, had it memorised in less than an hour. Maybe he shouldn't have given up acting after all. Fucking hell, he thinks, now's not the time. Viv is in floods to match the horizontal November rain lashing at the theatre doors. Rosy holds on to her, at that age where you're torn between being terminally embarrassed by everything your parents do and desperately wanting to protect them. Laurie's mother is sporting a new mantilla. Jo's parents didn't come.

'A man is coming to do the roof,' was the explanation offered. Jo accepted it gratefully.

Jo pulls at the cord and the tiny, ridiculous velvet curtains spring apart to reveal a plaque.

IN MEMORY OF LAURIE BLOUNT

A UNIQUE TALENT, A SHINING
STAR, A LASTING LEGEND

Presented by the Société Artistique of
the Rupert Street Theatre

Not Laurie's favourite theatre, by a long shot, but Tracey said you have to be dead at least a decade before the National will acknowledge you and the Young Vic was 'trying not to focus on death in the current economic climate' according to one of her contacts (who hadn't actually worked there in five years), so one of Ned's had to do.

Once both the applause and the tears dry up, everyone moves through to the bar for too-small glasses of commiserating tipples. Holden and Sian have brought the children, which feels inappropriate. Jo isn't in the mood for Holden's aphorisms and doesn't want to answer the kids' loud questions about the afterlife so he finds himself, for the first time he can remember, willingly gravitating towards Ned Lanford. Ned embraces him tightly, leaving behind his expensive scent on Jo's shoulder.

'You did wonderfully, dear Jo. Laurie would be so proud.'

Viv appears, wringing out her last tissue. 'Do you think he'd like the plaque?'

Ned purses his lips. 'Well, no, lovey, of course he wouldn't. He wouldn't want to be dead at all. This isn't for him, is it? It's for us poor souls left behind, gives us something to cling to.'

They stand quietly a while, as the odd peal of laughter cuts through the polite burble of chatter – second drinks are kicking in; the laughing will get longer and louder soon.

'How long now?' says Ned.

'Ten months next Monday,' Viv replies, far too quickly.

'I still can't believe it.' Ned's eyes are watery as he fingers his cravat. 'I was only talking to him a few ... I could've been the last person he spoke to.'

This is a terrible thought and Jo has to focus on an ugly painting on an opposite wall not to dry heave. 'I didn't know that.'

It's hard to tell through his permanent teak staining, which he pays a woman in Fitzrovia a tidy amount to paint all over him once a month, but Ned's face takes a definite plummet to the paler reaches of the colour chart. 'I'm sure I said.'

'What time?' There's urgency in Viv's voice, the sound of someone having a moment taken away from them for ever. 'I was talking to him. What would you two be talking about so late? While he was driving?'

'Business! I don't suppose it matters now.' Ned eyes Jo, as if inspecting him for ticks. 'Tracey tells me Laurie was working on a memoir. Do you know how far he got?'

Laurie didn't talk about projects until the end was in sight; he'd never walk into a room and announce he'd written fifty words that day. Jo doesn't like the thought of breaking that tradition, discussing Laurie's unfinished projects with Ned.

'Viv mentioned that. He never said anything.'

'Did you see any?'

'Laurie never showed anyone unfinished stuff.' He always said it would be like serving a half-cooked chicken; he preferred the juices running clear before sharing a draft.

*

Later, Tracey is cagey. 'We talked about it. There was no deal in place. I don't know how much he did. I never saw anything.'

'Then why did you tell Ned about it?'

Tracey's brows come together in concentration. 'I didn't. Or I don't remember. I've had a lot on.' Her wedding ring is off.

Rosy is more forthcoming. 'You know he recorded lots of stuff. There are some voice notes he was going to type up. Old audio of interviews as well. A few diary entries, the odd essay here and there, he said. He never showed me anything. All locked away somewhere. I don't know where.'

'Would Byron know?' Jo doesn't want to ask him, and potentially reveal that Byron has the upper hand in some small way, but, as he reminds himself: while Byron may be one of Laurie's oldest friends, Jo is the boss, not Byron's subordinate.

Byron smiles as Jo approaches. 'Oh yes, he kept diaries for years. I bought him a new set from Liberty every year. About this time of year, actually.'

Jo knows about those. Pages mostly blank save for names of restaurants so he could remember where he'd had dinner and who with. But once Laurie worked out the calendar on his phone, he stopped using them altogether.

'Not those. Was there anything else?'

Byron hops up onto a bar stool so he can look Jo directly in the eye. 'Some stuff in his personal documents, I'm sure, but I haven't looked through them. You told me not to. Shall I start?'

Something about the glint in Byron's eye, and the volume of the chatter in the room, and the lack of air, and maybe even the small glass of red he's been nursing the last half hour, gives Jo the courage he needs.

'I've been meaning to say, I'm downsizing Laurie's personal office.' He pauses for Byron's inevitable jaw drop. 'You've been, uh, invaluable but I know you're only staying on as a favour to me. You have your books, and so many other things going on.'

'Bu—'

'Tracey's picking up the press, Rosy's on admin, personal archive, socials.'

'Rosy?'

'Laurie would want me to look after you. There'll be a generous severance, help you focus on writing more. I'll get Rosy right on that.'

Fear fills Byron's eyes to the brim. He knows that cold, horrifying uncertainty when purpose is whipped away from you. Jo feels sorry for him in a way, but he'll live. Laurie always said Byron was even better at getting up than he was falling down in the first place. 'When's my last day?'

Jo holds out his hand, palm up. 'Let's make that new start today, on Laurie's special day. Can I take your keys? Rosy will box everything up and get it couriered over.'

When Byron drops the keys into Jo's hand, they're hot and clammy; he's been holding on to those all day, like he knew.

Ten
December

Jo

They know each other well enough now to order coffee without asking for the other's milk or sweetener preferences. Theo: oat latte, one sachet. Flat white with soy, no sweetener for Jo, who's struck by the sudden thought he can't remember Laurie's preferred coffee order when he came into the café. He will remember it later, at home alone.

Theo is impressed Jo owns a café. He's worked in bars, restaurants and burger joints all over the capital.

'Like Laurie,' Jo finds himself saying. 'He started as a waiter. Very bad at it, according to his friends.'

Theo laughs. 'My first job was chief chip shoveller up Wembley IKEA. I'd always give them less chips if they said no to lingonberry jam on their meatballs. Disrespecting the culture.'

Jo represses the instinct to correct that 'less' to 'fewer'. 'What did you really want to do? Or are you already doing it?'

'Write, I suppose. But before that ...' Theo hunches his shoulders almost up to his ears. Involuntary cringing at an imminent embarrassing confession. Jo guesses it seconds before he says it, recognises that spark of ambition that never caught aflame. 'Act. I wanted to be an actor. Well, a performer, really.'

Jo is so excited by this nugget of information, despite Theo's tortured face as he reveals it, he forgets to interject with details of his own less-than-illustrious acting career. 'Did you ever do anything about it?'

'Hmm. A few auditions. Whatever. I didn't finish drama school. The, uh, family stuff ... y'know.' The queue at the park café's hatch is moving slowly today. Someone at the front is ordering for hundreds. A couple of harassed-looking adults attempt crowd control on an entire nurseryful of children on the benches in the corner, noisily excited by the Christmas lights now twisting round the naked branches of select trees, and the gaudy, pop-eyed Santa dangling from the café roof, possibly once animatronic but now eerily still.

Theo is suddenly more sparky. 'It didn't feel like my world, you know? When you don't belong somewhere, you give off this energy. People pick up on it, drive you out, because if you don't get how things work straight away, you're too much effort. Know what I mean?'

Jo assumes either the drive was never there or it's been slowly squeezed out of Theo in the ensuing years. Jo recognises a fragile lid on a simmering pot when he sees one. He decides not to peek inside.

'I'm sorry that happened.' The noncommittal vernacular of a customer service chatbot.

They get their lunch, a damp samosa on a cardboard tray for

Theo, a Caesar salad in a plastic carton for Jo. The park looks rather unloved, and faceless, with no leaves on the bushes, the trees bare, and the paths damp and frosty. They move away from the children and their usual seat and head instead to a bench next to the mini Cenotaph.

Jo looks up at the weathered stone; it's bigger close up, he thinks, before realising that's a stupid thing to think. Of course it's bigger close up. Everything is. Maybe it's too close, though. Like sitting in somebody's grave. Viv has been on at him about a memorial for Laurie in time for the first anniversary which, Jo realises as if reeling from a paper cut, is next month.

'It's too late to do anything for his birthday now,' she said, pointedly, last time he saw her. 'I can't leave flowers at that ridiculous plaque in the Rupert. Wednesday matinee pensioners stomping over them for their interval drinks.'

He's about to ask Theo if they can move somewhere else when Theo starts reading the monument's inscription.

'The glorious dead. Hmm. Weird.'

Jo has an awkward sensation that someone he barely knows is about to surprise him in a horrible way, like the barista who was evangelical about fox hunting, or Byron's revelation that he voted Tory locally to keep his council tax low. 'Weird?'

'Glorifying people who fought in the war.'

'War makes heroes of the people who die for it, I suppose. They fought for us.'

Theo crams the last chunk of samosa in his mouth and licks his fingers. 'Glorious, though? I bet there's a few villains in there. Wifebeaters. Paedos even. Adulterers.'

'You sound quite biblical.'

'I've read it cover to cover, to make sure there was nothing in there for me. But you know what I mean? When people die they become, like, saints, but they're not, are they, not really?'

'Not always.' Jo glances at Theo. This is not about soldiers.

Theo takes a packet of cigarettes out of his pocket and lights one. Jo has never seen him smoke before. A mask is slipping. 'All this stuff about not speaking ill of the dead, it's rubbish, isn't it? Like dying lets you off being a shitty person when you were alive.'

Jo remembers Laurie's funeral, the half-hour tribute on the BBC he politely declined to be interviewed for, the tiny velvety curtains sweeping open to reveal his plaque, Rosy's speech. Laurie's myriad achievements – youngest playwright this, record-breaking that – but no hint of his soul behind them.

'The not speaking ill thing is for those left behind. Helps ease the pain of losing them. We remember the good things and forget their faults. They're not here to defend themselves, they can't change, can they, not now?'

Theo taps his cigarette, a tube of ash landing unbroken at his feet. 'Why should they get away with things just because they're dead?'

Jo wonders, not for the first time, exactly what this brother – who Theo will only say died in 'an accident' – has actually done. The man is dead, he's not exactly gone unpunished. It's not true what he's saying either. Death is not a guarantee you'll always be held in high esteem. Plenty of statues have been toppled, or miscreants exposed. 'Tell me about your brother.'

'He wasn't all good. Like men who went to war. The memorial makes them equals, doesn't it? Their personalities get stripped away.'

Theo is clawing his way down into emotions he doesn't quite understand. Unprocessed grief. It takes years off him; Jo can see the frightened young man he must've been when everything started to go wrong. He also sounds a bit like someone having a meltdown on social media.

'If you think about it, war memorials are pretty dark. Poppies, man, disgusting. People giving it rivers of tears and laying wreaths aren't thinking about the dead, they're thinking about war, heroics and . . . and . . . and women sitting at home weeping. Big emotional movie scenes, nothing like reality, turned on by bravery and misery.'

Jo isn't sure of his stance on war. He marched against the Iraq invasion, draped the café in a Ukrainian flag, wept in the Holocaust section of the Imperial War Museum. He thought a lot about people obliterated by bombs dropping on their houses, but never the soldiers who dropped them. He looks guiltily at the curling, sodden paper wreaths at the foot of the memorial. He forgot to buy a poppy this year. Laurie always wore one, each one more glittery as years went by; he thought they were camp, and that the least he could do was wear one, given he wouldn't have lasted two minutes in the trenches.

Theo is still going: 'Big tributes to the dead, but nobody respects the living, you're left to rot. But you've gotta die the right kind of death. What about Grenfell? Nobody called them heroes. Some posh MP who never worked a day in his life went on telly and called them dumb for not getting out in time, re-member? Memorials used to be warnings against making the same mistake again. But they're not, are they? They're trophies.' Jo is mildly disgusted to see spittle flying. 'We can't put heads on spikes any more so we lay big red wreaths in front of chunks of stone. We celebrate war, sent to your death by your country just to get your name engraved on a massive tombstone that claims you were glorious, whether it's true or not.'

This feels like a blasphemous conversation that would better suit a letter to the local paper, in green pen. Rhetoric like this could get you beaten to a pulp.

'I think glorious in this sense means they sacrificed them-selves for a cause.'

'To become fertiliser for poppies.' Theo sounds like an insolent child.

'I don't think many people like war. Whatever they did before
they fought, it doesn't mean they deserved to die. Same for your
brother.'

'Nobody deserves to die. It happens anyway, no matter how
good or bad you've been.'

Jo prepares to let that anger have some space, and says nothing. The park is quiet, the children and their guardians have
moved on. The December chill is working its way into the seams
of his gloves. But the door to what this is really about is ajar;
Jo feels a duty to nudge it open. 'So much is unresolved, isn't
it, when someone dies?' he finds himself saying. 'You always
assume they'll be there to answer you. But when they're gone,
the last thing you said to them, even if it wasn't anything important, it's like a huge question mark, just hanging there. Is that
how it was with your brother? Is that why you're so . . .'

'So what?' Theo's face is a ghost at a window.

What happened between those two? Jo can almost picture it,
but it doesn't feel like it's his place to invent a story of fraternal
discord, or a betrayal. He must hear it from Theo.

'You're angry. At yourself, maybe? At your brother, probably.
But not at this memorial, not those dead men and women. Does
it make it easier to believe that they're all the same, bad as each
other?'

'I don't think I know where to start. I seem to bring chaos
wherever I go.'

'That's not true.' Jo feels heat race to his cheeks. 'I find being
with you pretty calming, actually. Well, usually.'

A smile reaches Theo's lips. 'Someone told me once that grief
is love with nowhere to go. But there's another part, the bit they
don't put on the front of sympathy cards.'

'What?'

For perhaps the first time since they've met, the words flow freely from Theo. 'The hate's got nowhere to go either. How can you hate the dead? They're gone, they can't feel it. That's the whole point of hating someone, isn't it? You want them to know it. Stay awake all night thinking about it.'

So now we're getting to it, thinks Jo. Good old-fashioned guilt. 'Do you hate your brother? And wish you didn't, maybe?'

'I wanna know when I'm gonna stop feeling like this. There's too much of it, you know? It's like a grenade in my hand.'

Jo does know. 'Where would you chuck this hate, if you could? If you could pull the pin out, make it go away?'

'It's glued to my hand. The grenade.' His face is etched with every regret he's ever felt. 'I can't throw it anywhere. It's always with me.'

Jo has prodded the bear enough. 'Not always. It will get easier.'

Theo looks away. 'What about your husband? Laurie.' It's a jolt to hear his name. 'Was he a good man?' Jo would kill for something to lighten the mood – someone skidding on a banana, a clown car pulling up next to the park, anything. Theo turns back, clearly overcome with sudden regret that this has got so deep. 'Sorry.'

'It's fine.' Jo clenches his fists tightly to keep the cold at bay. 'He was funny and clever, people loved him.' It's refreshing to talk about him to someone who didn't know him, not to be interrupted with an alternative recollection. 'You don't normally say men are vivacious, do you? Women, usually. But they said that about him and it's true.'

Theo stubs out his cigarette on the bench and holds the tab end in his hand. 'Being dead, an important part of the conversation is missing. People might hold back, especially about someone so vivacious and popular, as you say. Nobody wants to go against the crowd, do they?'

'I suppose not.' Jo's hands and feet are totally frozen now.

Theo walks over to a bin, squeezes his tab end to make sure it's out, and carefully drops it in. 'Maybe I shouldn't feel guilty. Maybe we shouldn't mythologise the dead so much. Maybe we should speak ill, sometimes. Make them more human.'

Jo feels a flash of impatience; he thought this part was over. Theo's grief is too complicated to dissect over a mediocre salad. 'Laurie's got friends from way before I met him; they probably saw him entirely differently, have a few stories to tell. You don't need to know everything about someone. It's what they mean to you, personally, that matters. I'm freezing. Can we head to the Tube?'

Theo nods and circles the memorial, inspecting it, as if looking for a clue about the people it's commemorating. 'Know what it says on the other side?'

'I hadn't noticed.'

Theo blinks in the low sunshine. 'Their name liveth for evermore. That true, you reckon? We don't even know their names now.'

Jo thinks of Laurie's plays appearing on billboards and the front of theatres for years to come. Decades, even. 'We're all destined to be forgotten by those who come after us.' Not Laurie, though, he thinks. His name really will liveth for evermore – it makes too much money for anyone to let it be forgotten.

'I'm sorry. I don't mean to be insensitive. I find it all really confusing, but kind of interesting, I suppose. I get carried away. I'm sure your husband was a fantastic guy.' The rage is gone. He's the earnest, placid man Jo first met. 'It's just, it's not easy, is it?'

'Honestly, it's fine.' Jo recognises that expression. He's seen it for months and months, on Viv, and Rosy, even Byron. All searching for the same thing. He slowly starts to open his arms. Theo watches.

'Come here.'

Hugging him, Jo breathes in traces of fabric conditioner and a sporty deodorant. He can feel Theo's breathing change, then come the faltering gasps, in threes, as air tries to rush in through a tight throat. Jo can't see Theo's tears, but he knows they're there. The tension begins to drain away, a gently receding tide, until Theo's knees buckle slightly. This man, thinks Jo, has been waiting for this touch from someone – anyone, probably – for a very long time.

'Everything's going to be all right,' says Jo, as the choking sobs even out into a curative weeping. 'Promise.'

Plus One

Laurie

Regrettable and sordid as the Holden situation was, it had its benefits, and not just because his visits became sparser for the next year or so. I found myself energised with the zealous vigour of a junkie optimistic about their first year off the gear. I'd be the perfect husband, I decided, who stayed home, said no to parties, turned down boozy dinners, stopped at half a bottle of wine. I had Rosy over to stay more, so Vivi could have alone time with James. No, John. Julian? No idea who she was with; I'll have to check. It didn't work out anyway.

After a tense couple of years, the second café inevitably failed, choked by competition from two chains which opened before the ink was dry on our lease. He never said 'I told you so' but the dimming of those crystalline blue eyes was all the feedback I needed.

His displeasure found other outlets. He respectfully asked

that I stop directly lifting everything he said and placing it in my characters' mouths.

'Our marriage isn't a docusoap.'

'But you say the sweetest things.'

Jo fixed me with a scathing stare. 'They're never the things you quote me on.'

What could I say? I'd love to hear my own *bons mots* trilled back to me by an Olivier winner in a packed house, but I promised to respect Jo's wishes. Mostly.

Like a great white shark detecting the scent of blood fifty miles away, Ned got wind of my home life's change in temperature and dragged me to a charity event. A choir of all things. Gay men singing. It was tied to the Valenti award and with my (and Jo's) name all over it, I didn't want Ned representing me. His octopus arms were in traction of a kind, though. Since turning forty, or at least claiming to turn forty, Ned had a reverse midlife crisis and had met and, I assume, fallen in love with a director in his late forties who I won't name here because I don't want to give his shitty films any publicity. It didn't last.

'They do covers of nineties hits,' explained Ned. 'It's ironic. And fun!'

I felt too young for my teenage anthems to be repackaged as retro entertainment, but I tagged along, if only for the spectacle of seeing Ned have what he called fun. I liked being out again, among crowds, nodding at acquaintances and beaming at old enemies. (Always keep your widest smiles for your haters; it will infuriate them.) The singers ranged in age, shape and size, from cuddly old bears to scrawny young twinks with surprisingly capacious lungs and impressive octave ranges. Aside from the bears, who presented being large as an art form, I felt like the only man there with a wobbly tummy. The superhero look was taking off; Jo was doing something called body pump three times a week. My idea of hell but he looked stupendous in a tight T-shirt. As the choir valiantly harmonised 'Unbreak My Heart', I scanned the rows. I will weigh up any man, even if I'm not interested. I absorb them in a series of nimble glances – face, arms, arse, chest, package. Ever since William Fossett. Always in the same order. Signum crucis.

One made me pause for a longer look. Dark hair, swept back. The clear, orderly skin and features of someone in their twenties, yet to suffer sun damage and overzealous exfoliation. Round, dark eyes, a broad and proud nose, mouth in anticipatory pout – he wasn't yet singing, his part was obviously imminent. For the rest of the show, I didn't take my eyes off him.

I should've looked away. Never mind.

There was a party, in a poky room off the main theatre bar. There's always a party, isn't there? Especially at the fag-end of summer, when it's hot and sticky and everyone's had enough of the weather yet never wants it to end. Nights must go on. Taxis home, sunrises, working days all get in the way.

He was standing holding what looked like cranberry juice, little finger in his mouth, being bored to death by one of the more senior singers. On seeing me, the older gentleman seemed to instinctively know that whatever game was in play, he would lose, so as I approached, he conjured up an excuse and backed away. I introduced myself. First name only. I've never liked it when people, even famous ones, give you their full name like they're being herded through passport control in Sheremetyevo Airport. It instantly suggests a hierarchy.

'I recognise you.' I liked his voice. A hint of a drawl. But not cocky. This was someone who'd been ordered to speak more slowly by a terrifying director or, more likely, the manager of whichever bar he worked in when he wasn't doing this. His name was Teddy. I made no comment on this. I had learned my lesson.

In the presence of this youthful combustion engine I found myself acting unusually. Flirting, you might call it, but at the time it felt like I was being controlled from afar by the fucking Mysterons.

'I couldn't take my eyes off you,' I found myself saying. 'Your energy. Your eyes.'

'You could see my eyes all the way back there? You must have good eyesight.'

I certainly fucking do for gods like you, you cheeky little cunt, I thought. Twenty-twenty vision. But at least I now knew he'd spotted me in the crowd.

He told me which of my plays he'd seen. Too many for someone aged twenty-two. Twenty-two! I felt like I'd already experienced everything that was going to come my way by that age. It was the year I met Jo. This boy seemed like a newborn. His opening zinger was obviously his warning shot, because once I talked normally and stopped using the skeevy patois of a bus stop pervert, he relaxed.

He was in a short film, he said. 'It's coming out soon, if you fancy coming to the premiere?'

In those eyes I saw the hopes of a thousand starlets. Being wanted, or my opinion being respected, appealed to me.

'I'd be delighted.'

Teddy went outside for a cigarette. I resisted following. I was quite certain he'd come back. Ned Lanford, hovering by a door he must've assumed canapés would soon be appearing from, broke the world land speed record to be at my side.

'Who's that wonderful young man you were interrogating?'

'Christ, Ned, your tongue looks like the emergency slide hanging out of a 747. I thought you'd given up looking for cherries to relieve.'

'I thought you were married to the very handsome Jo. Whose

name is right there.' He pointed to the wall, and the poster for the event.

IN ASSOCIATION WITH THE VALENTI

The miserable shit. Brava.

'He's a fan, Ned. You wouldn't understand. He acts. Maybe he's a good shout for the Valenti. Be nice to pick the recipient myself for once. This is business.'

Ned backed off but kept staring between me and the doorway until I gave up waiting. I slipped out the stage door. Teddy was standing in the deserted alleyway and flicked his cigarette away as he saw me.

'It's so humid,' he said, his voice low and measured. 'You following me?'

'No. I'm leaving.'

'I thought maybe you liked them young, like your friend.'

God, I remember my irritation so starkly. Not the first time I'd been tainted by Ned's creepy aura. Youth held little allure for me, but I was always drawn to a handsome man with a smart mouth and total disregard for my feelings. On one occasion, I'd even persuaded him to fall in love with me. Those were the days, when all I wanted was a future that was Jo-shaped. But still, I felt the sting of Teddy's verbal uppercut. I was a mere thirty-four years old. A baby myself! Not that I wanted to tell him my age. When you're twenty-two and barely out of college, a thirty-four-year-old might as well be the Grauballe Man. They say youth is wasted on the young, but I don't agree. I'm glad they misuse it, devalue it. Once they've burned through it, they age – if they're lucky – and there's the shocking realisation of how much power they had, what could've been, and how it's slipped through their fingers.

Youth is a punishment, meted out retrospectively, when it's long gone.

'I don't "like them" any age. I'm married.'

He chuckled. Sparked another cigarette. I was transported back to another insolent young scamp with big dreams, who loved to push my buttons, but was now ten years older and, when I'd left him in my kitchen, varnishing a sideboard.

'Your wife not here tonight then?' I detected the distinct whiff of ego bolstered by a line of cheap cocaine, but I liked the back and forth. Nice to be challenged, so long as it stayed the right side of amicable.

'If you know anything about me, you'll already know I'd never have a wife. Why say it?'

A deep drag. I can hear it now. 'Just wondered if you were gonna correct me.'

My heartbeat picked up a bit. It was strangely exciting, being toyed with like this. I had no idea where this would go. I was not about to find out, however. Duty called. Home to Jo. I handed Teddy my card.

'Email me the details for the screening.'

'It's a premiere.'

I wondered how many times he'd made that plaintive clari-fication to indifferent parents or friends. Not a screening, a *premiere*.

'I'll be sure to wear a lovely frock. Good night, Teddy.'

Jo was waiting up and three glasses of wine down. He kissed me on the neck as I walked in, but I gently pushed him away, said I had some edits that couldn't wait, went straight to my writing room and locked the door as he plodded sadly up the stairs.

Eleven
December

Vivienne

When someone dies, there's a list of firsts that you must endure. Their first birthday dead. Your first birthday without them. First Christmas. First wedding. The first baby they'll never know. And the first anniversary of their dying, before the cycle starts again, and everything becomes the second time. Viv cannot believe it's Christmas already. The last year exists on two distinct planes: one a motion blur of indistinguishable horrors; the other a tedious calendar of life admin, trying to feel any other way than desperately sad. She has thrown herself into things – breath work meditations in an elite fitness club, Spanish conversation classes with a charming PhD student needing extra cash, a new multimedia project catching backstage bustle at huge West End shows – but once they're done, she's chucked right back to where she was. They are temporary, empty distractions, chewing gum when what she needs is chocolate.

Christmas, however, won't beat her, she's determined. There's something about the holiday season, and the looming pressure of New Year's resolutions, that forces you to acknowledge that the past is irreversible. She tries to brush aside the nagging reminder that January's renewal also brings an anniversary. She embraces Christmas shopping, tries all the limited-edition festive syrups in her local coffee shops; she drops off panettone and eye-wateringly expensive mince pies to Laurie's mother, but Belinda can't stay and chat because she's on her way out, to ambient Zumba. She arranges a date with a man she met on an app, a glass of wine at a local on the twenty-seventh – already vaccinating herself against the post-Christmas slump.

Viv invites Jo to spend the first Laurie-free Christmas with her and Rosy. They used to alternate houses, or occasionally diverge altogether and make the ultimate sacrifice – Christmas with their mothers.

Viv sends cheery season's greetings to Belinda on Christmas morning over text. She replies lightning fast, saying she's being spoiled rotten at her daughter's and thanking Viv for always being 'such a good friend to my precious Laurie'.

But was she? Can Viv honestly accept that compliment? Her mind searches for evidence for the prosecution. She once trapped Laurie's hand in a taxi door, after an argument about being unable to find a sitter for Rosy. Once she had a hot date with an even hotter actor, so lied that she had flu and missed the first night of . . . one of them. That she couldn't remember which play only further highlighted her phoney friend credentials. Sometimes she hadn't listened, she'd judged him, she'd ignored his calls if he'd been brusque the night before; she'd taken Jo's side even sometimes. Was she always a good friend to Laurie, or had their magic combination of selfishness and pettiness suited them both? They loved each other, she knew that, but they also dropped each other like a shitty brick if something more lucrative or attractive presented itself. Maybe that understanding was why they worked so well together. Best friends for ever, but please, *angel*, do step aside if cash, power or the promise of a bunk-up come calling.

God, Laurie, she thinks, hearing movement from Rosy upstairs, forever is such a long time. The weight of his eternal absence sits on her chest. These thoughts bother her until she no longer has the time for them, the gruelling Christmas cooking schedule a welcome diversion.

Viv always cooks as if twenty people are coming. Her festive displays are opulent and showy, her centrepieces the stuff of legend. Viv used to take great joy in making Laurie – usually unshockable – gasp with delight.

'Vivi, you've outdone yourself,' he'd say, every single time. 'One day I'm going to get you on set design for me.' This year, she's assembled a tall, white glittering vase of silver twigs and lush green holly, towering up to the ceiling almost. The cloth is sprinkled with sequins and embroidered snowflakes and fluffy snowballs. Tacky chic.

Jo arrives laden with packages that Viv can tell were wrapped in the shop by a professional and makes a great show of stamping his boots on the mat even though they're not muddy. As soon as Jasper is off his lead he bounds to the back of the house to find Rosy.

'Everything looks so gorgeous, Viv,' says Jo, taken aback.

Viv surveys her work with a faint smile. The show must go on. 'Dinner won't be long. I set a place for him, you know. Got quite far into the decorating before I realised.'

The way Jo pats her arm feels like a cease and desist. 'Poor Viv.'

Rosy slinks in from the kitchen. 'Hey, Uncle Jojo.'

He hugs her for a good couple of seconds longer than he did Viv. 'Hello, darling. Merry Christmas.'

Viv knows she shouldn't raise this now but can't help herself. There never seems to be a good time. 'About the memorial. We need something. For his mum, if nothing else.'

'I got my gardeners to plant a tree in her garden,' says Jo, like she's a wasp circling his pint. 'She loves it. I'm not big on memorials and monuments. They're a bit creepy, I think. No stone or statue could ever contain Laurie.'

Viv has never heard anything so ridiculous. She wants to tell him that she needs something, but not if it means his gardeners turn up on her doorstep with a silver birch.

'What about a service then? It's a way to remember him.'

Rosy peers over the top of her phone and catches Jo's eye. There's a lot of this now; the two of them have truly bonded. Rosy even goes over on her days off. They're each filling the hole Laurie left in their lives with one another, she supposes, whereas Viv's still gapes; it's a particular shape and the mould to fill it is long broken. She braces for the inevitable two-handed mutiny.

'You can remember him any time, Mum,' says Rosy. 'Doesn't have to be a big gravestone, or a church service. If you want to celebrate Laurie, let's have a party.'

'It's not a twenty-first birthday, Rosy! We need a church, otherwise it looks distasteful.' That said, few who knew Laurie will care about the optics. They'll be grateful to get to the champagne quicker. 'Jo, I understand about a stone, I really do.' She didn't. 'If I arrange a little service, you'll come, won't you?'

'Mum! We talked about this.' Rosy the traitor. Viv's mind wanders, imagining Rosy arriving for work at Laurie's office, heaving her bag off her shoulder, pouring two cups of coffee and handing one to Jo, and saying with gossipy scorn, 'You won't believe what she wants to do now! Some kind of weirdo requiem mass!' The pair of them sighing.

Jo now smiles the same smile that would greet Laurie and Viv when they staggered in drunk at 4 a.m. 'Of course I'll come, Viv, I'll have to. Otherwise *I* will look distasteful.' He hugs Viv and there's a second of stiffness between them before they both exhale. 'But not a church. Have a party, like Rosy says. No more eulogies, eh?'

'Of course,' says Viv with a brightness that leaves her almost spent. 'Now, let's eat.'

Later, Jo is loading the dishwasher. Viv hands Rosy her empty wine glass and sends her through to the kitchen for a refill. Suspecting Rosy and Jo will use this first alone time of the day to conspire, Viv hovers in the hall.

'She didn't just "realise", you know,' she hears Rosy saying.

Jo stops and closes the dishwasher. Viv can hear the top drawer buckling slightly under the weight of the crockery, so imagines he's glad of the pause to rethink the distribution – a dishwasher has never beaten him yet. 'What do you mean?'

Viv hears Rosy ease the cork out of the crémant. 'She set a place on purpose. For Uncle Lu. Wanted him to feel included, not forgotten, she said. She was being quite aggy about it. She wasn't even drunk.'

'She's taking this hard. Maybe harder than anyone.' Viv is grateful he's noticed, but patronised too. 'We should go easy on her, especially this time of year.'

'But it's weird.' Her own daughter. Viv has been siding with gay men against her own parents for decades, why should Rosy be any different? 'I told her she was being insensitive. To you.'

Insensitive to Jo? How can it be? He's flourishing. Viv has never been so fully aware of the chasm between them, how many stages of grief ahead of her he seems to be. She thought they'd be united by misery, but Jo has broken away in search of the support Viv's shaky foundations can't offer, Rosy slipping effortlessly into the role Viv has neglected. Why is it different for her? Did she love Laurie more fiercely than they did? Jo, going off to university, embracing a future unimaginable even a year ago. And Rosy, undaunted, unblemished.

She is stuck. She imagined today as sombre, a table of brave faces, maybe too much wine and clutching each other, bereft, remembering Christmases gone by. But there's been laughter, and gossip, and mild rants about the issues of the day. They're all wearing garish Christmas jumpers and golden foil hats, but Viv may as well be wearing black, and a heavy veil. It occurs to her that maybe she's forgotten how to be the person she was; Laurie is fused to her, threaded all the way through her being. How can she possibly let go of him without tearing away some of her own flesh? Easier to stay at a funeral for ever than leave it and live out some weird version of normal.

Viv peeps round the door as Jo kisses his fingertip and rests it on Rosy's forehead, an old Laurie trick. Rosy takes a deep breath and a tear forms.

'It doesn't matter whether she sets a place or not. He's always with me. But, uh, yeah, maybe it's weird. Let her deal with it in her own way.'

'That's the trouble. She isn't dealing with it. It's like she thinks we should *all* be sad for ever. Uncle Lu wouldn't want that, would he?'

Viv retreats, hand over her mouth, and takes her place at the table again. Why shouldn't they all be sad for ever?

Jo

Jo leaves Viv's two hours earlier than planned, can't watch her stare down into her wine any longer. It's dry and cold, the sky clear and hopeful, his favourite Christmas Day weather. He enjoys the sight of his breath swirling into clouds on the walk home from Brixton, Jasper tugging on his lead, eager to be home. As he turns the key in his front door, he gets a message from Theo.

Merry Christmas.

On a whim, not expecting him to say yes, but hoping he will, Jo invites him over. A fresh face in familiar walls, comparing notes on the strange customs we suffer in the name of the season. That's all he wants. He's certainly not expecting to have sex with Theo, but less than an hour after the doorbell rings in three shrill staccato blasts, he is doing exactly that, on the shaggy aubergine rug, on the floor of the back lounge. A milestone passed.

Jo's never imagined the first guy after Laurie, thought it was years off, maybe a one-nighter with a stranger off an app. Functional, not emotional, with no regret. Intimacy on this level has changed since he and Laurie last did it, the exact date Jo can't remember. Perfunctory rubbing and frotting against the clock in those last years, only focusing on the end goal. Mutual masturbation would usually be punctuated with 'Harder, no, not that hard. Christ, Jo, you're not ringing the Angelus bell, you'll pull it off.' In the most frantic moments, it wasn't unusual for Jo to be yanked out of his euphoric headspace by Laurie's plea of,

'Are you nearly there, Jo, my darling? My back can't take this any more.'

Theo, however, has all the time in the world and uses it wisely. His tongue has the ability to be in ten places at once, with untold strength and stamina, pummelling away like the jets in the short-lived hot tub Laurie installed during the first lockdown of the pandemic. As he focuses on not coming yet, Jo tries not to think of Laurie climbing out of it, swim shorts sopping and clinging to his pale legs.

It's thrilling and frightening to feel another person's body against his. He had a decent amount of partners before Laurie, but since, he's been programmed only for Laurie, adapting slightly as their physiques altered over the years.

Theo whispers in Jo's ear that he's 'so fucking hot' and it sounds ridiculous. Jo's visited the gym at least three times a week for the last decade and has smeared SPF50 on his face for even longer, but it's never occurred to him anyone would want to say this out loud. Theo is very beautiful, albeit in need of a good meal. Jo has never been one to moon over a man's eyes, but he likes the contrast between Theo's soft broad nose and the sharp angles of his chin, shoulders and jutting clavicles. Hunger looks good on him, all the way down to his hip bones where he turns from pointy to firm, his small but muscular buttocks – which Jo is surprised to find himself grabbing with the urgency of a teenage virgin who can't believe his luck – and his shredded thighs. Jo wants to tell him he looks hot too, but he can't, not in the heat of the moment. It feels pornographic, too open and aggrandising to pay someone a compliment while you're fucking them. Laurie used to do it when they were younger, though, Jo remembers, always telling him that he wanted him from the first moment he saw him.

And you got me, Jo thought then, and thinks now, as he gets close, driving his nails further into Theo's skin. You really did.

After, they crawl to the sofa and sit a while, entangled like pretzels, the fairy lights on the mantelpiece gently twinkling. Jo forgot this feeling, riding the wave of desire that melded them together, delirious joy that fizzes wildly before slowing to a comfortable simmer – there's an enzyme or a hormone or something that makes you feel this way, Jo can't remember its name.

There's something else, though. Guilt. His husband is ash and memories. Not even a year ago he was a real person, in this room, in a lopsided party hat, shovelling canapés down his throat. Now look.

Theo gets up to use the toilet and Jo forgets to warn him about the sticking door. He decides not to shout out, reluctant to dampen the electricity by bringing up such mundane housekeeping, so he waits a minute or so then pads out to rescue him, realising this is the first time in years he's been completely naked on the ground floor of this house. Theo doesn't need saving after all; he's already on his way back.

'You managed the door then?'

'No problem.'

'Can I get you anything?' There's a new formality, even though they're both standing with their dicks out.

Theo chuckles, leans in to kiss Jo, who tries not to recoil when Theo slowly runs his tongue over his top lip. He has forgotten the unabashed, minor perversions of the first time you do it. 'The host with the very most. Nah, I'm fine.'

Regardless, Jo needs to do something. He makes two strong gin and tonics. Instead of rejoining Theo on the sofa, he sits in the chair opposite.

Theo raises his glass, looks round the room as if engraving the moment on his memory. 'What you doing all the way over there?'

'Working out how I feel. It's been a while.'

'Me too, actually. I've … It's a long story.'

Now they've crossed a line, explored every centimetre of each other, Jo expects more insight, but having sex with someone is not seeing the real them. They're physically vulnerable, but emotionally everything is still behind shutters. It's like tasting a beautiful cake and being desperate to know what's in it. Maybe we're better off not knowing; in isolation, ingredients sound clinical and unappetising. He changes course.

'Are we still friends, Theo? I mean, I didn't plan this. I don't want you to think it's why I asked you here.'

Theo is trembling slightly. It isn't cold. 'I know you didn't. But it's why I came.' He reaches for his underwear, slowly slides the shorts up his legs and shifts slightly to pull them over his bottom, carefully tucking everything in. It's both awkward and erotic. 'Yes, we're still friends. We can call this a one-off, if you want. No judgement.'

Jo finds himself saying, 'What if I want to do it again?'

'Then we can.' Theo pulls his pants back off, and they do.

New Year comes and goes, January takes its first stumbling steps, and they're together whenever they can be. Although there's nothing to hide, Theo doesn't come round on days Rosy is working. Jo sees him in classes anyway. It's too cold to hang around in their park – which is how Jo thinks of it now, their park – so they sit in the pub reading or scribbling away in notebooks, before heading back to Jo's once the coast is clear. Jasper was instantly smitten; he nuzzles Theo's hand, looking for treats yet to appear, then sits contentedly at his feet, as if guarding him. Jo forgot about the intimate bubbles you inhabit when starting a new relationship. When you're still defining what it is, where it's going and, Jo remembers from his early twenties, whether this is a good idea. Some never emerge from this obsessive, utterly captivated stage. What makes this part so exciting for Jo is how private and special it is, sharing a world and a language of their own making, where all that matters is the two of them.

Jo's mind drifts sometimes to a Kennington rooftop, sleepless weekends with a talented boy who didn't realise how lost he was, soundtracked by sleazy disco and pleasure that dissolved on the tongue. Winding down with a shuffling slow dance to 'Silver Springs' or 'There Will Always Be a You'. Somehow sordid and romantic at the same time, morally it's a mass of weeds. Jo saw it as a rescue mission, if he's honest, saving Laurie from himself, setting boundaries, giving him something to focus on, measuring out the future rather than flooding Laurie's senses. Now, twenty plus years on, older and wiser, his time with Theo feels more innocent. Laurie could be suffocating at times, unashamed by the intensity of his feelings. Theo is less sure of himself, but where Laurie made a lot of noise to hide his insecurities, Theo acts like speaking will betray his.

Jo lets him smoke in the kitchen and the two of them hand books and newspapers to one another, with passages underlined. Not much beauty to behold within the beetroot-cheeked rage of opinion columns and nuclear doom of lengthy reportages, but occasionally words and ideas capture their imagination. Then they write assignments, or bits and pieces for pleasure. They tend not to show the other their work, except for a Dylan Thomas parody. They behave like poets, kissing by candlelight in a Paris garret. Jo, lost in creativity, hardly thinks about the café at all – Zosia and Alif are furious when he forgets a weekly meeting – and he bats away messages from Holden, Viv or Byron, saying he's busy with his studies.

Rosy tells him the memorial has morphed from a sombre dramatic reconstruction of the funeral into a charity party to raise funds for the Valenti scholarship. Jo has the wild idea of asking Theo to come. Would it be too scandalous? Laurie once recounted the story of his father's funeral, where one of the secretaries in attendance was crying too hard for his liking. He was still furious, said she may as well have been wearing a floor-length fur with nothing underneath. They'd all known exactly who she was, and hated that she thought she had a right to be there.

However, Theo is nobody's mistress and it's not a funeral. They don't have to reveal that they're together. Are they together? Is it too soon? Soon, as in they've only been having sex for about a month, and also soon as in he was with Laurie half his life, and has lived only a year without him. Jo is about to bring it up one evening when the doorbell goes. They both spring up as if caught with their hands in the till. Theo bolts into Laurie's study before Jo can blink. Ned Lanford is at the door, looking drunk and sad. He does this every so often, 'just calling in on my way home'. Unless he's been in Surrey, there's no way Jo's house is on the way to Ned's Hampstead flat, but Jo lets it go because there's a lot to be said for giving the lonely a few minutes of your time. He usually stays for a drink, tells one or two highly sanitised stories about Laurie, fishes for a compliment or two, then departs with a slobbery kiss that lingers too long upon Jo's cheek.

After pressing pause on Laurie's last work in progress, Ned's now ready to start things up. 'Laurie always loved sticking his oar in. Auditions, rehearsals. Am I right to carry on without him?'

'Of course. His last play. It's a huge moment.'

Ned takes a handkerchief out of his pocket to wipe away a tear which, inconveniently, has failed to materialise. 'If only there was some way of knowing what he wanted – with the

production company, I mean. What does the future look like?
Was there any indication in his diaries? Any unpolished works?'

'He never talked about it. But maybe I can help? Perhaps
there's an opportunity . . . '

'An opportunity?' Ned snaps back into character.

Jo takes a deep breath. He can do this. He deserves this. 'Now
I'm working on my own writing . . . '

Ned's mouth forms a perfect O. 'Why, lovely Jo, I forgot your
ambitions in that arena. How sweet that might be.' He gave a
hearty laugh. 'Of course. I mean, I suppose a Valenti alumnus
or two will be waiting for their big moment. That's what it's for,
after all . . . '

Jo feels stupid to have brought it up, that he presumed to
graze the surface of Laurie's genius. Nepotism was the lifeblood
of showbusiness, but some shoes could not be filled. 'Forget it.'

'No, I was going to say, who better than the man himself?
The original Valenti, continuing Laurie's legacy. It's got good
PR prospects.' He rests his hand on Jo's for a second or two
longer than is comfortable. 'I'll certainly think about it, dear Jo.
Anything to make you happy again.'

Once Ned leaves, Theo tiptoes back, slides on the sofa and
wraps himself round Jo.

'You shouldn't have hidden.'

'Who was it?'

'What would I call him? A friend? Business associate of
Laurie's.' He feels impulsive, like he needs a win after that embarrassing scene with Ned. 'Come with me. To the . . . I don't
know what it is. Charity disco of remembrance or whatever.
Meet everyone.'

Theo shakes his head. 'Not a good idea.'

'Why? Everyone was telling me to "get back out there"
months ago. So here I am. Out there.'

'Trust me, whether they know it or not, it's too soon for them.'

Jo is frightened something wonderful is escaping his grasp. 'We don't have to say who you are.'

Theo gets up and starts to gather his things. 'I'm just not up for it. It's a bad idea. Look, I'm going to head off.'

'See you around then.' The sharpness in Jo's voice makes Theo stop and look back with sad eyes. A rush of blood to Jo's head confirms this is getting serious, fast.

'Hey. Not "see you around". I do have to go. See you at uni. But the friends thing ... not yet.'

'We don't have to sneak around. I can do what I want.'

'Sure, but for your friends' sake, let's hold off the intros for now. I want them to like me, not resent me.'

He has a point. Jo imagines Viv, Laurie's representative among the living, unable to take her eyes off them.

'Okay, whatever you say,' he says, hoping it will make Theo stay. He leaves anyway.

Forced Errors

Laurie

I used to be good at keeping promises, so I went to see Teddy's film. His email was quite sweet – only two typos. There was even a little 'x' after his name. Everyone does that, though, don't they? It doesn't mean anything. Jo and I once creased up when the plumber sent over his estimate for a new cistern and signed off with 'xoxo' – Gossip Plumber, we called him, a reference I expect few of you will get.

The supposed premiere was badly organised, which always makes my arse twitch. They'd taken over one of those ugly cinemas on Leicester Square but forgotten to hire staff. You need someone front-of-house, an out-of-work actor with a kind face, making sure esteemed guests are filtered from the pedestrians, guiding them to the bar, or towards the step-and-repeat board on the red carpet (or mat, in this case) so you get lots of lovely free promo when they post their photos online hoping for an ocean of likes (but usually gaining barely a babbling brook). It's not hard. I'm guessing budget was a factor, but the lack of attention to detail went right to the bone: The London 'Breakthrow' Film Festival indeed. At least it didn't say 'fistival'. Vivi and I once had a terrifying, and expensive, afternoon back in our hospitality days grabbing back misspelled flyers we'd had printed for the bistro. '15% discunt' – mortifying.

Before the screening – sorry, premiere – started, I lurked by a nachos stand waiting for someone to notice me. I'm accustomed to unglamorous surroundings, I grew up in Greenford after all, but it had been a while since I felt so unimportant. I watched impertinent youths – cast, crew, and their acolytes, I assumed – milling about in the foyer like bacteria searching for a host. The place reeked of Daddy's money, but not his love. Finally, a door opened and a man with impressive cheekbones and pink hair said, 'Come on then,' and we trooped in. I found a corner. No sign of Teddy.

The movie was the usual art student fodder, the kind every young gay feels compelled to make. Queer misery. Blazingly unoriginal characters. Teddy's 125 seconds or so of screen time, as the kindly barman who masturbates over drunk customers' stolen bank cards, were the only highlight. I left the screen doubting everything I thought I knew about talent and opportunity.

'We're having an after-party,' said the young guy on the door. 'Do come.'

'The only after-party I'm interested in is hell, darling,' I quipped, to youthful indifference, but I went along anyway.

Teddy was less aloof than at our last meeting. The first time seeing yourself projected in giant form is a great leveller. I was a talking head on a documentary once – God knows who dropped out to make the knock-off Eames chair available for me. They screened it at the BFI, and I was supposed to do a Q&A after. I couldn't believe my eyes or ears. My wretched voice. My face, globular and moist, a Cornish pasty left on the dashboard of a car on a hot day. It was an instant cure for my vanity; I haven't watched myself on screen since.

I did what I always do for people who look a bit sad: I bought drinks. Vivi had never drunk a glass of wine until she met me. Teddy was having problems at home, the details sketchy, from his own discomfort rather than trying to conceal. He was looking for his own place. I recalled myself at that age. I'd been lucky. I worked hard but I'd known how to ask for help, skin like a rhino back then. Teddy wasn't like that – if he were, he'd have said no to that ghastly film.

So I spoke four words that would one day be my undoing. 'Let me help you.'

His face. Waiting for the catch. Instantly suspicious. Something we never take into account, when meeting someone, is how their view of us is tainted by past experiences. Everyone we've ever met has a hand in who we are today; I never touch prawns because a man I loved a quarter of a century ago ate nothing but, and I know Jo can't even look at Mickey Mouse because of Holden. We're always following in someone's footsteps.

'I'll lend you the deposit and a month's rent, get you going.' Money for things like rent and bills should be unimportant, it shouldn't mean anything. Life comes with too many burdens; if I could remove one, why not? 'What's your budget?'

'How would I pay you back? I work in a bar.'

'When you're a famous actor. I'm good for it. I can wait.'

It's annoying when you're trying to rescue someone and they won't let you. Take the cash, accept the gift, move on. So much easier for everyone.

'Teddy, I can write a cheque right now, and you can start searching. It's that easy.'

'You hardly know me.'

'I didn't know the man I bought my house off either but I handed him half a million pounds, no questions. All I ask is you spend the money on rent, not heroin or ...' I reached for the name of a clothing brand he might covet but my databank failed me. 'Or something frivolous. Definitely don't give the makers of this film any money. I want to see the flat, okay? Make sure you have somewhere safe.'

He was stunned. This boy's life clearly hadn't known many kind, untethered gestures. It's both a lovely sensation, and the saddest, to be the one breaking that curse. 'Why would you do that for me?'

'Why wouldn't I? Honestly, take that look off your face. I'm a weirdo. I get off on good deeds. Okay?'

Did I expect more? I don't know if I can answer that honestly now. I wanted to do something nice, not for publicity, or a balance sheet. This wasn't about my ego. I believed it then and I believe it now. I've always got a kick out of playing fairy god-mother, with more emphasis on the fairy than the god.

He emailed two weeks later bringing news of a studio in Mile End, somewhere I'd never been but knew was popular with younger queer people. I'd been spoiled by comparative luxury, so was mildly thrilled by the narrow and filthy front door and the charmless communal staircase to the first floor. Just one coat of magnolia over plasterboard – the rudimentary charm of a modern slum. The studio itself had a huge window, overlooking the kebab houses, betting shops and newsagents' that no British main drag would ever be without. It was tatty in an endearing way; it felt a good place to start. The furniture was a melange of standard landlord fire sale and junk shop chic. It had a proper bed, with a headboard. I could tell he'd very carefully arranged the pillows and supplementary cushions. The deep creases on the bed linen gave away the fact that usually, the bed wouldn't be looking so pristine. Looking round it with a sympathetic hauteur, I'd never felt more like my mother in my life.

'I thought you might've got a flat share, lots of other actors, like your own little sitcom.' I couldn't bear to be in the house alone longer than an hour; I needed to know someone was in another room somewhere, even if I only heard Jo's muffled cough two floors up.

'I wanted peace and quiet.' He made me tea in a slightly scratched mug with 'I Walked the Pennine Way for Cystic Fibrosis' on the front.

I sat on the one armchair. He perched on the bed.

'What does your mum think of your place?'

He shrugged. They don't like questions, do they, the young? Unless they're asking them. I used to love people showing interest in my life, grateful for the chance to talk about myself. Only recently, I've less to say. I digress. I told him I'd been thinking of him. Concern washed over his face.

'No, I think I can help you. I help run a scheme, for actors. Writers too. Do you write?' I explained about the bursary, the access to esteemed producers and directors, helping out at rehearsal rooms, how they could be in, or work on, one of my productions. All stuff that would have stars shooting out of even the most cynical eyes. Nothing. Not even a shrug this time. 'You should apply.'

'Apply?'

'You know, fill in the form and whatever. Have you got a showreel? Good, you'll need that. You know the drill.'

'You want me to apply?' I couldn't work out whether he was disappointed or relieved.

'That's how it works. People apply. There are interviews, and a workshop. I don't make the final decision but I promise I'll say positive things when asked.'

He flopped back on the bed, exhaled deeply, then sprang back up. 'That's all I have to do?'

The penny dropped. Everyone had stories of being chased round a dressing room by a pervert in a gaping silk robe, but I never dreamed I'd be suspected as one. He thought I'd come to collect on my debt. I felt quite revolting for a moment. As I said, we're always battling the ghosts of whoever came before us. I was relieved to be taping this particular chat.

'I'll leave it with you.' I read him the website address off my phone, thanked him for the tea and left.

When I got home, Jo was at the kitchen table with red eyes staring blankly ahead. I did a quick reference check in my head. What might be wrong? Dead parent? Another staff member quitting? New Rihanna single not quite what he was hoping for? Then I remembered, the second café was closing for good that day.

'I thought you were coming.'

'I got held up, sorry.'

He wasn't listening, grabbed his coat, said he was off to Holden's.

I stayed in that night, not even bothering to message Vivi and Byron to cancel our plans, keeping the phone free in case everything fell apart. He'd bided his time, but this would be Holden's perfect opportunity, wouldn't it? Take my boy, fuck me over beside the café's deathbed just as I'd ruined Jo the day I signed the lease. I was curled into a ball of tense nervous energy when Jo strolled in after 1 a.m., a little drunk, but not bitterly so.

'How was your evening?'

He smiled. 'Oh, fine. Sian cooked.'

I tried to swallow my anxiety, stop my voice cracking. 'And Holden?'

'Was uncrastically ... nope, hang on, uncharacterised ... eeehm, un-cha-racter-istic-ally – phew – sympathetic. Told me at least I gave it a go. That life isn't all about making pots of money.'

I should have known that lily-livered little shit wouldn't have thrown a spanner in the works. Access to my purse meant far more to Holden than revenge.

Twelve

January

Vivienne

The party was a bad idea. Like a birthday bash where the guest of honour doesn't show up. Viv keeps walking round, aghast at how much fun everybody seems to be having. Jo looks stunning. Velvet jacket. Deep green. She hasn't seen it before, must be new. She can't bring herself to go shopping. She hasn't set foot in Selfridges once since Laurie died. She can't even face Morleys for a quick scoot to the MAC counter. Doesn't feel right.

Anyway. It's a mistake. Byron is talking nonsense to whoever will pretend to listen, at triple decibels. He's stopped running the lint roller over his trousers – Laurie would've crucified him for that. Holden and Sian are hovering, wearing their usual pious smirks; no doubt it helps them clean up when collecting sponsorship for their charity hikes. Jo must've invited them. She certainly didn't.

Holden has a face she'd never tire of punching. 'You know anything about Jo's new friend?' he says, with a wolfish grin.

As he predicted, she has no idea what he's getting at. Holden spends ten minutes detouring round the fucking point before telling her Jo is seeing someone.

She hates to bite, but bite she must. 'Has he told you that?' The wine in her glass is too warm, so she knocks it back to be rid of it, flinches at the vinegary rush as it hits her throat.

'There was a packet of cigs on the microwave,' says Sian. 'And the smell of smoke in the kitchen.'

'Not just one cigarette,' Holden says, 'it smells like an ashtray in there.'

Jo gave up years ago but Laurie gave up drinking years ago, didn't he, and, well, he certainly wasn't zealous about it, not that Jo ever knew.

Rosy joins in, something suspicious nestling back a few paces behind those outwardly innocent eyes. 'Oh yeah, I've smelled that.'

Viv starts to get a blinding headache, fuelled by rage that they're gossiping at Laurie's party. So unchic. She feels like her own tongue is itching to say something outrageous, so she bites it, gently.

'You must've noticed Jo has a spring in his step, Viv,' says Holden smugly.

The implication being, of course, that Viv has no such spring, because she's still wading through shit, alone.

Prickles of sweat appear on her forehead. She glances over at Jo, talking to Ned Lanford, who's stuck to him like honey to fucking toast. Hang on. Ned always had his eye on Jo. Jo has eyes, so it was always unlikely, but now Laurie's gone, and Jo's probably lonely.

She pauses for a waiter to refill her glass and marches over, silently cursing as the thick carpet causes her leg to bow just as Jo turns to see her approaching. 'You two. Sly devils.' She only realises how drunk she is when Jo's eyes narrow in confusion.

'Sly?'

Viv watches Ned smirk uncertainly, and tries not to think of him smoking cigarettes in that beautiful kitchen when the rest of them have to stand outside and smoke and freeze. 'Over here, plotting.' She attempts a giggle; it sounds like a hiccup. 'The game's up, gentlemen. I definitely detect ... a frisson?' She makes herself say it, even though it's not the right word. All Christmas Day she was made to feel like some crazy irrational neurotic woman drowning in grief; she's not having that again. She can be playful, light; it used to be her factory setting.

To her surprise, Jo laughs, and Ned's smirk disappears. 'Viv, you're not ... me and Ned? Really?'

Jo's instant dismissal, as if Jo and Ned being a couple was the maddest thing on Earth, crushes Ned. His face reminds Viv of the painting of *Saturn Devouring His Son*, but in wax crayon. Worth tottering over just for that, except now they'll have to watch her walk away again.

She laughs it off, a fraction too long and too loud. The perfect time for everyone else to stop talking. Shit. She feels sick. 'No, I was joking!' Her voice is high, slightly crazed. God, she needs to be somewhere else. Outside. Under a rug. Outer space, anything. Every time she breathes, or moves in this room, the situation snowballs. 'Too much vino. Just off for a ciggie.'

She tries to glide away. The carpet's unforgiving shag betrays her again and she buckles, yet doesn't spill a drop. How could she think Jo would be interested in Ned? But if it isn't Ned, then ... who? And how long? And why hasn't he told her? 'It's probably nothing, Vivienne,' she mutters to herself as she blunders through a fire exit, out to a charmless bin store. She takes out her phone and scrolls through old messages, imagining that he's leaning over and whispering them in her ear.

> One of us needs to remind Byron that he's not pretty enough to drink Coke straight out of the glass bottle. X x x

> Who the hell was that guy leering over you last night? He had the personality of an air fryer. X x x

> Thank you for today Vivi. You looked A-list gorgeous btw. Meant to say. We've still got it baby. X x x

She sighs and opens her contacts list, defeatedly tapping her screen.

'Hey, this is Laurie. Thanks for your call which, sadly, I've missed. Please don't leave a message after the tone, text me instead. Or email. Or try again later. Or call my office. But if you do leave a message, make sure you say the important stuff in the first five seconds because that's all I can bear. I'm sorry. Love you, possibly.'

Day by day she is realising how the force of Laurie's presence airbrushed away her own inadequacies. She can't believe she ever resented it; it was his gift to her, every time she drank wine. She ends the call without speaking.

Golden

Laurie

A message from Teddy, asking to meet in Hyde Park. He looked more groomed than usual, smelled of lavender and amber and optimism. He had a new job with better hours, in a vegan restaurant.

'A vegan restaurant? What the hell do they serve?' I've always been unfashionably, unimaginatively carnivorous. 'Sorry, I mean ... wonderful. Well done.'

'I'm saving. So I can pay you back.'

I didn't say anything, couldn't do the whole 'I won't accept it' dance like two grannies arguing in a tea room about who pays for the Cherry Bakewells. He had something he wanted to show me. We left the park and walked up one of the streets off the Bayswater Road to a square, grand and framed by stuccoed houses, save for one side, which had obviously fallen foul of a V2 rocket and now featured a jolie-laide sixties apartment block. In the middle was a private garden, fenced off with tall, imposing iron railings, and fastened to them, I now noticed as we approached, was a bicycle, spray-painted gold.

'Is this an installation? Is it yours?'

Teddy gazed at the bike, eyes vacant, utterly still. 'My brother was killed here. Just over there. Knocked off his bike by a lorry taking a shortcut.'

He looked so broken, so desperate and alone, that I wanted to fold him into me immediately. I reached out for him and he almost fell into my tight hug. I patted the back of his head softly as he tried to make sense of the grief that had a hold of his throat. 'You poor angel.' I can't imagine much worse than being splatted by a lorry. It made me shiver.

'I've been struggling a bit. Depression, you know how it is.' I didn't, not then, not really, but Vivi and I had often tried to make sense of what she was feeling. I knew it could be a lonely experience, and it explained why I'd not seen much more of that bravado from the first night we met.

'They're only supposed to stay for a year. The bike, I mean. The residents' association or the council or whoever, they leave it, for about a year.' He blinked at me through those sad, dark eyes and long lashes. Quite feminine, aren't they, usually, but still so attractive on a man. 'I don't have anywhere else to go, to be near him, you know. We don't have a headstone or nothing. Just this.'

'No, right, of course. And it's lovely, it really is.' I wasn't lying. Better a true expression of who the person was than a vandalised gravestone or crude marker with vital statistics on a cheap gold plaque. 'You should be very proud.'

'My mum wrote them a letter. They were nice about it. Someone had a fundraiser.' I could imagine the kind of grating, moneyed do-gooder with a white saviour complex patronising

Teddy's mother for the sake of altruism. Although maybe I was no better with my no-strings loans. 'Me and my friends do maintenance, make sure the paint doesn't chip. I mean, it's not ugly. Kind of nice, right?'

I had to admit, in that square so full of grandeur, overlooked by the homes – or more likely second homes – of people whose biggest problem was probably choosing which Yves Saint Laurent suit to wear, there was something beautiful about that flash of gold, the insistence of the modern and urban way of life, encroaching into these expertly maintained gardens.

'If you need any help to keep it up to scratch, just ask; I can cough up for the paint, or whatever.'

I decided to have a word with Ned Lanford, make sure the bike stayed where it was. There wasn't a single thing Lanford money couldn't buy.

'That's so nice of you,' muttered Teddy, burrowing himself deeper into my coat, an almost inaudible high-pitched whine setting his tears to music.

'Come on,' I said, as he sighed the last of his emotions into the cashmere. 'Let's get you home.'

There's no way back from what came next. I know that.

That afternoon, I think, I remembered who I used to be. We undressed each other with deft tenderness. As mortifying as I found my body, Teddy took control at first, touching me as if I were beautiful, never pausing or shrinking from the parts I found difficult to be alone with in the shower. I'd always advocated for body positivity – I still won't go see a show if everybody in the cast is skinny – but found it hard to apply it to myself. Teddy, though, helped me feel desired, and free. His body had a few of its own imperfections, easily counteracted by his youth, a stark contrast against the determined, sculpted frame Jo was cultivating to ward off age. I was transported back in time, loving and laughing with the same ferocity as those days of the fire escape up to the rooftop.

After, I lay with the covers round my midriff, daring not to pull them right up to my chin. I reached out and ran my index finger up his spine to the nape of his neck. Jo didn't like to be touched, not immediately after, always said his skin was too tingly.

I'd been out of the game so long, I forgot all those nights writhing under strangers before Jo. The game that kept my sadness at bay. It wasn't just the thrill of the chase, or wanting them because they were beautiful, or because what was in their trousers was hard or huge or pretty. It was that instant moment of possession. It's easy to see a naked body these days, mere clicks away. It used to take effort, there was a sense of achievement in a man undressing for you. I'm a dinosaur, a relic, but I still believe the first time you see a lover's naked body, you should be able to reach out and feel skin, and their life-force, not a glass screen and data. You should be ready to take everything from them, their fear, pride, strength, and be willing to give up yours in return. It's all in your hands. Or mouth. Or inside you. Owning each other's space. That first fuck, or even suck, is an audition. You're trying out for the role of permanent keeper. If they trust you, their heart might follow, and you'll hear their secrets. And if they don't, you're damned to wonder. This is where it fell apart with Jo, I suppose. He'd given me everything already, there was nothing new to tell. Teddy, however, poured forth. Little did I know how quickly I would begin to drown.

I ended up writing a vague approximation of that (minus the references to Jo and Teddy) in my *Stage & Literature Digest* column. Upon reading it in the vets' waiting room, my mother phoned the magazine's front desk, hysterical, and begged them, for her sake and my own, to sack me. Jo never saw it. Obviously. Since we passed the ten-year mark he hasn't read a word I've written and probably never will again. Maybe he knows all he needs to know.

The Halo Crack'd

Laurie

Everybody wants to be a good person. We talk about it constantly, don't we? Politely refusing cake when on a diet, putting the expensive coat back on the rack, or saying no to a cocktail before 6 p.m. 'No thanks, I'm trying to be good.'

I've always tried to be good. Not just for appearances' sake, but because I know, in the long run, striving for the good makes you feel better about yourself. But there's a downside, one we never talk about. To truly live as a good person and do only positive deeds, you have to be unselfish, deny yourself the things you really want. The cake. The coat. The cocktail. You must leave yourself wanting. For ever.

I used to take myself back to that teenage summer, my simmering sexuality. Imagine how life might've turned out if I'd ignored propriety, and grief, and rather than sit mourning my father behind my mother's dusty Venetian blinds, I'd put myself out there, bitten into the cherry. So often in my life I'd acquiesced, done the right thing, and I was through with it. From the outside you may not have noticed, but inside me came a revolution. Maybe I became obsessed by Teddy, I don't know. There was a paradox at work here, I guess. I was doing something for my own gain, but with what I told myself were altruistic intentions.

Making dreams come true, that was my thing. When we're chucking donations onto the silver tray at church, or gently placing coins in a sleeping homeless guy's lap, to the casual observer it's selfless, but the benevolence gives us a buzz. It feels good, doesn't it, to play a part in someone else's flourishing? That's why I helped Jo get that first café, set Vivi up with everything she needed for her photography career, and sent Rosy to the best school I could afford. Hell, it's even why I gave in and tried to coach Byron. To watch mighty oaks grow from my acorns. Since I'd got everyone I loved up and running, I worried I'd run out of fairy dust. What use was I if I couldn't change someone's life?

So, that summer, maybe I was revitalised by Teddy needing me, looking after him, taking him wonderful places, introducing him to people. You could say I was getting careless. Brazen, even. In my head, taking Teddy under my wing counted as being a good person. A *Pygmalion* complex, perhaps, but what I got in return was priceless. It reminded me of starting out with Jo, someone excitable and impressed on my arm. Over the years, I often wished I'd bottled that feeling, the spark between us that lit up our early years. My boy and me, elbows brushing in the jump seats, pushing him forward from the small of his back to shake the hand of someone I wanted to make jealous, gazing over at him from my sun lounger, tracking the sweat running down his back. Before we became ships that passed in the hallway, a relationship carried out over scribbled notes on the kitchen counter, reminding one another about dental appointments, or in the coagulating pots of leftovers on the hob. I never realised how much I'd missed the silly rituals – almost, but not quite, like a courtship – of messaging each other and your stomach thrumming with excitement about seeing them. Teddy and I spent a weekend in Brighton, fingertips touching as we watched the sky give in to sunset, not minding the uncompromising pebbles under our bare feet. Not since my days hanging around outside the sandwich shop for Jo had I felt such a profound sense of being on the cusp of something wonderful. And Teddy was such a crisp remastering. None of Jo's amused detachment, or rules of engagement, true – Teddy simply enjoyed being – but I felt so free.

When I first fell in love with Jo, it never occurred to me how young I was, how there might be so much else out there for me to get my teeth into. I suppose I fell into his arms all the faster because the stability he offered excited me. You can only live on the edge so long before it becomes mundane. But, as wonderful as my life was, I'd become stale. I could've travelled more, lived in different cities a while, met new and interesting characters instead of staying welded to my own clique. Now I saw everything through Teddy's eyes, a window into who Jo and I used to be, or who I might have been if I'd chosen a different path.

I was heading for a January opening – potentially disastrous but Ned liked a challenge and the bastard was right in the end – and Teddy would come watch rehearsals sometimes. I'd catch him gazing at me in wonder, tapping his front teeth with his little finger, one little habit I adored. A few times, he came to my office. Always through the garden door. I didn't have a full-time assistant then; I'd yet to take pity on Byron. I toyed with giving Teddy the job, but his organisational skills were lacking: his electricity was always running out – he topped up his key meter with the smallest amounts he could. No sex in my and Jo's bed, though, that wouldn't have been right. Good person, remember. Not on the desk either, too many reminders of Holden's sweaty head, face down, sarcastic mouth slobbering into my Post-its. So, the spare bedrooms. Front lounge with the blinds down, on the hard floor. Even a bizarrely thrilling standy-uppy or two in the tiny downstairs loo with the dodgy door. We made it count, whatever time we had. Whether reading, fucking, eating or just talking, we learned something new about each other every time. Sometimes I play back my recordings of those days, just small snippets of our dialogue, and I feel a rush of excitement for the ignorant fool I once was, and a rumble of dread for the man he would become.

Jo was getting to the stage most relatively active gay men hit in their mid-thirties: constant 10ks, assault courses through swamps, fun runs and vague murmurings about marathons. Holden, tragic and similarly aimless, was training with him. Sian was chief touchline supporter. Even Vivi went sometimes, so Rosy could get some fresh air. I couldn't think of anything worse than watching a load of men confront their midlife crises clambering over a stile in a 'tough mudder', but Vivi claimed it was a nice day out if you took a hip flask and remembered to layer up. I would sponsor generously and my involvement ended there, aside from waving Jo off every Sunday.

He'd look like a little schoolboy in his winter getup. Long woollen coat, slim legs poking out the bottom, gloves, statement scarf, topped off by a colourful beanie. Green was my favourite. Backpack of gym kit strapped to both shoulders. The only betrayal of his age was a lack of chubby, rosy cheeks and spittle bubbling at the corner of his mouth. Instead, under that hat he was chiselled, eyes bright but deep, skin, if not in the full flush of youth, glowing with careful maintenance. He'd lean down for his dutiful peck on the cheek and I'd smell the aggressive, synthetic aroma of high-end barrier cream. For the millionth time that week, I wondered what on earth he saw in me.

'Don't forget to eat,' he'd say, with parental affection.

'Look at the size of me. It's like telling me to remember to breathe.'

'There's nothing wrong with your size. Bye.'

The door would click shut and I'd reach for my phone and call Teddy before Jo's car had even pulled away.

To Jo, my comings and goings were barely different; the real losers of my infatuation were Vivi and Byron, shunted from my diary for more time with Teddy. Vivi had often jilted me at the dinner table for various boyfriends, but she wasn't happy on the receiving end.

In Selfridges one afternoon in the run-up to Christmas, as we prowled the length of the beauty hall, day-drunk and scooping up fragrance samples, Vivi came out with it.

'Why don't I see you any more? Been months since we had a proper night out.'

'I'm huddled over my laptop every evening, trying to make the next one work,' I lied. 'I'm really up against it. It's not flowing as naturally these days.'

'I call by, you're never there. Jo says he's not sure where you are.' The fear in her eyes, I'll never forget it. Jo and I were the concrete harbour her little tugboat needed to feel safe. 'Since when has Jo never known where you are? Is everything all right between you two?'

'Tickety boo. I didn't want to say anything to him but I can't concentrate when he's in the house, knowing he might come in. Obviously I can't tell him that.'

'But you've always hated being alone in the house. You like having someone nearby. Like at the bistro.'

'I'm older. I've changed.'

She dropped it, once I paid for a huge bottle of her favourite fragrance, that heavy Tom Ford one that comes into a room a whole hour before she does.

Byron wasn't so easily mollified. He'd found a publisher for his sci-fi novel and with a child's naivety, expected it to be an instant bestseller. Maybe it was my fault, maybe I made success look easy. He trawled bookshops, searching the shelves. No train journey was complete without Byron darting off to browse the tiny station bookstore, combing through the smut, crime and millennial fiction set in expensive kitchens, searching for his masterpiece. Usually, pride of place, was a similar book – in genre only, not artistically – by a more attractive writer which came out around the same time as Byron's.

'It always gets a table,' he would say.

'It's a bestseller, By,' I'd reply.

He made the mistake many writers make, comparing himself to others and assuming everyone got an equal shot, as if readers' appreciation was irrelevant.

'But the writing! The wafer-thin plot! That awful protagonist! To hell with the bastard. It's so terrible! Isn't it, Blount?' Same thing every time.

But the rival book was not awful. It was genius. A slim, coruscating tome that stayed with you for weeks. I imagine his agent was rock-hard after receiving that humdinger. Yet duty prevailed. That good person hormone kicked in.

'It's not that great, no, By. Not at all. I bet the film will be terrible.' I did some work on it in the end; I never told Byron.

I'd play the good friend, dining with Byron at my club before pretending I was going home, telling him I'd pick up the tab – you've never seen anyone move so fast. Beyond rent, I've no idea what he spent his money on, but it certainly wasn't clothes, grooming or dinner. Once Byron had scampered home to stick pins in plasticine effigies of fellow authors, Teddy would meet me for a few drinks after his shift at the restaurant. Sometimes we'd go to his, and sometimes we'd part like lovers with an ocean widening between them, kissing in the street and gripping one another. However late or early I got in, Jo would always be in bed and would never comment. I can't decide whether I wanted him to notice or not.

Ned Lanford, however, had plenty to say. One night in the new year Teddy and I were gathering our coats to leave when Ned sidled up and sat at our table, blocking our exit in one perfect fluid motion. He was good at hemming men into corners.

'How lovely to bump into you boys. Join me for a nightcap?'

Teddy looked startled, eyes darting from me to Ned, but I'd seen Ned's Shere Khan act too many times to be intimidated. Ned played the perfect gentleman, asking Teddy lots of innocent-sounding questions about his social life – Ned collected information on young men's favourite watering holes like 1950s housewives swapped cupcake recipes.

When Teddy managed to excuse himself to use the toilet, Ned swivelled round to me, his dead loveless eyes searching mine for guilt, and kompromat.

'People are talking about you and this ... waifish young man.'

Ned himself was looking skinny at that time. Jo once said there was something innately sad about a man who manages to stay rake-thin past fifty, but given he spends three days a week in the gym and raises cans of beans above his head while waiting for the dishwasher to stop, I'm not sure I should listen.

'Waifish? He's not exactly fresh out the workhouse, Ned. Who's talking exactly?'

Ned dismissed my question. 'You're probably a little too famous and a lot too married to be sitting in public, and God knows where else, with a man very much not your husband.'

I wasn't famous, not remotely. I firmly believe you're not truly famous until you've had a doll made in your likeness – so far Mattel have yet to call.

'I sit with you in public all the time. And Byron. Are people talking about us too?'

'I've been telling them, those who ask, that he's a Valenti mentee we've stayed in touch with.'

I was impressed Ned had bothered to lie for me but annoyed he'd done so without asking. God, was this my future? Sitting in velvet booths bickering with Ned Lanford? The last two swingers. Like Gore Vidal and Tennessee Williams in *Palimpsest*, stumbling round Rome together on a futile cock-hunt?

'Teddy is a friend, Ned. An actor. I have dinner with dozens of actors week in, week out. There's no need to make excuses.'

'But not the same actor. Day. In. Day. Out.' Ned brought his head closer. He'd been drinking whisky earlier, which he always drank when in a bad mood. 'I'm worried about you. Call me old-fashioned, but there's something déclassé about dining with your tart, surrounded by your peers, while your handsome husband sits home alone. I will die on that hill.'

'Weird hill for you to die on, of all people, but, hey, at least you're dead.' I laughed. 'Jo isn't home alone. I bought him a dog.'

Jo was, obviously, furious I'd made another 'huge life decision' without consulting him. He called her Liza and cried with joy every time she ate a biscuit out of his hand.

Teddy returned, dropping his gaze as he shuffled back into his seat. Ned and I made a bad job of pretending we hadn't been talking about him.

'You're lucky to have Mr Blount as a mentor,' Ned purred. 'We should make it official. Let's discuss getting you on the Valenti sometime.'

'I'd like that,' muttered Teddy, with the strangest look on his face.

Ned stood up, so we felt we had to do the same.

'I'll get the bill on my way out,' he said. 'My treat.' He turned to Teddy then, head smoothly rotating like an owl with its eye on a mouse. 'Delightful to see you again, young man. Any help you need, let me know.'

'That was nice of him,' said Teddy, shakily, once Ned had gone. His brow was slicked with sweat, even though it wasn't particularly warm.

I didn't say anything. I went straight home that night.

Thirteen
March

Jo

Sometimes it's like they're a teenage couple. Theo's tastes are adolescent. They watch superhero movies. They go to a club on a Sunday night and neck in a corner. Theo suggests they buy some weed.

'Have you ever ... done drugs before?'

Jo stifles a laugh. Has he ever done drugs before? For the first two or so years with Laurie, he did little else. Your drug history is such a private thing, though; it's like you have to 'come out' as someone who took drugs back in the day, whenever that day happened to be. Jo remembers getting wasted as a bonding experience – maybe it's why he still feels tied to Viv and Byron long after his patience with them has run thin – but he doesn't want to be one of those middle-aged men who drones on about all the times he got high.

'I've dabbled.'

It is one of those days March occasionally gifts you. Temperate, bright, a tease of summer to make you long for it all the harder. They take Jasper to Brockwell Park and sit on the grass and get stoned, laughing at smooching couples and dog-walkers. Once the hysteria dies down, Jo asks Theo if he does this a lot. The atmosphere changes immediately.

'Why do you ask?'

'No reason. I thought this might be something you do with your friends. When I'm not around.'

'I don't have many friends.'

But he knows where to buy drugs from, Jo thinks. Not that drug dealers tend to be friends, not the ones Jo remembers anyway. Theo is either a solitary beast, or avoiding introducing Jo to his coterie. That's when the glaring anomalies surface, isn't it, when you shuffle into the centre of the Venn diagram, force everyone together?

'You must've had friends once? What happened?'

'I suppose I've focused more on myself, chasing my own light. Connections aren't as important to me.'

That weird therapy speak he uses sometimes, it's disconcerting, evasive. Theo lies back on the grass and closes his eyes, exhales slowly and drums his fingers on his chest.

'I had a lot of problems. Some people couldn't deal with it. Some people I just needed out of my life. I've never been close to anyone.' His eyes open. He smiles. 'Except you, of course.'

It is an unnecessarily schmaltzy addendum but Jo is charmed by it all the same.

A woman passes walking a cockapoo. It's wearing a tiny hi-vis jacket with 'NERVOUS' written on the side, to warn other dog-walkers away. If Theo wore one of those, Jo decides, it would say 'TRUST ISSUES' – it's probably carved through him like a stick of rock. He feels the urge to hug him, tell him he's sorry things went so badly, but doesn't want to come off as patronising, so instead they watch the dog totter by, trying to cock its leg while the oblivious owner drags it along, scrolling through her phone. Jasper tugs gently at his lead, eager to pick up whatever message the cockapoo is leaving for him.

'What about you?' Theo hugs his coat round him. It's still too chilly to be outside this long, and that coat is too thin. Jo wants to buy him a new one, but that would reveal he'd noticed his inferior outerwear; there's a fine line between considerate and controlling.

'Me?'

'Your friends. When you've been together as long as you were with Laurie ...' It's a jolt again, for Jo. Goosepimples spring up, not just from the encroaching chill. 'You must share a lot of friends.'

'They've been very supportive.' It's true. As needy as they are, they haven't kept their distance. 'We've helped each other through.'

'It's a fitting tribute. The strong friendships he's left behind. Right?'

'Right.' Jo desperately wants to change the subject. He calls for Jasper and hugs him tightly. 'Roll another. Let's check out completely.'

One evening, they go to a roller-skating club. Jo hasn't done this for years, and roller rinks have certainly smartened up their act since. It's all plush velvets and mood lighting, vintage mirrors and Americana pastiche. Still the same sweaty old hired skates, though. It's the kind of place Rosy might go. For a moment, he thinks he sees her, and is worried Theo might react like it's an ambush. The girl turns round and has a completely different face from Rosy. How would he feel to be seen with someone else, by someone who loved Laurie so fiercely?

Once home, Jo makes hot chocolate and finds Theo in the front lounge, picking up an award, a heavy, charmless icicle from a now defunct ceremony.

'Laurie nearly left that in the taxi on the way home.'

Theo chuckles. 'One too many? Must be weird to be surrounded by this. Like, these awards telling him how great he is. Was, I mean.'

Laurie never needed this stuff, though. Not really. Critical acclaim was welcome, but bums on seats and houses roaring with applause fascinated him much more.

Theo was examining another award. 'Broadway! Wow. I'm impressed. What was he like at home?'

The question catches Jo off guard. 'What do you mean?'

Theo is running his hand along the frame of the Hockney next to the fireplace now. 'Like, these achievements. You read about them on Wikipedia but you never know what they're really like, do you? I can't imagine what famous people are like in downtime, can you? Well, I suppose you can.'

Laurie hated being called famous. 'He was pretty ordinary. Messy. But thoughtful.' He can't do this. He understands Theo's interest, which seems to come from genuine curiosity and not the first sparks of jealousy, but Jo doesn't want to be in this room, a mausoleum without a body. 'Let's go through to—'

'But a good man, yeah? At home as well as in public?'

'Yes,' says Jo, unable to stop himself blurting out, 'You'd have liked him.' It's true, he would've. Everybody did.

'Was it open? You and him?'

There is curiosity, and then there is intrusion. 'What do you mean?'

'I know a lot of gay couples, like, older ones, been together a long time. They open things up. Did you?'

It's such a whiplash turn Jo isn't sure what to make of it, so he reaches for a joke. 'Oh, is that what older gay couples do? I had no idea.' The subject was broached once, by Jo, in a very offhand way; Laurie hit the roof and it was never discussed again. 'Why do you want to know?'

Theo shrugs and smiles awkwardly. 'Futureproofing, maybe.'

Jo's turn to smile now. So Theo is imagining a future. This is more than just classmates with benefits. 'No, we weren't open.'

'Ah,' says Theo, carefully placing a BAFTA back on the shelf. 'That's sweet.'

Another afternoon, they stop at Jo's café. He's been neglecting Zosia, Alif and now Kris too. Theo is reluctant to come in at first.

'My sourdough toasties are to die for. You don't want to miss out.' Jo walks around and opens the passenger door, holds his hand out to Theo. 'Come on.'

It's not too busy, but not worryingly quiet. Zosia looks up from wiping a table and bounds over to greet Jo, starting back slightly when she realises Theo's not just another customer, that they're together. Together, together.

'So great to see you.' Jo notices her cloth needs changing. Zosia follows his gaze and puts her hands behind her back. 'Let me get you something. What'll it be? Flat white with soy for you, Jo, yeah?'

Few understand better than baristas and waiters that warm, fuzzy validation a customer feels from their favourite order being remembered. It thrills Jo every time. 'Please. And an oat latte for . . .' He hesitates. What should he say? His name? My friend? My lover? God, no, so dramatic, too outré for 4 p.m. in a coffee shop. 'For him.' There, perfect.

Zosia nods and scurries away, while Jo and Theo take a table near the window. Alif waves while he serves customers. Kris has their back turned and is busy grappling with the machines making caffeinated magic. Theo looks about nervously. Yet he's impressed, Jo can tell. They've talked so much about Laurie's achievements, Jo feels a swell of pride to finally show Theo one of his own. He'd give anything to see this place through new eyes, buy another ten minutes of that excitement. Every second he's spent in it is emblazoned into his brain, though. Whenever he walks in, the same home-movie stutters into life in his head. The agonising decision over which plates to buy, and how often to change them – every five years. The endless trials before they found the right focaccia provider. The refurbs. The staff he's loved and lost.

'Must be hard work, running this place.'

'I do it on autopilot. Not that I do much of the running any more.'

'You ever thought of expanding?'

Jo sweeps crumbs off the table. 'No.' In case the lie shows in his eyes, Jo looks over to the counter, remembers perching on it all those years ago drinking from a mini bottle of champagne with Laurie. 'I'm happy with what I've got. Always have been.'

Two drinks appear before them. Jo looks up to see Kris beaming, but not at him. At Theo.

'Oh my God! Mate! How are you?' they're saying, as Theo looks up, open-mouthed, before jumping to his feet.

'Kris. Hey.'

They hug, but Kris's embrace is definitely more enthusiastic. Jo watches every twitch of their muscles for signs of how they know each other. Could Kris be one of the old friends who couldn't take the heat when things got rough? Surely, out of everyone, Kris would understand, after losing their mother.

'Haven't seen you at group for a while,' Kris says. 'You been busy?'

Jo tries to show no emotion, but his ears prick up like Wile E. Coyote hearing Roadrunner's distant 'meep meep'. Group. There's a group?

Theo glances at Jo. He seems genuinely happy to see Kris, but awkward too. 'Aw, I don't know, I think I'm kind of done.'

'That's great you're in a better place. Miss you, though.' Kris is suddenly aware that Jo is their boss and sitting right there. 'Hey, Jo, lovely to see you too, obvs. I didn't know you knew each other.'

'Yeah, we're doing the same course,' mumbles Theo.

It's reassuring, yet dispiriting, to see Theo has as much difficulty defining what the hell they are to each other. Jo watches Kris doing mental gymnastics, and perhaps sensing there's more to this iceberg, they scuttle back behind the counter. Jo waits for an explanation. None comes. Jo blows on his flat white even though it isn't hot. Theo sips his latte.

Finally, Jo breaks: 'What's "group"?'

Theo doesn't meet Jo's eye. 'Huh?'

'Kris asked why you hadn't been to group. What is that?' Theo's face drops, Jo backtracks. 'If it's personal, you don't have to tell me.'

Theo shakes his head. 'Grief counselling. Sorry. I'm not ashamed, it was just weird seeing Kris here, out of context.'

'Ah, okay. That's how I met Kris. Well, Viv did, at a counselling session. A group. She only went once. But it did get me a fabulous barista.'

This line of conversation is clearly not something Theo is keen to pursue. 'It's not for everyone.'

They finish up, say their goodbyes, Kris noticeably less animated. Theo needs to get home, wants to finish his essay. He rejects Jo's offer of a lift, and runs for his bus all smiles and winks and waves, like everything is okay. Because it is, surely? Jo walks to his car, is about to open the door. He can't help himself. He turns round, heads back to the café.

Kris is surprised to see him, their eyes gleam with mischief. 'Forget something?'

'No, no, wanted to see how you were doing.' A lie. 'Theo said you were at grief counselling together.'

Kris's smile dips slightly. 'Ah, right.'

'I didn't realise what happened affected him so badly still. It was such a long time ago.'

Kris's eyes narrow in confusion. The tiniest amount. But it's there. They look over at the door as if wishing for a coach-load of customers to come through it.

'I mean, not that I'm judging. Grief is a very individual thing, isn't it? I mean, look at poor Viv, for example. I ...' He's babbling, making it obvious Theo has told him zero about what happened. 'I just want to make sure Theo is all right.'

'Um ...' Kris watches Alif flip the sign on the door to closed. 'I kind of ... whatever happens in the group is, like, I can't really talk about it with outsiders.'

Jo's never been good at probing, this was Laurie's forte. 'I'm not an outsider.'

'I know, but, well, it's a confidentiality thing. Look, I'd better get on. I'm meeting my cousin later.'

Kris leaves Jo standing by the counter. He instinctively reaches for it, as if he needs to steady himself. Would you really need grief counselling for a decade? Jo knows every inch of this man's body but when it comes to what's going on inside his head, he's a total stranger.

No Heroics

Laurie

Never start anything without having some idea about how it might end. Books, plays, events, refurbs, marriages even. You should know where it's going, even if you change your mind along the way. You should also bear in mind that 'for ever' is a concept somewhat at odds with reality. This was my mistake with Teddy; I thought it could go on indefinitely. Overnight stays in Brighton, reliving my youth and putting my back out on dance floors under the influence. Seeing the world through another's eyes – it's like being immortal. Teddy darting round the hotel room, looking at everything in wonder.

We'd drive out to the countryside, raking through rails of polyester in second-hand shops and cooing at antiques in dusty windows, making old ladies stare at our interlocked fingers under the table of respectable frou-frou tea rooms, taking long lascivious licks of towering ice creams as we strolled cobbled streets. Much older gays would look with envy from me to their crinkly, snow-capped partners, wondering which wrong turn had marooned them in their lane instead of speeding ahead in mine. Jo seemed happy enough with his pedestrian evenings with Holden and Sian, or hanging out with his café crew. If I'm honest, this made everything all the more jarring.

It occurred to me, every marital breakdown I'd ever written about had missed the mark. I'd concocted blazing rows and painful, aching silences, couples tearing at each other's throats, and stalking out of rooms as the other entered. When imagining the death of love or fidelity, I'd erred towards apocalypse, but it wasn't the case between me and Jo. We got on perfectly well, barely argued. We still read the weekend papers in bed, did our Sunday lunches and took Rosy out for the day. The silences were comfortable, our routines bonded us tighter and the shared jokes and pet names and joys were as abundant as ever. You carry on, I realised. You don't have to be hateful, or dislike each other or, if you do, you don't have the energy to show it. He still left a glass of water for me on my side of the bed every night, picked up my dry cleaning, continued to send me links to furniture he was thinking of buying, or holidays we should go on. We had a beautiful week in Porto. He was too intelligent to be oblivious, so I interpreted it as permission. He never asked where I'd been, why I was late home, only if I'd had a good time. Perhaps he didn't care, or was determined not to show me. A phoney war. Yet I still looked at him and felt that familiar pull. My beautiful boy from the rooftop. Forever in his grip. It was such an education for me. You can still get on, do nice things for one another, love each other even, as everything disintegrates.

There were hints of decay elsewhere. Teddy asked if I might leave Jo. I'd wondered about it. Idly. Vaguely. Dismissing it within seconds. Where would I go? Rock up at Teddy's tiny studio with my gold Samsonites, and sit on his wobbly bed watching him prepare beans on toast? I couldn't. Nobody would forgive me; everyone I know loved Jo like a saint.

'You wouldn't want me full-time, pet,' I said. 'I'm a nightmare.'

'You're not. You're fun.'

'You say that now, but you don't have to pick up my dirty socks, or trip over my shoes in the hallway, or dance round the smoke alarm wafting a tea towel when I forget about the toaster.'

'I don't have a hallway. Don't you want to be with me all the time?'

Killer question. The truth was ... no. I didn't. Jo might be an awkward consort at times but he knows how to behave, can hold his own in a conversation even if only nodding and smiling. Alone together, Teddy and I had beautiful chemistry, and music to everything we did. How would that tune sound out of the bubble, when I couldn't protect him? It seemed incredible to me now that I'd ever thought Teddy and Jo were alike. Jo always kept me at arm's length, he was in charge of the schedule, always self-sufficient, turned his phone off for days on end. Teddy was needy, and craved progression, to have 'the talk'. Jo never asked anything of me back then; he'd kept me waiting and wondering until I couldn't stand it any more and had to have him with me all the time. I handed Jo the keys to my heart; it was beginning to feel like Teddy was sneaking behind my back to a locksmith to have his own set cut.

'You go home to your husband,' he said, another evening. 'I don't have anyone.'

Teddy was always at pains to portray himself as a loner. I was never sure how true it was. Every waiter I've ever known – biblically or socially – has been a tremendous gossip, out every

night, and he was still a peripheral member of the choir. Panic
gripped me.

'You don't talk to your friends about me, do you? You don't
know who they'll talk to.'

His lips curled in amusement. 'What friends? Anyway, we're
seen together all the time.'

'It's not the same. My friends are . . . ' I wanted to say they
were proper grown-ups. 'My friends don't pry.' Not that I gave
them a chance. 'Yours might . . . use it. Gossip is valuable cur-
rency in the theatre world.' Asking young men to keep secrets
for me made me feel uncomfortable.

'I don't. I promise.'

Maybe it was a blessing he had few friends bending his ear
about my bad influence, but it also meant I was his entire focus.
These occasional complaints – what if that was his default, and
the rest of the time spent with me was a performance?

He got to me, though. Why should my life stay the same?
Maybe I could go travelling, more than my standard four weeks
a year lazing on beaches or feigning interest in local culture. I
began to get fantastical notions about roaming the world, Teddy
at my side maybe, injecting new vim into the tired and jaded
persona I was frankly sick of carrying round. I didn't need that
house, I didn't need the dinners, and the first nights, and the
shows. I could be a digital nomad – I'd read about them in
magazines at the dentist.

A denouement started to formulate. It consumed my
thoughts, this new version of myself. I'd be at dinner with
Vivi and Byron, having the same conversations we'd been
having since we were twenty, but dreaming of Teddy feeding
me fresh pasta in a scuzzy, charming backstreet restaurant in
Sicily. Byron would usually snuff out my fantasy by revealing

deathly dull titbits about himself as if he were being profiled in *Vanity Fair.*

'Would you like to know another fascinating fact about me?'

'Another?' shrieked Vivi. 'Still waiting to hear a first, By.'

He wasn't deterred. 'I only like blueberries when they're rock hard, like bullets, but juicy and fresh.'

Vivi almost choked on her rosé and nudged me. I'd normally have interjected by now. 'Have you heard this?'

'My, how remarkable and exotic, By,' I said. 'How do you like your toast?'

'Golden, why?'

'Ah, shame. Same as me. I was thinking you might have two totally unique attributes. Just the one then, never mind.'

'Oh, to hell with you both,' he muttered, scowling.

All I could think about was my new life waiting to start. Living simply, beautifully. My imagination was full of billowing silk, beaming sunshine and golden sand. Everything was so bright there.

Yet it was raining the day it started to come crashing down. Teddy texted me. Wanting 'to talk', again. Oh, talking, humans do so much of it and never say anything of use. One thing I liked about Jo was we'd never really done big emotional showdowns. We didn't 'work through issues' like soap opera characters, or sit at the kitchen table for transformative conversations about 'the future of our relationship'. We got on with it. Obviously, living now as I do in a world where even your taxi driver is burdening you with his emotional traumas, I realise this isn't the best course of action for a healthy, flourishing relationship, but it suited me fine. Why sit whining about the state of your existence when there's wine and cigarettes and pornography to blank it out? But Teddy was from a generation weaned on watching the casts of various scripted reality TV shows get deep and meaningful in the deodorant aisle of a pharmacy, so I accepted my summons to his studio for the inevitable 'what are we?' interrogation.

He stalled when I arrived, made a great fuss of making tea I didn't want, then going to the shop for the vodka I did want. When he came back, he sat on the edge of the bed, hunched over, forearms pressed into his thighs, a hangdog expression, and asked if we would always be friends. All I remember thinking was that rain had got into my shoe and damp was slowly creeping up my sock, but it would be bad form to take them off while faced with such a cliffhanger.

He repeated the gripe that he was always left alone when I went home to my 'handsome husband'. How did he know Jo was handsome? Maybe he'd googled, found some old red-carpet photos. Maybe it was more sinister. Had he followed me? I couldn't blame him for being curious.

He wanted to know whether he was expected to be 'exclusive'. Ah, the return of that emotional muscle I'd so admired when we first met. But as everybody knows, personality shifts don't happen in a vacuum, there's usually an outside influence. Either Teddy had his eye on someone new, or someone had expressed an interest and Teddy was weighing up his options. Internally, I furiously flipped through all possible ways I could prevent this becoming unmanageable. Could I really go home, now, tell Jo it was over, that I was taking off with a man young enough to have never owned a landline? I needed to buy time.

'Let's go away this weekend,' I said, trying to sound authoritative and reassuring. 'Or tonight, maybe? Scoot off to Oxfordshire, to my club's country outpost. I can say I've got meetings. Talk this over.'

I kissed my fingertip and pressed it to his forehead. Like a daddy wanting baby to hush. Who'd turned that little head of his? A foxy new waiter at the restaurant, maybe? I cursed myself for never having visited and done a recce of potential threats.

'I'll go home, sort this with Jo now.' I was already half out the door but I turned back. 'Teddy, is there someone special you want to tell me about?'

His face flushed. 'Would you care if there was?' Then I saw it. He wanted to know whether it was possible to hurt me, whether he mattered. Maybe there was someone else, maybe there wasn't, but he was testing my commitment.

I knelt before him, cupped his face. 'Baby, I would be devastated. But I wouldn't blame you. I'd fight for you.'

Finally my shoes and socks came off.

It was still pouring when I got home. I expected to find the house in darkness but the lights were blazing and Jo was sitting in the back lounge, head in hands. This is it, I thought. Someone's seen us and told him. Flowcharts and spider-grams unfurled in my brain. I was about to deny everything when it occurred to me he hadn't actually spoken. When he looked up his eyes were raw and red. Despite everything I'd done, and said, miles away in a poky studio, there was a rush of love. My boy.

'My gran's dead.'

He hugged his knees and his body jerked with frenzied sobs. They'd been close. She'd always known he was gay, let him stomp about the house in her high heels when nobody was around. I liked her. At our civil partnership, she'd told a brilliant off-colour joke about wedding night sex, to a table of rapt actors. I held him as he cried, realising we didn't touch that much any more, not like this, not in an affectionate way that wasn't sexual. We were still having sex, once or twice a month. Functional, but not unpleasant; I still took great delight in making him come, although it occurred to me, as our bodies began to change, that he might be fucking me out of pity.

So I enjoyed that moment, so tender, feeling his blood course through his body. I absorbed some of his tension, and his crying became more gentle.

'I'm heading to Derbyshire tonight.'

'I'll drive.'

He didn't protest; he'd wanted me to offer, but would never have asked.

I transformed into that super-organised person I become in the darkest of situations. I methodically packed our bags, and called Vivi to come and get the dog. I cleared my diary. I made hot sweet tea for Jo and showered and groomed myself to look like the adorable, dependable husband I would need to be over the following days. I drove swiftly but safely north, listening to my love tell stories I'd never heard before about this marvellous woman who'd been his only ally and had sworn like a sailor at anyone who crossed him. We laughed, we cried, we screeched along to terrible pop music on the radio and we shouted, 'Oh, do fuck off!' whenever a traffic report interrupted us.

The one thing I didn't do was send a message to Teddy and tell him I wouldn't be coming back.

Fourteen

March

Vivienne

She is thrilled that Eugène is on the desk when she arrives, and even more so when he recognises her, lifting her hand to his mouth and letting his lips hover for a second or two, in that way she used to find on the distasteful side, but relishes now.

'Ah, Madame Vivienne! So wonderful to see you again.'

She laughs like a nervous schoolgirl. 'It's been a while.'

'But you are back with us now. I have your regular table. Monsieur Miller is already there.'

'He is?' Byron has never been early for anything. She was hoping to arrive first. They haven't had lunch in a formal setting alone together for so long it's starting to feel like an alien concept. She arranged today to break the seal. All morning she's rehearsed her facial expressions, workshopped greetings, had it all mapped out, imagined herself rising from the table with

194 Justin Myers

statesmanlike poise as Byron lumbered towards her. Trust him to go rogue and spoil it.

Byron is sitting to the right-hand side of the curved sofa, his usual spot, staring into his laptop as she approaches.

'Hello, By-By!'

If he is weirded out by being back here after so long, he doesn't show it, but he dutifully gets to his feet and plants a pinched kiss on her cheek. 'Grainger.'

Viv used to hate the way Byron called her and Laurie by their surnames, but now she enjoys the fondness the habit suggests. She sits down next to him while Eugène dispenses menus, takes requests for table water and snacks, before disappearing in a haze of irresistible cologne.

'I know exactly what I'm going to have.' She's rehearsed this too, but Byron doesn't have the script and carries on typing. Small talk it is then. 'Are you putting that away?' She signals to the laptop. 'What are you working on?'

'Next round of edits,' huffs Byron, with strained resignation. He always makes such a meal of writing books, as if it were a forty-year stretch in the gulags. Viv doesn't know why he bothers. Laurie claimed he knew Byron's editor; apparently most of the artistry happened when Byron was out of the room. 'It's getting to a really exciting stage. I'll be sharing it with you soon.'

'Can't wait to read it, By.' She read his first one, and the weird self-help books – spare copies of which are still in a box in her attic – but she hasn't bothered with the others. There's just no time. She buys copies for everyone she knows and applauds at his launches, the important stuff. 'Isn't this nice? Lovely to do something just the two of us.' Byron slips her the side-eye. She covers her hand with her mouth. 'I don't mean that as in, at long last or ... you know. Obviously just the three of us would be better, but ...'

Byron isn't listening. He's scrutinising the menu, even though he always has the same thing. They all used to. Except, today, Viv is going to be different.

Byron closes his menu. 'You'd think they'd take away the chair.'

She hadn't noticed. The empty chair. Laurie's chair. In the last few years, he preferred to sit with his back to the room, less chance of catching the wrong eye and being forced to talk shop. Byron and Viv developed rudimentary sign language to warn him of any approaching invaders. 'Shall I ask them?'

'No, it'll make us look weird.'

'We should have invited someone else along.'

Byron snorts. Nobody else likes it here. Rosy refuses to be in the same room as anyone eating snails.

'I'm going to have Laurie's usual. Thought it would be a nice tribute. Are you having the halibut, as per?' The 'as per' circles Byron a few times before landing. He rolls his eyes. 'Remember Laurie's whole skit about your halibut being your soulmate or something?'

'Of course I do. He never shut up about it.'

But when Eugène takes Viv's order, he shakes his head sadly. 'Alas, madame Vivienne, the sweetbreads is off the menu.'

'*Are* off the menu,' mutters Byron from behind the cocktail list, clearly looking only for effect, as he always orders a sidecar.

'Do you not ... It's just that it was Laurie's favourite.'

'Pardon, madame, we have not served the sweetbreads for some time.'

'He died,' she says, in her smallest voice.

'You don't have to pretend to like that shit just because he did, Grainger. Just get your risotto like always.'

'I thought it might be a nice touch, that's all.' She orders the risotto.

Byron spends most of the main course prattling on about the next book, and the strongly worded emails he's been sending to his publisher over trifling matters. Viv can't take any of it in. She keeps expecting Laurie to interrupt any minute with a contradiction – he was good at those – or a better anecdote, of which he had millions.

'Have you found anything else then, By? Since Jo let you go?'

'Let me go? There was no job left to let me go from, Laurie died.'

Viv takes that as a no. 'I can ask around if you like. Sometimes I need an extra pair of hands on a shoot if my regular can't make it. I've loads of stuff coming up, I'm really getting back into my—'

'First Laurie offering me his crumbs, now you stepping in. Appreciate the thought, Grainger, but I've got some feelers out.'

'Oh.' They chew a while, in silence, until Viv thinks she must speak before she screams. 'Is it true Laurie was writing a biography?'

'An autobiography, you mean? He was always hammering away at something. Why?'

'Just wondered.'

'You worried he might have revealed your secrets? Or worse, not mentioned you at all?'

Byron is really delighting in that extra space on the podium, but she won't rise to it. 'I'm not worried about anything. Ned Lanford was asking.'

'Ugh, to hell with that human embodiment of a stain on the carpet.'

They laugh together for the first time in over a year, halted by Eugène topping up their water glasses unnecessarily. Viv hasn't touched hers.

'You must miss him almost as much as I do.'

Byron sighs and lays down his fork. 'Things certainly aren't the same. My potatoes are cold.' He makes a great fuss of fluffing out his napkin. Everything Byron does feels like stage directions. 'Don't you wish you'd met someone? Settled down?' He looks at her with those deep cow eyes.

For an awful moment, Viv wonders if Byron might be about to propose, and, worse, whether she would actually say yes. She holds his gaze until he looks away and busies himself with his cold potatoes. 'I've never been short of boyfriends.'

'We all know that.' Viv can practically see his tongue fork as he says it. 'But you know, your person, a soulmate, your halibut if you like. The One.'

'Laurie always said there was no such thing as The One.'

'Well, he would, wouldn't he? He already had Jo, he found his. More or less.'

'What do you mean?' Her natural urge to defend Laurie even when he isn't being attacked resurfaces. 'Do you wish you'd . . . I don't know. Was there someone?'

He doesn't answer. When it comes to romantic affairs, Byron keeps his cards close to his chest, probably because he's got such a lousy hand. There's never been any introductions, just the odd time he's been 'unavailable' for dinner, weekends away he won't talk about. Occasionally, she and Laurie wondered if Byron might be gay and repressed – Laurie was convinced there'd been a 'try before you buy' stage – but then Viv watched him chat up a variety of actresses at Laurie's memorial with a confidence that made her uneasy. She remembers now, more clearly than she'd like, a very pretty actress, Eva something, chatting to Byron and, the whole time, keeping the top of her champagne flute covered with her hand. Viv has never heard anything seedy about Byron, but she never talks to actresses at events; she finds them vapid, synthetic, always looking over your shoulder for casting directors.

Viv looks to the empty chair, as if willing it to say something. The punchlines, she misses them. Where is she supposed to go for them now? Viv excuses herself and sits very still in a cubicle in the restaurant bathroom. She can feel the earth spinning. *The One*. What nonsense. She never had time for anyone else, nothing serious anyway. She supposes she should be grateful she's still got Byron. You don't make friends at her age. Circles won't open up for you, schedules don't align. She's never liked cliques. Hated them, in fact. Such a narrow way of living, gossiping and taking delight in excluding outsiders. Then she found her own. Imperfect as it was, unequal and unreliable, she found her space in a tight circle. Now Laurie is a footnote in her memories, and Byron's too wrapped up in his own spirals of doubt. The pair of them are lyrics stripped of their melody. Just words on a sheet of paper, unsung.

When she returns from the ladies', Byron is sipping an espresso and has asked for the bill.

Death Knock

Laurie

There's something about watching a velvet curtain engulf a coffin rolling into the abyss to the tune of 'Fly Me to the Moon' that makes you want to get your life on track. The good person complex rearing its head again. You want to make sure, maybe, that when mourners watch your oak overcoat glide away, or wobble into the ground, they'll truly miss you, and have only beautiful things to say about you at the do afterwards, which will be held somewhere you've never particularly liked, with catering you'd never have eaten.

Jo urged me to go for a walk or take an hour to myself, but I played limpet, without a hint of resentment. It was only after tearful goodbyes garbled through an open car window and assurances to crepe-skinned aunties that no, we wouldn't wait for another funeral before visiting again, that I realised I hadn't heard from Teddy, save for one missed call the night after we arrived in Derbyshire. True, I hadn't tried contacting him either, but it would've felt indecent. Infidelity on the same timeline as a funeral feels like a hanging offence. Still, it seemed odd, not even an angry text to lambast me for standing him up.

Ned Lanford had the answer. Back home, he came round one afternoon, to the house, something he never normally did. I'm not a huge fan of making house calls unless you really must. I don't particularly like being invited to friends' for dinner, hanging out together like students or the cast of *This Life* – a reference Teddy did not get – pretending to like their cooking, or their decor, or their children. Restaurants exist for a reason. Anyway, Ned had his serious face on so I poured us a drink and prepared to hear that he was terminally ill or had lost all his money in a phishing scam. I wasn't sure which would bother me most. I was still regularly taping conversations, but it was difficult to reach for the recorder under Ned's watchful eye.

He wanted to talk about my 'young friend Teddy'. For a terrible moment I thought Ned was here to tell me Teddy was dead. I could tell Ned was enjoying the suspense but finally he came out with it. He'd run into Teddy, trying to get into my club, looking for me. 'Making a scene, if I'm honest.'

My blood ran cold. I imagined Teddy shouting my name, insisting I wouldn't mind being disturbed, that he always dined with me there, to the blank faces of the drones on reception. I kept everything behind my mask. Ned went on. 'I took him home. To my home. Calmed him down a bit.'

There it was, that shiver down my spine. I broke. 'Back to yours?'

'Yes. He stayed over.' He looked pleased, so prim and regal, like butter wouldn't sizzle and blacken within ten feet of his tongue.

The bastard. The bastard. The bastard. Even now, I want to

fly into the most ridiculous rage, smash things, choke to death the first fucker I see. Years on, holding it in for those next few minutes will haunt me for ever.

'Ned, Teddy is very young. And vulnerable.'

A sneer escaped from the corner of Ned's mouth before he reined himself in. I knew what he was thinking, that I was a hypocritical, lying piece of shit.

'He seems to have something of a crush on you. I think he was worried that you'd be mad, when you heard about us.'

Us?! They were an 'us'?! I felt queasy.

'I know you two were only friends, of course, you told me that yourself, but I, eh, got the feeling you were very close.'

I wanted to rocket to my feet, unleash my fury, but I couldn't let Ned see he'd got to me. I folded my hands in my lap and cradled my now empty glass, which I was desperate to fill right to the top.

'So you've had sex, Ned. Congratulations. Why are you telling me this?'

'As a courtesy, being a gentleman.'

Honour among cunts. How touching. 'How did it happen?'

He was hoping I'd ask. He smoothed out his trousers as if laying a napkin across his thighs.

'You know, he reminds me a little of your Jo. Not now, of course, but when he was younger. So full of energy and ideas and ... what would you call it? Spunk, I suppose. I'm quite bewitched.'

'Teddy isn't my property, Ned. We're friends. He can have a one-night stand with whoever he likes.'

That's when he laughed. Not his usual forced bellow saved for the auditoriums of struggling comedies, but his proper vicious, self-satisfied laugh only ever deployed at someone else's expense. My turn.

'Not one night. I don't want you to feel hurt, but Teddy has been my overnight guest on numerous occasions recently. I've been assisting him with his Valenti application. Helping him get a decent showreel together. All very innocent. At first. Business. Much like you. But I'm only human. One thing led to another and ...'

My stomach dropped. He had to be lying. He couldn't have done it more than once. No way. Ned leaned over with his phone, showed me images, video, the odd selfie of the two of them. Teddy smiling, but with medicated features. Sunken eyes behind greasy cheeks and jowls loosened from over-chewing and anxiety babbling. The pupils slightly too large and the smile too wide and slack. The joy could be interpreted as sincere, at a push, but the expression was filtered through pharmaceuticals. It could pass for happiness if you didn't know him, and even in such a state he seemed unblemished and perfect next to Ned's pillowy face. I've never seen anyone look so different in every photograph taken of them as Ned, and ugly as fucking sin in every single one. The thought of this rat, this beast, this turd in an Oxford shirt, defiling Teddy's wholesome mind and beautiful body. This was some showreel all right. I wanted to die, right there.

'Was he drunk?' Then, a terrible thought. 'Did you put something in his drink?'

'Are you kidding?'

The thing I admired about Ned was he never fluffed his lines. It was excellent for important meetings to have an unflappable, imperious smooth-talker next to you. It hadn't come without a price: thousands of pounds on school fees and many a night spent crying in a freezing cold dorm because his parents didn't love him enough. On a personal level, there was something disgusting about it.

'Laurie, I'm the richest person you know. I don't need to lace anyone's drink with hypnotic powder to get my end away.'

How did he manage to make me feel guilty for asking what seemed like an obvious question? Ned laughed. 'Listen to us, like the *Sex and the City* gals debriefing each other on our sexual exploits. Except of course there's no overlap here. You and Teddy are just friends.'

Those cold, dead eyes. If eyes were the windows to the soul, Ned's curtains had been closed for a long time.

'Speaking of which, can I get another drink, Laurie? You're being a monstrous host. Worried I'll tranquillise you?'

I took the chance to slip my hand into my drawer and hit the red button on my recorder. 'As a friend, I'm concerned about Teddy.'

'Oh, Laurie. Let's not do this, shall we?' A knowing smile crept onto Ned's lips. 'I know about you two, it's blindingly obvious to anyone with a central nervous system. If it makes you feel better to believe Teddy was an unwilling participant, go ahead. I assure you, we've been together drunk and sober, many times now, stretching back further than your little northern sabbatical. I even went to his charming little ... what would you call it? A room? A garret? I've no idea.'

I heard myself say, 'Studio.'

'A bleak little cell, but still barely manageable on a waiter's wages,' said Ned in that cool, flat way he spoke in meetings when he knew he was winning. 'Not a very tidy young man. Unmade bed. Ketchup bottle on the occasional table. Common.'

I began to rise out of my chair.

'Sit down, Laurie, unless you want to be in *Popbitch* this Thursday. You've had your fun, I don't judge. But you have a husband, and not just any husband. Jo. Handsome. Clever. Pure. Not like the other flakes and wannabes everyone else we know is married to. You loved him so much you named our scholarship after him.'

I lowered myself back into my seat. I was suddenly aware of my clothes on my skin, the tightness of my collar, the elasticated band of my sock cutting into the flesh of my ankle, my belt holding in my miserable, worthless and now sunken gut.

'I've often wondered how things might've turned out if I'd made it across the room to Jo a little faster.' Ned's voice was low and musical. A lullaby, or an incantation. I tried to focus on his face. My lips started to tingle and beads of sweat began to gather on my forehead. 'I bore you no ill will. But this is pure greed, Laurie. The kindest, most sensible thing to do would be to put an end to it before Jo finds out. Why can't I have a little paradise like you?'

'Jo isn't going to ... there's nothing to find out.'

'What if I invited Jo to dinner? At your club? Do you think he'd come? He might. Imagine if we happened upon you and your ... friend.'

I slowly formed the words, trying to talk through the onset of a panic attack. 'Why would you do this? I swear, we're just friends.'

Ned threw his head back now. 'I hope you didn't send any dirty little pictures. Last thing you want is photos of your cock and hole all over Teddy's phone. He's not very responsive, is he? Can't even get a cheeky sext out of him. Shame.'

I hadn't sent Teddy anything, but in a moment of madness, I'd shut myself in the ensuite (most flattering lighting in the house) and contorted my way through a dangly nude photoshoot. Ned couldn't have seen them, could he? They were deep in my own phone.

'I'm doing you a favour, Laurie. You're getting careless, and your writing isn't what it was. You're distracted. You got in first with Jo and I accepted it with good grace. Maybe Teddy and I have a chance, but not with you hovering like a bluebottle.'

'Is this to get back at me? For Jo?'

That laugh again. 'You flatter yourself! I find Teddy utterly charming. You should've seen him the first time I took him away for the night.' He registered my look of horror and it charged his battery even further. 'Oh yes. Fingering the cookies and sugar sachets on the tea tray, asking if it was all free. Blasting his atrocious music on the wireless speakers. He couldn't believe there was room in the shower for at least four people.' He paused dramatically, delighting in the flip of my stomach as I imagined how far into depravity Ned had taken Teddy. 'Got so excited by finding an iron in a cupboard, as if he'd discovered a lost fragment of the Turin Shroud. I even pretended not to notice when he tipped the soaps and the gins from the mini bar into his little backpack.' He smiled at the flicker of recognition on my face; Teddy had done exactly the same when we went to Brighton together. 'Imagine never having stayed in a hotel until your twenties!'

I knew when I was beaten. I wouldn't let him see me cry. Not that day, not ever. 'I'll never work with you again.'

Ned patted my arm. 'We both know that isn't true. You've led a charmed life, Laurie. I've been happy to help make it happen. We work well together. This is for your own good. End your . . . friendship with Teddy. Definitively, no going back. No promise of reconciliation. Harsh as you can. I'll look after him.'

I remember watching Ned leave, biting into my lip and thinking, that fucker, that miserable, spiteful fucker, I hope he's found dead on the toilet.

I bolted my office door and drank a bottle of vodka to myself that evening, listening back to my showdown with Ned. He sounded even more in charge on tape than he had saying it to my face. I had lost. I heard Jo come in, late, after a night out with his two zip-mouthed besties, no doubt. I held back until I was sure he'd be asleep before heaving myself up the stairs. But he was waiting, watched me wobble into the bedroom, nodded towards the glass of water I knew would be there.

He'd been thinking, he said, and there was something in his voice that startled me into instant clarity. So it's happening, I thought, his gran's dead, he's reassessing his priorities, it's curtains for me. I couldn't begrudge him, really. But that wasn't it. Not at all.

'I want to get married.'

'Huh? Who to?'

'To whom, so-called writer. To you, of course.'

'We are married,' I slurred.

'I want to upgrade. Now we can do that. From civil thingy to full marriage.'

Full marriage, as if the last decade had been a half-measure. Fairly astute of him, really.

'I want it to feel real, Laurie.' He looked so serious. It felt ridiculous. Him sitting, sober and angelic in his David Rose pyjamas, me pathetic and drunk with my jumper halfway over my head.

I found myself saying I wanted it too. Of course I did. Who wouldn't want to be married to Jo? If I didn't, someone else would, likely with half my money to send them on their way.

'I want to spend more time together,' he said, brushing away loose cotton from his thigh with irritation. 'We're like flatmates sometimes. Ships that pass in the night. Don't you want that too?'

I swear it was on the tip of my tongue to reveal everything. I even felt a pre-emptive wave of relief, like the first rumble of

a storm after a month of sweltering heat or the smell of chips
before you spot the glowing shopfront. Then he started crying.
His classic deflection.

My phone buzzed. Teddy. I wanted to cry out, call him immediately, say I was in a car coming over. But I had to seal the
deal with Jo, soon to become my double husband. My insurance
policy, my rock, the authenticity certificate that proves I am
good, can do good. I turned the phone over.

'I want whatever you want, Jo. I want you.'

Boom!

Laurie

Teddy told it differently, but not differently enough. I buzzed and buzzed until a neighbour let me in the street entrance, and was about to shoulder-barge the studio door when Teddy opened it, looking younger and smaller than ever, in a T-shirt two sizes too big and in need of a wash. Sadness cloaked him; his eyes darted round me but didn't find my face.

I walked into that tiny studio knowing it would be the last time. That tatty furniture, the greasy, tantalising waft of fried chicken, and the shouts, laughs and complaints from people on the street below. Teddy sat on the bed, cross-legged, tapping his front teeth. The noise went right through me.

'Tell me about Ned,' I said.

'What did he say to you?' I'll never forget his look of horror and shame. Did I look like that when I went home to Jo? That dreamy, damaged expression. Eyes doing all the talking, mouth paralysed. Ned was kind, at first, he said, when they spoke for the first time, not long after I'd first met him.

'Never mind what he said. I want to hear it from you.'

Teddy nodded slowly, as if summoning up the strength. 'We talked about acting. He took notes and said he'd write up an application for me. He put me in a cab home. We met for lunch the next day.'

'Where?'

'What?'

I had to know how big an impression Ned had tried to make, how much persuasion Teddy had taken. I'd seen Teddy go into fucking raptures on finding a mini can of Heineken in a hotel room fridge; Ned's usual lunching spots would've blown his mind.

'Mr Lanford said I could choose. We went to Wagamama.' I almost laughed, imagining Ned prodding at sloppy yaki soba with splintery chopsticks. 'He showed me the application. It made me sound great. He told me to let it breathe a day or two, then send it. He said he'd be in touch.' So far, so innocent. Then, Teddy realised he'd lost his phone. 'Thought I'd left it in the cab. Or it had fallen out of my pocket. Someone had left a message at my work. Ned. Said he must've picked it up by accident.' Bile rushed to my throat – Ned and Teddy's phones were nothing alike. 'I went to meet him, at one of his restaurants.'

Home turf. Ned would've pulled out all the stops. As beautiful as it was hearing this love story unfold, I wanted to commit a murder. I didn't need to hear any more. I had a strong compulsion to be very nasty indeed. Naturally, I picked the easier target.

'So out of gratitude for finding your phone, you fucked him? A thank you would probably have done. Or a box of Roses. Do people still do that?'

Teddy's entire face changed. He shuffled as far up the bed as he could go without melting into the wall. 'It wasn't like that. Honestly. I didn't look at him that way. I knew he . . . I guessed there might be more to it. He'd been so kind, I was confused. I thought of you, and what you said about him.'

'Never mind what I said. Tell me.'

'I don't know how it happened. I must've been drunk. I hadn't eaten much, I suppose. I had a margarita before I left work, only had one drink at dinner, I swear. It went straight to my head. Next thing I know, I . . . I can remember bits. I woke up in a bed, his bed, no clothes on, he was next to me, saying he'd had a terrific time, that we didn't have to tell anyone, it could be our thing.'

I prayed for a superpower to help me take away Teddy's confusion and self-hatred and tell him everything would be all right. But that wasn't why I was here.

'Teddy, I'm getting married.'

His face pixellated into crisis. I wanted to go to him, touch him, run my fingers through those curls and pull his head to mine, our necks locking into place together. I couldn't. I'd rehearsed what to say in the car, and decided not to deviate, hesitate or answer questions, no matter what happened. Ned had a point. I belonged with Jo. I knew it when we held hands during his grandmother's funeral. I knew it when I looked into his eyes when he said he wanted us to be married. I'd known it all along. You can't recreate that sense of belonging, that duty, the need to be a good person. Teddy was a beautiful facsimile on the surface, but that's all he was. However much I cared for him, no matter how my feelings for Jo fluctuated, whether I was in love with him or not – at that point, no idea, honestly – I couldn't, in all conscience, be a good person if I continued encouraging Teddy's fruitless dependency.

'I'm getting married and that means I can't see you any more. Wouldn't be right.'

Teddy was crying now. 'I only ... it was only because I felt I should. I didn't know how to get out of his house. I wasn't sure what might happen.'

If I'm honest with myself now, I didn't want to delve too deeply into what this actually meant. There was something ugly, cataclysmic and irrevocable staring me in the face and I could only look away. A coward, certainly. A disgrace. I have punished myself for this on many a long night. I spied the bottle of ketchup still there on the coffee table.

'It's none of my business. I have Jo, and now you have Ned.'

He was aghast. 'I don't have him. It won't happen again. You have to believe me.'

'It doesn't matter if it happens again.' I hadn't even taken off my coat. 'I'm leaving now. I'm not coming back.'

'But Laurie! Please! I won't see Mr Lanford again. I'll apply again, normally, like everyone else, like you said I could.'

A switch flicked inside me. Ned wouldn't put this kid on the Valenti, not now he'd got what he wanted. Not a chance. 'That's not happening. Forget the scholarship.'

The fear in his eyes, the iced-over disbelief of a loser. 'What am I gonna do?'

I looked him right in the eye, saw deep into him, the fear and confusion. I felt heartless but perhaps that's exactly how I needed to feel. This was my punishment. 'I've a feeling you'll be just fine.'

I must've been in there ten minutes. Ten minutes to terminate one of the strangest, happiest times of my life, not even making it to a second summer. Like spending hours preparing a huge roast dinner, that's quickly demolished once served up. No sense of occasion, nothing to show for your valiant effort but slop and scrapings. I glanced up at the window as I hailed a cab, knowing his ghostly face would appear.

I listen back to that conversation sometimes, Teddy's voice small and defeated. Can't believe those words coming out of my mouth. I'm no stranger to being cruel, but there's always a punchline, or swirls of affection somewhere within. This was cold. I listen to remind myself I was capable of the most awful things even back then. How might his life have been different if I'd fought for him a little harder? Where might mine be now?

When I got home, Jo greeted me with a scowl. The dog had been sick and he'd spent an hour cleaning it up. I poured us some wine and we sat on the sofa while I stroked Jo's head and told him I was sorry he'd had a bad day. I felt like Princess Leia having to listen to Luke Skywalker drone on about Ben Kenobi, ten minutes after she's been forced to watch her home planet of Alderaan explode into dust.

Fifteen

April

Jo

Jo likes it when Theo cooks, watching his hands as they chop, the way his tongue pokes out of the corner of his mouth as he 'guesstimates' how much chilli a sauce needs, how he jumps back when the pan spits, looking to check if Jo saw it too. He seems adventurous, carefree, in contrast to how he acts in restaurants, removing lettuce from his burger, or picking out flecks of mushroom from his pizza. Never critiquing with words, but unable to achieve a poker face if his pasta is overcooked. Jo tells him he'd make a good chef.

'I've worked in kitchens. Too many rules. Strict portion sizes. No chance to experiment. Cooking is my therapy.'

Jo wants to ask about actual therapy, the group counselling sessions. He's even toyed with the idea of turning up to one, to see his reaction, but stopped himself. That would be a gross breach of trust, against both Theo and Kris. If he wants to know what's going on inside Theo's head, he'll have to get him to open up.

'I kind of stopped cooking after Laurie died,' Jo says.

'No point cooking for one, right? I'm the same.'

'No, not that. Laurie hardly ate at home anyway.'

So many people brought food after Laurie died, warned Jo he needed to keep his strength up. Stacks of lasagnes and curries in the freezer. Viv, too, always round with a bag of ingredients she'd turn into something magical, watching him eat, telling him, 'I'm not having any, I ate at home.' Jo's grown to associate food with misplaced sympathy, eating now a function, not a pleasure, so he's graduated to warm-ups of beige food in foil trays, or pretentious Marks & Spencer meals that lose all their dignity and grandeur after three minutes on 900 watts and a forlorn beep.

After dinner, Theo goes to the hallway to retrieve something from his bag and returns with a Tupperware container. Inside, what look like slightly dry brownies.

'You bake?'

'I get baked.' Theo's grin is mischievous and infectious. 'They're space cakes. Wanna get lost for a couple of hours? Adventure time.'

Adventure. Jo's not a huge fan. It's for people who turn up late, miss trains, wing it. Jo has never winged anything in his life, except perhaps this relationship. They eat one each. Theo wants to go to the cinema, stoned, but there's nothing on at the Ritzy that Jo feels able to handle. He stands in Windrush Square, observing human traffic spilling from fast-food outlets, lighting up cigarettes and hugging each other. He'd have done this when he was twenty, with his flatmates. He's suddenly hyper-aware of his age. They jump in a cab, and London rushes by in a blur of buses, trees, other people's lives. In a bar in Soho, Theo rubs up against Jo and puts his fingers in his mouth and it's both horny and disgusting. Jo can taste salt and the brownie on Theo's fingers and he has a sudden vision of Theo as a care nurse, feeding him pudding. He stumbles to the toilet and expects to see an ancient man in the mirror but instead finds only himself, slightly paler than usual, eyes a little wider. Somehow this is more disappointing. He tries to throw up but nothing comes.

'What am I doing here?' he asks his reflection, which can only stare back, helpless.

Standing at the bar, a man approaches, wearing a lecherous smile. He's about Jo's age, buff and Botoxed. Laurie would've said something derogatory and Jo would've shushed him, were he here. But he's not.

'Hello, boys.' Despite the plural, his eyes are trained on Theo. 'In every relationship, as the great Teena Marie said, there's one who loves to love, and one who loves to dance. Which one's which?' He drags his fingers down Theo's chest. 'I bet you love to dance.' He turns to Jo. 'You agree, Daddy? You the boy who loves to love?'

Daddy. Jo's always hated that internet vernacular, cribbed from bad porn. Laurie used to find it hilarious.

'It was Tina Charles,' barks Jo. 'I'm the one who loves to be left the fuck alone.' Surprised by his ability to channel his dead husband's venom, he elbows past the guy and pulls Theo out into the street.

'I think he was trying to be friendly. Are you not having fun?' Theo looks worried. 'You don't seem yourself.'

The weather is warming up, so it's busy. People shove into them as they pass, tell them to move, tut at having to step off the pavement and onto the road. It was exciting to be among it back in Brixton, but here, now, it feels oppressive.

'I'm not myself.' He hasn't been this version of himself for a long time. Twenty years. More. He doesn't want to complain, but he doesn't want to stay either. 'I wanna go home.'

Later, in bed, Theo apologises, and asks Jo about his weekend plans. 'Let's do something that's fun for you. Whatever makes you happy. I mean it.'

Jo longs for a normal activity, not something that feels like a day out for underprivileged teenagers.

'Cook for me,' says Jo.

'Is that it? Easy!'

'But . . . let me invite some friends. Show you off. Make it real. Does that make sense?'

Theo is silent for a while. Jo watches his stomach rise and fall as he breathes. Thinking. 'Who?'

They've never got this far before. 'Rosy and Viv. Maybe Holden and . . . or Sian if they can get a sitter. Haven't seen them in a while.'

'That it?'

'I think so. How about someone you know too. Kris?'

'Uh . . . no, let's keep to your circle. If it makes you happy, I'll do it.'

'Uncle Jojo . . . he's so handsome!' whispers Rosy as she helps Jo make lethal bellinis.

'Oh, is he? I hadn't noticed.' He feels giddy and happy, flushed, not just from booze. 'Do you think it's going okay?'

Rosy nods, but he knows already. It started shaky, with Viv more subdued than usual as she stepped over the threshold, but she gave Theo a warm hug, and sounded genuine when she said it was lovely to meet him. She's warming up fast now; Jo wonders whether the goodwill can last until the end of the evening. Theo was trembling with nerves doing his prep; if cooking really was therapeutic, tonight would set him back a few sessions.

'Do you seriously not have a griddle pan?'

'I've never griddled anything in my life.'

'Not even in the café?' It was interesting to see this new, slightly impatient side to Theo, but Jo wished it wasn't over a pan.

'No! We've got a panini machine. It's not a barbecue.'

Holden has come solo and for once is managing to keep his clever asides to himself. It helps that Viv has never been interested in anything Holden has to say. There are many risks introducing your best friend to your partner's best friend: they might prefer each other to either of you; they may share your secrets behind your back; they may hate each other and begin to question your taste in friends; or, as in this case, they might be largely indifferent yet slightly in competition with each other.

'Theo, let me know if you need a hand,' Viv said within seconds of Holden's arrival. 'I know where everything is.'

Theo takes his interrogation well.

'I don't know why Jo's hiding you away,' says Viv a few wines in. 'We're not monsters! We don't bite ... not without taking the money upfront, anyway.'

Rosy nudges her mother for the sixth or seventh time that evening but Jo catches her eye and signals that it's fine. Let Viv be Viv.

'Dinner was delicious! Loved those skewers. The chicken was so tender. And that, what was it, the sauce they were on?'

'Smoked sweetcorn guac.' Theo's face ripples with shyness. It suits him.

'Guac,' repeats Viv. 'Yes. Lovely. I know you're studying creative writing but, well, nobody makes any money from that, do they, Holden? You still plugging away?' Holden's mouth opens but no sound comes out. 'You should be a chef!'

'That's what I said,' says Jo, trying to read Theo's expression.

'Would you fancy that, Theo?' says Viv. 'Maybe you could open your own place.'

'I'd like that. Be my own boss.'

Jo is so surprised by this about-turn that his drink goes down the wrong hole. Theo has a lot of things he'd like to do, Jo's noticed, all things he'd probably be good at. He's heard him singing in the shower, trilling mini operettas and belting huge ballads, and he is a beautiful writer. For a man of many talents, it seems a shame he's never made much of them. Then again, as Laurie always said, people who haven't quite made it are what keeps pubs, restaurants and front-of-house at theatres running.

'You've plenty of time,' says Viv, holding out her glass for her daughter to fill. 'A toy boy, Jo! Laurie would laugh his head off.'

The atmosphere shifts ever so slightly. 'He's not exactly Leonardo DiCaprio, Mum,' quips Rosy, clearly calculating when to order the cab to make sure it arrives before her mum descends into tear-streaked nostalgia. It may already be too late.

'No, let me be serious a minute. Shush, Holden.' Holden looks round the table in protest; he hasn't said a word. Viv continues: 'It's been very hard since Laurie left us in such a ... a stupid, stupid way. He was such a bad driver.'

'Mum ...'

'Wait! I know he'd be so glad to see us together, enjoying this lovely dinner cooked by Leo ...'

'Theo.'

'Yep. He'd be so happy we're still in touch, and that ... well, maybe not with you Holden, he wasn't that keen, but I know you know that and I'm sure he was fond of you in his own specific way, but now Jo's found someone new and I hope Laurie is looking down—'

'Mum!'

'Let me finish!'

The doorbell interrupts her. Ned Lanford skulks on the step, a bottle of champagne with a ribbon round it in his hand. Jo stands a while, not sure what's happening. It's 10 p.m. Ned isn't drunk but looks clammy and edgy, like he ran here.

'I don't mean to intrude. I bumped into Vivienne and she said you were having dinner so I thought I'd drop this off for you to celebrate with.'

'Celebrate?'

Jo has no choice but to show him in. Viv, not usually so enthused to see Ned, throws her arms round him with the fervour that only spying someone with a bottle of champagne can inspire. Holden nods curtly, Rosy gives a tiny wave with the tips of her fingers, and Theo doesn't move a muscle. Jo can read his mind. Ned wasn't on the approved guest list, he's broken a promise. Jo tries to catch his eye, to mouth that he didn't know he was coming, but Ned gets in his way as he reaches out his hand to Theo, who stands and shakes it.

'Well, hello there, mister.' Ned does a full body scan, logging Theo's every contour. Jo's flesh turns pimply.

'I'll clear these, you catch up,' says Theo. 'Go through to the lounge, away from me banging about.' He gathers an armful of crockery and heads to the back of the kitchen. Ned's gaze follows.

Ned doesn't stay long, and Theo comes through to the lounge only once, to drop off champagne glasses. When Ned leaves, the others decide to head off too.

At the doorstep, Ned clutches his hand. 'Terrific to see you happy again, lovely Jo.'

Viv hugs Jo with such violence, he almost tips over. 'Say buh-bye to the toy boy. Okay, I promise not to call him that again. Does that make you a cougar? Or is that women? Good old sexism, alive and well.' She takes Rosy's arm and totters a few steps down the path, before turning back. 'I want to say, I'm glad he's so different from Laurie. So ... unrefined. Wouldn't be right, would it, to replace him?'

Poor Viv, thinks Jo, not for the first time. Romances are relatively easy to find, best friends are harder to come by. 'It's early days, Viv.'

'I hope you're not replacing me either!' Rosy is hurrying her along now. 'We can go for lunch sometimes, you know. I'm almost as entertaining as my daughter.'

He heads back to the kitchen. Theo isn't there. Then he hears him, in the downstairs loo, coughing deeply. Jo knocks on the door, asks the usual questions. Theo emerges, now an expert in opening that awkward little door, sweat nudging at his hairline, eyes red and strained.

'Don't say you've given yourself food poisoning? I feel fine!'

'No, I'm okay. Just something went down the wrong way.'

Later, Theo makes camomile tea, sets the mug down on the table with great purpose. Jo looks up from his book.

'I need to tell you something. I don't know why I didn't before.'

Because you don't really tell me anything, thinks Jo. 'Go on.'

'I applied for that scheme. That one. Your husband's.'

Jo feels something shift inside him, like a roof of heavy snow responding to the first sign of thaw. 'The Valenti? When?'

'Years ago. I didn't get it, obviously. But I, uh, I think I met your friend, the one who came late. I met him before. Did he say?'

'Oh. No, he didn't. I didn't invite him by the way.' Jo wonders how embarrassing Theo's audition must've been to warrant
keeping this to himself so long. 'Why on earth didn't you say?'

'I should've. I'd forgotten about it. It was only when I saw
your friend . . .'

Pretty much every drama student or ambitious amateur applied for the Valenti these days. It had been a roaring success,
which meant more failures in its wake. Theo is one among
hundreds, yet Jo feels his world shrink just a little.

'Didn't you know who I was, that first time we met?' Jo
isn't keen on their origin story having a director's cut. 'How
far did you get? In the process, I mean. Was Laurie in your
interview?'

Theo lights a cigarette. 'No, I didn't get to that stage.'

Jo gets up to open a window, not because the smoke bothers
him – although it does – but in the hope that doing something
rather than speaking will get Theo to tell him more.

'I thought you might think I was a weirdo, for not mentioning
it. For long enough, I didn't clock who you were. Then, once I
did, well, the longer I left it . . . y'know how it is. It was a long
time ago.'

Theo's riddled with embarrassment; Jo decides not to dwell.
He doesn't want it to become a thing. Everybody holds back at
some point, don't they, if they prize what they have, when they
don't want to risk losing something good? Sure, it would be nice
to meet someone who had never heard of the Valenti scheme,
the nettle hiding in every flower he tried to pick, but Jo hates the
thought of Theo nursing a secret that, in the scheme of things,
doesn't matter, not at all.

'Oh, don't worry. I know what you mean. Every time I walk
into a bar I meet ten guys who tried out for the Valenti.'

He eases a smile into place and sees Theo's worry lines melt away. Jo shakes his head lightly, as if resetting, or dispersing the fog of his thoughts. The main thing is, the hard part is over. Theo's met everyone who counts, they like him, and the future is finally in motion.

World of
Bright Futures

Laurie

How lucky was I to have not one, but two so-called happiest days of my life? We called it our 're-up', because it made us sound young and vital after all these years together. My mother was going through a phase of watching emaciated Americans and bawdy Essex bikini waxers on reality TV shows, so kept telling everyone we were 'renewing our vows', which made Jo grind his teeth almost to dust. Interesting how much it amused me; I'd usually have sided with him. I didn't resent Jo, I still loved him fiercely – this is the confusing thing – but it was a struggle to see him as anything other than an obstacle to my happiness, a bungee rope pulling me back from exciting danger and into the routine and safety of his embrace. A chokehold, really. And Ned was right. We carried on working together, once he'd made me chuck out the play I'd just written and start again.

'Too nostalgic,' he said. 'Don't fall into that trap. The ageing gay writer combing over past glories, while the soundtrack to his youth booms away in the background? So tacky and obvious.'

'Nostalgia is big.'

Ned shook his head dismissively. 'Not as big as you are. Frankly, it has Teddy all over it. If you want to step back in time, Jo makes a more suitable muse, don't you think?'

I couldn't disagree, annoyingly. If Jo was the mould, Teddy was a wonky, misshapen pressing.

Ned mentioned Teddy only one other time, to tell me he'd 'scarpered from his little flat'.

'You said you'd look after him.'

'I did. I tried to cheer him up. Took him for dinner. Sent him shopping. It was actually very romantic. I realised ... oh, it did pain me, I promise, but it would never work. I called to see him one day and ... someone in a stained towelling robe told me he'd shipped out.'

Certain as I was that I'd made the right decision, I still searched for him. Selfish reasons, maybe, wanting closure, a chance to sleep at night without drinking three vodka and tonics. But Teddy wasn't in the restaurant. He'd quit his choir. No social media profiles. He'd vanished. I felt so helpless. As a project, as a balm for my soul, Teddy had been a failure. For the first time, instead of making dreams come true, I'd created a nightmare. Yet the juggernaut of my wedding continued.

Jo took full control and gave up any pretence of sophistication; he wanted to go super-sized. Country house hotel; coordinated, but not matching, suits; silver service dinner; table decorations designed by Vivi as our wedding gift, towering to the ceiling. It was formal, opulent, very much not us. Or not who we used to be.

'We were babies then, low-key made sense. Things have changed in the last seven years.'

They certainly had. I missed those babies. Jo got it as close to the anniversary of the civil partnership as he could – out by one day, 26th July – claiming it would help me remember, but I'd never forgotten. He acquired a short beard for the wedding, picking at it all morning while getting ready.

'I'm not sure any more,' he said, even though he looked front cover-ready. We good-naturedly jostled for space in the mirror.

'Ned once told me beards were only for people with something to hide,' I said with a smile. 'If that were true, that rancid bastard would have one longer than Father Christmas.' I felt a flash of happiness as Jo giggled in response and patted his face in satisfaction. Nothing to hide for my boy, oh no. An open book. Perhaps that's the trouble.

Oh, Jo. Being awestruck by him almost cancelled out my bitterness. There's never been any denying that he's beautiful. He always hushes compliments, and has been known to hurry out of a room if he senses someone going gooey over him, but sometimes I wonder whether this modesty is actually a way of showing off. He does everything so right; even his mistakes – like the beard, which was gone by New Year – are charming, and he learns from them. There is nothing I can teach him myself, however, nothing he can reveal that would shock me. Everything he does, he is good at, but he is smart, he keeps his world small. If you don't dare, if you don't get hypnotised by ambition, you can't fail. He's never shown any sign of playing catch-up, of being fascinated, or intimidated, by my supposed power. I saw then how raw, how green Teddy was in comparison. Already, his mistakes were calamities. How impressive and frightening my celebrity, my ability to make things happen, must've seemed to his innocent eye. Watching me in the theatre, wielding my tiny toffee-hammer of influence. His astonished face when I demanded a better room at the hotel – risky, really, but like I said, I became bold. Maybe I'd liked that a tad too much.

'You're very pink.' Jo began pawing at my face with some kind of cosmetic pad. 'You caught the sun yesterday.'

I didn't tell him how, that I'd tried to call Teddy, only to hear the soulless 'this number has not been recognised' bot, and in a fit of despair bought a bottle of petrol-station rosé and downed it in Regent's Park, before falling asleep for the sun to roast me alive. Not a good day to have sunburn. There were cameras glued to my face, I could never let my smile drop – quite challenging when your skin feels like the taut crust of a Cumberland pie.

Rosy looked beautiful in her bridesmaid dress; Vivi had her phone pointed at her the entire day.

'Is there a hashtag? For the wedding?'

I watched Rosy twirl dutifully. Behind the scenes, she had begged to be allowed to wear a jumpsuit but Vivi baulked at the idea. Considerable bribery had forced Rosy into that ball of titanium-grey silk.

'Hashtag? No, there fucking isn't. I don't want anyone filming the ceremony, or our first dance, or anything horrendous like that.'

'Everyone likes gay wedding videos, Uncle Lu,' said Rosy, perhaps disappointed her chances of going viral were disintegrating.

'I know, sweetheart, but this is our day, private for us. I want us to remember it. Proper memories, not out-of-focus video. We've got a cameraman anyway; he's got two Emmys.'

Vivi whistled. 'How'd you manage that?'

Unusually for me, this wasn't a favour I was calling in. 'Jo did. The guy goes into the café for a dark cherry mocha every morning.' The cameraman was very cute and very gay. I wondered how hard Jo had batted his lashes to get him here.

'Her favourite thing at the moment is reaction videos,' said

Vivi, losing interest in me and refocusing on her daughter through her phone. 'You could be in one. "Tearful pensioners react to cute gay couple dancing to . . . " What's your first-dance song?'

'"O Fortuna" from *Carmina* fucking *Burana*. Mind your own business. You'll find out soon enough. Why do people need to cry at strangers to feel something?'

'Idiot. It's the same as going to a play to "feel something". Except you don't have to pay the actors.' Vivi popped her phone in her bag. 'You're very shirty for an ecstatic groom. Slap on some aftersun.'

Jo wanted our mothers to walk us down the aisle, but his refused, probably because it involved close physical contact and she hadn't touched Jo since 1987. We walked hand in hand together. Jo was trembling; I could sense him stealing quick glances at me. I was frightened to peek back, in case my despair rose to the surface. We exchanged vows, and trotted back down the aisle to the whoops and cheers of our friends, frenemies, dependents and obligations. All through the speeches, I imagined growing old with Jo, and having soggy cornflakes gently and lovingly spooned into my mouth, exchanging gummy smiles that tore back the years and made us youngsters again. So long as he never finds out the truth about me, of course. Otherwise, there's every chance the task will be delegated to someone who never knew or loved me or, worse, still done by Jo but under duress – jamming the spoon in sideways, impatiently and roughly scooping up any dribbles and cramming them into my mouth.

I think about this a lot. Sometimes I imagine my Rosy as an old woman and it crushes me. Will there be anyone around who remembers this tour de force? People hardly look at photographs they don't appear in. Who'll know how magical, how wondrous she was? Rosy will keep my memory alive, but when that's gone?

When the people who remembered you forget, what happens to you?

My heart was heavy but my feet were light. I danced through heartache, just like in a bad pop song. Only left the floor for wine refills. Locomotions, Lambadas, Macarenas, the dreaded Gangnam Style, ABBA's back catalogue, and slow-dance smooches with Rosy tiptoeing on my Gucci loafers. Anything to avoid sitting down, having to think, or being trapped in a corner by Ned Lanford, who was coked up and becoming the kind of talkative nightmare that terrorised smoking areas of clubs, inflicting ceaseless braggadocio on people too wasted and polite to interrupt. When my body couldn't take any more, I grabbed a bottle of champagne from a fuckable waiter and found a quiet corner outside, away from the smoking and flirting on the terrace. I called Teddy's phone again and again, as if a miracle would happen.

Jo, a heat-seeking missile, located me in minutes, catching me mid-swig, dabbing at my tears with my tie. I had food down the front of my shirt. My zip was undone. I was the polar opposite of a catch. Jo looked immaculate, as ever, his shirt still brilliant white, tie poker straight. He pushed his glasses back over the bridge of his nose and leaned against the wall next to me.

'I don't know what's going on, but I want you to know it's fine, and I'm here.'

'Erm, bit emotional. Big day.'

Then he said it. 'I want you to stop drinking. You're out all hours, boozing with Vivi, and Ned, and Byron, and the actors and crew and God knows who else. I want you coming home to me sober. Do you think you can do that?'

Bit late for an ultimatum, the ring was already in situ. I looked at him in the soft, warm glow from the lights on the terrace and was struck again by how handsome he was, much more than Teddy even. Not that he'd take my word for it. Why did he stay with me? Didn't he believe me when I said he was beautiful? Would he one day choose to believe it from someone else, and leave me? Maybe he already knew he could do better, and stayed out of pity.

I found myself agreeing, hand on heart and everything, that my drinking days were done, I'd even go to meetings if that's what he wanted. I poured the champagne away, onto the pebbles. We both watched the foam catch the light as it gushed from the bottle, glints of excitement in the night, that we were both leaving behind, right here.

Sixteen

April

Vivienne

She hasn't been able to concentrate on anything since that dinner. The one with Jo's new man. Sometimes she says those three words to herself in the mirror, or while waiting for the parking meter to cough up a ticket. *Jo's new man, Jo's new man.* They sound impossible in her mouth. Ugly, ugly words.

Viv pushes the trolley round the supermarket. To any outsider she's browsing the soft cheese section – 'dairy for beginners', Laurie used to say – but the shelves are a blur. Her mind is replaying a movie. Jo's warm, gentle laugh as he spoons out the vegetables, the delicate touch of Theo's shoulder as he leans over to pour the wine. Scene after scene of what would, a year or two ago, have been science fiction, but was now reality, as if those weddings never happened. Yesterday she tried on her dress from the second one. It still fits.

The whole dinner, she could hear herself laughing and complimenting Theo on his cooking – pretty good, actually, not that this would be easier if he'd burned everything – and making jokes and sparring with Holden like the old days. But inside, one step removed from that reality, she could feel strong, insistent hands pressing down on her shoulders, pushing her into the earth, other hands moving her mouth for her, even raising her eyebrow at the right moment, as if she knew that one false move could banish her to the margin of Jo's life for ever.

Viv realises a security guard is taking a special interest. How long has she been standing there? She moves on a few paces, picks up some butter, examines it, pretends to read the nutritional information of what is essentially a tub of yellow lard – but she's not really there at all.

She never quite put a shape to how this version of the future might look. Jo 2.0. She's only ever known him in the context of Laurie, and assumed it was a case of Jo being handpicked and instantly smitten, rather than Laurie slotting into any existing criteria. In a way, she's disappointed she was wrong about Jo and Ned. She would understand that, a sympathy bunk-up or mad moment of morbid insanity. Jo vulnerable, Ned swooping in. Ned always has a look in his eye of someone who got the last cookie out of the jar seconds before your arrival, and Rosy said he's been sniffing around. But, no, this is a proper someone, from outside.

And Theo already looked so at home. 'Can you believe he doesn't have a griddle pan?' in that low, playful voice. Yes, she can believe it. She knows those kitchen cupboards better than her own mother's face. There was a familiarity about Theo she couldn't quite absorb at the time. It was like when you gaze at a newborn baby's serious, crumpled expression, staring in quiet concentration, and claim 'he's been here before'. Their chemistry didn't feel new. Theo had the air of an over-rehearsed understudy, whisked on stage for his big moment, while ushers hurriedly pinned up cast change notices in the foyer.

She should be grateful, she thinks, tossing the butter back on the shelf and wheeling the trolley back to its friends, unable to complete this mundane task today. Jo could've gone full Ned Lanford, taken up with some young, desperate tart, a gold-digger who'd sit around Laurie's house, wearing cheap fast-fashion, touching all those beautiful things. Or he could've bussed in a Laurie clone, some mid-forties creative with enough money and a ready-to-go crew that would tolerate her, but keep her on the fringes.

She sits in the car, motionless, for five minutes. She didn't account for this. She knows he is gone, of course, but maybe there was some distant hope buried within her that this was all a dream, or a temporary glitch, and that Laurie would suddenly appear, one morning, at lunch, as if nothing had happened. She'd dreamed of them growing old together, holidays in Italy, mooching round antiques fairs, convincing one another they still looked fabulous. It's been stolen, all of it. Now Jo's new man will move in, probably, start to put his own stamp on the place. Who'll let her wander around her personal museum of a friendship that is, now, nothing more than artefacts and anecdotes? They'll pack Laurie away, one memento at a time, until all traces are vanished. Move forward, move forward, Rosy is always telling her. She gets it, she does. But she thought they'd all be moving in the same direction; Jo's veering off course.

She smokes a cigarette with her eyes closed before wheeling slowly to the car park exit, grateful to feel the sunshine warm her face as she drives through the open barrier and out, to whatever the hell her life is now.

The Cruelty
of Daylight

Laurie

When you're older, every movement has a consequence. Reaching to plug in your phone – your back will remember. There's no escape. This is why hangovers worsen as you age. Like those nights you have only two drinks, maybe smoke a cigarette, and get to bed around eleven but the next morning feel like you went on a three-day crystal meth bender. Payback for the good times. Every debt gets called in. Now I was sober, there was no anaesthetic coursing through my veins. The physical side, bizarre aches and pains I'd never felt before, I could deal with; I rattled with paracetamol. But I struggled with the unwelcome emotions, the weird paradox of having it all – amazing husband, nice house, a job people would kill for, bums on seats – yet feeling like I'd lost everything.

Jo's body wasn't ageing, but his emotions were bubbling up too. I'm still not sure what started it all. Realising he was sick of my shit, perhaps. A supporting wall buckling at last. Most of the time he's a placid lake; we glide along the surface. Sometimes there's fire. Storms. I feel responsible. Like he learned it from me. We've become each other. I know there were rages when he was growing up, but his impatience became a deathless presence in any situation where we were alone. I found myself shuffling round the house. I started to become more forgetful, walking away from half-made cups of tea, losing phone chargers and scarves, hunting for things I was adamant I still owned. Jo would help me look, never complaining, but tetchily opening cupboards and drawers, and making great noise when peeking behind jars on the kitchen worktop.

'Are you sure you didn't throw it out?' became his mantra, hovering by the door because my scattiness was making us late for one of the activities he was insisting we do together, now more practical rather than cultural. I accompanied him on big supermarket shops for the first time in years, complaining I didn't really have the right clothes to trudge round cooked meats. He'd look at me with a mix of affection and pity.

'You're not Joan bloody Crawford. Just wear jeans and a jumper.'

Supermarkets. They'll survive any atomic blast. Cockroaches will roam their aisles of canned goods and cheap baby clothes long after humankind has been blowtorched off the planet. I trailed after Jo as he shlepped up the aisles, examining jars and packets and trays of pale meat with the same shatterproof concentration he reserved for reading the tiny labels on exhibits in the Tate Modern. A few people caught my eye. A slightly harassed-looking young woman with a baby in the trolley seat, banging away on the shiny steel with their rattle. A gay couple in graphic T-shirts, mouths tight and embarrassed as they bickered softly by the tenderstem broccoli. One little old lady with a warm smile but anxious eyes pulling one of those cumbersome tartan-print trolleys that I've banned my mother from ever getting. I can't have her lugging her ciabattas and sauv blanc home in one of those shonky carts; she takes taxis on my account.

Jo had a system, I noticed. Things had to go in the trolley a certain way. I was shooed away several times when trying to arrange heavy bottles or oddly shaped vegetables. This didn't surprise me; I'd long since known of Jo's habit of rearranging the bathroom shelf to his liking, and he was very particular about the number of times a doorbell should be pushed (twice). My only part in this production was to present my card for payment. He didn't want help packing, even; he didn't say it out loud, but he didn't trust me to do it right. I wasn't sure why he wanted to share this moment. Maybe he wanted to demonstrate what happened behind the scenes, while I was off having fun. Domesticity. Methodologies honed without me, but for my benefit, to keep cupboards and fridges stocked, so I never had to ask 'Do we have any ...?' He hefted the bags into the car unaided too, but he allowed me to roll the trolley back across the car park and chain it to its fellow inmates and retrieve the £1 coin. Jo would hold his hand out primly, and I'd drop it into his palm with a bow, which would make us both laugh out loud and briefly remember why we were in love.

When the internet was down at home I tottered along with Jo to his gym and sat on a glacial Wi-Fi connection in its godawful juice bar, overlooking the main fitness area. Seas of treadmills. LED screens. Dark-grey pulley systems and gigantic barbells (I had to look that word up). It was like the main loading bay of the Death Star. I spied Jo in one corner, pulling a lever so some blocks – weights, I assumed, but they could've been house bricks for all I cared – moved up and down. His arms changed shape as he pulled, rippling and convulsing into forms I'd seen only on statues. A few metres away, a younger man watched him. I was surprised to feel not just jealousy but mildly turned on. They all wanted Jo, didn't they? When done, Jo wiped himself daintily with a bright neon green rag – where on earth does he get this stuff? I never see it in the house – and strolled to the next machine, ignoring his spectator completely. So poised. After, Jo came with me to see that charming Stephanie Stein play about a working-class woman who wins a lifetime's supply of Fortnum's hampers and gets gout. There were plenty of seats free.

After the play, I stopped to smoke a cigarette while Jo dealt with some staff crisis. I watched a group of young friends stagger past the theatre drunk, limbs rubbery, voices loud and high with excitement. That used to be me, I thought, but now I was the guy lurking outside in the rain, smoking and watching the rest of the world have a good time. They didn't notice me. I was barely forty, but already invisible. I felt an instant jolt of fear I'd end up being that pasty old toad, staggering from one canapé tray to another, making young men wince in sympathy, dreading catching my eye. No. So I called a moratorium on anything deep fried and swore from then on my diet would include 'leaves' – the kind that come suspended in animation in a plastic bag from the chiller cabinet.

Jo, trying to keep me out of pubs and bars at the weekend, decided we should focus on the garden, a pastime I felt could wait at least another thirty years. There were trips to the garden centre, a place I hadn't been since my father was alive on his monthly jaunts to buy weedkiller and discounted bedding plants that barely survived the journey home. Jo and I rubbed shoulders with retirees and knackered parents with toddlers lured there under the pretence of meeting an epically unhappy man paid minimum wage to stand by the entrance and wave like a lunatic wearing a foam gnome suit. The stink of the place would cling to my nostrils, soil, foliage and chemicals mixed with the faint pong of dried-up carbonara and scones from the inevitable café, which Jo would insist on visiting once we'd finished pretending we gave anything near more than one fuck about herbaceous borders.

He'd pour the tea, naturally. I was allowed to butter my own scone.

'How do you feel?' he asked once, in that way he asks his customers if they've had a good day. 'Now you're not drinking.'

How was I supposed to feel? I suspected the correct answer was like I could run a marathon, or dream up a cure for cancer before lunch. I actually felt like a layer or two of my being had been stripped away. It was a blow to realise that while alcohol didn't necessarily mean having more fun, it had made me more fun to be around. It made me interesting. My jokes zinged harder. My work was, arguably, more incisive and vital when written with a mild hangover. Drunk, dance floors felt inviting, not frightening as they did now.

Alcohol takes so much away, I know. It ruins lives. But it enhanced mine. Every successive drink was a turn of the dial. It was, ironically, a sobering idea that so much of my personality came from a slick of poison in a heavy tumbler or a dainty glass. Jo never really asks questions out of curiosity, he's more interested in confirmation of the answers already in his head, so I replied that I felt 'different', ambiguous enough to placate him.

'I'm proud of you.' I was surprised to hear this. I knew he was proud of everything I achieved, he said so, but this time I hadn't done anything of note. I suppose it was more what I hadn't done. I couldn't take my eyes off how he buttered his scone. Right to the edges, with tiny scrapes and sweeps, like he was adding the finishing touches to a canvas. 'You've turned a corner. You should try getting back out there.'

'Back out there? Isn't that what people say after a divorce? Where am I getting back out to?'

His face never twitched, but my sarcasm annoyed him, his finger lightly tapping his side plate. 'Start going out again, do what you used to do.'

'I thought you wanted to spend more time together.'

'I did. I do. It was a suggestion. I don't want you to feel you're missing out.'

Then it dawned. Having me around wasn't working for him either. Vain of me to assume it was one-sided, I guess. I moaned too much about the quality of the scripts on movie night. I sulked about coming last in the local pub quiz (where I'd sit with a lime and soda, eroding my stomach lining, while everyone else cheerfully knocked back pints). I was useless in a garden centre, didn't know the plants' names or care when they flowered.

'I'm not a plant gay.'

Jo's tongue dabbed urgently at a sliver of butter in the corner of his mouth – the smell of butter under his nose long after he'd eaten something always made him gag – and, once cleared, he smiled and said, 'No, I know, and that's okay.' An acknowledgement, maybe, that the attempted transformation from paunchy souse into bright-eyed gardener had been too swift to be effective. 'I'm not either, really. How many peace lilies have we killed over the years?'

'Are you saying you want me to drink again?'

'No!' He winced at the sharpness of his reply. 'I mean ... I can't stop you.'

His experiment had been a failure, and he was expecting me to fall back into my old habits.

'I'll see if Vivi wants to go to dinner tonight. Do you want to come?'

He shook his head. 'No, you have fun.'

I hired a gardener the following week.

Factotum Ascending

Laurie

It felt like we were celebrating, but I didn't know what. There was something in Vivi's voice as she babbled away about starters and whether she could break her 'no bread on a weekday' rule. Excited, but edgy. Rosy was with us, which ruled out the news being a new man – any potential romantic lead was run past me way before Rosy got to hear about him. Byron was ebullient in an unnerving way. I assumed he'd pushed over an old lady or seen a house fire on his way to meet us. Unusually, Jo was there. It wasn't our anniversary, was it? Couldn't be, it was months off. Seven years, almost. Or fourteen, if you counted the first one. Seven years since I'd seen Teddy then. How hollow I'd become in that time, every emotion safely muted; I was an old TV on standby, nothing but a red light glowing in the dark.

Earlier that day, I'd heard the door slam and sloped upstairs, surprised to find a selection of shoes laid out next to the bed, and him in the spare room, steaming a nice shirt, instead of changing into his usual loungewear.

'You going somewhere?'

'Not going, coming. With you. Vivi called. Dinner. You were supposed to ask me to come. Did you forget?'

'I didn't. She's covering because she forgot.'

'What trousers with this shirt? Trainers or shoes?'

'You always look great in everything,' I replied, not meaning to sound bitter.

The restaurant was one I'd been eager to try. We were seated by a waiter just the right side of obsequious at a round table on one of those huge semicircular banquettes, which had the marked disadvantage that we'd all have a perfect view of each other. I prefer a long rectangular table: you can lean back, duck out of the conversation, escape the madness. Maybe Vivi was dangerously ill and announcing how long she had left. Dishes and glasses came and went and I knew Vivi wanted me to ask what was going on, or make a remark, but I couldn't be bothered. I knew they'd tell me when they were ready. I was sick of performing. Years of filling silences created by people duller than me had left me drained.

Vivi ordered a bottle of champagne. 'What would you like instead, Lulu?' Her face motherly and lightly patronising. 'A mocktail?'

Round table. All eyes on me. 'I'm fine with what I have.' I tapped the side of my bottle of booze-free beer, which tasted like floorboards.

Vivi nudged Byron. He gave a thin, sickly smile and immediately flushed deep magenta. The champagne arrived and there was a minute or two of delicious awkwardness. The pompous ceremony of laying out the champagne flutes; me deciding not to protest when one was placed before me; the clank of the ice bucket being set up on its stand; the waiter struggling a little with the cork and wincing as it popped loudly; the indelicate pouring of a smidge in Vivi's glass so she could taste; our eyes burning into the glass waiting for the foam to recede so she could try; her nod that it was fine; further indelicate pouring; my hand sliding over the top of my flute so he'd miss me out; another clank as the bottle went back into the bucket; the flourishes as the waiter draped a brilliant-white napkin around the bottle. I live for those little agonies beyond your control, when silence throttles you. It harks back to watching my mother serve dinner for five through the hatch between the kitchen and the dining room, and gritted teeth.

Finally, I caved. 'Well?'

Vivi nudged Byron again and he reached under the table, into a bag I hadn't noticed, removed a hardback and handed it to me. It looked kind of familiar; I'd seen it in a bookshop window, maybe.

'Is this for me?' I ran my hand over the embossed gold lettering of the title, *Summer of Love in the Countryside Disco*, over an illustration of a beautiful landscape with a bright, embossed neon sign in the distance, saying 'DISCO'. Below, the author's name, Mimsey Potts.

'I don't think you've ever bought me a book before, By. Bit early for my birthday.' I looked at Jo, who smiled back vacantly. This felt like an ambush.

Whatever Byron wanted to say was lodged in his throat, so Vivi stepped in. 'It came out last week. Byron wrote it. We're celebrating.'

Why on Earth was Byron trembling? The moron. I opened the book, flicked through the pages. 'You wrote another book? Had it published? Why didn't you say?'

Vivi and Byron's eyes met, wracked with conspirators' shame. Out of the corner of my eye, I saw Rosy down her champagne.

Vivi spoke. 'We wanted to see how it did first.'

I'd underestimated Vivi's ability to keep secrets. But Byron, who blurted out mundane trivia about himself without any encouragement whatsoever? No mention of the first draft, or sending it out on submission, or the deal itself? Not a sausage? Books took at least a year to edit and market before hitting the shelves. I closed the book, its pages slapping together harder than I'd intended. 'Who's Mimsey Potts then? Did you ghost-write this? Is that what you mean? Why the secrecy?'

'It was my grandma's name, Blount. I wrote it all.' Byron looked at Vivi for encouragement. They were ganging up on me; that wasn't usually how it worked. It was always me and Vivi teaming up to give Byron a pasting, or, occasionally, us boys dismissing Vivi's psychodramas. This was new.

'What do you mean, you wanted to see how it did?'

Rosy sighed deeply, beckoned to her mother to pass the bottle. 'They wanted to make sure it was a success, Uncle Lu, before showing you.'

They. Plural. A conspiracy. I felt like I'd walked in on someone trying on my clothes.

'It's just . . . ' Ugh, that thing Byron did, often, pausing before he was about to say something, to make sure you were listening. Made me want to plant his face in a cake. 'You're such a . . . you're very successful.'

'You're a lot to live up to, Lulu,' said Vivi from behind the safety of her champagne flute.

A gust of courage hit Byron's sails. 'Sometimes you're not very . . . understanding, Blount. When things go wrong. Failure, I mean.'

Finally, the elephant in the room coughed and asked for peanuts. I glanced at Jo, now staring into his glass. This was ridiculous. Hadn't I always been supportive? Hadn't I read untold pages of Byron's clumsy sentences and tortured adverbs? Didn't I send him on a course to improve? Didn't I give him a part-time job to help subsidise his endeavours? Didn't he have direct access to my work and my help, any time he liked? Hadn't I always enthused about Vivi's photography – even during the blurry-arty years that truly sucked? Didn't I get her the leg-up she needed? Didn't I set up Jo in his own business? Hadn't I paid for Rosy's education to make sure she didn't end up smoking cigarettes behind the Co-op like her own mother had done? Hadn't these bastards basked in my hard-earned greatness for decades, and now I was expected to clap politely, like a proud mama bear on school sports day, because Byron had managed to shit out a book? I know our lives together hadn't been all magnolia blooms against a cerulean sky, but I'd done my best by them, given them everything. The ingratitude. It screamed mutiny, on a ship I had no idea I was captaining. I couldn't help being a success. I couldn't help being better than them at everything. To hell with them.

I crammed down the lid on my volcanic fury. 'So it's doing well? It's a bestseller?'

'Well, not top ten, no. It got to about number seventeen. We're really happy with that.'

I should've held up my glass, proposed a toast and left it at that, sat eating my pudding like a good boy. But, no.

God.

I got it. I knew what they told themselves. I was intimidating. I got my success easily. The fuckers. I was rancid with irritation. What a shame he'd missed the top ten. He'd done all he could, it seemed. Used a fake name. Completely sold out. Written something so nakedly commercial, lowered himself to my level, something his supposed artistic sensibilities would never have allowed him to do before. He'd kept this from me so he could present it like some weird humiliation or intervention. The poison leaked out.

'So you've finally debased yourself with an airport novel, but still can't whack "Sunday Times Bestseller" on the cover? Sorry for your loss, By.'

'Nothing wrong with writing something popular,' chided Jo, in the voice he usually reserved for reminding me I'd forgotten to flush the downstairs loo.

'Yes, I know!' I hissed. 'I've been doing it for years.'

'Debasing? Silly Lulu! It's a cute story, he's found his niche.' Grainger now, morphing into a disapproving village elder. She said it 'nitch', like an American. Good old Vivi. No shine she can't dull with her praise, which runs on a scale from 'muted' all the way up to 'faint'. She had nothing to say to me about debasing. I'd seen her sponsored posts on social media. 'Renowned photographer plugging scented drawer liners'? Give me a break, Grainger.

I couldn't fill my lungs with air fast enough. I gripped the table. How dare they talk down to me like this. To me! Without me, none of us would be able to afford to sit at this fucking table ordering champagne that I couldn't drink.

'They didn't mean anything by it, Uncle Lu,' said Rosy, draining her glass again. 'It was supposed to be a nice surprise.'

I read it as something else. A coded message my entourage was shifting to another orbit. I saw Vivi and Byron inch closer, steeled for my next outburst. This was what they wanted, wasn't it? To have the volcano explode, vindicate them? Just me being me. It's always terrifying to catch a glimpse of how others see you, even those closest to you, who you've shared everything with. I raised my beer bottle and wasn't entirely unhappy to see Byron and Vivi shrink back the tiniest amount, their faces a masterclass in 'Have we pushed this too far?'

'Sorry, Rosy, my sweetheart. I was playing a bit rough, I agree. I'm just so surprised. I'm happy for you. I am. Truly.' I wasn't. They knew I wasn't.

'I wanted to see if I could do it myself,' said Byron. 'Show you that I'm capable, not just a hanger-on. Does that make sense?'

If only Byron had had this epiphany two decades earlier, he might have saved me a fortune. I connected my bottle with his glass. 'Course it does. But, By, honestly, you should've just opened with that.'

As my pulse returned to normal, the earlier scene seemed ridiculous. I still find it hard to reconcile the lonely but sparky little boy I was with this strange monster I've become. When did that bitter tang start to seep into my blood? My mother always insists I was a sweet child, which must be true because she never says it about her other two. Not that I remember much about Evangeline and Ray's personalities growing up – they were just there, faded anaglypta in human form. Where did he go? All those hopes and fears. That vitality. It's so sad when everything that happens to you ends up as footnotes.

We finished dinner and even went for a drink afterwards, but I felt an imbalance not in my favour. I left the book in the gents' toilet and, three weeks later, told Byron I'd read it and that it was fabulous.

Seventeen

July

Jo

Jo's planning a holiday, to make the most of the summer break. He planned to surprise Theo with a ticket, but remembers Theo's jagged smile and anxious eyes when Ned Lanford turned up at dinner uninvited. This guy doesn't like surprises. Money is an issue. Theo doesn't have much, still lives with his mother. Jo hears little of life inside their flat in Ladbroke Grove, aside from the odd snatch of an anecdote – Theo was once late because his mum needed a hand with something, which on gentle prying turned out to be adding fabric conditioner to the washing machine.

'She pours it in manually. Doesn't like leaving it in the drawer. I've never asked why. Secret mum reasons. You've got to listen for the rinse starting. She had to go out, so I stepped up.'

Jo becomes fixated on this rare morsel. He wants to ask more about his mum, his dead brother, and whoever's hurt him so deeply he can only live so firmly in the present. What he wants most is to ask what happened when Theo applied for the Valenti. Coincidences happen all the time, sure, the world runs on people turning up in places you might not expect. But when Jo asks for specifics, which he has done, twice, it's a teenage shrug, and clichés like 'That's how it goes' and 'I didn't have what it takes.' Not even bitter, or particularly evasive, just pragmatic, gently rolling down the shutters, almost back to how it was when they first met. Jo understands, reminds himself there are plenty of failures he doesn't want to relive. Anyway, mystery is both an aphrodisiac and a foundation, and the shutters can easily roll up again. Hence the holiday. Nothing like sunshine and unfamiliar surroundings to help you open up about the world you've left behind. They need to be away, that's all that matters.

Jo approaches it like a business proposal. If he can pick the location, identify a hotel and shortlist potential travel arrangements, Theo will go along with it, surely. Jo settles on Madrid. He spent so many holidays poolside while Laurie nursed hangovers, trying and failing to reanimate him before cocktail hour, when he'd demand to be whisked to the coolest rooftop bar within driving distance. A city break presents distractions if conversation falters. Laurie always used to say you never really knew a lover until you'd been on holiday with them. If you could survive two weeks in Ibiza or three days getting piss-wet through in a tent in the Lakes, in close proximity, you were meant to be together.

As expected, Theo is worried about money. 'I'm kinda broke right now.'

'Don't worry about that ...' Jo stops himself from embellishing, that he has plenty of money, or that it's on him. Theo has precious little power and wants to hold on to the crumbs he does have. 'I need the break. I want you to come. You can get the next one.'

Jo expects Theo to brighten at this, but his frown lines deepen. 'I think my passport's out of date. What about somewhere closer to home?'

Whatever happened to that earnest enthusiasm of the early days? Jo won't nag, but he'll be firm if necessary. 'Get it renewed. I can shout you the cost, I'm the one dragging you away. You do it online. Just send in your old passport.' His long-dormant organiser gene is reawakened, almost as dominant as the one that forbids him from taking no for an answer.

'I don't know where it is.' Theo smiles weakly and Jo is exhausted at the thought of another protest coming. And then he realises this is not just about money. Theo's never had a passport. He breathes in the richness of defeat.

'Closer to home? Okay. How about Brighton?'

Theo's eyes darken for a moment but he soon dredges up his best smile. 'Cool.'

Jo masks his disappointment. 'Brighton it is. I know a lovely place.'

Since Theo met everyone, it's less intense. Now they have the luxury of security, physical distance isn't threatening. They don't have penetrative sex – what Laurie would've termed full in and out – every time they see each other now. They still can't keep their hands off each other, but it's tender now, less urgent. Theo seems happier; there's less bowling, and more cooking at home, or comfortable silences in the pub. Jo wonders if he's making Theo old before his time – what was stolen from him when he was younger that's made him cling to youthful rituals? Jo watches Theo carefully, wondering when it will come out, and whether he'll be ready when it does. Their summer assignment is to write a short story. A 'pivotal moment' in a thousand words or fewer. Theo claims he hasn't started yet, but Jo's caught him scribbling notes. Jo's done a first draft. It's something, maybe, but he doubts it will see the light of day. Too real.

The night before they're leaving for Brighton, on one of the warmest days of the summer so far, Byron invites them to a book launch – not his own, a stablemate. It's obviously to get a look at Theo, having missed the dinner for no reason other than wanting to appear unavailable. Theo doesn't take much persuading, which would've been astonishing only a month ago. Jo feels a pang of guilt for his own past reluctance to attend events like this. Towards the end, Laurie gave up trying. Jo lends Theo a nice shirt that's too big on him but still looks great because, well, it's hard for things not to look great when they're on Theo.

'Don't you remember this bar?' says Theo as they enter the throng, an hour later than they were supposed to arrive. 'We did space cakes in here. That guy freaked you out, remember?'

It wasn't the guy who had 'freaked him out', but his own reaction. And eating 'space cakes' in his late forties, like some tragic midlifer hanging out with teens at a rave, as Laurie may well have said.

Jo spots Byron and Viv across the room tipping wine from a small glass into a bigger one that's already half full. Viv freezes, embarrassed to be caught.

'The wine's not even warm,' she says, teeth clenched ventriloquist-tight, double-cheek-kissing them both. 'What kind of book launch is this? You're in luck, you missed the speeches. Very naughty of you, though.'

Jo surveys the room. 'Where's the scribe?'

'Around somewhere. You can't miss him, dressed like a Christmas tree,' says Byron. 'You know, he hasn't thanked anyone for coming, has he, Grainger? All he said was, "Nice to see you." Laurie would've been horrified.' He holds out his free hand to Theo as if expecting him to kiss it. 'So what is it you do, Theo?'

'I'm a student.'

'Oh, yes, of course, the writing.' Byron glances at Jo and breaks into a thin smile, before going back to Theo. 'But what do you do for money?'

'Oh, uh, bar jobs mainly.'

Byron locks eyes with Jo. 'That's how we started. All of us. Then Laurie found his generous benefactor and the rest is history.'

Someone unseen in a far corner of the room taps hard on a live microphone, and once everyone's gasps from being jolted into cardiac arrhythmia have settled down, announces there will be karaoke in half an hour.

Byron's eyes bulge. 'What is this, a book launch or a hen night?'

Viv takes a leisurely swig of wine; she forgets to pull a face at its sourness. 'I love karaoke. We used to do it all the time back when it was the thing, remember, Jo? Do you sing, Theo?'

'He does!' says Jo. 'Very well.' Theo turns, with a half-smile, his cheeks reddening. 'I've heard you in the shower. You're great.'

Theo laughs now, snakes his arm round Jo's waist; their bodies slot together perfectly. They're both so relaxed, their bones could be jelly. The room hums with good moods, everyone's eyes are bright and faces excited, the bad wine is hitting as it should. Theo's hand is fanned out against Jo's arse; this is heaven, he doesn't want it to end.

'So have you ever performed? Professionally?' Byron, as always, readying himself to envy someone he hardly knows.

'Uh, kind of. I was in a choir.'

Jo is anxious to catch these trickles of information coming his way. 'Choir? Were you?'

'What, like at school?' says Viv, her eyes misting over a little. 'Rosy was in the choir.'

'Nothing worse than listening to a load of brats murder your favourite carols,' hisses Byron, watching Theo, who laughs politely.

'No, no,' he says, 'it was a gay choir, a big group of us. We did shows and events and openings and stuff. Proper harmonies.'

'Oh, West London Gay Voices?' squeals Viv. 'We knew a guy in that!'

Theo's arm tenses immediately. Where it once rested on Jo's back, it digs in.

Viv is oblivious to the change in temperature. 'Byron, big gay Dave, remember? Why did you give it up?'

Jo recognises the disengaged look on Theo's face, same as at the dinner party, the fear he's got too personal, wanting to stuff the words back in. Down go the shutters.

'I, er, it was a big commitment and I had some stuff going on.'

Jo's close to unlocking more, he can taste it, but Byron decides to switch the topic to his struggle with his next book, which sounds awful. 'I've booked an Airbnb in Perpignan,' he says, mispronouncing it. 'Going to hide away and wrestle with draft five.'

They stay for two more drinks, out of politeness. Byron is doing all the talking, but Jo doesn't hear a word he says. He suggests to Theo that they leave. Theo smiles awkwardly, but agrees.

Viv pouts as they kiss goodbye. 'I've barely spoken to you. Why do I never see you?'

'You absolutely do. All the time. Bye, Byron.'

'When do we get to see some of your writing?' Byron's tone is bright and upbeat but Jo senses a lacing of salt.

'What do you mean?'

'Well, you must have an aim? Otherwise why study? Is there

a book? Not plays, surely? You could write about Laurie! Has that memoir turned up?'

Not this again. 'I'm not ready to write a book.' He nods at Theo. 'Shall we?'

'Shame you have to go.' Viv puts her hand on his arm, gently, but with determination; he'd have to shake it off – and be seen doing so – to get away. 'Laurie would've torn tonight to shreds, wouldn't he? I do miss him.' She gestures around the bar, white wine escaping from her glass in the process, before glancing at Theo. 'Sorry. I don't mean to go on in front of you.'

Theo shakes his head. 'I don't mind. I understand.'

Admirable how he never flinches, thinks Jo, never intimidated by the constant reminders of Laurie. Clearly not scared of ghosts.

'You certainly wouldn't have come out of it unscathed, Grainger, not with that plunging neckline,' quips Byron.

It's an attempt at Laurie's playful, gently skewering manner, but it doesn't land; it feels mean. Jo wants to tell Viv that Laurie would actually have loved her plunging neckline, which is probably true, he would have.

Regardless, Viv either isn't listening to Byron or doesn't care; instead, she strokes Theo's arm now. 'I'm sure he'd have adored you. And you him.'

Theo twitches this time, his arm tensing again as Jo tugs it to move them nearer the door. Viv is taking off to the more sentimental corners of her mind and he'd rather escape before she lands. They emerge from the air-conditioned chill of the bar into the oppressive, sticky night.

'I love this time of year.' Theo, evidently relieved to be outside, beams as he looks up and down the street. Jo feels a surge of affection, then a tinge of sorrow. 'The fag-end of the summer, isn't it?'

'Laurie used to say that.'

Jo remembers this time last year, how dark and oppressive summer seemed even on the brightest afternoons. Trudging for cocktails by himself, talking to strangers. And now look at him. So much to look forward to. Something's not right, though. Maybe it's going back to Brighton in the morning, remembering last time he was there. How many years before Laurie died? Five? Six? Laurie sulking because it was raining, complaining Jo hadn't booked somewhere within walking distance of the hotel for dinner, huge argument before bed. It's a novelty to have a memory that's not rose-hued, but real, how things could be sometimes. Comforting in a way. Over eighteen months of heartfelt eulogies have worn him out.

Theo and Jo walk in silence through Soho's chaos as if protected by a force field.

'You all right? God, this hay fever.' Theo coughs. 'Hey, I wanna show you something.' Theo grips Jo's hand and strides ahead. Jo feels like he's three again, being dragged behind his mother in the supermarket, mittens dangling from his sleeves. Hitting Regent Street, they jump on a bus, which swings left and crawls down Oxford Street, picking up shoppers, post-work drunks and tourists gobbling American candy. Theo seems nervous; Jo, on autopilot, does not ask where they are going.

They get off somewhere along Bayswater Road. Theo leads Jo to a square, typical of the more well-heeled parts of London. Jo has always fantasised about living somewhere like this. Wrought-iron fencing encircles a well-tended garden in the middle; key holders only, no doubt. Hundreds of windows face onto it but nobody would ever look out – when you're that rich, living somewhere so beautiful, you have a duty to take it for granted.

Laurie preferred a fixer-upper, not this carefully curated

perfection. He wanted to be near chicken shops. Pubs. Bus stops. Pavement vomit. Places he could see the world happening, not a weird millionaire ghetto.

They walk slowly; Theo clearly knows the way. It's almost silent save for the light hum of traffic only a block away, noise dulled by the sturdy, expensive houses in between.

'Theo, when exactly were you in the choir?'

Theo is distracted. 'Oh, ages ago.'

Jo sees a chink of opportunity. 'Why did you leave, really? What was the stuff you had going on?'

'Oh, you know, family shit, misspent youth,' he said, his voice almost ghostly. 'Got in with a bad crowd.'

Jo tries to keep his voice as even as possible, mimicking Theo's almost, to avoid spooking him. 'Is it around the time you applied for the Valenti?'

Theo stops and turns to Jo, slowly. 'Here we are.'

Fixed to the beautiful railings of the square is a bike, painted in gold. It looks like it's been there a very long time. The paint is chipped, one of the wheels is buckled as if someone's tried to prise it from the railings, and the seat is askew. Tied to the handlebars is a small bouquet, wrapped in cellophane, the flowers inside reduced to mouldy twigs. There's a card attached, but the writing has faded in the sun and smudges of ink suggest it's endured plenty of rain showers too. Theo inches forward and runs his hand along the chassis, occasionally brushing off dirt. 'I should've brought wet wipes. I didn't know I was coming.'

Jo doesn't move. He waits.

'This is where my brother died. Well, over there. A lorry was making a detour, going way too fast. Knowing my brother, he thought he could beat him. He didn't, though.'

There's a pause where Jo is obviously supposed to say

something, but he doesn't. He's not sure he can speak. Not this. Please, not this.

'I was grieving. I didn't have any direction. I was trying to make it as an actor, but not really trying. Didn't have the energy. I joined the choir. Trying to be good. Trying to cancel out everything my brother was. He did bad things. Stupid things. He gave my mum nothing but trouble, but when he died, it was like he'd been someone else all along. This incredible saint, gone too soon. The slate got wiped clean. I wanted that. To wipe everything. Start again.'

Again, Theo stops, looking for comforting words, reassurance maybe. Jo stays mute, eyes boring into the bike, his heart thumping.

'I put my trust in someone. He promised me that he'd help me. It went wrong. I had ... I don't know what you'd call it. A breakdown, maybe.'

Jo takes a deep breath. He's missed his cue twice now but he won't let this one pass him by.

'So it is you. It really is you. Fuck. Stop talking.'

Theo appears mildly startled by Jo's sharpness. There's a voice inside Jo he's been resisting, but it fights its way out now, angry.

'Is this how you reeled him in? Brought him to your pop-up graveyard?'

'What ... ?'

Jo sighs and closes his eyes. His hands tingle. There's a chill down his spine, even in this heat. He can imagine it. He can see Laurie falling for this. He thrived on an emotional backstory, pain and hardship in something beautiful. 'He loved writing about sad little boys like you.'

Theo still doesn't understand. Jo wants him to enjoy these last seconds of ignorance so the contrast of what comes next hits him all the harder. He's ignored it long enough. Got caught

up in romantic ideas, instead of what was staring him in the
face. He thought Theo's cageyness stemmed from dealing with
trauma; it made his eagerness to be friends more unexpected
and charming. Jo almost congratulated himself for managing
to perforate Theo's protective shell but now that slow opening of
the bloom feels cheap and fake. Theo wasn't being mysterious,
he was scared of being caught.

'You know, Laurie took everything at face value. Gullible,
even. Maybe I overthink. Things that don't mean anything on
their own start to add up, turn into something huge. What are
we doing here?'

Fear dawns on Theo's face, sweeping over him like enchanted
mist. His breathing quickens. 'Jo, please, whatever it is you think
I've done . . . '

Jo's head swims with the deceptions. 'I can tell you what
you've done. You've given yourself away. That final piece. Fuck.
I'm so dumb. Nobody goes up to a forty-six-year-old man in
the park and asks to be their friend. Most people who've never
been in my front lounge before walk in and stare in wonder, like
someone seeing their first Caravaggio up close. Nobody picks up
those awards for the first time without saying how heavy they
are. *Nobody.*' Theo opens and closes his mouth without sound.
'Nobody ever manages to open that sticky toilet door without
being shown how. Nobody ever waits that long to tell me, of all
people, that they applied for the Valenti. I hear it in the first five
seconds. Nobody hides from Ned Lanford unless they've already
met him. All that sixth form debating society shit about dead
soldiers and memorials. And now your choir, and your bike.
You sick fuck.'

'Jo, I was going to tell you.'

'Yeah, in about ten minutes, probably.' The clarity of his
thoughts! Jo is a pilot sticking the landing. 'What's your grift?

You must be really backed into a corner to play your ace now. To show me your magic memorial death bike.' Jo pauses to make sure Theo is still breathing. He begins to croak out a reply so Jo forges ahead. He has to say this, he has to survive this moment. 'Did he have tears in his eyes? Laurie, I mean, when he saw your bike, took you home? Did he call you his boy? Did he make you go on top so he could watch himself inside you? He liked that, didn't he? See this is the thing, Theo, Teddy, whatever your fucking name is. I knew that bastard inside out. Even if I hadn't heard it from the horse's mouth, I can tell where Laurie's been. He leaves, like, this trace behind him, space dust, an energy. Germs, you could say, but slightly less poetic. I can see where he's been, I know who he's touched, and I can hear his voice in everything they say.'

Theo bends over, folding almost in half, and takes long, loud breaths. 'How did you . . . ? What do you mean, horse's mouth? Did Laurie talk about me?'

'Oh, little baby Theo. Spin a fairy tale to a storyteller and it'll always go in the bank for later. He wrote it all down, Teddy.'

Realisation now. 'You don't understand.'

Jo is not done. 'You thought you were special, I bet. The first. Or the last. You weren't. You're a dot in a crowd scene. Laurie and me were tied together in tight knots. You can't compare to me, you could never replace me. Whatever you're doing here, this weird fucking shadowing trick, your sick project, it's over.'

Theo stands up straight. 'Please, I can explain . . . '

There's relief in this high voltage confrontation that seems like immortality; Jo has an urge to call everyone he's ever met and tell them what he thinks of them. This must be what it felt like to be Laurie.

'And now this, bringing me here to make me feel sorry for you. Were you worried Laurie might have let slip about his little choirboy, huh?'

Theo's face is contorted with shock, the death mask of the guilty. 'You don't understand,' he shouts, as Jo begins to walk away, feeling more alive and disgusting than he ever has before.

'Stop saying that. I don't want to understand.'

'I love you. I do. I'm ... honestly.'

What a moment for the three little words to make their debut. Jo stops. Turns around. Takes in all of Theo, who's breathing fast, clutching on to the back wheel of the bike for support, tears streaming down his face.

'Well, I don't love you. And I never have.' Jo carries on walking and does not look back.

[Untitled]

Laurie

So, you read it. I knew I couldn't trust you. You've always been good at making me believe that you're untainted by my world, that gossip is beneath you and creativity is above you. Yet here you are, reading where you shouldn't. I picture you as a child sometimes, never speaking, ears flapping, taking in all the grown-ups' secrets.

Apart from going gooey over sunsets, we take it for granted that the clouds and the sky are beautiful. That's what I've done with you. We've never really confronted our shallow foundations, have we? I was attracted to your looks and your in-difference and you were interested in ... well, I've never worked it out. Maybe my life seemed glamorous? Maybe you get off on being a dependable sidekick? My strong right hand, my stay, my oil on stormy waters, cheap straighteners taming the wildest of curls? I find joy in your beautiful face, I feel lucky you're mine, but maybe I hate you for it, too. I can't escape my DNA, I don't work as hard as you do at it. You won't be beautiful for ever. I've seen what happens to rich and thin men when they get old. All those needles and serums and laser treatments. Not nourishing but preserving, like formaldehyde. Their skin's texture oleaginous and synthetic, like Benecol.

I don't know how much you've read and in what order. I've been careless; I suppose I underestimated your appetite for getting inside my head. Have you ever just watched someone, the way I watch you? You should. I can tell what you've seen from how you act. You've slipped up a few times, mentioning things you couldn't possibly know. William Fossett. I've never told you about him, but you mentioned him, at lunch that day with By and Vivi. And something about the bistro days; you weren't there. Little turns of phrase, too. Staunchly analogue. I've been observing you for years, my darling, squirrelling away things you say, things I used to find so amusing. We used to be like that, do you remember? Two little parrots teaching each other how to talk. My boy. Now you're using my own words against me. Maybe I idolised you too much at first, debasing myself for you. I needed stability. I never made a secret of that.

We could've been anything we wanted, as long as we had each other. Adventures out there for the taking. But you wanted to be like everyone else. Conform. Dim the bright lights, turn gloss to matt, live sugar-free and low-fat. Basic. I'm sorry, but there's something about eating a hamburger with a knife and fork in a chain restaurant that makes me feel like a crippling failure.

You've been good at making yourself indispensable. Respectable face, playing into my Anglican guilt, the same narrow thinking that made my mother cut the crusts off my sandwiches in case the other parents at the school gates thought she was neglectful. No wonder she adores you.

What happened? What if I looked inside your head? Let me peek behind that poker face. Why don't you write anything down? You're not a closed book, you're a blank page. The way I felt about you then, I've never felt about anybody. But your contempt for my chaos seeps out of you. Rearranging my shoes in the hallway, straightening my toothbrush so it's just so, reading out a charge sheet of the previous night's misdemeanours. Slicing your tomatoes so evenly. I hate tomatoes.

Do you remember being young? I think about it all the time, try to equate the man I see now, chugging on his charcoal shot and smoothing the T-shirt down over his hard body, with the smart cookie who'd sit next to me and blow smoke rings into the sunrise. Whatever you liked about me then I've either lost, or you simply don't like any more. Your tastebuds have changed. Somehow, without either of us noticing, it became more important to be right about something than it did to make each other happy. Maybe I should have left you after that first night, like I did all the others; stopped calling, drifted out of your life. A fleeting halcyon moment. Instead, I kept you close, brought you into my home, preserved you in amber.

I came close, once, to something original. Imagine I'd come home that night, when your grandmother died, and said what I was about to say. Where would I be now? Where would you be? Imagine how happy we might both be if the last ten years had never happened.

We never stood a chance, you and me. I let daylight in on magic. It could never have worked.

Eighteen
July

Jo

One night, Jo made a huge mistake. One we're all doomed to make if our curiosity outguns our willpower. A message flashed up on Laurie's phone, and Jo, idling nearby, swirling a teabag round a mug, read it. It was Viv.

> oh just make something up, tell him it's work. we should celebrate!

It's unsettling to discover how people talk about you in your absence. We do it all the time, break confidences, offer light character assassinations, exchange pitying looks, but we think that once we leave the room ourselves, we're immune to it. Had this happened a few years earlier, Jo might have tackled this head on. 'So what are we celebrating?' he could've said, or made vague, informed enquiries to get Laurie to reveal it. But being portrayed as standing in the way of a good time, in a private conversation between two people who'd known each other longer than he'd been around, made him reluctant to pry. Laurie was staying out later, sometimes not making it to bed at all – Jo would often find him passed out on the sofa in the back lounge. That night they were supposed to be seeing Sian and Holden, plans Laurie was obviously keen to evade. Why didn't Laurie just say, rather than make him out to be a shrew?

Jo placed a cup of strong black coffee on the bedside table and watched as Laurie battled from dreamland to the waking world. He seemed puzzled, trying to process why Jo was waking him and not his alarm's incessant siren.

'The dog isn't dead, is he?' They'd just got Jasper – a tumour had done for Liza a couple of months earlier.

'No. Your phone's been buzzing.' It made a dull clunk as Jo placed it on the table, Laurie's red eyes flashed to it briefly. There was definite relief to find the screen blank. 'Good night?'

'Er, yeah,' he said, his voice a croak. One cough. Two. The smell of the smoking area at the Groucho started to fill the room.

'I was thinking, I'm gonna cancel Holden tonight. I'm tired. Might get an early night. Unless you want to meet them without me.' He tried not to laugh; Laurie wouldn't go as far as the ensuite to see Holden and Sian without Jo.

'Sure. I might see Vivi then. Won't be late, though.'

Jo went back downstairs, hoping this benevolent act might sweeten the next messages about him.

He put it out of his head, didn't think about it for years. But it's a drug, seeing how you're perceived. Every so often, he went looking for trouble. One night, a couple of years before Laurie died, Jo wandered into the office, sat at Laurie's desk, blinked in the mechanical glow of the screen. Laurie kept everything:

fan mail, work emails – even two-line replies – half-finished manuscripts, brain dumps. He was a hoarder of words, terrified of running short of new ones one day.

He found a short essay Laurie had written about his father. Jo already knew most of this story, but it was illuminating to read it rather than hear it in Laurie's dismissive drawl, before quickly changing the subject. It was like opening a window just a crack, feeling the light stream of fresh air, and wanting more. Jo imagined him tutting and rolling his eyes as he hammered away at his keyboard. Reading about their early days together, in Kennington, and discovering how fondly Laurie looked back on that period made Jo want to bring that feeling into the present somehow. On the rare occasions they ate together, Jo would look across the table at Laurie's smiling face – winking at him even, in the amber glint of the candlelight – and wonder how he could live so many lives inside his head. Laurie would blow hot and cold, be up and down, go from distant to clingy. Reading Laurie's thoughts on ageing, his confusing relationship with his own talent, and a couple of pre-him flings where he had acted much less gallant than usual, Jo saw the essays as a cheat sheet and took a few cues from what he'd read to smooth the oncoming waters. He slipped up a couple of times, betrayed his knowledge, but Laurie didn't seem to notice. Guilt kicked in and after a couple of weeks of nipping in the office to sneak a glance, Jo backed away, stopped snooping.

A week or two before Laurie died, Jo dared one more look. Laurie had been preoccupied, jittery; Jo told himself it would be the easiest way to understand. The tone had changed, however; Laurie seemed to have written these newer notes under a much darker sky. Jo saw the name Teddy appear again and again. This time, Jo wasn't prepared to hold back.

But he doesn't want to think about that now.

Since Laurie's death, he's been back in, reading whatever he finds, puzzled by glaring inconsistencies, ones he can't face right now. Is this the infamous memoir? What about the things that are obviously untrue? Yet enough of it is authentic enough to show him the life he thought he'd known is in ruins, and the new one he's trying to build is turning to dust before his eyes.

Theo. Teddy. Whoever. The long con is too gross, too horrible. It's chilling – you can be inside someone, have them inside you, explore every part of someone, yet never know what's happening inside their head. First Laurie, now this. Do men with dark secrets seek out Jo, or is he drawn to them? It's been a hell of a couple of years; Jo has made a good mark for any opportunist.

And Theo – maybe Jo wanted to believe what they had was real. He'd read about trusting widows swindled out of their savings by dewy-skinned chancers they met on holiday. Theo – grizzled, messed-up, fragile – may have been in deeper cover than a charming flaneur or a hung Turkish waiter, but he was still on the make.

The complication? Theo is refusing to accept he's been caught. The calls persist. Over the last couple of weeks since he was found out, Theo's come to the house every other day or so. Jo hasn't told Rosy what's happened, but she covers for him like she's giving one of her girlfriends an alibi, with the same excuse, that Jo isn't there, even though the car is parked outside. Zosia messages Jo every time Theo comes into the café. He chats to Kris a little, Rosy says, asks about Jo; they never tell him anything.

'What you looking for? Can I help?' says Rosy, bringing yet another cup of tea as he stares into Laurie's screen.

Unlikely, thinks Jo. 'I'm not looking for anything. I'm supposed to be writing. My summer assignment.'

'Oof. How long is it?'

'A thousand words.'

'That's nothing!' Mercifully she stops before stating the obvious, that Laurie could knock up the same number of words before his morning shower.

Rosy pads over to the armchair in the corner and sits with her knees brought up to her chest. 'Remember the last time you decorated in here?'

Jo can see her now. A scrawnier teenage version standing on Laurie's desk, long roller in one hand, paint dropping onto her head and over the computer monitor. Her protests of 'I wanted to help' echoing off the walls as her mother dragged her away to get cleaned up, Laurie and Jo doubled up laughing. 'You chose that chair, didn't you?'

'My orange phase. I miss that big old sofa. Look, you're in no fit state to write.'

'Aren't I?'

She sighs. 'Uncle Lu wouldn't want this. You should work things out with Theo.'

Jo knows from experience that when someone is telling you how you feel, you're best letting them get it out rather than argue. Never interrupt an armchair psychologist.

'Delayed grief. Comes in waves. It's not linear. I read that.'

'Online?' That sounds snarky and Jo regrets it. As if books carry more weight than the internet. Laurie said the knell for traditional publishing as a respected medium sounded when Byron got his first book deal.

She ignores the jibe. 'Mum has good days and bad days. She talks to him like he's still there. Phones his phone.' They exchange a look that each can immediately translate – they've both listened to at least one of those voicemails.

'I delete them,' Rosy insists, 'so there's room to leave more. Do you want me to have the number cut off?'

He shakes his head. Let Viv have her free therapy sessions with the Vodafone messaging service.

The doorbell rings. They both know who it is. Jo feels closer to Rosy than he has for a long time. Every time he's looked at her and thought, Now she's a grown-up, properly, she's gone on to surprise him, become even more worldly.

'You have to let him in eventually. He's not giving up.'

Jo feels like a stupid teenager. Screening his calls. Not answering the door to disgraced boyfriends. Pathetic, really; he's nearly fifty. Since when was he scared of talking to a boy? Then, a voice, through the letter box, faint. Jo creeps into the hall, Rosy a few steps behind.

It's Ned Lanford, his clipped vowels reaching out to them. 'Rosy, sweetheart, you there?'

'What the fuck does he want?' whispers Jo. Rosy shrugs, but the answer comes in a flash. 'I'm supposed to be away, aren't I?'

Jo wrenches open the door hard, so Ned flops pathetically onto the step and has to prop himself against the wall for support, his arm sliding on the tiles. It reminds Jo of Theo leaning on the bike, watching him go. Or Laurie, arriving home drunk. Two men he will never see again; he'd quite like Ned to make it three.

'Jo! Darling! How terrific to see you! I swung by to say hello.'

Rosy fixes Ned a drink and they pretend it's totally normal Ned would stop by at 5 p.m. on a weekday when Jo is supposed to be away on holiday. Ned is distracted, eyes tracking towards the office, like a child in a restaurant pretending not to stare at someone eating ice cream on the next table.

'How's your new friend? What was his name again?'

'Teddy,' says Jo, never taking his eyes off him. 'He's good, thank you.'

Ned smiles widely. 'Teddy, that's it. Sure. Yup. Great.' What a dreadful spy Ned would make, thinks Jo. Imagine having no cover story. But he's never had to lie; Ned can buy himself out of any situation. 'And you, Rosy, how are you?'

After more of the excruciating small talk that really comes into its own when everyone else in the room has so much else they'd like to say, Ned excuses himself to go to the bathroom. Jo has a feeling he can't shake, remembering the day of Laurie's funeral, Ned lurking in corridors, the random visits since. If Ned has any plans to snoop, they're soon thwarted by the good old gammy door of the downstairs loo.

Rosy calls out instructions. 'Bang it. Turn the knob now. No, bang harder. Now turn!'

After a few attempts a florid and bumbling Ned is released, claiming he has to hurry along. Jo's gut churns as he remembers never having to liberate Theo from the loo – not even on his first visit. What a ridiculous way to be caught out.

Slipping on his straw hat, which makes him look like a politician sneaking into a brothel, Ned asks chirpily, 'You and your new man got any holidays planned? Not much of summer left.'

Ned must be desperate if he's borrowing conversation topics off his barber, but Jo humours him, to make it clear the house won't be empty anytime soon, in case Ned has any ideas. Tells him he's busy with a college project in preparation for the new term. Renovations at the café. Sorting through Laurie's stuff. His mouth moves, but he can't get out of his head how Ned didn't even flinch that Jo used the wrong name, Theo's 'other' name. Because he already knows. It's obvious. He's worked out exactly who Theo is, and he knows why he's back. Once Ned's gone, Jo goes into Laurie's office and closes the door behind him.

Nineteen
July

Vivienne

Viv is shooting an actress for a Sunday magazine. They've met before, she was in one of Laurie's plays around the time of his wedding, but the actress either doesn't remember her or is pretending not to. Stars do that sometimes.

'This is nice,' she says, with a chill, chugging from a huge metal water bottle. 'They usually send a man. You get a different look with a woman photographer.'

Viv has encountered this before. Some people only trust a man to make them look beautiful. She thinks this is ridiculous, but has always found flattery is the most soothing balm.

'These shots will look incredible. You already do. Makes my job a lot easier.'

It works. She softens. It's hot in the studio, no air-con, windows are flung wide to zero effect. Yet the actress relaxes with every costume change; Viv suspects there's vodka in that ridiculous bottle.

As Viv and her assistant adjust the lighting, she feels the actress's eyes roaming her body like she's searching for a barcode.

'I was sorry to hear about Laurie. He was terrific fun.'

Ah, so she was pretending. 'Yes.'

The actress swigs from her bottle. It sounds dangerously close to empty. 'Horrendous when something like that happens. So senseless. Was he speeding, do we know? Drunk, maybe?'

The 'we' irritates Viv. As if this woman is a concerned, intimate friend, not just someone hunting for gossip. 'I don't think so.'

'My husband died in a car accident,' says the actress, fiddling with her hair as the stylist sucks air through her teeth in annoyance. 'He was always speeding. Idiot. He was on a machine for weeks. I was angry for a long time.'

Viv hates this byproduct of bereavement, having to pretend you know, or care, how everyone else feels, being front row for someone else's grief story. She tells Viv more than she wants to know. The change in breathing at the end, the row with her then-teenage children over whether to close the blinds in his room, out of respect, or leave them open so he could gaze at the sky as he faded away.

'It must've been so hard for you,' she says. 'I understand.'

She doesn't. Viv knows people mean well when they say this; there is kinship in shared experiences and grief is inevitable for anyone who loves. But she wants to shake this woman. She doesn't understand, of course she doesn't. She lost her husband, yes, it was sad, yes, but she didn't lose Laurie. She can't possibly know how Viv feels because there was only one Laurie. Her loss is unique, the Big Bang of grief, the unicorn – it's never happened before, it will never happen again.

The actress sniffs up and a sob escapes; the hair and make-up team swoop to obliterate all signs of emotion. Viv remembers the woman's husband now; he once cornered her in an accessible toilet, toyed with the zip on her dress. As she watches the woman cry, Viv thinks, as she always does, that Laurie said it best.

'The thing about horrible people, darling, is they're always loved by someone, somewhere,' he once told her, 'by people who either don't know how horrible they really are, or don't care.'

Once the shoot is over, the actress thanks her. 'I'm sorry this has happened to you, that Laurie's gone. Things like this change you. I remember a lot of our time together back then. You seem kinder now. You needed to be. Are we done?'

Viv watches her go, and wonders, not for the first time, how other people saw her and Laurie. Were they unkind? Was she? Was she a good friend to Laurie? She feels the need to prove her worth.

She's telling Rosy about the actress the next morning, as she makes sandwiches for her daughter's lunch.

'She was in something I saw the other night. On ITV. It stank,' says Rosy, over her mother's shoulder. 'No cucumber. No.'

'You can't have tuna without cucumber. You always have it.'

Rosy wrinkles her nose. 'Cucumber is just a glass of water you can chew. Makes the bread soggy. When was the last time you made me a sandwich?'

'Not that long ago. I'm coming to Jo's with you.'

'Mum, I'm not sure he's up to visitors.'

'I'm not "visitors". Anyway, I've made him some Moroccan houmous.'

'I thought all houmous was Moroccan. What's the difference?'

Rosy gets her interrogational skills from her grandmother;

Viv can hear her voice now. 'My one's got chickpeas on top, and onion. Toasted almonds.'

'Chickpeas? Houmous is already chickpeas. Why would you put chickpeas on it?'

Viv always imagined having one of those mother–daughter relationships where people told them they seemed like sisters. She imagined Rosy coming on shoots with her, or booking surprise trips to a spa. She wanted it to be everything her relationship with her mother wasn't: easy, supportive. But, as Laurie always said, you can't run from DNA.

'It's how you do it. Chickpeas on top, along with the other stuff. So do you want a lift or not?'

'It's like having dough balls as a pizza topping.' Rosy looks at her mother with a mix of pity and suspicion. 'Jo might not be there. Wednesday is his café day.' Rosy realises Viv already knows this; she hopes she hasn't blushed. 'Mum, you're not just gonna walk round the house like Mrs de Winter, are you?'

'I'm taking houmous. It's my best friend's house. I'm allowed to be there.'

'I don't mean to sound harsh, but he's gone now.'

Fucking hell. 'I was talking about Jo. He is still my best friend. Stop acting like a bloody guard dog. It's not up to you. I'm coming.'

'If he's there, try not to gloat.'

'You don't really think I want Jo to be miserable, do you? I don't.' She's telling the truth: she wants Jo to be happy. But it doesn't mean she isn't relieved Theo's apparently off the scene. And it won't stop her. 'You should keep your loved ones close, Rosy, you never know when something might happen.'

Rosy scoops up the sandwiches into a plastic tub, and clips down the edges with a force that says a thousand words – not that she's done speaking. 'All the more reason to keep your distance, then you won't feel so awful when it does. Keeping Laurie close didn't do you much good.'

At the house, Viv places the houmous in the fridge and scrabbles around for a pen and some paper to write Jo a note.

Sorry to have missed you. Moroccan houmous in the fridge. Enjoy!

She pauses, reads it back. No warmth whatsoever. How should she talk to Jo now? She takes the lid back off the pen.

Love you. See you soon? xx

Then she goes upstairs.

Five minutes later, she sticks her head round the office door and makes Rosy jump.

'You looked engrossed there. You type even louder than Laurie. What are you working on?'

Rosy's face is clammy, she seems disoriented. 'I was just . . . are you leaving?'

'Yes. I was gonna wait, but—'

'Okay, well, see you then. I'll tell Jo about the houmous.'

She's about to say there's no need, that she wrote a note. But then she stops. Maybe he'll assume Rosy brought it round. He won't have to know Viv was there.

'Okay.'

She screws up the note and heaves her tote, heavier now than when it arrived, onto her shoulder, closing the door carefully behind her.

Twenty

August

Jo

Betrayal is a bomb that destroys everything in its path; there's always debris left to be cleared, survivors who need counselling. Actual bombings bring about the need to understand why it's happened, however, while personal betrayals invoke an impulse to exile people from your life, or refuse excuses or clarifications. One morning, Jo decides to stop acting like he doesn't want an explanation. Over a bowl of granola that Jo keeps forgetting to chuck out because he doesn't like sliced Brazil nuts, he decides that next time Theo knocks at the door, he'll let him in. He won't summon him here; he'll let fate decide.

Theo doesn't contact him that day, or the next, and Jo goes to bed starving, too anxious to eat. Losing Laurie in the blink of an eye has taught him nothing about leaving things open-ended.

The following afternoon, it's Rosy's day off. Jo's in the office editing his summer project, feeling vicious and unkind about his work. A proper writer at last. Four light taps on the door. He ambles to the front of the house, willing whoever it is to give up and go away. He's relieved, and excited, to see Theo's silhouette through the translucent panels.

The door creaks comically as Jo opens it and they both glance briefly at the hinge they imagine to be responsible before locking eyes.

'You're actually in.'

'I've always been in.'

He looks tired. The beard is a tad longer. This, Jo decides, is how someone who wants you to believe they miss you would present themselves at your door, and the only truth Jo knows about Theo is that he's a liar. Yet he shows him through to the kitchen. Last time they were in this room, they were shouting out ideas of what to do in Brighton. Log flume! Bargain hunting in the Lanes! Ice cream from the right ice cream place, not the wrong one. Now this is happening, Jo isn't sure he's ready to hear it. Doesn't he already know everything? It's all there, a few metres away, on Laurie's computer, scattered breadcrumbs of time. Theo's had days to construct his own version.

'I should've told you I knew Laurie before. I don't know why I didn't.'

Jo can't look at him while that lie hangs in the air. He turns away to make coffee. 'You know why.'

'You said Laurie wrote about me. What did he say?'

Jo is glad of the kettle's horrific industrial din. It needs descaling. 'I don't think you get to ask questions.'

'Right. Okay. Can I sit?' The chair scraping the tiles adds to the torture. 'What do you want to know?'

A tinkle of a teaspoon in the cup. So, so ordinary, all of it, except for the conversation. He wants so badly to be tender, but the situation demands savagery. 'Why did you do this? Isn't it enough that you fucked my husband? Why come after me? Is it a fetish? Completing the set?'

Shock and panic blazes across Theo's face. 'What? Who said that? Nothing happened between me and Laurie. I swear.'

Jo was so desperate to hear this, yet the denial makes him angrier. So stupid, pointless. A toddler saying 'it wasn't me' with green fingers, next to a pot of paint, and a wall covered with handprints.

'So you weren't in love? You didn't have an affair?'

Theo shakes his head, eyes pleading. Jo recognises that desperation, that fear of not being believed. He's seen it before, in this very room, from Laurie. 'No. My God. No. That's not what this is about.'

'It's not a happy accident, is it? That we met? That I've embarrassed myself. I thought I loved you. Christ.'

Theo's mouth drops. 'Last time I saw you, you said you didn't. Never had, you said.'

'I said a lot of things.'

'For what it's worth, I meant it when I said I loved you.'

It's worth a lot, Jo only wishes it wasn't. He focuses on the task at hand, sips his coffee. 'Let's hear your version then. Everything. How you met.'

'He came to see the choir. I was in a choir, like I said. West London Gay Voices.'

Jo realises the colour must've drained from his face. He'd hoped for an early discrepancy between their accounts, something to negate quickly anything that happened after it. 'So that part is true.'

'I can only tell my side, the truth. There was, like, an aftershow thing. I met him there. With your friend Mr Lanford.'

'Not my friend.'

'Okay.' Theo looks relieved to hear it. 'We got talking. They made me laugh, they were funny. Mr Lanford was quite bitchy and mean, but I liked that, like a queeny old uncle. Laurie sort of the same, but kinder vibes, you know?' He looks embarrassed. 'Course you know. Sorry. I was in this short film. A really shit one. Laurie said he'd come see it. He seemed genuinely interested. I've met a lot of men in the industry, especially gay ones, sometimes older, they act like they know everything, and look down on me. Especially then. I didn't know anything.'

Jo knows that feeling only too well, lingering at Laurie's elbow while someone 'important' talks right through him.

'But Laurie wasn't like that. He didn't patronise me or pretend the film was good. I'd heard of him, obviously. Went for dinner. I wondered . . . I was a bit wary. Laurie made me feel, uh, interesting and important. Mr Lanford too, in a way, but I did wonder if they might be after something. Nobody spoke about it openly then, really, did they? Just rumours. This is before MeToo. I'd heard stories. Not about Laurie, other important men. Slippery hands. Anyway, Laurie said if I needed help with anything to give him a call.'

It sounds so plausible, so Laurie. Or it would, if Jo hadn't read Laurie's startling, contradictory account.

'He paid your rent.' Theo's face falls. 'Laurie was a charitable guy but he liked a return on any investment.'

'Things weren't great at home. I asked him to be my reference for a landlord. He offered the deposit. I didn't ask.'

'Out of the goodness of his heart?'

Theo looks surprised. 'You were married a long time. He was generous, you must know that.'

The little fuck. How dare he. 'Sure. You know him so well, I get it. Am I Elaine Paige or Barbara Dickson?' Ripples of confusion across Theo's face. 'Oh, stop it, you know who they are, you're not seventeen. So, a sweet, platonic bromance. Fine. Sounds delightful. He pays your deposit, oops, and not forgetting your rent, and all you have to do is smile sweetly.'

'He only paid the first month.' Theo's chin dips to his chest and he lightly raps his front teeth with his index finger. Jo imagines him as a younger man. He can see, almost, why Laurie was suckered; he hated to see anyone obviously hurting, unless it was distress he'd intended himself. 'By then, Mr Lanford had ... I got to know him quite well. We would meet sometimes. He paid the rest, something to do with Valenti funding, he said. Investing in me. Laurie did warn me, he said the last thing I needed was to be in debt to Mr Lanford, but I'd already said yes.'

Jo doesn't know what to think. Laurie's notes didn't mention this arrangement. Laurie certainly never held back about Ned. Maybe he hadn't known about it. The threads of Jo's certainty are coming loose, but he owes Theo the opportunity to dig his grave faster and deeper. 'So if you weren't shagging, what were you doing?'

'Laurie would take me out. Cinema. Theatre. Or just dinner, if I was feeling down.'

'And he'd come over, right?' Jo can see the little studio now, replaying Laurie's description over and over. He wrote about it with such reluctant affection, as you might gush about a childhood home you didn't actually miss. He imagines them, writhing in that fleapit, having deep conversations, drinking tea from chipped mugs, Theo performing this same little-boy-lost act.

'Not really. Two or three times.'

'What about your magic golden bike? Assuming there is only one. Maybe you've a few dotted around for some other chump.'

Theo looks hurt. 'I showed him it once, yes. He took me home in a cab. Stayed with me a bit, made me tea, ordered a pizza. That's all.'

Jo is shaken by this version of events. He's always believed in the printed page, that written words mean something. Right from his stacks of *The Face* when he was a teenager, up to the inscription on Laurie's memorial plaque. Words are godly. 'You're saying nothing ever happened?'

Theo seems to get smaller and smaller in the chair, like his side of the table is drifting into outer space. 'No, but ...'

Ah, here we go, thinks Jo, now we get to it. 'You don't have to draw me a diagram, I know what goes where. Just yes or no.'

'You sound like him, a bit. I've realised that the more I know you. You say the same things. I had a bit of a crush, if I think about it. But I never did anything about it. It was too late anyway.'

'Too late?'

What can only be described as utter devastation tears across Theo's face. 'Mr Lanford.'

Jo's skin begins to crawl, knowing that at least some of what Laurie wrote is about to fall into place. 'Ned.'

Theo stops tapping on his teeth and lights a cigarette, his hands shaking. 'He said he'd look after me. Could help me get the Valenti.'

Jo feels saliva rushing into his mouth, vomit's five-second warning. That fucking scholarship has brought nothing but trouble. 'What happened?'

Theo flinches as if reliving it. 'What do you think? I'm not the only one with a horror story about Ned Lanford.'

Despite everything, the lies, the deceit and the sleaze, Jo wants to grab Theo's hand, tell him he understands. Jo knows he's lucky not to have met Ned Lanford first, how different everything could've been. So many women he knows, and other gay men, have a man like that lurking in the far reaches of their timeline. 'Tell me.'

'I think he put something in my drink, or slipped it into my food. The first time anyway. After that it was persuasion. Not so gentle either. He filmed me a few times. To this day I don't know where the videos went. He said I owed him, he'd done so much for me. My head was gone. I told myself this was how it worked.'

Everyone has stories. Jo's met a few colourful characters in his time, men and women, who scatter innuendo through conversations like landmines in the hope of scoring a random hit. 'Theo, that isn't how it works. He took advantage.'

'I know. Dangled promises. Tossed me aside. I lost myself, had to disappear. He found out where my mum lived. Eventually he sent a letter saying I'd been unsuccessful for the Valenti. I'll never forget it – "we'll keep your name on file", it said.'

In a flash of selfishness, Jo considers whether that rejection was on Valenti-headed notepaper and actionable in court. 'But you met Ned here. You never said a word! He didn't even know you!' He remembers Ned barely blinking on hearing the name Teddy when he called round to see him. Out of sight, out of mind.

Something in Theo changes, like he's pulled himself out of that bad memory, reliving it has made him stronger. 'Too many feelings, I still don't really understand them. I've been talking to other Valenti guys. He might not remember us, but we remember him. There's a lot of dirt on Ned Lanford.'

Jo knows what's coming next. The wind has long changed in the entertainment industry, and it's only a matter of time until the sharp bristles of this broom reach its darkest corners, no matter how much filth like Ned clings to the walls. Jo has to ask, even though he already knows the spoilers. 'And Laurie?'

Theo shakes his head, even manages a smile, remembering him, maybe. 'No, nothing like that. Anyway, I don't know what

Mr Lanford said to him, but he told me I was coming between Laurie and his husband. Well, you. He said I should cut all ties. I'll never forget his face. Laurie said he was sorry he let me down. I didn't see him for a long time.'

Jo tries to piece everything together from what he's read, the things that check out, and Theo's contradictions. 'I know you came here just before he died. That wasn't the first time you'd been in my house, was it?'

Theo shakes his head. 'He showed me his awards after lunch one day.'

'You had sex here.'

'No.'

'Last time you came here, to see Laurie, you wanted money.'

Theo looks hurt. 'No! I know I've kept things from you, but I'm not who you think I am.'

'I don't know who the fuck you are.'

'I came by because I'd been thinking about him. I wanted to take Ned Lanford down.'

Jo is excited about this, in a way. No better accelerant to a cause than revenge. Is there part of Jo that's always wanted to be the one crocheting next to the guillotine when Ned's head rolls into the basket?

'I know Laurie recorded conversations,' says Theo. 'Listening to real people. For inspiration.'

'And for security,' says Jo. In Laurie's line of work, nobody's word was their bond and handshakes were buttons at the bottom of the charity tin.

'Sure. I wasn't sure if you knew or not. I wanted him to help me. I'd been working up the courage to come see him.'

Jo understands now why Theo never talks about his past. The scars are being torn open; the physical effort of telling the truth has left him slumped in the kitchen chair, broken, drained. Jo's reminded of something Laurie always used to say, usually on a first night, that you never appreciate how hard acting is until you see someone who absolutely stinks at it. And Theo doesn't stink at it, not right now.

'Being generous, I think Laurie was in denial about Mr Lanford. Everyone I spoke to told me the same thing. "He likes them young." "Watch your drink." It's treated like a joke. We've all said it, even I have.'

Jo quickly replays the last twenty years of his life. Ned's endless parade of young boyfriends who'd evaporate and never be spoken of again, some turning up years later in service jobs with washed-out smiles, all dreams totally extinguished. The parties, the cars with dark windows, the photo blackouts, the nightcaps with young hopefuls, the cursed Valenti scheme. Jo gave his name to a production line of Ned Lanford's next conquests, and Laurie bankrolled it. What a bucket of ice water to the face it is to confront your own stupidity among the bleeding obvious. For an awful moment Jo wonders if Laurie was fully complicit. Did it make a difference? He enabled it. Jo needs to corroborate that last entry he read. 'So you didn't ask for money?'

'No! Just his recordings, his cooperation. I said I'd keep him out of it. I gave him a couple of weeks to think about it. I kept messaging him, to remind him.' Out of nowhere, Theo breaks down in tears, rivers of pent-up shame, anger and horror flooding from his eyes, but it's hard to feel sorry for Laurie's secret lover and his dead cheating husband right now.

'So how did we get here? Why did you take me to see your brother's bike? Were you testing me, to see if he'd mentioned it?'

Theo doesn't seem to know the answer at first. It finds him, eventually. 'Talking about the choir reminded me, I suppose. I wanted to show you. I want to share everything with you.'

Jo bites his tongue. Oh, he showed him all right, showed him exactly who he was. 'What are you doing on my writing course? What do you want?'

Theo shakes his head emphatically. 'I wanted to talk to you at the funeral. I couldn't think of anything to say. I didn't dare come near.'

'And the counselling group, with Kris. You weren't there for your brother, were you? You're grieving for my husband. Bit over the top, for someone you haven't seen in years? Just an old friend?'

Theo starts to tap his teeth again. 'Laurie was the first person to treat me like a human being and not expect anything. I wanted to be friends again, I was scared to show it. I was angry as well, though. Confused. I think he was frightened I was gonna cause trouble.'

'None of that explains why you're studying the same creative writing course. What's your game? How are you even paying for it?'

'Laurie's agent set it up. I've got savings. That's it. It is, honestly, a coincidence. I felt bad about Laurie. The last time I saw him wasn't particularly friendly. I was cut up about it, I had a rough few months. So when we met, it felt like a sign. I could make it up to him maybe. Check in on you. I know how he felt about you. And now, it's something else. It's you and me. I swear to God I'm telling the truth. I loved Laurie, yes, but like an uncle or something.'

Jo stares into the dregs of his freezing cold coffee. He can't hold it in any longer. As wholesome as this sounds, there are dark visions, so expertly scripted by his husband. He pictures them laughing at him while they gazed at a Brighton sunset. Making pacts that things would be different one day, once Laurie left Jo behind. The thought curdles his goodwill.

'How can I believe you? You lied to me. You said you didn't know Laurie.'

'I never actually said that.'

The attempt to smooth out the lie enrages Jo. Time to hit him with the evidence. 'Did you know Laurie kept a diary? He said he fucked you, and you liked it. Pages of confessions, everywhere. I don't think I've even scratched the surface.'

Theo rears back at this switch from spark to flame. But he's not shocked. The fog, Jo's rage, begins to clear. Instantly, Theo no longer appears the amiable, paranoid loser in a permanent battle with the world; he's a calculating supervillain.

'Oh God. You knew about them, you just didn't realise I did. You wanted to get into his diaries, through my pants. Desperate to see what kind of write-up you got? Oh, from the few bits I've read you get a glowing review. Five out of five for every fuck. I'd have you at a four, but Laurie was generous, like you said.'

This venom has simmered a long while in Jo's belly; it's both relief and agony to spew it into the open, so he doesn't stop.

'All that time making your polite enquiries about my life, you already knew every detail. Well, you wanted to see if your version and mine matched up. If *I* matched up.' Jo screws up his face in mockery. '*What was he really like? Was he a good man? Ooh, he must've been this, I imagine he was that.* Pathetic.'

Theo's long sigh betrays an impatience. 'I was asking what he was like with you, what you thought of him. I never said I didn't know him. I didn't know him, not really, not the way you did. You said so yourself, the other night.'

'Oh, so you're getting off on a technicality. Hiding is lying.'

'No.'

'What's the endgame, Theo? You've tried Ned and Laurie, you want me to get you on the Valenti, I suppose? Too fucking late, you're too old, you're done, you're history, you swallowed for nothing.'

Theo is shaking when he stands up. 'I should go. You're angry, but I know you don't mean this. I don't know why you don't want to believe me. I knew he kept recordings, that's all. And, yeah, maybe I wanted to find out how much you knew about Ned. But I swear, I didn't have sex with Laurie. Anything he said, or wrote, about that was made up. He was a storyteller, like you said. Maybe it was wishful thinking, I don't know, but he kept things respectable with me. I didn't plan this. I wanted to get to know you, find a piece of my old friend. I never imagined we'd hit it off. You shared your life with a legend, I was nobody. You were just an idea in my head back then, all I knew about you was, uh . . .'

'What you learned when you and my husband were laughing about me in your crummy fuckpad?'

'No. Laurie always said nice things. Then, once I got to know you, the real you, I fell in love with you.'

Jo wants to spit at him. 'I'm sorry for what happened to you. I really am. You've been through a lot. I don't even understand my feelings for you right now. But I know I can never trust you.'

Theo shakes his head. He wants Jo to believe, his sad eyes are doing their best to break him. 'I'm guilty of lots of things. I hid the truth, but me and you were real, Jo, I promise. It is real. Believe what you want, but I know the truth and I'm not giving up on you. I'm going.'

Jo's mind races, on full alert, reminding him Theo is a confirmed liar, and yet his stupid heart, perhaps embarrassed by being thoroughly duped, wants so badly to believe that Theo's version is the truth. Regardless, the head is too angry, and overrules. 'Fine.'

He pushes past Theo into the hall, and opens the front door wide. The air rushes in, humid and oppressive, bringing fresh flickers of doubt. Who should Jo believe? A man he hardly knows, or the one he lay next to for two decades? As painful as the truth is, it's all there in black and white, blinking out from a screen, available whenever he likes. Laurie may never have told it to Jo's face, but he'd never lie to himself, when nobody was watching. What Laurie wrote has to be true, because somehow the chance it isn't is even more awful.

Jo can't help but breathe in the scent of Theo as he leaves. Laurie would've done exactly the same, thinks Jo. We are exactly the same. Were.

Infra Dig

Laurie

I've spent so many years in restaurants wondering if my next waiter might be Teddy. Ridiculous, really. Only the very best waiters – or the very worst – actually remain waiters for a long time. For everyone else, it's a stopgap. I'd resigned myself to never seeing him again, stopped getting excited whenever I felt a presence at my left during dinner. The further away in time Teddy became, the more closely I examined the dynamic. Like the line of scum round a bath, the feeling I'd done something grubby and noxious began to lay heavy on my chest. Then, barely two weeks ago, the day after we took down the Christmas tree, Jasper started barking and there was a knock at the garden door. A ghost. Teddy. Jasper jumped up at him excitedly.

'Hello, Laurie.' Voice deeper, but still that gentle musicality to it. 'Can I come in?'

Teddy hadn't aged, he'd evolved. Shiny, quilted jacket instead of his tatty denim. Scruffy brown boots where his regulation trainers would have been. A vague approximation of a beard, the kind men in their thirties feel obliged to grow to prove their days of wanking into socks and playing video games are over. His eyes, though. The same. Round and dark with flecks of hazel, daring me to say no.

I felt very small stepping aside to let him in. He was obviously eating well, looking after himself, even if some of those lines and grooves felt ahead of their time. Smoking regularly, I supposed. His features were beautiful before but now they made sense. Maybe I was lost in the memory of who he'd been, as if he had been locked away in a cupboard these last ten years, waiting to be used again like an old colander or stockpot. Yet he'd lived, seen things, maybe even loved again. What must he have thought of the cheap photocopy of myself that opened the door? Laughable, now, that I ever thought of myself as past it in my mid-thirties, watching my youth circle the plughole. If he'd grown into his face, I had burst out of mine, its features trying to escape to every corner, as if my nose was brandishing a knife.

I ushered an excited Jasper into the main part of the house while, behind me, Teddy headed to the office. Knew the way. I couldn't think of anything to say so I said his name. He flinched. He'd been to the café to check Jo was there, he said. The thought of Jo and Teddy being in the same room made me want to claw my own eyes out. The idea of them talking, even if only to order a latte, was disgusting to me. That must never happen. Never.

He read my mind. 'I didn't speak to him.' He ran his eyes over me. 'Do you still tape people?'

'How did you know about that?'

'You told me once. You tape Jo, use what he says when you're stuck. Do you? I don't mind. You can tape this one.' He tapped his pocket.

Ten years I'd imagined our reunion and never once had I predicted such a carpet of frost over it.

'Where have you been? I have thought of you. A lot.'

He nodded, pleased, but ignored the question. 'I cycled past a few times. Saw lights on. People coming and going. Not you. A girl. That your niece?' ·

'Sort of. She's my assistant now. Grown up. She'll be back soon.'

'I'm not staying.'

Maybe he was here to blackmail me. Did people do that in real life? Would he haunt the café and pedal by the house on his boneshaker until I capitulated and ... did what? He was yet to set out any demands. I was too afraid to ask, make it official, so I clung to small talk. 'Where are you living?'

'My mum's. She wishes I had a car, not a bike. For obvious reasons.'

I'd never returned to the gold-sprayed memorial. If I really wanted to see him again, that's where he'd be. What stopped me? It was his turf, I supposed; I wouldn't have any authority there, like I might in a restaurant, with him as my waiter. I felt nauseated at the thought of it. 'Are you working?'

'Yeah. Saving to go back to university.'

'Acting?'

Teddy smirked. 'Got my fingers burned there. Nah. I wanna study English or something. Be a writer, like you! Well, not like you, obviously.'

I couldn't help myself then. 'Teddy, I'm so sorry. I behaved badly.'

He laughed, but not the carefree chuckle I remembered, or even his nervous little laugh. It was bitter, knowing. 'No shit.'

I couldn't read him. What was he here for? Did he want me

to buy him a car? He sat in my orange chair, a bank manager's smile painted across his face.

'You still in touch with that piece of shit Ned Lanford? No need to lie, I know you are.'

'He told me he'd look after you.' I didn't sound convincing. How had I ever believed it myself?

'Look after me? After you chewed me up and spat me out, you mean? Passed me along like a soggy joint? Come on.'

I didn't say anything, just let the accusation – and the truth of it – settle.

'You know Ned's conquests, right? The little men dangling off him. First nights, after-shows, creepy Christmases in St Lucia. You ever know their names?'

Creepy Christmases? 'Yes, if we were introduced.'

'Do you remember them now?'

Everything I could say next felt like a wrong answer. I chose honesty. 'Maybe not, but there's a lot I don't remember.'

'That's why you record everything, right?' Teddy smiled. 'There's a lot I do remember. There's a word for what happened to me back then, you know,' he said, eyes trained on mine. 'Took me a long time to process, still working on it, really. Do you think you and Ned were the first to have a go? Plenty like you out there. Rich white guys with colonialism fetishes. Read too much literary fiction. Fantasising about aristocrats getting topped by their servants.'

His vocabulary had evolved too. As painful as the content was. If the past was another country, what was this? We had travelled galaxies. 'It wasn't like that for me. I cared for you. I was confused. Ned, he not quite threatened me, but ... I had to think of my marriage.'

'Fuck you. Don't make this about you. You left me feeling like I'd done something wrong. Like I was dirty.'

It was horrible to watch this stranger I'd once known so well, as out of place in this room as a skyscraper in a Turner landscape. This hulking fridge of a man in a Teddy costume, and a frayed, damaged one at that. 'I cared for you.'

'Yeah, you said.' Teddy sat back and surveyed me with a hateful curiosity, borne of years of brooding and replaying scenes over in his head. He'd practised this moment many times. 'Ned groomed me, Laurie, and you let him. You could say you did too.'

I felt bile rise to my throat. 'I don't think I'd call it that ...' I reached for my phone to start recording.

'Oh, go for it. I want you to listen back to this one, or I can send you my copy, I suppose.'

'Even if it's on tape, it doesn't make it true.' I was shaking, I desperately needed a drink. My throat was closing up, spots and stripes danced before my eyes, the warm-up act for a three-day migraine.

'Don't make it a lie either. You ever thought what it was like for me?'

Hearing your actions relayed to you from another perspective is sometimes amusing, when it's a drunk story, say, or being caught picking your nose at an awards ceremony. But the lens Teddy used to recount our history was terrifying. He'd been targeted after the choir show, he said, Ned Lanford and I both almost breaking our necks to get to him before the other could scoop him up. The offers of money, paying his rent, the assurance there were 'no strings', the repeated bait of interviews for the Valenti, exploiting him in a vulnerable moment after visiting his brother's memorial. There were Ned's photos and lewd messages, which, he said, made him feel uncomfortable, pressurising him into being overtly sexual. The repeated requests to reciprocate, he said, Ned never leaving him alone, desperate for something I had. There was the expectation Teddy would always be available to me, in that poky studio, and being shot down when talk of Jo ever came up. He said I was only caring when he complained, or looked like he might try to change the dynamic of the relationship, and he'd fallen for it every time. There were the broken promises, insistences not to listen to friends or ever talk to them about us. And then, he said, once I'd tired of my chew-toy, I tossed him over to Ned Lanford. He'd had a breakdown, lost his job, friends, everything. It was only then, as he teetered on the edge of oblivion, that his mother pulled herself out of the grief that had suffocated her for years and helped the one son who was still living.

When the full catalogue of our actions was laid before me, I couldn't fight it, I couldn't deny it. This was no great love, it was a fantasy. I was lost in a fevered infatuation, high off the buzz I used to get from making dreams come true, but actually thinking only of myself, and building a prison for Teddy. I had been searching for a reboot of my marriage, but I failed. Teddy was not Jo. It's like that first recast after the original run of a show; you long so hard for the original actors but you try to make the best of it. Maybe I enjoyed the gratification from having my cake and eating it, seeking someone more fragile than Jo, more impressionable, someone to make me feel important and needed, who couldn't survive without me. I could claim now it was a coincidence, that there were a million young, attractive, assertive men I could've had an affair with, but I'd chosen Teddy because at first he reminded me so much of my Jo. Targeted him, as he put it. I'd become everything I hated. I was Ned Lanford in more respectable packaging. What could I say?

'I'm sorry, Teddy. I didn't mean for any of this.' I couldn't shrug this off. I owed Teddy the knowledge that he was not imagining what had happened. 'I accept what you say. I feel terrible.'

'You accept it. Right.' I think he almost pitied me. There was no anger in his voice, his body was loose and open in the chair. 'This is the trouble with people like you. You think feeling guilty, or terrible, undoes the bad thing you did. But it doesn't. It eases your conscience, but it doesn't change anything for me.'

What did he want me to say? That I was a monster?

'I asked around. Nobody had a bad word to say about you. People genuinely like you. They trust you. Imagine how special I feel, that you picked my life to ruin and not anybody else's? Like a proper winner.'

This was the wrong moment to feel proud that my reputation was, more or less, intact, but I did. I'd tried to be a good guy, always. That's what they all say, isn't it, on the way to the chopping block? I'd lost my head over Teddy and now I would be relieved of it one last time, for good.

'Can I explain? I didn't mean to do the things you say I've done—'

'That you *have* done.'

'Yes, that I have done. All of it was a mistake, from the very beginning. I've been a mess these last few years. Me and Jo, when you've been together as long as we have. There are peaks and troughs.'

'Am I supposed to feel sorry for you?'

'No, not at all. I just want you to know that what I did was about me, not you. I didn't set out to hurt you, I was only thinking of myself. I know nothing I can do can change what happened. I'm sorry.' I've never wanted someone to believe an apology so much in my life.

'I've had a lot of time to think about how to fix this, move on, get it out of my head. I'm not here for an apology.'

'Do you want some money, is that it? Or maybe I can help with your writing career. I know a woman who—'

He held up his hand. The room was silent a while. Teddy drummed his fingers on his thighs. Through a tear in his jeans I saw a small patch of what looked like eczema.

Finally he spoke. 'You have an opportunity, you know, to do something good.'

Money, then. How much was my problem worth? Did I really want him to go away? What if he wanted more? I'd taken everything from him, maybe he'd try to do the same to me? He might tell Jo. The way things were, did that even matter?

He read my mind. 'I'm not interested in hurting you personally,' he said, *tap-tap-tapping* on his thigh again like the rhythm was keeping him calm. 'I want you to help me. Expose Ned. You could get the narrative out there first, plant a seed. Once people start talking, it's over for him. People will believe you.'

People had been 'talking' for years, albeit in hushed tones and dark corners, yet Ned's ascent had never stalled. 'Or they'll hang me too. I've worked with him for over twenty years.'

'You're the only one big enough to discredit him. Ned's done it plenty of times. His little rumour mill. You know how it goes. Oh, so-and-so is difficult backstage. Drug problems. Mental health issues. And that's that, they're fired out of a side door, career over, smeared for ever. Remember Elliott Bannerman?'

Suppressed suspicions flashed up in grisly detail. 'He did have a drug problem.'

'Eventually, yeah. Self-fulfilling prophecy once that octopus has finished with you. Trust me.'

'You have to be careful,' I said, stomach roiling. Who frightened me more? Ned or Teddy? 'Ned has a lot of influence.'

Teddy shook his head in disappointment but I could tell he wasn't surprised. 'That's a no then? Not even one little recording? Help me start a whisper?'

Whether I helped or not was irrelevant. It was highly likely Ned already knew about this revolt and was making manoeuvres to crush it.

'He'll probably fuck you over soon, you know that, right?'

'I'm sorry.' Ruinous for me as this was, I couldn't bear to close the door on Teddy, not after a decade of wanting to make amends. 'I will think about it, though. Are you going to tell my husband?'

'I liked the coffee in Jo's place. I'll definitely pop in from time to time.'

I reached for my phone and asked for his bank details, made some transfers.

Teddy rose and made his way to the door. 'I'm not coming back here. Don't worry. I know you'll think about today until you die. But that's not enough. We're not quite done.'

Our conversation lasted almost as long as it had taken me to cut him off, that day in his little studio, as he sat shaking and tearful. I'd thrown him to the wolves, and deserved a much stronger punishment. I considered getting on my knees. Then I said it. 'I did love you, Teddy.'

He stepped into the dark. I heard the scrape of his boots on the paving as he whipped round to look at me one last time. He smiled. Shook his head. 'You know the sad thing is, I actually believe you. You'll hear from me again. I'm not giving up.'

'I know.'

I went to sit in the chair, still warm from his body, noticing he'd left his cigarettes behind. How pathetic I must've looked from this angle. What a fucking idiot, considering any of this remotely romantic. And what a coward, too, terrified it would all come crashing down. Yet part of me hoped it happened sooner rather than later. Maybe I owed him my downfall.

*

That evening, I watched Jo slicing olives, before calmly wrapping cling film round the slimy tub and placing it back into the fridge. Next, cucumber. Slowly, to a set rhythm, he cut even slices. Methodical, beautiful boy. I used to love watching him, but something about this scene rattled me.

'Use the chopper thing. The guillotine.'

'Mandoline,' he corrected. 'I prefer this way.'

The sound of the knife hitting the chopping board was pinching my throat. Executioner's sword thwacking the block. 'But it takes much longer.'

He stopped and gathered the sopping green discs into a pile before slicing the lot in half in one smooth sweep. 'I use all that labour-saving bollocks at the café. I like to take my time when I have it. You know me, staunchly analogue.'

My lips started to go numb. 'How was work today?' I said, convinced my voice dripped with insincerity and guilt.

He looked at me as he wiped the knife with kitchen roll. 'Same as ever. Zosia burned three croissants.'

He reached for a punnet of tomatoes to start the wearisome routine all over again.

I left the room, fists clenched.

Twenty-one
August

Jo

It feels like the right thing to do, to sit in the half-light of the office and wait for Rosy to arrive. There's a bit of drama to it. Then he remembers Rosy is not a character in a soap and if she walks in to find him waiting in Laurie's chair with curtains drawn and lamp off, she might think it's a ghostly visitation, and scream the place down. So when she does turn up, late, he's making coffee. He watches with affection as the smell hits her and she inhales exaggeratedly. He wants to make a joke about the Bisto Kids, but she won't get the reference and he'd rather look stupid than out of touch.

'Mum got me this amazing thing that squirts water up your nose and cleans the gunk out of your sinuses.' Her bag thuds on the table, her denim jacket is draped over a chair and, as it always does, immediately slips to the floor. 'I can smell everything now. Paint drying on the Eiffel Tower. Doughnuts frying in New York. I feel like a superhero.'

He doesn't want to have this conversation. But he has to.

'You never asked me what happened between me and Theo.'

She stays with her back to him as she hunts in the fridge for a snack, but she definitely tenses up. 'It's none of my business, Uncle Jojo.'

'Have you read Laurie's diaries?'

It sounds like an accusation – maybe it is – and Rosy's face drops, as if caught with her hand in a charity collection jar.

'You're not in trouble. I'm not mad. I just want to know. I need to talk to somebody about them. I can't keep it in.' He rehearsed that. Funny how assuring someone they're not in trouble sounds exactly the opposite. Laurie would say it to Rosy when she was smaller, when she broke something, or lost a toy, or money. When you've known someone all their lives, you never stop treating them like the child they were.

Rosy nods slowly. 'A bit. I wouldn't say ... I don't think they're diaries. I'm not sure he wrote them while he was living it. Do you know what I mean?'

'A memoir, then?'

Rosy nods again and sits down. Jo places coffee in front of her. Every movement feels like a cliffhanger. 'He made notes, all the time, about everything. Voice notes in his phone as well. So he could remember stuff. I told you.'

The thought of Laurie's voice saying those words, those poisonous outbursts about him and declarations of love for the past version of Theo – disgusting, heartbreaking. He's almost glad he's only read them to himself. 'You did tell me.' But you also told me you didn't know anything about the memoir, he thinks. 'Have you listened to them?'

She claims not to know where they are. It's like a cross-examination.

'I transcribed a few bits, but I can't find them now. There are so many drives and folders and file sharing systems and the cloud and Dropbox or whatever; he wasn't very organised. Didn't like me routing through, in case I made it complicated.'

'I bet. When did you read them?'

'Ned Lanford asked me to dig out something. Something to do with a show. Not long ago. I found something then. How did you find them?'

'I was doing my summer assignment.' He doesn't want her to think he's been brooding over this, waiting for her to tell him. *A pivotal moment in one thousand words.* Ha. Doesn't get much more pivotal than this, does it?' Jo sits opposite her. In this kitchen he's watched her eat cereal, kick her shoes against the chair, and grow into this woman capable of keeping secrets. He should've known she'd be loyal to Laurie; death has only vulcanised their already impenetrable bond. 'What did you think of it? What you read?'

Rosy shrugged. 'I honestly didn't read much, it felt wrong.'

A sharp pang of guilt tightens Jo's stomach. It does feel wrong, all of it. He hates that her view of Laurie, of their perfect life, has been tarnished. 'Did it shock you?'

'I don't know.'

Jo remembers Theo's pleading, his face going through four seasons as he denied the affair. 'Did you guess it was Theo?'

Rosy looks like she's concentrating really hard on a crossword. Unreadable. 'What do you mean?'

Jo doesn't want to take a hammer to any more of Rosy's memories about her beloved Uncle Lulu. But he has to. 'It's easier if I show you everything I've seen.' Cradling cups of now-lukewarm coffee, they head to Laurie's office, and print what they can find – some of it Jo knows he's read but can't locate now, so labyrinthine are the branches of Laurie's system. Jo sits in the orange chair while Rosy reads at Laurie's desk. They don't speak. He gets up every now and again to make more coffee, heats up soup at lunchtime, and he lays it next to her as she reads, even though she won't touch a drop.

When she's finished, she makes a fuss of neatening the pages, even though her mind is no doubt scattered like space junk. 'I don't know what to say. What are you gonna do?'

Jo begins to tremble. Trying to suppress the anger and sense of betrayal is taking everything he's got. 'I'll send it to Tracey, say we found the memoir. Then everyone can see for themselves. The real Laurie. Unfiltered.'

Rosy leaps out of her chair. 'You can't! You're joking! It makes him look really bad!'

Maybe he was really bad, maybe everyone should know, and Jo can absolve himself, finally break away, crawl out of the shadows. 'So what?'

'Because ... because ...' Rosy's eyes have gone wider than Bambi's. 'Because it doesn't match up. Not all of it. Maybe it's not real.'

Jo didn't expect this. What does she know? 'Theo confirmed some of it did actually happen. How they met, that golden fucking bike. All that.' Jo thinks back to Laurie's cheerful 'Honey, I'm home's – now hollow echoes, meaningless.

'Maybe someone broke into the computer.'

'Rosy, are you suggesting a burglar tiptoed in there and wrote it, pretending to be Laurie?'

Rosy gulps, as if trying to get a handle on her breathing. 'No. Remotely, I mean. Other people can get in there. The cloud thing. Laurie's shared drives with production managers and editors and all sorts of people, for years and years.' She's breathing heavily, sweat's forming on her brow. She taps on the keyboard, swishes the mouse around its mat. Jo is struck by how dull it is to watch someone else work a computer. 'Or, how about ... maybe it's a novel or something? Autofiction, right? Like when you've got a reality show but the producers are making them say shit for the cameras.'

Even if Laurie planned to change the names, he could never have released this, the avatars are so obvious; it would have caused a sensation, destroyed his career, friendships, marriage.

'We're clutching at straws here, Rosy.' Memories come flooding back. All those times, with a cut knee or a splinter in her finger, running first to Laurie, sometimes straight past Jo. It is her natural instinct to protect her beloved uncle's reputation.

Rosy looks utterly defeated. 'You asked if anything shocked me.'

'Yeah?'

'What about the things he said about you, that nasty part?'

He wasn't expecting her to mention that. Jo shivers, remembering reading it for the first time, caught out. '"Sugar-free, low-fat and basic", you mean?'

'Yeah. He'd never talk about you like that. That's why I didn't tell you about it. He told me every day how happy you were! Weren't you?'

This is the hardest thing. If asked, Jo would go on record to say that, on the whole, they were happy, despite the ups, downs and long periods of plateauing.

'And ... and! No way would he cheat on you, Jojo, not like this. Not with this ... Teddy guy. And definitely not with Holden. I mean, Holden? No way. No offence, but he hated that prick.'

This is the one part that makes the least sense. This is the one glimmer of hope that Theo is telling the truth and that

Rosy is right. The Holden story doesn't hold up. That night played out very, very differently, and it couldn't possibly have happened when Laurie claimed. Had Laurie got mixed up, screwed Holden some other night, or was it not true at all? A weird exposé masquerading as total fiction? Jo stops himself. He doesn't want to remember that night, not now. He knows the truth. So maybe someone else did have a hand in this.

Rosy finally spoons soup into her mouth and makes a face. 'Is it gazpacho? Oh. Have you shown it to Mum?'

'No.' Viv could easily confirm it was true. Maybe that's what he's so afraid of. Jo can't decide which is worse, that Laurie lived a double life, really did think those terrible things, suffered that loss, hated him – or that it's all lies, and he's not only lost his husband but sent Theo away for ever, for nothing.

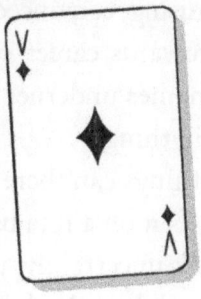

Twenty-two

August

Vivienne

Viv glances up at the theatre's marquee, decades old but still
bright enough to be seen from outer space.

LAURIE BLOUNT'S

THE CRUELTY OF DAYLIGHT

RETURNS TO THE WEST END

Returns. Not exactly the prodigal play. The last version closed
three years ago. Another revival, perhaps the most bankable of
them all. People really do love this show. Laurie downplayed it,
said he 'shat it out over three weeks on my Kennington rooftop',

but Viv saw how many hours he spent at his desk, or at a free table in the Sonata, agonising, convinced every word he sweated over was edging him towards career oblivion. Viv recognises only one of the actors' names underneath, but Tracey's assured her they are 'the next big thing'.

'How many next big things can there be at one time?' says Jo, as they arrive together. 'Is it on a rota basis?'

Viv watches him blink uncertainly, taking in the lights and posters and noise. Jo hasn't been back amid the schmoozy, aggrandising argot of the theatrical world for long, so hasn't yet relearned to tune out the bullshit.

Tracey waves at them, wedding ring now permanently removed. Ned Lanford, scowling at his phone in a corner in an unforgivable tux, switches immediately to a mile-wide grin when he spots them and bounds over. Jo recoils from Ned more forcefully than he has before. Putting on a show, maybe? If he hasn't already, Ned will surely have another crack at Jo, assuming what Rosy told her is true, and Theo really has been eliminated.

'How scrumptious you all look. What a trio. No Byron?'

'I'm sure he's on his way,' says Viv, embarrassed on Byron's behalf, because he certainly won't be.

Viv entertains the fantasy of slipping off to the theatre bar until it's all over. Despite the show's plaudits, Laurie's talent for characterisation was in its infancy when he wrote *The Cruelty of Daylight*, so, for her, being in the audience is like watching five Lauries spar with one another – lovely yet devastating. Viv notes the actors are definitely wearing less in this production; Laurie was never keen on nudity on stage.

'If the punters have read the reviews and know what's on the way, they won't relax in their seats until they've seen the cocks and tits.'

Thankfully, after the show, Ned passes on dinner, claiming he has a hot date.

'How old is he?' asks Jo, bitterly, which makes Viv gasp. He's said the quiet part out loud, as Rosy would say. Rosy stares.

Ned, accustomed to getting away with murder for years, Viv assumes, shows no sign of discomfort. 'Twenty-four,' says Ned.

'That's the same age as me,' says Rosy flatly, staring down at her sequin-covered Doc Martens, specially customised for this evening. It's like the oxygen is sucked out of the room.

'We're friends! Someone I'm helping out.' Ned's perfect, paid-for teeth gleam like the windows on a skyscraper. 'By the way, meant to ask, are you all on the same phone numbers? Jo? Vivienne?'

'Yeah, why?'

'I got a message before. Don't recognise the ... uh ...' Ned peers into Viv's soul; she sees traces of doubt in his eyes. Fear, even. Bad day at the stock exchange maybe? Ned's smirk doesn't reach his eyes; he's been buried in that phone all night. 'Just trying to work out who it was. Anyway, duty, and booty, calls.' There's a round of air-kissing, a salacious wink, and off he darts.

'I hope he's found dead,' says Rosy. 'In a toilet.'

Viv looks at her daughter with horrified curiosity. 'Laurie used to say that. About him.' It's like the past has reached out and poked her in the eye.

The restaurant is uncomfortable and ugly in a way that feels very noughties but not remotely current. Too much concrete; the seats are reformed breeze blocks.

Byron arrives after they've already ordered, with no explanation other than, 'Arriving on time is non-U; it wouldn't have done for a Mitford.'

Viv watches Byron pick his nose, roll his findings between

his fingers like he's preparing a taco, and flick the tiny missile across the room. There's a whole tiresome performance while he's furnished with a menu, a young waitress hovering while he decides. Every move so mannered as if cameras were upon him. Laurie would have destroyed him for this. Once done, Byron looks round the table exaggeratedly. 'Where's your young man?'

Jo tries to shrug but it doesn't really work sitting down. 'We're not together.'

Viv is utterly ashamed by how relieved she feels. Although, this might make her life harder, once she tells Jo what she's done.

'Oh.' Byron peers at Jo over his glasses. 'Too soon after our Laurie, maybe? What has it been? A year?'

'Nineteen months.' Viv reaches for her wine glass and takes a huge gulp. She's only just stopped counting in weeks. She knows she makes them uncomfortable, that they think she's being hysterical, glaring at her through a misogynistic filter. She doesn't care.

Byron slides his hand to the left and wraps his fingers around her hand. 'Oh, Grainger.' His hands are clammy, she is desperate to remove hers. Jo and Rosy exchange a look. 'Well, Jo, I'm sorry it didn't work out. Shame. I suppose that's what happens when reality ruins a perfectly good fantasy. Letting daylight in on magic ... kills it every time. Not every love can bloom like magnolia under a deep blue sky, right?'

There's something. It clearly unsettles Jo. Viv too. She can't put her finger on it. Something about Byron's swagger, arriving so late, swerving the performance altogether. So disrespectful to Laurie's memory. Being so blasé, pretending he can't remember how long ago Laurie died. And this flowery talk, like he's some romantic soothsayer. This is an act without an audience. Viv notices Rosy looks queasy, and as if marionettes suddenly being operated, both she and Jo rise, shakily, at the same time, saying they're off to the bathroom. Rosy dashes away, covering her mouth. Weird.

Jo follows.

'I should check on Rosy,' says Viv.

Byron's head is focused on his screen. 'Sure.'

Viv tosses her napkin at him, the miserable little shit, and leaves the table. Now's her chance. Time to say what she needs to say, tell Jo what she's done.

Twenty-three
August

Jo

Rosy is too fast for Jo, ducking into the toilet before he has a chance to ask her why she nudged him so hard before racing off. Still, while he's here, he might as well go too. Middle age has taught him never to miss an opportunity to get one step ahead of his bladder. On emerging, he finds Viv perched on a breeze block embellished with hand-knitted hearts, fiddling nervously with the clasp of her handbag.

'I took the box. Laurie's box. The ashes.'

'What?' Is that why she's so jealously guarding her handbag? Did she bring Laurie to dinner and a show? 'Viv. Why?'

She looks so tortured and miserable. She's only been operating at half-speed since Laurie died; it's like he took some of her with him.

'I couldn't sleep thinking of him shoved at the bottom of

the wardrobe like an old pair of Reeboks.' Her voice trembles. 'He deserves to be pride of place. Can't you look him in the eye?'

What is she on about? 'You could've talked to me about this. I know you're ...' How can he say, delicately, that knowing how long Laurie has been dead to the exact day, as he knows she does, is perhaps a sign things are not going well? 'I know you're working your way through it, but we could've discussed the ashes together.'

'Working my way through it.' Viv's mask slips, repressed emotions hurtle to the surface. 'I don't want to intrude, you've moved on. *Worked through it*, as you say.'

Intruding has never bothered her in all the decades he's known her. She has walked in on him on the toilet over ten times. 'Viv. It isn't about moving on. It's moving forward.'

'I know the terminology. And I know how it feels. They're not the same thing.'

'You're welcome at the house any time you like.'

'Any time I like.' Her bottom lip is protruding. Laurie always fell for this trick. 'An open house isn't the same as an invitation.'

She's right. They've tried being around each other, just the two of them, but there's a space. Always. Literally. They leave one naturally, between them, walking down the street, or circling each other in the kitchen. A gap where Laurie should be.

Viv finally puts her handbag to one side. 'You say I can't move on. Sorry, forward. But what about you? You've always been a passenger. Everything you are is what Laurie made you.'

This is brutal. How long has this resentment lain dormant? More scarily, why does it sound like she's right? 'I make my own money.'

'I'm not talking about money. You go through life like it's just happening to you, and you have no control over it. Would you ever have got off your arse and opened the café if it wasn't for Laurie?'

'I'm doing my own thing. My studies.'

'Tracey sorted that for you! Laurie again! You say you're moving forward but you're not. You've moved sideways, playing at being Laurie. It's like Byron said, this was never your dream. You never wanted to be a writer.'

Ah, Byron, dripping poison in her ear. Jo drifts back to warm summers long gone. Laurie running his tongue up Jo's torso, asking his truest desires, telling him to forget the café idea, that he tasted better than any doughnut, that his sweat had the definite tang of bestselling author, that they should make it happen. Was that actually how it went, or is he an unreliable witness? Jo's the only one left. If he wants it to be true, it can be true.

'There's me thinking Theo was a cheap replacement, how wrong was I?' drawls Viv, staring through time. There's a point in most discussions where everything could explode if we let it. We should walk away from those moments more, but Viv has no intention of doing so now. 'You're actually replacing Laurie with yourself. I never used to see you at launches. Always "too tired", spoiling it for Laurie. He'd spend the night wondering if you were okay. Worrying you were lonely . . . or not so lonely.'

'I've no idea what you're talking about.' But he does. And she knows he does.

'Now you're out schmoozing and smarming at first nights, as if it was anything to do with you. I watched Laurie write *Cruelty* in every single lunch break. Greasy thumbprints, balsamic vinegar stains on the pages. Graft. That's my voice you hear in Debbie. And a bit of Miss Galloway too.' The best characters in the play. He should've realised. Laurie stole every bit of dialogue he ever wrote. 'That's what's been getting on my tits, and I couldn't work it out. You think you *are* Laurie. You're even obsessing over young hot . . . what is Theo? A writer? A waiter?

At least Laurie didn't fuck his silly crushes.'

Didn't he? Would Viv lie for Laurie even now? 'Viv, I know you're upset.'

'Twenty years with Laurie and you're onto the next within a year? Laurie said you could be cold. Did he really mean nothing to you?'

Jo can imagine their hushed, disapproving whispers – he witnessed Laurie and Viv slate plenty of others, no reason for him to be immune. He wants to tell her to fuck off, but in a way he understands, because he's wondered too, whether everything happened too soon. There's no rulebook, only a vague guardrail. Queen Victoria sat glum, in full mourning regalia, for over forty years, but if Theo's bedroom eyes had drunk her in across a crowded room, she might have shrugged off the widow's weeds sooner.

'Vivi ... Viv. I could've waited two months, two years, two decades. It will still feel as awful as it did the night the coppers knocked at the door and told me he was dead. I won't ever get over it. I won't ever move on. I don't want to, not really. But I have to live my life.'

'Do you?' Maybe she'd be happier if Jo died too, or let himself go to ruin.

'Laurie is dead, but if he were alive, he'd be living life to the full. I owe him, we all owe him, actually, to live our best lives, don't we? We have this opportunity, he doesn't. We can't grieve for ever. What's the point?'

She comes closer, as if to intimidate but also get a better look. 'You didn't actually wait for him to die before you, er, lived your best life, though, did you? You and Holden, for instance. Byron's birthday. Another night ruined by one of your ridiculous strops. Laurie never got over finding you two at it, you know. Poor Sian, out for the count upstairs. He tried to convince himself he was hallucinating, that he was too pissed.' There's glee when she spots the shock in Jo's eyes. That's why she moved closer, for the sport, to see his reaction better. 'Ah, you didn't know I knew. See? Told me everything. That's how I know you've never, ever thought of being a writer until he died and cleared a space for you.'

He has an urge to push her, but knows there's no coming back from that. 'I didn't know he'd seen us.' Jo's stomach thrashes. The disgust he felt then, that night, the second it was over, returns tenfold. Laurie had caught them. He knew all along, Viv too, and they never said a word! Just watched him all these years, knowing what he did. The guilt, the shame. Jo has carried this anvil on his shoulders for years. He feels exposed, his skin suddenly transparent, his insides rotten, trying to escape his body. 'We were drunk. Laurie and I were going through a ... I don't know what to call it. Not a rough patch.' A period of ignoring one another, being sharper than usual over the phone. Late nights out for Laurie, too much wine with dinner for Jo. One night, a movie night, Laurie went to Byron's birthday, slamming the door behind him. Sian, Holden and Jo drank the house dry. Drifting downstairs in the early hours for paracetamol, Jo caught Holden in Laurie's office, snooping. Holden did his usual trick, laying into Laurie, doing bad impressions of him while he minced round the office, running his finger over everything, searching for dust like a demented mother-in-law from an old sitcom. A cheap dig about Laurie's bank balance, turning quickly from a stupid row into something even stupider. There's a line with bad tempers, changes in air pressure from the threat of violence that both parties know isn't meant with true hatred, that will never be fatal. Just a cloud of anger. Jo thought it only happened in films. He'd fucked Holden hundreds of times when they were together – this miserable rematch didn't make sense then, but now, Jo understands. He was lost, he couldn't tap into Laurie's feelings, too distant. Jo was frightened it was ebbing away.

But he could read Holden like a book, knew how to push his buttons. It was actually what he liked about Laurie, the unpredictability. Maybe Jo got too staid, regressed too far into Laurie's shadow, wanted to wrest back some control. So he fucked Holden, hard and angrily, with zero passion or affection, on Laurie's desk. A power trip.

The guilt the next day was a biblical cloud that wouldn't shift. Laurie was quiet, Jo assumed sulking after having to go to Byron's party alone, so Jo made a great show of being happy about the café after all, and cornered Holden in the guest bathroom that morning and told him they should never speak of this again.

'But ... what about us?' Holden said, reaching out to touch in between Jo's legs.

Jo was almost disgusted to see a spark in Holden's eyes. 'I am not this person. I don't do this. I love Laurie. I don't love you. It's friends or nothing.'

Holden took the friends option, as Jo knew he would – he was working up to asking for a loan for a new kitchen extension.

Jo shakes the memory away. He's had to make peace with his shame, but it doesn't let Laurie off the hook. 'How about the affair Laurie was having for years? At least one. You knew about that, right? He told you everything. No?'

Viv immediately reddens. 'No.'

'Oh, maybe not the specifics, but you must've had an inkling. The waiters, the theatre kids? The same ones coming to shake my hand at his ridiculous funeral tea while you stood watching.' Jo wipes spit from the corner of his mouth. 'You two and your private jokes, right to the end.'

'It wasn't like that. Laurie wasn't like that. He wouldn't cheat. He never laughed at you.' She looks so lost it's impossible not to believe her. That truth appears to hurt her more, that Laurie really did have secrets.

'It's all in black and white, Viv, he wrote about it. The ins and the outs. I've read it.'

'I don't believe it. Laurie wouldn't do that, you've made a mistake. Laurie didn't have time to write a diary, are you mad? We were too busy living.'

'And that's exactly what I want to do, Viv! Live! Would you rather I sat in the dark for ever? Talk only about Laurie, like he was my whole life and I had nothing else? Like Yoko?'

Viv is recovering from her shock; her face goes to war once more. 'At least Yoko has a talent of her own. You've stolen Laurie's. You're entitled to leave him behind, but I won't. So he stays with me.'

Leaving Laurie behind – hardly. They've just come from a performance of one of his plays, for God's sake. 'Viv, I live in the same house. Laurie's still everywhere. I'm not proud of what happened with Holden. I've tried to forget it. But Laurie was no angel.'

'I don't care. You don't deserve him. You've moved forward. I understand. But I'm not going to let him down.'

Jo knows she'll feel different in the morning, apologise, insist she was lashing out. And he knows he will forgive her, despite everything she said. He watched Laurie and her do this to each other, week in, week out for as long as he knew them. That's how they showed their love, exposing each other's secrets or flaws and bonding over them, two sides of a wound gradually meeting and closing and melding into thicker, stronger scar tissue. That's what this is about: Viv's wound can't heal on its own. He'll let her keep the box, do whatever she wants with it.

There's no escaping the truth: she has more of a claim on Laurie than Jo's ever had.

Rosy steps out of the ladies' bathroom, looking pale and drawn. 'You're both so loud. Embarrassing. Is it true, Uncle Jojo? About you and Holden? Why did he say he slept with him then? I don't understand.'

Jo breathes slowly to coax his heartbeat down from the danger zone. 'I don't know. Viv?'

Viv sits back on the awful breeze block. 'He despised Holden. We all do.'

'It was so spiteful,' says Rosy, reaching out to touch her mother's shoulder. 'Just not Uncle Lu's vibe at all.'

At least not the vibe he showed to the world, thinks Jo. Either way, Laurie would never have gone near Holden, not after he found them together, and certainly not on that night; it was impossible.

'Did anyone else know about ... ' Rosy can barely force the words out. 'About you and Holden?'

'Nobody knows,' says Jo. 'I didn't even know Laurie saw us.'

'Byron,' says Viv with a sigh. 'I had too much to drink one night and told him. I was so mad. I begged him not to mention it to Laurie. He knew.'

Rosy steadies herself against the wall, trembling. 'Did you hear what Byron said? About magic and daylight?'

Jo and Viv turn to look at her; she looks ill. 'Yes, why?'

Rosy covers her mouth. 'I thought I was gonna be sick. I knew I'd heard it before. In the memoir, um, in that horrible bit, where he knows you've read some of it. It was so vicious and violent. Byron must've seen it. Why else would he say something like that?'

'No idea.' Jo has never stopped to think too deeply about how Byron's mind works; he's always been too afraid of what he might find.

Rosy paces the floor as a woman scooches past her to get into the ladies'. 'And the part when Byron surprised Laurie with his book. So nasty. None of that happened. We were all there. Laurie was fucking delighted for him. And the bit about magnolias, what he said just now.'

Viv stands up. 'What's going on? What's this about?'

'But now I'm thinking, remember I said it didn't add up, it wasn't like Uncle Lu to say that about you?'

Jo tried to put it out of his mind, but his brain keeps it on flash cards, deployed when he least expects it. 'Yes.'

'It's like he wanted us to know he's seen it,' says Rosy. 'I don't think Laurie wrote that. I really don't.'

A whip cracks inside Jo's head. There's a chance Laurie didn't cheat, that Theo is telling the truth about what happened to him. He desperately wants to grab it. The evidence is flimsy, but it's all he's got. His heart thuds against his ribcage.

'Byron. He had more access than anyone. He wrote it. And God knows what else.'

Twenty-four

August

Jo

This must be what it feels like to stalk an animal, thinks Jo as he walks slowly back to the table, flanked by a seething Rosy and a bewildered Viv. Knowing what you have to do, not sure how it'll end, but absolutely certain there will be blood. Byron, the serial underachiever who finally got lucky, sits looking pleased with himself. The starters have arrived; he is forking calamari into his mouth as they approach.

'What were you doing in there? Or shouldn't I ask?' He winks at Jo and it's so disgusting Jo cannot contain himself any longer.

'I found some of your writing. On my computer. Well, Laurie's.' Jo awaits the Edvard Munch expression of a liar uncovered, or a theatrical gasp, but there's not even a protest of ignorance. Instead, an awkward smile creeps over Byron's face, like freshly upchucked vomit pooling on a kerb. Rosy was right: he did want them to know.

'Ah, that. I was wondering when you'd twig.'

Rosy is breathless with nerves. She hasn't seen many confrontations other than glossy reality TV face-offs, while Jo feels like he's done nothing but instigate showdowns for the last two weeks. 'You're not denying it?'

Byron's eyes twinkle while he chews. 'Doesn't seem much point.' He sets down his fork, only too happy to explain, like a killer unmasked in a touring production of an Agatha Christie knock-off. 'It started as a harmless prank,' he says. 'I was his assistant. It's not like I broke into his computer with a crowbar. Laurie liked a joke.'

Jo hates to see how much Byron is enjoying the spotlight. 'What made you do this?'

Byron breathes deeply, his lips curling in satisfaction. '"Society's most captivating critic and lovable cynic since Joe Orton." He dined out on that, didn't he? That was the *Guardian*, wasn't it?'

'*Sunday Times*,' says Viv. 'And he dismissed that in his next column. He didn't need to talk about how good he was. He always said it was for others to say and to think.'

'Oh yes. "Watch me and decide for yourself."' Byron snorts. 'I never got it, to be honest. Didn't find him that special. Look, we were old pals. We helped each other out from time to time.'

'Laurie didn't need any help from you,' says Viv.

Byron raises an eyebrow. 'He confided in me, as it happens, that Tracey was nagging him for a memoir. Poor old Blount didn't know what to put in it. He wasn't sure how honest to be. How grisly he should get. So I made some suggestions.'

Viv laughs so sharply it's like a cough. Spittle lands on Byron's face but he doesn't flinch. 'Laurie asked you to write his memoirs? You? I don't think so!'

'Don't be stupid. Blount's writing had one priority: make him look as good as fucking possible, and to hell with anyone else.'

He is an ugly drunk, thinks Jo.

'Uncle Lulu wasn't like that.' Rosy sounds younger, more naive.

Byron laughs drily and sloshes wine into his glass, revelling in how revolting he must appear at that moment. 'You know fuck all about him, Rosy. Anyway, I had a quick peek, see if I got a mention.' Jo can't help but smile as he imagines Byron scanning the documents for his own name, and the inevitable 'the only thing worse than being talked about . . .' moment. For Byron, it came when he arrived at the day of the lunch to celebrate publication of his first novel. 'Two or three lines. My name only once. Once! That day was supposed to be about me. So . . . I filled in a few blanks, switched things about, made them more interesting. I thought it would be funny to show him anybody could be him.'

'You made him sound like a total bastard!' complains Rosy. 'He was thrilled for you that day!'

'Sure, on the outside. He liked to be a rung higher than the rest of us, though, didn't he?'

As vile as this scene is, it's exciting. If Byron is behind this, Theo could be telling the truth. Maybe Laurie wasn't that unhappy. His life wasn't a lie. The sweat from his clash with Viv is barely dry, but Jo feels most sorry for her right now. Her eyes dart from Jo to Rosy to Byron, so far confused and clueless.

'And what about the rest?' says Jo.

'The rest?'

'The other stuff. How much of it is you, and how much is Laurie?'

Byron dissolves into laughter; he's waited a long time for his moment in the sun. 'How much have you seen? Rollocking read, isn't it?' He beams at the waiter as his empty plate is removed, before reaching over and grabbing a prawn from the starter Viv never got to start. 'Old Laurie, eh? What a raconteur. I thought he'd see the funny side.'

'Why the fuck would you do that, Uncle Byron?' What a joy to hear the full force of Rosy's anger, standing up for herself and for Laurie.

'You make too much noise,' snarls Byron. And then it comes, the inevitable blaming of the one man who can't speak up for himself. How it wasn't easy being in Laurie's shadow, watching people lap up everything he did. 'He wasn't the only one keeping a diary, you know. Anyone of us could write a spicy memoir about the old days. My work was just as good as his. Clearly. Jo, you must get this. I used to wonder if you were jealous.'

Maybe, sometimes. There were good days and bad days, but on the brightest, Laurie made being himself look so easy. 'You sabotaged his work.'

'Don't be silly, just a few hundred words hither and thither.' There's a faraway look in Byron's eye. It tells of sleepless nights, feeling embittered by failure, being kept awake by the brilliance of Laurie's star. Maybe. 'You see, it isn't about talent. Really, anyone can mimic anyone. He didn't have anything unique, I proved it. You read it yourself, and never said a word, to him or me. So you believed it.'

Jo is engulfed by guilt. What a strange, unforgivable violation. 'What did Laurie say when he saw what you'd done? I can't believe he was still talking to you.'

Finally, Byron's smirk evaporates. 'Well, nothing. He, ah, he never read it. Don't think he even saw it. Didn't open it once. I checked the tracking history. A lot.' All that showing off, desperate to get Laurie's attention, and he never read a word. 'You looked, though, I saw that.'

'Which parts are you?' Jo has to know. Did Byron rewrite

Laurie's relationship with Teddy to be sexual? Did he change that night with Holden to make Laurie look like the villain?

Byron smiles again. 'You can't tell? So it *is* good. Thank you. I can't even remember what I said. My laptop went the way of the dodo six months ago. I lost everything. My access to Laurie's network went too. I haven't looked.'

Horror breaks over Viv's face; she's finally realising what Byron has done. Her phone rings. She ignores it. 'Why would you be so disloyal to Laurie? He cheered you on every step of the way! He gave you a job!'

'Ah, come on, Grainger. Laurie could be a prime dick, you know that. Me and you made him look good. Liked to keep me on as his lackey. I wanted him to see it could be taken away any minute, and that even if it's bullshit, people believe what they want.'

One thing Jo doesn't understand. 'Do you mean you wrote those awful things about yourself? Why?'

'I know what he said about me behind my back. In fact, I read it for myself. You're not a writer, you wouldn't understand. Underdog gets the reader's sympathy.'

'It didn't work. I hate you even more.' Rosy laughs. 'You'll notice he never slates Mum, not once.'

Byron turns to Viv now. 'He really doesn't, Grainger. He loved you most. Nobody came out unscathed, except you.' There's a tremor in his voice. 'But what about me, eh? When do I get my flowers?'

Viv's face is set hard with disgust. 'Same time as everyone else, Byron. When you're dead.' Viv's phone rings again. 'It's Tracey, I'll take this.' She makes her way outside.

'One day she'll wake up and realise how much he held her back.' Byron clicks his fingers for the waiter. 'You all will. You should put this memoir out, Jo. Tell the world about Ned. Take Laurie down too as a special treat for me.'

Jo has never hit anybody before. It would be satisfying to watch Byron's square, pasty body fly a few feet across the room, see him splayed out in spatchcock dishonour, with food down his shirtfront. But what's the point? Byron is pathetic, a cardboard cutout third-rate villain, twirling his moustache and laughing into a strong wind, without even half an ounce of Laurie's wit and originality.

'Every second you've been in our lives, you've outstayed your welcome,' Jo says. 'You've no idea what you've done, have you? I don't know what's real and what isn't any more.'

'Oh, relax!' says Byron, realisation dawning that this jape hasn't landed, that there's no coming back. 'I can help you unpick it. No harm done.'

Jo is about to tell him he's wrong – very, very wrong – but he sees Viv gliding back towards them, phone in hand. She grabs a wine glass off the table and dashes its contents in Byron's face.

'I'll never speak to you again as long as I live. Laurie loved you.'

'Grainger, I can explain ... it was a few words, it was a joke. I didn't mean anything by it. Laurie would've found it funny.'

'Shut up. Rosy, we need to go. I ...' Viv laughs, but it's not a joyful laugh, it's one of shock and ... excitement, maybe? 'That was Tracey. Ned Lanford. He's dead. Heart attack.'

A bolt of lightning travels up Jo's body. The moment is surreal. 'We just saw him! Where? When?'

Viv laughs again. 'Sorry, I don't mean to ... Garrick. In the loo. He really did go and die in a toilet.'

Rosy clamps her hands to her mouth. 'Amazing.'

Bryon's face gapes. There are tears in his eyes. Nobody behaves how you expect when someone dies. 'I'm not crying, it's not for Lanford. I just ... I ... I really wish Laurie were here to see this.'

'I never want to see you again, Byron. Dinner's on you.' Jo rises from the table, and strides away, as they all stare after him. There is hope. Theo. He has to get to Theo.

Twenty-five
September

Jo

People can be stingy with forgiveness, struggle to hand it over even though they desperately want to. Luckily Theo is generous with his and Jo decides he should be too. There isn't time to be bitter, not if there's a chance of going the distance. But even two weeks after the beautiful reunion, earnest promises that secrets will never come between them again, and fevered make-up sex that has the headboard clattering against the wall, there's persistent doubt. One night, Jo sits up in bed and switches on a light; he doesn't want to think about this in the dark.

There's a slight, satisfying resistance as Theo slowly peels his arm from across Jo's torso, like they're both made of Velcro. 'What's up?'

'Nothing, go back to sleep.'

He can't say it to Theo. That it makes him feel sick, angry

and lost that he'll never know for sure which voice was Laurie and which was Byron. When he was reading, he imagined himself inside Laurie's head in a way he'd never managed before. Now he's questioning everything. The parts where Laurie is alone with his thoughts, no witnesses to corroborate; there will always be room for uncertainty. Was Laurie showing the reader who he really was – it doesn't help that Jo has no idea who the intended reader was supposed to be – or was Byron meddling with a version of Laurie to tarnish his name, make himself look the innocent and Laurie the pathetic, nasty creature on far too many of those pages?

The real killer, however, is not knowing whether Laurie really loved him or if it was just an act. Laurie said he did, all the time, but people do. They say it when they need to, to keep the peace, to reassure, to give an ego boost, during orgasm – any declaration can be explained away by circumstance.

Theo has suggested showing Viv the diaries, but Jo can't do that to her. She needs that perfect memory of Laurie to hold on to, especially now Ned is dead. Whatever Viv's feelings about him, Byron's banishment is another hit to her already small circle, and empty tables get harder to sit at the older you get. If there's something after this life, what might Ned and Laurie be doing now? Blaming one another? Hiding from each other? Or sharing a bottle, neither of them quite saying what they're thinking, as they watch all of creation from their cloud?

Wherever they are, Jo is still here, choking on the fallout. He's forgiven Viv, because Laurie would, and she had a point. The day after Byron's excommunication and Ned's expiry, Viv came to the house. She and Jo sat, hands interlocked over the kitchen table, like a prison visit, tears streaming, promising things would be different, and believing each other. They've made plans to scatter the contents of that box, and he's promised

Justin Myers

her a headstone, whatever she wants, whatever it takes to help her find her chapter two.

Jo switches the light back off and lets him himself sink into the sheets. Theo brings him closer. Jo breathes in his scent. He must get him to change his anti-perspirant; it's too teenage and synthetic, not musky or spicy enough.

Then Theo says it. 'I love you, Jo.'

As cover versions go, it's not bad.

The next morning, Rosy breezes in while Theo and Jo sip coffee in dressing gowns. She briefly scans to see whether either gown once belonged to Laurie, but on seeing they're both Jo's, she visibly relaxes, greets Theo warmly.

'What you two up to?'

'Daydreaming, when one of us should be working on that summer assignment,' says Theo, a mischievous smile as he catches Jo's eye.

'You still not done that? You start back soon.'

'All right, Mother!' Jo smiles. 'Still just that rough first draft. Think I need to start again. Change the angle.'

'You can't edit a blank page,' says Theo and they're all quiet a moment, in acknowledgement, perhaps, that blank pages are never as big a problem as the words that eventually fill them.

Later, Jo idles at Rosy's desk.

'Busy?'

'Pretending.'

He's already run his doubts by her. Of everyone, Rosy is the most like Laurie, spent almost as much time with him as Jo did. But the uncertainty remains. Rosy encourages Jo to embrace logic.

'You'll definitely know the difference if you read them again. Now you, uh, know everything.'

'I don't know everything. I feel like I'll never know everything.'

'Look, Byron wasn't a bad writer. Not really. But he's doing a bad Uncle Laurie impression. I'll put it all in some proper order, do some cross-referencing with his appointment diaries. I can find a way to recover the unedited versions, before Byron got his hands on them. There's still other stuff we haven't found. I come across it all the time. I guarantee you'll think you were nuts ever to believe a word of it. He absolutely loved you. Okay?'

How can this wise young person be the same one who once tipped a bowl of spaghetti hoops into his manbag when she was four? He feels the same person he was that day, but she's undergone a thousand evolutions. 'Are you sure?'

'Definitely. Because . . .' She trails off. 'Never mind.'

Jo won't let it drop. 'What?'

'I found something in one of the folders. One Byron couldn't access. Written not long before, uh, you know. It's about you. I didn't know if I should show you.'

Not more. Not again. Jo can feel everything unravelling in an instant, the happiness he felt in Theo's arms dematerialising. 'Is it bad? Is it definitely him?'

'Oh, it's him. It's not bad. It's pretty full-on. Do you want to see it?'

He does.

He doesn't.

He does.

'Yes.'

She prints it out. 'I bet there's much more of this in his files, you know. The real him.'

Jo takes it, wordlessly, to the sofa under the window overlooking the garden, curls his legs underneath him, and begins to read.

Encore

Laurie

This city. At my age. Man, every day is a fight. Life. Getting out of bed, knowing I've got to bump some heads. The infinite to-do list scrolling inside my cortex, the hurdles I must clear before I even start breakfast. This house, my job, the café, our success, everything we built and bled for – though it seemed easy at the time – and everything that comes with it. People who need pleasing, or who depend on us. Arses that want to be kissed. Bills that need paying – I know Jo does pretty much all that, but even knowing the debts are accruing somewhere is burden enough. I get anxious thinking about atoms swirling in a far-off room.

It's a cliché, but I long for simplicity. I don't think I realised how fleeting my youth would be. I wasn't ready to be ripped so hard and so fast from being at the centre of everything. I wonder if Jo misses it. Our old lives, before everything mattered.

Sometimes I want to wind it back, be in the little flat again. Jo has never been that interested in 'remember whens', so I don't mention it. He'd probably tell me I'm being silly and shatter my illusion that it's the best we ever were. I know what he'd say, that we'll be bigger and better again and again, new zeniths always await, many stairs left to climb and worlds to conquer.

But I imagine it.

Back to Kennington, that shitty flat. With its mice, scratched floorboards and horrible spotlights that dangled out of the ceiling like oxygen masks in an emergency landing, so bright you felt like you were in a dentist's chair, so we never turned them on. The washing-up we never did, that stupid tabletop dishwasher, does he remember it? We could only fit two plates in it. Useless. Noises from every compass point, madness beyond each shared wall. Bonkers Claire below, playing R&B morning, noon and night. The two bears who went clubbing from Thursday to Tuesday and waved at us, wasted, from their balcony but blanked us on the dance floor. The little kid with the gappy smile from the big flats, who'd tell us they liked our jeans, and ask us where we were going. That kid will be a grown-up now, somewhere. Do I pass them on the street ever? Get served by them in Starbucks? They could be an MP now, for all I know.

I want to go back to that feeling of observing the world, and being majorly fucking impressed by it. Back when things were simple because we didn't yet know how to make them complicated, or if they were complicated, it was because we chose chaos, instead of having it foisted upon us. I miss my old body and how it used to move, and feel in the shower, in clothes. The stuff I can't fit into any more. I miss how Jo used to look at me, and touch me, and be ... not dazzled. I was never on his level, but I could feel his desire. Passion has a glow, and a scent; it leaves you coated in itself. I know it's still there, in its own way.

I suppose I miss the rush of it. I don't get headrushes any more, unless I stand up too quickly.

I tell myself that if we had that again, if we could spend even one weekend climbing those treacherous metal stairs to the rooftop, and sat and watched one more sunrise, I'd feel brand new. It wouldn't matter about the truth waiting in the mirror, or my waistband cutting into my flesh. My grey hair would colour again for him, for the memory of us. We can't unlearn things, or unsee horrors, or undo hurting each other, but we can find ourselves again.

I went back, recently, to see the flat. Just to have a look, find out what it meant to me. They've built a room where the open rooftop should be. That place we sat, lounged, staggered, kissed and held each other. They've taken that fresh air, and perfect endless sky, and boxed it in with bricks and cheap double glazing, and shiny laminate, and filled it with a bullshit sofa and bad furniture from the King's Road. A chintzy tomb for our gorgeous sunrises.

I swear, as soon as I get a hint that the owners are tired of it and want to sell, I'm gonna buy it. We don't have to live there, or even visit more than once, but I'll rip out that monstrous shit, tear down that ugly extension, let the sky back in, and I'll take Jo there in the middle of the night, in summer, when it's humid and the noise of the city syncs with your heartbeat and the air makes the mercury bubble.

We'll watch, sweating, holding hands, sharing a Marlboro, as the space above us turns to fire, making a silhouette of those creaking old gas towers. One night in Kennington will wash the years away.

I love Jo, with everything. I forgive him for everything. I'm sorry for everything. He is my everything.

For ever.

Twenty-six

September

Theo

Knowing for sure that Laurie adored him hasn't helped Jo at all. He lies curled up on the sofa, like half a croissant, for hours, Jasper by his side, clinging to the sheet of paper until it's soaked with his tears. Theo tries to remove it from Jo's grip, promising he'll print a fresh one. Jo doesn't reply, or look up, but he unclasps each finger, one by one, from the paper. Like most mourners, he's crying for himself, thinks Theo; things he'll never get to say, responses that will never come. Crying because the rest of his life is for ever marked by what it can never be again. Sad story.

Theo backs out of the room, eyes fixed on Jo, then heads for Laurie's office. Rosy's left the file right there on the computer's desktop, as if expecting someone to come looking for it. His eyes roam the letters on the screen. Laurie's voice, but not as he remembers it. There's another voice harmonising in the background. He clicks to print and watches the blank paper slide into the feeder tray and emerge the other side, marked with Laurie's lament. Theo looks up to see Viv standing at the door.

'I came to check on Jo, but he's asleep through there.' Viv picks up the sheet of paper.

'Good. He's worn out. Beautiful, isn't it?'

Viv doesn't say a word, she places the paper carefully back in the out tray.

'It really means a lot to him,' says Theo, not taking his eyes off Viv for a second. 'That last ... I don't know what to call it. Last chapter. I mean, it's kinda destroyed him but ...'

Viv smiles, uncertainty lingering at the corner of her mouth. 'It'll be a comfort eventually.'

'Hmm.' Theo turns away. Best to break eye contact for his next trick. 'Shame Laurie didn't write it.'

She doesn't twitch. Nerves of steel. He knew it. 'Byron didn't write that.'

'I didn't say he did.' He wonders how long to wait.

Viv steps fully into the office and closes the door behind her, her expression unreadable. She's decided, wisely Theo thinks, not to deny it. 'How did you know?'

'The gas holders at Kennington. Or towers, as you call them. There's one now, not two.'

She's alarmed. Theo gets a kick out of it. 'What?'

'They knocked down the others. Built flats. Only one's left. You'd think going back for one last look, Laurie would've spotted that.'

Viv seems almost relieved. She sits in the large orange chair, brushes imaginary dust off her bare arms, and sighs. 'Are you going to tell Jo?'

Theo can't remember the last time he felt so powerful. It frightens him in a way, how easy it would be to topple this fucked-up Jenga. 'No. It's good, sounds just like him. Why did you do it?'

'Jo needed to hear it. Rosy told me he was driving himself mad after reading all that other stuff.'

Theo has a pang of envy. Nobody's ever gone to that much trouble to ease his own misery. 'But it's yet another lie. It's not him.'

'It is him,' Viv hisses irritably, before getting a hold of herself, sitting back. 'Let me tell you something. He might not have typed it out, or said it to Jo's face, but we talked about it a lot. Last time I saw him, in fact. We always talked about going back to basics, before everything. Before you.' She does not say it with malice. 'It's all him.'

He's surprised she's not a little sorrier to be caught. On the few occasions they've met, Viv's been instantly readable, sad but sweet; this is a turn to the dark side. The last couple of weeks have hardened her. What she's done is a huge risk. She must know how Byron's supposed embellishments have left Jo horrified and disoriented. Theo's fascinated. 'Jo's not stupid. He might work it out.'

Viv tenses. 'I thought you weren't going to tell him.' She sounds offended he would even suggest it. It's like the idea has never occurred to her. Is she for real?

'I'm not. But if he finds it on the computer and reads the metadata, he might see the creation date is way after Laurie's death.'

'Metadata! Go say that word to him now and see how he reacts.' The tension dissolves. 'Why would he check? He can barely do FaceTime. And it's what he wants to hear. I don't deceive him lightly, believe me.'

He does believe her, that's the thing. 'So you're doing this for Jo?'

'Maybe myself a bit. I said some horrible things to Jo the day Ned died. Awful. Laurie would've been so mad at me.'

'Laurie's not here any more.'

She laughs sharply. 'Wrong. He's everywhere. Even now he's surprising me. I read the lot, everything. I always thought I knew what he was thinking.'

Must've been quite the eye-opener; he almost feels sorry for her. 'You might never know. Thanks to Byron.'

'Byron didn't, uh, tinker that much. I can't believe Jo was ever taken in by it.'

Theo can feel a shift. Control transferring. Just like that, the gears grind in the opposite direction. 'What? Can you tell what's real and what's Byron?'

'Of course I can. I've known those men half my life. And there's your metadata, remember? I can see who's edited what. Like mucky fingerprints everywhere. A lot is untouched, totally clean.' She looks at him pointedly; he can practically see the relevant chapters reflected in her eyes, which pierce through his blank expression. 'Let's make a deal. You keep my secret, I'll keep yours.'

'I told Jo. Nothing happened.' Theo tries to keep a lid on his nerves, his voice steady. 'Laurie's overactive imagination. He was famous for it. That's why we're both sitting in this nice house. He made up that stuff about Holden, after all. Or was that Byron?'

She shakes her head. 'God knows why he took responsibility for that. A coping mechanism, maybe. That was his thing, he always found his therapy in fiction. Can't deal with it in the real world, make up a version that you can put behind you.' She pulled a face like she'd smelled something nasty. 'He'd rather slit his own throat than ever touch Holden, though. Mind you, if Jo and Holden hadn't . . . well, Laurie would've probably never looked at you.' She seems to realise how frosty she sounds. She manages half a smile, softens her gaze. 'He didn't always show it, quite the opposite, we've all read it now, but he was devoted. You clearly meant a great deal to him. I'm sure it was the same for you.'

'How do you know what he said about me wasn't what you just said, therapy in fiction?'

Theo realises he is playing Laurie-themed chess against a master. 'Because you are exactly his type. To the letter.' It's as if she has dirt on her hands she's desperate to clean off. 'I'm not an idiot. I don't need to believe your story. Only you and Laurie know exactly. But I can guess. I've seen what Laurie had to say.'

'But he never told you about me?'

'No.'

It stings, but Theo will not cry, he'd rather die right here than give himself away. 'I thought he told you everything.'

'I get it now. He was protecting me. He knew I couldn't keep it from Jo. Didn't want to burden me. That must be it.'

Theo says nothing. His jaw hurts from clenching.

'Don't look so scared. I won't say anything. But all this doubt and confusion ... it's best if I make all this go away.'

'Go away? What do you mean?' What had she come up with? A suicide pact? Time machine?

'Rosy has promised Jo she'll dig out the original versions, before Byron got his hands on them.'

'You just said they don't exist.'

'But they will exist. That's my next project, to fix this and give Jo and Laurie the right ending.'

'Fix it?'

'Yes, so we can move forward, like Jo says.' A hint of bitterness there, Theo notes. 'I'm going to work through it all, make a few changes, then show Jo the unedited version, the true Laurie.' She presents this plan as if reading out a recipe on daytime television.

'You're cleaning them up?'

'Exactly. It's the only way, isn't it, really?'

The tears finally spring to Theo's eyes. Tears of anger, and frustration. Every muscle in his body is taut. She can't just erase history like that. Who else would ever take the time to tell Theo's story? He's prepared to fight. 'But you can't.'

'I've already made a start. Imagine if this got into the wrong hands and was treated as gospel. He'd be finished. I've a lot to do but, you know what, it's actually quite healing, putting myself in Laurie's shoes. I'll blame Byron for the spicier stuff and everyone is back where they should be.'

'How is that moving forward? It's total fiction.'

'It's the best outcome. For Laurie, and Jo, and you, really, when you think about it. What do you reckon Jo would do if he thought you and Laurie were actually involved?'

It would be the end, Theo knows that. Jo's opted to believe Theo's version, willingly accepting Byron as the villain because he never liked him, not really, and it's easier than facing the alternative. Self-preservation. Theo gets it. He has no idea how much Jo knew about Ned's deeds, but the ghosts of the wronged Valenti alumni will haunt him for ever.

'Why would you protect me?'

'I owe it to Laurie. I'm trying to be a good friend. Sometimes I missed the mark when he was here. I know he could be vicious, but that wasn't the real him. He never, ever meant it. We all say things we regret. I can show Jo who he really was. The Laurie I knew.'

Suddenly Theo realises what else will be lost. 'There's evidence in there! You can't sanitise it. What about Ned? He was a fucking predator. He ruined people's lives. Do you know what happened to me? He can't get away with it. Maybe neither of them should.'

'Evidence. Hmm.' She looks at him with pity now. 'Look, Theo, Ned's heart exploded in a toilet cubicle. He's in the express lift to hell right now. Maybe Laurie is there too, with a glass of bubbles, and saving me a seat. I mean, I hope not obviously. But what good will it do, dredging it up? They can't be held accountable now.'

'Laurie was going to help me. I know he was. Maybe he'd want me to see it through.'

She wrinkles her nose ever so slightly to show Theo she knows better. 'He's gone, though, sweetheart.'

'Don't call me sweetheart, we're not friends.' He doesn't have to lie down and take this. She's not interested in helping Jo, she wants to keep the house lights shining, cling on to Laurie's fame. 'What are you going to do then, work the red carpet at Ned's funeral like all the other hypocrites?'

'You're right, they're hypocrites. Nobody wants to hear it. They'll crucify you.' She gazes off into the distance as if imagining the fake smile she'll paint on as she does circuits of Ned's wake. It makes Theo feel sick. 'I'm being realistic. You're not ... important enough to make the right kind of noise. You're not a credible witness.'

The nape of Theo's neck starts to tingle. 'Not credible? What are you talking about?'

'Your brother didn't die in a bike accident, for a start.'

Theo tries to catch his breath. Maybe this is what being a ghost feels like, watching life play out before you, powerless. Best to say nothing, to see what she's got on him.

For her part, Viv doesn't seem happy to be telling him this. 'Your tribute, the, uh, ghost bike, is it? It's in memory of someone who got killed cycling across Asia; the square's residents paid for it. You have an unusual name, Theodore. Anyone wanting to check up on you could, easily.'

The fucking bike. Almost his downfall. Too clever. Seemed like a good idea at the time. Actors need a backstory. If you want doors to open, the kind with no handle on the outside, the sadder the better. It always worked too, bar the odd misstep.

'Did you ... check up on me?'

Maybe she never liked him. He was fooled by those bright smiles that reached her eyes and the gentle pats on the hand. Man, showbusiness – the home planet of the born liar.

'No, it never entered my head! Ned Lanford told me. He had his eye on you. You were sending him those messages, weren't you?'

Theo remembers this feeling of helplessness; it makes his blood surge. The last time Laurie left his studio. The miserable morning he first woke up next to Ned. The doors slamming in his face ever since. The collective amnesia of every other man he's asked for help. Being in this room, last year, seeing Laurie that final time, and yet more disappointment. He thought Viv might be different. He should've known. Why shouldn't he scare the shit out of Ned every now and again with a little anonymous message? 'Are you blackmailing me?'

Viv gasps. 'Don't be so silly! Blackmail! Honestly. I don't want more trouble, I'm trying to smooth it over. But you have to see, if Laurie's name was trashed, Jo wouldn't be able to handle it.'

'He was set to publish the lot until he found out about Byron.'

'He didn't mean that. I know him. If he found about your ... situation, it would break him.' The pain must show on his face, because Viv's tone becomes almost motherly. She looks like she might touch him. 'Tell me what you're thinking, sweetheart.'

The residual guilt is twisted, corroding barbed wire in Theo's gut. 'Maybe it was my fault. If I'd left Laurie alone, not come back, he might not have crashed. I was calling him, bugging him to make a decision.'

Viv shakes her head. The jewels in her ears rattle as if reminding Theo he has nothing. 'I've been there, don't do that to yourself. We could all have done things differently. He was with Ned that night. I don't know why, he didn't answer my messages and Ned wouldn't say. Now I've seen all this, er, writing, I like to think he was standing up to Ned, don't you? Threatening to expose him. I'm not even sure Laurie would've been able to pull it off. Rosy says a lot of Laurie's audio files are suddenly harder to find. I don't think it's a coincidence.'

Theo is struck first by the heroic vision of Laurie cutting all ties with Ned, squirrelling away the evidence for Theo, out of harm's way, and then comes the less romantic one, Laurie forming a plan with Ned to save their skins, scorching the earth behind him. Like Jo, he can only choose which version to believe.

'Theo, I understand you want blood, but what you have with Jo is much more valuable. I've seen Jo in love before, I was there. He loves you. And I can tell from Laurie's words that, well, whatever he did, he loved you too. You must have had some feelings for him? He won everyone over in the end.'

'You wouldn't understand.'

Theo is in permanent conflict. He doesn't know how to feel. The truth is a wavy line, cutting through fog and light and reaching high and dipping low. It's illegible, in strange handwriting with more than one author. The question of what is real and what isn't goes back way further than these rich assholes passing round papers, playing with his life like it's a game of Consequences. Theo is annoyed he can't straighten it all out,

frightened by the reality of loving someone yet hating them
to their bones. Laurie's tenderness and warmth, then his cold,
calculated stare as he turned and left the studio, they're all part
of the same story, impossible to untangle.

When he read that Laurie had died, it all hit him at once.
The betrayal of his youth, the continuing injustice. It was like
losing everything all over again, and somehow the breakdown
was much tougher now he had that life experience behind him.
Knowing you can survive the lows doesn't make them any less
painful. Day after day, spooning his mother's scrambled egg –
microwaved, too runny – into his mouth in front of daytime
television, barking out answers to quiz shows in crackling
monotone. His mum would hover at the door, watching her
only son, making pleasantries, light encouragements that he
should go outside and see the tulips, or anxiously calling the
cab to his counselling appointment a whole hour earlier than
he needed it, just to get him out of the house and find peace. It
was only the letter from the university, the reminder of the last
good thing Laurie did for him, that brought him back above
water, that made him remember Laurie's original kindness. He
wanted to harness that feeling, pay it forward somehow. What
would Laurie do? he asked himself. When he saw Jo was in
the same class, the answer was obvious. He must look after Jo.
Theo didn't mean for things to turn out like this, but he must
love Jo, right? Otherwise why would he be here? So why bring
it all crashing down? The urge to protect Laurie and the drive
to see Ned's reputation ruined, opposing forces that threaten to
tear him apart.

Viv reaches over and rests her manicured hand on Theo's
knee. She smells expensive and comforting, of sunshine and
caramel. He squints as the September sun hits the gems in her
rings. She regards him a moment. She's trying to understand,

he can see, but there's no explaining that fine line between love and anger, the way it darkens and fades at will. Viv has always been absolutely certain of her love for Laurie; even now, it's unwavering. He made it easy for her.

'I imagine it's confusing to be you,' she says. 'I'm sorry for what you went through. You should think about starting up counselling again. I am. Look, Laurie was a good man at heart, I believe that. I wouldn't do this otherwise. Losing him has been hard enough; I can't lose his memory too.'

She has won. He won't challenge her again. 'How do I know you won't blow this up one day? You don't owe me anything.'

Viv stands, rearranges her bag, standing much taller and stronger than she did earlier in that doorway. 'Whatever I think about it all, Laurie would want me to look out for you. I owe him one.' She looks at Theo with genuine warmth. 'He always said I was bad at keeping secrets, but I'm good at promises. I believe in doing the right thing, I always have. And this is how it has to end.' She leans, places her hand on Theo's shoulder, and squeezes.

Theo is surprised to feel a flash of optimism that makes him trust her, like he can confess for the first time. 'I loved him and I hated him.'

'I get it. Me too sometimes,' she says, but he knows she's lying to make him feel better. She can never hate Laurie, no matter what he did. 'I'll fix the bit about the gas tower, thank you. When Jo's calmed down, he'll be happy. His perfect memories of Laurie will still be there, and he'll have you to build a future with. Look, I'm not defending Laurie and certainly not Ned, the bastard. I feel for you, I do, but you have a real chance here. Don't waste it.'

'Just like that?'

Viv nods. 'I'll pop back later to see Jo. Give him a kiss from me. You can do this. Jo deserves peace, so do you. And we all deserve Laurie's art. I'd hate to live in a world that's airbrushed him out completely, wouldn't you?'

Thing is, he would. Even so, he's not sure he wants to be bonded to Viv for ever by a lie. He tries to imagine how life would've turned out if Laurie had lived, but he can't conjure up a single scene; he was meant to be here, in this room, making deals to protect the Devil.

He waits to hear the garden door click before creeping to the back lounge to find Jo still asleep. Jasper stares back at him, totally still, save for the odd twitch of his tail. Theo watches them for a couple of minutes, trying to find calm in the rhythm of Jo's breathing. It doesn't work.

He has a scrap of fight left. It can't be over. There must be some notes left, recordings, something. Maybe he can pull this back.

Tiptoeing back to Laurie's desk, he searches through files. He goes through everything, even the most innocuous-sounding folders. Viv has already started her rehabilitation project, it's all gone. He'll never see it again. Unless . . . Might Jo have sent the pages to himself? Does he even know how to do that? Why is he so bad with tech? Is it intentional? Maybe living offline makes it harder for the truth to catch up with you.

Theo darts into the kitchen and fetches Jo's laptop. He searches for a few minutes. Coursework, assignments Theo recognises, but nothing of Laurie's.

And then, in a folder marked 'Jasper pet insurance', he finds a document that looks like it doesn't belong. So he opens it, and reads.

A PIVOTAL MOMENT IN 1,000 WORDS

JOSEP VALENTI, BA (HONS) CREATIVE
WRITING, NORTH LONDON UNIVERSITY
SUMMER ASSIGNMENT
TUTOR: DR LAURA PARR

The Barista can't take it any more. He can't spend
another day shaking with anger, keeping the
words in. The Genius is on his way out, coat over
his arm, looking at his watch when the Barista
tries to talk.

'Stay for a drink. A proper drink.'

The Genius looks surprised, suspicious, like it's
a trap, but he's intrigued, so he slings his coat on
the floor as usual, and comes back. He sits, really
slowly, not taking his eyes off the Barista as he
pours. On taking his glass, the Genius pauses, like
he's waiting for permission. The Barista nods, and
the Genius begins to sip.

'I'd forgotten how it tastes.' He lies so easily. So
many nights the Barista has stood at the window
looking down as the Genius slaloms up the garden
path after nights out with the Photographer and
the Failure.

The Barista tells him to drink up and prepares
another, slightly stronger. How easy would it be to
crunch something up and slip it in? he wonders.
It's what they do in movies. But he wants him
awake.

'Is something wrong? With you, I mean?'

The Barista smiles. It's touching to hear concern

in the Genius's voice. Maybe he does love him
after all.

There's nothing else for it but to lay out the
betrayal so they can pick over it, like mudlarks.
Even now, the Barista doesn't like to see the
Genius on the back foot. It's rare to have him at a
disadvantage. It feels wrong, but the only way he
can ever outstep the Genius is with the truth.

This man has taken half the Barista's life from
him. Made him believe he was everything he
wanted. All that time he was venting his poison
and dreaming of escape, ripping everything
apart, sliding between the sheets with others, too
cowardly to tell him to his face. Yes, the Barista
made a mistake, one horrible mistake, one night, in
anger, but the Genius could've released the Barista,
left him to find his own happiness, but it suited
him to keep him around, either for revenge or as a
shield, maybe, from the inevitable firestorm.

The Genius drains his second glass, rapidly,
then a third. Now, with his crimes nailed to the
wall for him to see, he begs.

'I'd get down on my knees if I could. I need you.'

'Go on then.'

The Genius eyes the ground, thinks about it. 'It's
not what it looks like.'

All those words at his disposal and the Genius
grabs at the stupidest cliché. Messages come
through. Insistent vibrating. The Genius ignores
them. Calls, then, also go unanswered.

The Barista has to say it. 'Is that Teddy
calling?'

The Genius's eyes go huge. The Barista can tell he has many questions but is too afraid to ask them. He gets to his feet, says he's late, that he has to go. 'I'm not going to him, I swear. I have to do something. It's important. I'm going to put this right.'

'It's over,' says the Barista, calmly, but not without sadness. 'You and me.'

'You're not divorcing me, Jo. Not like this. I can explain.'

'You don't need to explain. I've read every word.'

'No, you haven't. You just think you have. This isn't about us. I have to help him.'

'Are you going to leave me? For Teddy?'

The Genius's reply doesn't come fast enough. He's thought about it. 'I really have to go. I will make all of this right, I swear to God.'

'You don't believe in God. "Dog spelled backwards", we've always said.'

'Jo . . .'

'I know what my name is. Must make a nice change for you, calling out two syllables in bed. Sciatica willing, of course.'

'I have to go. Back as soon as I can. I swear.'

The Barista lets him leave, because he knows what's coming next. The damage is done. He's had the drinks. He's over the limit now. All the Barista has to do is call the police, tell them the Genius left in a state, is drinking again, and that he's worried. They'll pull him over, he'll be in court, it might even make the papers. And he'll know not to fuck with the Barista. Not again.

However.

He has doubts now. What will it solve? He
doesn't want to walk out, doesn't want the Genius
to go, to be abandoned and humiliated. What's the
best way to make someone pay? Let them leave,
or force them to stay? Maybe if his wings are
clipped, he'll realise without the Barista, there
is no Genius. Does the Barista even want to be
let go?

The Genius's humiliations belong to the Barista
too; he couldn't bear to see him hurt, as much as
he wants to hurt him. So he doesn't make the call.

This is the part of the story he always comes
back to. The one he'll replay over and over until
his timer finally runs out of sand.

Maybe if he'd called the police, things would be
different.

They might have pulled him over before he
crashed.

He might not have been so anxious, kept his
eyes on the road.

His last words came as he closed the door,
calling back up the hallway: 'I do love you, Jo. I
do. I will make this right.'

I didn't say I love you back. Or call him to say
sorry. Didn't tell him to be careful. I let nature
take its course, straight into a wall. Drunk, by my
hand; perhaps dead by it too. That truth pressing
down on me, like I'm being crushed by a car. His
car. I imagine him in the tangled metal, in those
final moments. Is he awake? Is he frightened?
Does he look up at the stars and cry out for me?

I'm sorry, Laurie.

We always said, right at the start, that secrets kill a relationship. And now look at us.

A secret didn't kill you.

I did.

Twenty-seven
September

Theo

Whoa.

Theo closes the document, breathes in deeply for five, and out, slowly, for six. Yoga breathing. Well, well, well. Quite a read. That explains the ferocity of Jo's tears. And why he was labouring over it so long – it clearly didn't come naturally to him. A wise man once told him, in bed, that you can't buy talent in a jar.

After a few minutes of middle-distance staring, cogs turning, his stomach finally settling, Theo tiptoes to the back lounge. He finds Jo slowly waking up, wiping the crumbs from his eyes and blinking his way back to reality. No more secrets indeed. Not that it matters now.

Maybe Theo needs to play the game, reap the rewards. Laurie has damaged them all enough; they've earned their futures.

So much ugliness has brought them here, but it doesn't mean what comes next can't be beautiful. Viv is right. They can make something out of this.

Who says that secrets only kill a relationship? They're as good a foundation as any.

Theo smiles at Jo, reaches out for his hand, and lets his mind wander, imagining the fun he's going to have with all this lovely fucking money.

[Untitled]

Laurie

'Rosy, petal, can you type up this small section of audio? It's an out-take from the Guardian *interview, never published. Am repurposing for my column on death scenes. Thanks, treasure. Don't bother transcribing all the times the rude bastard yawns.'*

[begin transcription]

INTERVIEWER
You've been around a while now. Are you getting to the stage where you might start picking up lifetime achievement awards?

LAURIE
[sharp intake of breath]
Been around a while! Just say, 'You're old,' it's

quicker. I've said no to a couple already. It's flattering but, you know, I'm not ready to put a lid on my career yet.

INTERVIEWER
No, course not.

LAURIE
I'll take posthumous ones instead, save me sitting through the ceremony.
[laughter]

INTERVIEWER
Do you ever think about how you might be remembered? About your legacy?

LAURIE
Fuck, no, I'm forty-two. I must be looking extra rough today. I'm saving that for my high-backed armchair and drooling into a *Woman's Own*. Decades away.

INTERVIEWER
What about a tell-all exposé?
[a few moments of silence]
Um, an autobiography, perhaps?

LAURIE
I've dabbled with putting a memoir together but it's never felt like me. Too great a temptation to blur out a few sensitive images. Or spare people's feelings, you know. It's like staring at yourself in a mirror too long: eventually you get morbid, think about the workings

underneath the skin. I've written a play about it all instead. Well, most of it.

INTERVIEWER

And when can we expect that?

LAURIE

Oh, after they've lowered me into the ground, angel.
[laughter]
I don't want to be around for that time bomb. I'll leave it in a safe pair of hands for now and then when enough time has elapsed ... boom. Actually, better not put that bit in. That okay? To take that out? Spoilers.

INTERVIEWER

Sure. You've written about this kind of thing before, though, haven't you? What the dead leave behind. In *Daddy Issues* [sic], for example, or ... wasn't there a scene in *The Gleaming*?

LAURIE

You're thinking of Sonja in *Infra Dig*, I think.

INTERVIEWER

Oh yes, that's right, sorry.

LAURIE

[laughter]
God, don't be. You're not an encyclopedia. But, uh, I mean, look, yes, sure, I suppose ... sometimes I wonder what the world will make of me when I'm gone. I mean, I haven't always been kind, but I've never ... I don't

know, I've never gone out of my way to be unkind,
know what I mean? I've led as wholesome a life as,
uh, circumstances have allowed. I hope the world will
forgive me. I read a quote once, something like, 'You
live as long as the last person who remembers you', but
when you've produced a body of work, your reputation
lives on even longer. I think it's up to you to ... uh ...
to kind of, uh, make sure your reputation is in the best
possible shape. But you're right, I find this fascinating,
something we have no control over, that could come
for us any time. The randomness. It does freak me
out sometimes. But that's me being a bit dramatic, I
suppose.

INTERVIEWER

How does this influence your work? Do you channel
this ... what would you say it was? Insecurity?
Anxiety? Do you channel that every time you write a
death scene?

LAURIE

I prefer to think of it as curiosity. And, y'know, for me,
it's not about the death scene itself. Showing someone
croak isn't very interesting, dramatically. It's ...
horrible, obviously, and painful and traumatic. But
ultimately mundane.

INTERVIEWER

What about deathbed confessions? They're not
mundane.

LAURIE

Not super fascinating either. Sorry. But the
ramifications ... definitely. That's what I like to
explore. The aftermath. Silences. Darkness of the soul.
Knowing nothing's gonna be the same again. That's
what attracts me, that's the perfect scene. Everything
changing in an instant, the future suddenly a scary
and exciting place. You've just lost someone and now
you live in this world they will never know. The story's
just beginning. The before and after, I can do. The
during? Not so much.

INTERVIEWER

Tell me about the before.

LAURIE

Well. *[sighs]* When you leave your house in the
morning, you, uh, you never stop to think it might
be the last time, do you? You know, going through
the motions. Reach for your coat, check your hair in
the mirror, pull at the squeaky handle with the loose
screw, and get annoyed with yourself for not fixing
it yet, just as you do every single morning. Blah di
blah. You step out into the day, and it's weatherless,
an, erm, an expanse of January grey. It never crosses
your mind that, already, you've done something for
the last time. Rolled your eyes 'cos there's no milk left,
or laughed out loud at a stupid joke on the radio. Your
newspaper lands on your mat with a great thwack but
you'll never pick it up. Nobody will.

INTERVIEWER

That's quite poetic. And terrifying.

LAURIE

Well, darling, I'm a writer, that's my job: lure you in
with my poetry, then scare you to death. I mean, you
don't get to decide how it happens, but as long as I don't
expire while I'm on the toilet, I'll be happy. You know?
Nothing poetic about that.

[laughter]

[end transcription]

Acknowledgements

The Glorious Dead has been a long time coming. This story brewed in my head for years, until it became impossible to ignore any longer. Sometimes it's not about finding the right time, but the right people. I'm so excited I finally did this, but I didn't do it alone.

Thanks to my agent Becky Thomas at Lewinsohn Literary, for patiently waiting six years to read the book I told her I was going to write one day, the first time we ever met. She has always been my biggest champion and I'm thankful we went for that coffee.

My editor Alexa Allen-Batifoulier, for backing *The Glorious Dead* and its cast of horrors right from the jump. Her insight and passion lifted it to another level. And my publisher Christina Demosthenous for taking it to the finish line. Her tips, tricks and love for the story really made this one shine. I've learned so much from you both.

Huge thanks to the talented Meg Shepherd for my stunning cover, which I love, to the sales and marketing teams for helping to get this baby on the road, and to Eleanor Gaffney in production and copy editor Lorraine Green for that vital last kick of the tyres. I'm so happy to be working with everyone at Renegade and the wider Dialogue family for this next adventure. The belief you've all shown in this book means everything; I can't wait to see what the future holds for us.

To my partner Paul for always letting me get on with it. To my cousin Joanne for lending me an ancient nickname. To my friends for always being interested in what I'm doing (and constantly asking when this one was coming out): Catherine, Claire, Neil, Ian, Kim, Lily, Mel, Dom, Hil, Tim, Deb, Roz, Olivia, Owen, Ilana, Adam, Rob, Darren, Laura, Amy, Charlotte, and Steve over in NYC. And to Nichola and Sarah: we miss you.

Thanks, as always, to Dom Wakeford, Anna Boatman and Cal Kenny for your part in my journey.

To all the booksellers, festival organisers, book clubs, reviewers, bloggers and influencers who talk up my books and inspire readers. You are hugely appreciated.

And finally, thank you to everyone who reads my work. Your eyes are the ultimate prize.

Bringing a book from manuscript to what you are reading is a team effort.

Renegade Books would like to thank everyone who helped to publish *The Glorious Dead* in the UK.

Editorial
Alexa Allen-Batifoulier
Christina Demosthenous
Saida Azizova
Eleanor Gaffney

Contracts
Stephanie Evans
Sasha Duszynska Lewis
Isabel Camara

Sales
Megan Schaffer
Kyla Dean
Dominic Smith
Sinead White
Georgina Cutler-Ross
Kerri Hood
Jess Harvey
Natasha Weninger-Kong

Design
Meg Shepherd
Sara Mahon
Sasha Egonu

Production
Narges Nojoumi
Amanda Jones

Publicity
Izzy Warner
Annabel Robinson

Marketing
Katy Blott

Operations
Jairiza Rivera

Finance
Chris Vale
Jonathan Gant

Copy-Editor
Lorraine Green

Proofreader
Saxon Bullock

RAISING READERS
Books Build Bright Futures

Dear Reader,

We'd love your attention for one more page to tell you about the crisis in children's reading, and what we can all do.

Studies have shown that reading for fun is the **single biggest predictor of a child's future life chances** – more than family circumstance, parents' educational background or income. It improves academic results, mental health, wealth, communication skills, ambition and happiness.[1]

The number of children reading for fun is in rapid decline. Young people have a lot of competition for their time. In 2024, 1 in 10 children and young people in the UK aged 5 to 18 did not own a single book at home.[2]

Hachette works extensively with schools, libraries and literacy charities, but here are some ways we can all raise more readers:

• Reading to children for just 10 minutes a day makes a difference
• Don't give up if children aren't regular readers – there will be books for them!
• Visit bookshops and libraries to get recommendations
• Encourage them to listen to audiobooks
• Support school libraries
• Give books as gifts

There's a lot more information about how to encourage children to read on our website: **www.RaisingReaders.co.uk**

Thank you for reading.

---

[1] OECD, '21st-Century Readers: Developing Literacy Skills in a Digital World', 2021, https://www.oecd.org/en/publications/21st-century-readers_a83d84cb-en.html

[2] National Literacy Trust, 'Book Ownership in 2024', November 2024, https://literacytrust.org.uk/research-services/research-reports/book-ownership-in-2024